W I C K E D N E S S

He knew that he deserved this.

"I want you to look around here," Mama said, waving her arm in a short arc above her head. "Look around this house, this house where you grew up. Every night I ask myself, how could a man like you come out of a home like this? I don't understand it."

"What did I do wrong?" she continued in her steady timbre. "Tell me what I did, son. What was it that made you turn out the way you did, with all your wickedness? It just hurts my heart. I ain't never told you but I'm tellin' you now. It hurts my heart. I can't hardly sleep some nights, I just lay there in my bed prayin', wonderin' what kind of trouble you got yourself into now. Are you in jail? Are you hurt? Are you dyin'? Are you dead? I never know. Lord, I just never do know.

"All that evil, all that devil's work, all those demons that you've walked with for these years. All the people you've hurt, all the people dead because of you. What number of men have you killed, Boone? Don't tell me. I don't want to hear. My soul can't take knowing. Maybe you even killed your own brother. Don't think I haven't thought about that on some of these nights, don't think for one second that I ain't wondered if you was capable of that kind of wickedness."

She paused in her speech, breathing hard. Her cold stare tore through Boone's guts. He knew that he deserved this.

SEWERVILLE

by
Aaron Saylor

POINT NINE PUBLISHING

Play it low, in the background:

"The Funeral" - Band of Horses
"Enough Rope" – Chris Knight
"Go Down" – AC/DC
"Shanty Town" – Matt King
"Before the Blues" - Colin Linden
"Springsteen" – Eric Church
"Killed Myself When I was Young" – AA Bondy
"Depersonal" – Joplin Rice
"Easier" – Joe Purdy
"Methamphetamine" – Son Volt
"Lucky Now" – Ryan Adams
"Endless Ways"- Ryan Bingham
"Oxycontin Blues" – Steve Earle
"Wicked Gil" – Band of Horses
"Blossom" – Ryan Adams
"The Graveyard Near the House" – The Airborne Toxic Event
"The Unrepentant" – Steve Earle
"The Mountain" – Matt King
"The Mountain" – Steve Earle and the Del McCoury Band
"Send a Boat" – Chris Knight

For
Leslie
Mom
Dad
Nan
John
Mike
Sis
Sue
Pat
Karen
Brinton
David
Anthony
Daylan
Kevin
Chris
Daxon
Cory
Matt
Greg
Steven G

and you..

Once, he thought, I would have seen the stars. Years ago. But now it's only the dust; no one has seen a star in years, at least not from Earth.

-Philip K. Dick
Do Androids Dream of Electric Sheep?

PART ONE
FAMILY BUSINESS

VULTURE

Boone Sumner sat in his pickup truck, gnawing the same thumb nail that he always gnawed when his nerves went a-jitter. He didn't want to go into the Slone house, that great sprawling structure which loomed before him. Through the tall front windows, he could see his wife, Karen, seated at the dining room table, all the way at the back of the house. She counted through loose stacks of cash and wrote numbers down in old-fashioned ledgers, while her father watched with that cold look which Boone knew too well.

I hate you both, Boone thought. It wasn't the first time that day the notion had occurred to him.

He had to go in.

He didn't want to go in.

He had to go in.

Not yet, though.

So, he waited. For what, he couldn't say. He sat there, watching his wife and her father through the windows as they counted their money, and he waited.

Walt Slone - Boone's father-in-law - lived in this airy home of six thousand square feet, three times the size of any other house in Seward County. The structure loomed over the valley from astride a well-manicured hill, behind a phalanx of immaculate Bradford pear trees which grew to such splendor that passers-by could see only the very tops of the house's first-floor windows.

The house of Walt Slone existed as a great modern masterpiece of brick and glass, an imposing facade the earthy color of bread crust, split by windows that gleamed like sheets of diamond. At night, the illumination from the house's tall windows could be seen from Main Street. Around Christmas time, the red and blue Christmas tree lights in the living room were visible from the county courthouse lawn down by the center of town.

Some outside observers – snotty academic types from the universities in Lexington, or Louisville, or Ohio, or Virginia - would say the enormous house was an insult to the community, a monster in keeping with the monstrous man who lived within. They'd say it was a vulgar display of wealth. They'd call it a crown of gold on the head of

11

a rotting corpse, built high above a valley filled with boarded-up businesses and sad mobile homes that were rotting on their foundations. They would say that Walt Slone's house loomed above Sewardville the way a vulture loomed above a dying rabbit, waiting to feed as the rabbit made its last desperate kick. But people who would say this came from other places. Tennessee, California, the *New York Times*. They didn't come from Sewardville, didn't understand places like this.

Boone kicked open his truck door, got out, breathed in the chilly night air. *It's awful damn cold for October*, he thought. If the weather kept up like this, in a couple of weeks his black leather jacket, white thermal underwear shirt, and blue jeans might not be enough. They were enough now, though.

He rubbed his face, felt the bristly beard that was the color of wet sand. He thought about Halloween. He always thought about Halloween on nights like this, when the wind had just the right amount of razor bite and the air was thick with the smell of dying leaves.

He still didn't want to go in the house.

He knew that he had to go in the house.

Karen and Walt went about their business, and he watched them. They were far back, at the other end of the house, seated at the kitchen table with several green accounting ledgers stacked in front of them. Only one small orange bulb glowed soft over their heads, yet still Boone could see them in there, Walt Slone and Karen Sumner, the father and the daughter.

He didn't want to go in. He had to go in. He couldn't go in. Sure, he'd driven up here to the house. Sure, he needed to talk to Karen, or at least at one point he thought he needed to talk to Karen. But maybe now he didn't. Now, as he watched her in the kitchen, writing in the ledgers while her father counted through stacks of hundreds and fifties and twenties, Boone recalled only painful times and suddenly he didn't feel such a strong need to see his wife, after all. Tearful arguments, slammed doors, wasted moments.

He leaned against the truck, and he waited, and he waited, and he waited. Finally, he had procrastinated enough, and so he headed for the front door.

"Goddammit," he spat into the October night, pulling his coat collar up around his neck. As he walked, he looked skyward and saw that all the stars were covered by clouds.

A breeze blew cold and crisp across the front porch of the sprawling brick house, much colder than any other October wind that

Boone could remember. The weather forecast called only for rain that night, though, and he could remember snow in a few Octobers past so it couldn't possibly be the coldest ever. But it was getting there.

He cupped one hand against the door's inlaid glass, peered into the house, and saw Karen and Walt still in the kitchen, still counting money, still writing in the green ledgers.

Tap-tap-tap

went Boone's fingers on the window. Neither his wife nor father-in-law looked up. He tapped harder on the door

rapp-ppap-pap

but got no better response and so he banged

BAM-BA-BAM-BAM

and kept banging, until his wife looked up from the kitchen table and saw him.

Half a minute later, Karen opened the door just enough to stick her head out.

"You're home early," she said.

"This ain't home," he answered.

She just looked at him. Her caramel hair fluttered soft in the bitter wind. She didn't hide the utter antipathy she felt about his visit.

He asked, "Are you about finished?"

"Not yet," she said. "There's a lot to be counted."

Boone nodded, slowly. "When do you think you'll be finished?"

Boone's question bounced off his wife's hollow expression like a raindrop off concrete. "Did you make all your rounds?" she answered. A question with a question, that was her style.

"My rounds?

"Yeah, your rounds. You know. Did you take care of everything you were supposed to take care of?"

He shrugged. "Sure I did. I always do, don't I?"

"Did you collect from the bootleggers?" she asked.

"Yeah."

"The bookies?"

"Yeah."

"The cash register down at the Bears Den?"

"Mmm-hmm."

"Did you meet that truck from Florida? We had a lot of merchandise on that truck."

"I got it. The merchandise is already delivered. Don't worry about it."

She squinted, trying not to forget anything. *They will respect what you inspect,* that was what her Daddy always told her. After a long reflection, she said, "What about the quarter machines? Did you clean them all out?" Her voice dripped with acid and disgust.

"The quarter machines?"

"You gotta get those, too, Boone. You know that. How long have you been doing this?"

Boone Sumner hated a lot of things in the world, but very few of them did he hate more than the goddamn quarter machines. Walt Slone had them tucked away in a back corner of every store in the county. To Boone, those machines represented the absolute zero of the human race, sucking lives away one silvery coin at a time. He'd seen plenty of people cash welfare checks and feed the money into dollar-changers, just to get some loose change to fritter away in those infernal machines. All day every day, the sorriest of the sorry-sack degenerates plugged three or four hundred dollars worth of quarters in there and if they really hit big they might get twenty bucks back. Not that they really cared about the math.

He called them quarter machines, but other folks called them "bulldozers." They consisted of a glass case that held two shelves, with one higher than the other and a flat metal bar on the top tier that swept back and forth like the grater on one of the state DOT's big Komatsus. People dropped their quarters in the slot and tried to hit the 'dozer bar just perfectly enough to push their quarter into the other quarters already on the level. Hopefully this created a chain reaction that would then push at least one quarter onto the bottom level, where it could push a few more coins into the catch basin where they could be retrieved by the lucky winner.

It was a stupid game. People put a lot of quarters into it, though. And Boone collected those quarters. Every day, he collected those quarters and took them back to Walt Slone. That little bit of money from the quarter machines meant about as much to Walt Slone as a thimble of liquor meant to a raging alcoholic, but still Boone collected from them every goddamn day.

Before Karen could ask again, Boone said, "Yes, honey. I cleaned them all out."

"All of them?" Karen said. "Are you sure?" His wife had a way of asking questions that made Boone think she never believed him about anything.

"Every last one. I'm sure," he said. "I have thousands of quarters in my truck. Literally, thousands. If you want to look for yourself, go the fuck out there and have right at it. I swear to you, the fucking quarter machines are empty."

"Your attitude is not the best."

"Are you and Samantha coming home tonight?"

His wife only shrugged, and looked at her feet. "We're still workin'," she said. "There's a lot to do. A lot of money to count, a lot of numbers to check. That's how we like it, right?"

Boone looked at her, but did not answer the question.

Karen said, "Just go on home and I'll be there when we're finished."

Boone looked at her.

The space widened between them.

"You know, the numbers, we have to get the numbers finished," she continued, just to fill the space. "We always have to get the numbers. It's probably going to be a while."

"That's okay, I'll just wait in the house," he said. He stepped forward, towards the door. But his wife opened the door no further.

"Are you *sure* you got all the quarter machines?" she asked.

So this was this. Of course he got all of the quarter machines. How could he not get all the quarter machines? Of course he got all of the quarter machines. The goddamn quarter machines.

"Go home, Boone," she said quietly.

"What about Samantha?"

"She's upstairs, asleep."

"Can I see her? Can I see my daughter, at least?"

Karen's eyes drooped. She didn't really want to answer him.

For three solid, sober minutes, a canyon of silence widened between them. The cold wind kicked across the front porch again, raking their faces like sandpaper.

"I'd better go," said Karen, at last. "Daddy wants to finish up the numbers." She glanced up at Boone again, but said nothing else, as she backed away from the door while closing it at the same time.

Through the glass in the door, Boone watched his wife walk into darkness, her small frame silhouetted against the gentle orange light that glowed from the kitchen beyond. When she reached the table, she sat down, opened the top ledger, and began punching numbers in a calculator while her father waited for the figures with an unmoving expression.

Boone watched a little while longer. He thought about knocking on the door again, even raised his hand to do it. But he didn't. Instead, he just headed back to his truck, and got out of there.

BUSINESS

After Boone left, they sat at the kitchen table, Walt Slone and Karen Sumner, the father and the daughter. A twenty-inch flat screen television hung from beneath the cherrywood cabinets, silently broadcasting the news from WTVL, the NBC station in Lexington, which was fifty miles away but still about as local as television got for Sewardville.

The ledgers were open in front of them, stacked six high on the table's flat oak surface.

Walt knew they were old-fashioned - archaic, dusty remnants of business, long usurped by the technological age. He liked them precisely for that reason, though. He found comfort in the little notebooks with red binding and green cloth covers; they were solid, dependable, always there when he needed them. The ledgers did not require broadband connectivity, or flash drives, or terabyte hard drives so they could function; they required only sharp pencils and basic mathematical abilities. He provided certain pencils, but he trusted Karen with the mathematics.

While his daughter wrote, Walt stayed quiet. He leaned back in his chair with his meaty, weathered hands folded on his lap. The silent television caught his attention for a moment, but not long.

Across the table Karen punched numbers into the calculator, scribbled figures on lined paper. The clock marched towards midnight.

Walt preferred that they always checked the books just before bed. It helped wind him down. So every night, after his various business establishments closed, the people who minded businesses - teenagers, dropouts, people from the margins of life - counted the cash, and totaled all the receipts. Shortly after the receipts were totaled, the bag men arrived. These men had large heads and wide shoulders, and wore bruised leather jackets and work boots. Some came in pickup trucks, some in old sports cars, some in off-duty police cruisers. The margin people met them at the store entrances; the receipts and the cash got collected. All of the money and all of the receipts came back here to the house, where the cash was counted, the ledgers filled, the figures reconciled.

Before he retired for the night, Walt Slone knew the numbers. Usually they made him happy. Usually.

"How'd we do today?" he asked.

"Not good," she said without hesitation. "The numbers are down."

He nodded. "Let's start with the girls."

"Mmmm-hmmm," Karen said. "The girls seem to be hittin' it pretty hard. No pun intended. Best night they've had in six months. Almost fifteen thousand between the seven of them. Danielle brought in three thousand on her own."

He took a breath, exhaled, tapped his fingers on the table. He felt unsure which one was Danielle. That redhead from Prestonsburg? Or maybe the blonde who used to work at the Dairy Queen? He barely knew the difference anyway. The girls came and went, a smear of forgotten faces and hazy flesh. Some of them made a living in his spare rooms, but none of them made a career, and he found that an acceptable arrangement.

Karen turned over another page in the ledger, punched more numbers into the calculator, scribbled some additional figures on the lined paper.

He noticed for the umpteenth time that she had her mother's fine cheeks.

"What about the bookies?" he asked.

Karen said, "There's just no way around it. They keep coming up short. Barely two grand tonight. They haven't cracked ten thousand for a whole week since the Super Bowl."

"You think they're takin' from the till?" Walt asked.

"Probably. Don't you?"

He nodded, slow, sure. Of *course* the bookies were taking from the till. He made them keep ledgers, too, but was not such a fool as to believe they actually entered all of their transactions in those ledgers. Mostly he let it go, but over time these off-the-record side bets added up. Something would have to be done to bring them back in line.

Walt said, "Call the sheriff in the morning, tell him to check it out." He thought some more. "How much you think they really owe?"

"If I had to guess, I'd say maybe a couple hundred a day for what, nine or ten months now?"

He winced, and repeated. "Call the sheriff in the morning."

She shrugged, wrote down a reminder for herself on a yellow post-it, stuck the post-it to the front of the ledger.

The business talk continued from there, like they were checking off items on a grocery list. In a sense, that was exactly what they were doing.

"How about the grass?" asked Walt next. He never worried too much about this one. If anything, marijuana stood as their one constant. Never too up, never too down – people were always willing to smoke themselves into a safe haze. Pot was safer than pills and needles, more acceptable in the culture at large. Movie stars smoked pot, comedians smoked pot, neighbors smoked pot, teachers smoked pot, everybody smoked pot. Hell, now and again came news that one state or another might consider legalization. The cigarettes, the gambling, the pussy business, the numbers on those jiggled up and down like a fisherman's float on a pond surface, but not marijuana. The numbers for marijuana could be counted on for long-term consistency.

She bit her lower lip and stared at the ledger.

"Don't tell me our pot business is off, too," he said, incredulous.

"The numbers are down," she said again.

This made for a shitty evening.

He thought she must be getting close to finishing for the night. If she wasn't close, he'd have to turn in early and get the update in the morning. He could feel his mind fogging, overcome with harsh figures.

Just as he was about to say good-night, she closed the books and handed him a piece of paper with a single number written on it: the total take for the day.

He took the paper, read it, raised an eyebrow in her direction.

"You're sure this is right?" he said.

"I'm sure," she said. "The numbers are down."

"Hell yeah they're down. Obviously they're pretty damn far down." He pushed his tongue into his upper lip, a nervous habit. "Is it Elmer, is he making a dent in us?"

"I don't think it's Elmer."

"Well if it's not Elmer, then what the hell is it?"

"It's not Elmer."

Walt Slone believed it was Elmer. Period. Five years ago Elmer Canifax was a piss ant who mostly drew his market from the kids that gathered around his farmhouse like crows in winter, hungry for cheap beer and bags of marijuana mixed with pencil shavings. But that was five years ago and in the Slones' business, five years was a geologic era. A lot happened in five years. The kids were growing up. Now, the kids must want more than cheap beer and a quick toke. Now, Elmer could make a real dent in their business. That had to be the answer.

"I don't think it's Elmer," she repeated. "The numbers are down all over. It's not just one thing or the other. It's everything."

He shook his head. They'd worked so hard. Laid groundwork, made money, worked on the details. Diversified, made sure they weren't painted into corners. The portfolio was both wide and deep. How could they be down? They couldn't be down. It made no sense. "The car wash? The quarter machines?"

"Down."

"Both the convenience stores, all the rental property?"

"Down."

"The Bears Den? Surely they're not down."

"They're down."

He hesitated, not sure he wanted to ask the next question. "Even the pills?" It would be a bad sign if the pills were down.

"The pills are down," she said.

She saw the expression in his face and knew that his frustration would soon boil over. She slid the ledger across the table so he could look at it. He trusted her with the mathematics but sometimes he liked to see for himself. "It's right. Right as can be," she said. "Not good. I understand that. But right is right. The numbers don't lie. They're damn sure down all over. I'm sorry."

Walt got up from the table and paced around the room. The news burrowed into his heart.

The pills were supposed to take everything to the next level, spread their business the length of I-64, into West Virginia, Indiana, maybe all the way to St. Louis, who knew. The pills were the Next Big Thing. Hell, by now they were the Current Big Thing. Kids, parents, grandparents, whores, soccer moms, construction workers, preachers, cops, criminals — everybody loved pills. This was the great wide-open market; anywhere there was a mouth that swallowed or a nose that inhaled, there was a home for pills. Vicodin, Lortab, Oxycontin — the father, the son, the holy ghost. Everybody loved pills. Look at the news. People were dying out there. How the hell could the numbers be down? What about the damned pills?

She looked at him, expecting the blow up would come any second, fast and hard. But her father only walked over to the window and peered out at the night.

"You think it's the meth?" he asked without turning around.

"I don't know," she said.

But they shared that same feeling.

"It's that goddamned meth," he said, shaking his head in complete disbelief. "You got people cookin' that shit up on their own time, layin' around the house all goddamn day mixin' house paint, cough syrup and Miracle-Gro. You got six year olds huffin' drain cleaner before breakfast. It's too easy, that's what it is. Hell, it makes me wanna suck on a toilet cake and see if I can pop a chubby. Of course our numbers are down. What the hell do they need us for if they got the fuck all high of their life underneath the bathroom sink?"

"The stuff moves on the street," Karen said. "Maybe we should look into it." She hated mentioning it. She'd mentioned it before. The answer never changed.

"Hell no," said her father. "Forget that shit. You wanna talk about medicine, we got weed, we got pills, that's all the medicine anybody needs right there. We can bounce back on that. Don't need meth. We ain't down that much."

The answer was always the same. The numbers were down, but they weren't down *that* much. Not yet, anyway. Weed and pain medicine, those were government tested and approved. It was strictly a matter of distribution from that point. Meth was different, though. Meth was seedy, evil, an abomination cooked up by miscreants in shoddy trailers and rundown shacks. Meth was ruin. The Slone family wanted no part of ruin.

Walt bent his head back, shook his shoulders, loosened his body up, then went to the table and sat back down.

He looked at her for a moment. Then he said, "Did you know some of these kids snort bath salts now?"

Karen nodded. "I've heard that. They're not really bath salts, that's just the name."

"Bath salts. Whatever. Pretty soon these little bastards are gonna be smokin' Windex and bourbon whiskey."

"They probably already do," she said.

"I heard some of the worst ones shoot meth straight up their own assholes. They get a needle and cook it up, then stick it right in. Can you believe that?"

She nodded. She could believe it.

On that note, the conversation went quiet. Walt's attention drifted back towards the soundless television and he watched it for longer than he really wanted.

Karen closed her final ledger, set it on top of the stack and then pushed the stack to the edge of the table, out of their way. She clasped her hands and looked at him for a long moment, then finally decided it would be best to change the subject.

"Election's coming up next year," she said.

"Yeah," he acknowledged.

"We should start talking about that soon."

"Don't want to."

She shook her head. She was the only one who could get away with shaking her head at him. "Fine. But if you want to keep your chair in the courthouse, you might want to start thinking about the election. We've got to get the signs printed, the baseball caps, the extra bottles of liquor."

There stood little chance that he actually might not get the votes he needed come either the primary in the spring or the general election next fall, but they still needed the signs, the baseball caps, and the liquor. These were the fuel that kept the machine running. The election meant little; the machine meant everything. The machine meant support. Support meant customers. Customers meant good business.

He understood all of this. Still, he said nothing, only looked down and inhaled deep, through his nose. She knew he was thinking especially hard, whenever he breathed that way.

Several minutes ticked away before he cast his eyes back towards her. "I like my chair in the courthouse," he said. "The chair helps us, don't you think?"

"I'll order the signs tomorrow morning," she said.

PART TWO
THE GONERS

BEARS DEN

On the southern edge of Sewardville – the opposite end of town from Walt Slone's house – stood a ramshackle old bar, constructed of cement block painted beige. It was the only place in the county that served alcohol by the drink (the only place that did it legally, anyway). A Vietnam vet named Ray Hoover opened the place in 1976. He painted a gigantic Old Glory flag on the outer wall facing the parking lot. It just seemed right. The sign out front announced RAY'S BAR, but it wasn't much known by that name

A decade later, Ray Hoover died in front of that flag. A biker from Ohio slashed Ray's throat with a busted Miller Lite bottle, the culmination of a drunken brawl that started in the men's room and spilled outside. The next week, Ray's daughter Lorna took up the place, and she'd run it ever since. The sign out front still said RAY'S BAR, but nowadays most everyone who went there called it the Bears Den. Not a soul could explain why, since no bear of any sort had been spotted in the area for at least thirty years.

Whatever the name, the concrete-block little bar with the giant American flag painted on one outside wall was the favored haunt of Sewardville's drinking finest. Boone Sumner's brother Jimmy went there more than most; he was indeed the finest of the finest when it came to drinking. Every night, Jimmy stayed belly-up to the bar until either he couldn't hold his head up or Lorna tossed him out the front door, whichever happened first. If a day went by that Jimmy didn't show up at all, Lorna would call Harley Faulkner's funeral home to see if he'd turned up there instead.

Tonight, though, brought no need for such a call. Jimmy Sumner sat in his customary spot atop a stool at the left end of the bar. He wore a ratty old army jacket, pulled the collar up just beneath his thin, pockmarked face with locks of salt and pepper hair spilling down onto the camo cloth. He sat not far from the jukebox, which was mostly filled with Steve Earle and AC/DC discs, and also a few from the singer-songwriter types like Springsteen, and Ryan

"Lucky Now" drifted across the room, melancholy, lonely, brokenhearted. Jimmy figured it was one hell of a good time for another drink. He ordered up another shot of bourbon whiskey. Lorna brought it, and Jimmy slammed it back, setting the empty shot glass on the bar in front of him.

"The lights'll draw you in, and the dark will take you doooown, and the night will break your heart, but only if you're lucky now," sang Ryan Adams. Jimmy joined him for the next line, barely in tune, *"And if the lights should draw you in, the dark will take you down, and love will break your heart, but only if you're lucky now.*

Jimmy traced his current state of obliteration back to around four-thirty that afternoon, when he belted down the day's first taste of straight Maker's Mark. That was seven hours ago; yet now, even though the clock headed towards midnight, he still felt like he was just getting started.

Then again, Jimmy always felt like he was just getting started.

"Hey Lorna. Bring me some more of that brown liquor," he said to the hefty woman behind the bar, a plump lady twice Jimmy's size.

She was pushing fifty now but looked ten years older than that, if one judged by the wrinkles in her haggard face and the nicotine-yellow sheen on her teeth. "Where's your brother?" she asked, pouring him another shot of bourbon.

Jimmy smiled. "Boone? Fuck Boone," he said. "Why you gotta be askin' about my brother anyway?"

"Somebody ought to come get you, Jimmy. You finish up that drink and get on out, you hear?"

He bit his lip, swished the bourbon taste around in his mouth. Bourbon carried a sweet burn, which he liked. "Yeah. Brother ain't comin'. Fuck him if he did." He swallowed a thick curl of saliva. "Boone, he's prob'ly sittin' at home, whinin' about his baby girl or some shit. Y'all think he's such a goddamn bad ass."

"Nobody said Boone was a bad ass," Lorna said.

"Fuck they didn't. Y'all think he's a real shitkicker. I know. I know what y'all think. Now give me some more Maker's, why doncha?" He tapped the empty shot glass on the bar.

"You don't need no damn Maker's," said Lorna. "You don't need anything but to go on home before you get yourself or somebody else hurt."

Said Jimmy, "You don't know what I need."

Said Lorna, "You don't, either."

But Jimmy heard her, and when he did, he went quiet. He looked around the bar, saw a couple of ragged old men that sat in the same corner every night, figured he would sit in that corner himself whenever they died.

He came back at Lorna one more time. "Just one more shot. That's all. One more little shot. Then I'll git."

"Nah," she said. "You'll git now."

But Jimmy wouldn't git now. Two fifths' worth of bourbon coursed through the veins in his wiry body, and it still wasn't nearly enough. Most folks would be passed out in the floor or puking in the bathroom sink, but not Jimmy Sumner. Jimmy Sumner thought two fifths of liquor was nothing but a head start; check back when he got through another half gallon. It so happened that in Sewardville there was only one good place with enough alcohol and good music. Jimmy came to the Bears Den so he could sit with the rednecks and the coal miners and drink Maker's Mark bourbon and listen to the by-God old jukebox and fuck if that wasn't what he was gonna *do*.

Ryan Adams faded out of the juke, and soon some dirt-fuzz opening licks from Angus Young's guitar cut through the Bears Den atmosphere in much the same way that a rusty machete hacked through a briar thicket.

Bon Scott wailed "Go Down" across the grimy room for the eighth time that night. The song played so much on this jukebox that sometimes one patron or another felt the need to ask if the machine was stuck. Jimmy liked it that way - the same song, over and over and over and over. He often told people it just plain fit his compulsive personality.

He slid his empty shot glass across the bar, towards Lorna. Dog-drunk and determined, he said, "Fill 'er up."

She watched the plain little glass come her way, shook her head, but had no other visible reaction.

"I'll trade you half a pain pill for a drink," he tried again.

She just looked at him.

"Come on, Lorna."

"You ain't suited for a beggar," she said.

He waited. Lorna showed not even the smallest sign that she felt at all inclined to do as Jimmy asked, but still he waited. And waited. And he waited some more.

While he sat there and he waited, he stared at Lorna's hefty cannonball breasts, each one bigger than his head, the pair of them barely contained by her dark red turtleneck sweater. He imagined his head could rest between them perfectly, that they would look good in the moonlight that shone through his bedroom window. He thought he might ask if she'd take him out back and show those beautiful titties off for a dollar. Maybe for five he could cop a decent feel.

Before he could make that mistake, a tall, rugged sumbitch walked into the Bears Den. It was Deputy Caudill, a lifer in the Seward County sheriff's department who'd come into law enforcement twenty years ago with Sheriff Slone, and since earned every ounce of his skull-cracker reputation.

CAUDILL

The deputy wore a loose, dark blue sheriff's department uniform that looked like a paramilitary outfit, only with a badge pinned on the shirt. He had a permanent look of discordance. Red gin blossoms spidered around his nostrils and disappeared into his thick sandpaper mustache, a monster of bristly facial hair that looked as though it might have shined shoes in a previous life.

When Caudill sat down, he showed Jimmy a cold smile, curled up beneath the hair monster, although calling the brief gesture a smile was like binding up dead tree bark and calling that a book.

Jimmy paid no mind. "Bring me some Maker's, dammit," he told Lorna one more time.

"Jimmy, you done drank all the Maker's," she drawled back, while she was already walking over to serve Caudill.

"Rot gut, then," said Jimmy. "Don't matter. Just bring it."

"Go home," Lorna said. She pulled a glass from under the bar, set it down in front of Caudill and filled it with cheap Beefeater gin. His favorite.

"Thank ya, honey," the deputy said. He took his drink in one hand, had a pull, then showed Jimmy a stiff middle finger.

Jimmy twisted on his seat. He felt a creeping illness. He rubbed his eyes, hoping the sudden slosh in his stomach would go away, but it did no such thing.

The sick orange light of the Bears Den smeared across his brain; neon beer signs mingled with the cigarette smoke and fluorescent overheads. The walls and ceiling slid around. For a second he thought he might fall to the floor, but grabbed on to the edge of the weathered maplewood bar and pulled himself back from the brink.

"Lorna. Lorna! Hey, Lorna!" he said.

She occupied herself with Caudill.

Jimmy tilted back on his stool and reached for the little blessings he carried around in his jacket pocket.

The pills.

His hand closed around the amber plastic of a medicine bottle half-filled with Oxycodone. Suddenly everything felt right with the world again.

He closed his eyes, raised both eyebrows and held them in that high position. He did that a lot when thoroughly hammered the way he was thoroughly hammered right now. Rolling the pill bottle in his palm, he thought about telling big bad Deputy Caudill to suck a long hard one. Instead, he just whispered, "Hell with this," because he knew nobody in the room was listening. He'd been in this spot enough to know that nobody *ever* listened to him.

But this time Lorna did. "Fine. Hell with it," she agreed.

"Hell yes," Jimmy concurred. He popped open the Oxy bottle and caught a single white gem with a deft motion he'd honed over the last several years. OC's, Lortabs, Vicodin, Xannies, these were his friends. He knew how to handle his friends.

"Whatcha got there, Jimmy?" Deputy Caudill asked.

"Oh, you know, just a little of papaw's medicine," Jimmy said.

"Is that right?" said Caudill. "Papaw's medicine, huh?"

"You bet your ass it's papaw's medicine," said Jimmy. "It don't get no righter than that." He climbed off his seat and immediately drunk-tumbled to the floor, landing hard on his bony ass.

Lorna exhaled. She muttered under her breath - the words *dumb* and *motherfucker* and a couple others Jimmy couldn't quite make out - and then she came around the bar in an angry rush. Before his addled brain could fully register just what was happening, Jimmy sensed the pressure of her meaty hands in his armpits, pulling him upward. He reached for the Oxycodone again, a protective reflex to make sure he didn't lose any.

With barely any struggle, she stood him on his feet.

The moment slowed for Jimmy. He felt the floaty sensation of being encased in gelatin. He swayed left, right, back to center, but this time he didn't go down and felt like that was an accomplishment. He looked at Lorna and grinned, showing a wide mouthful of yellowish teeth. His eyes became happy slits.

"You smell like a batch barrel," she told him.

"Baby, I'm-a buy you a ring," he said. "We're gonna get married."

Caudill laughed out loud.

"Really," Lorna said, disinterested. "And what kind of ring is that, Jimmy?"

"A big one," he said. He waited a moment, broadened his smile, "A great big ring, to match your great big fat ass."

Lorna measured him up, and smacked him a good one under the ear, and another one on top of his head, boom boom.

He was too drunk to feel anything. He laughed at her. Then he spit in her face.

Deputy Caudill jumped up and came at him. He grabbed Jimmy by the back of the hand, smacked his face down on the bar and dragged a greasy spot across the wood for three feet. Jimmy's nose shattered like a dinner plate on a tile floor; bloody snot poured across his lips and chin, red torrents. Lorna screamed obscenities that curled the paint on the wall.

It all ran together – the blood, the curse words, the bad bar light.

Jimmy saw stars and tweety birds and thanked God that the Oxycodone hadn't already started working. He could still halfway think for himself, with the narcotics not quite flowing through his system. A truck driver with more hair in his mustache than on his head - Jimmy hadn't seen him in his life until just that moment - held Lorna from behind, his arms around her waist, his biceps bulging out of a cut-off flannel shirt as she fought to get another shot in.

Meanwhile Deputy Caudill wrenched Jimmy's arm backwards, yanked him up and shoved him towards the door. The deputy put a violent torque on Jimmy's wrist, driving it up and into his liver.

Now *this* hurt. Hurt like all hell.

The drugs didn't work so well now. Jimmy saw fire and smelled brimstone. He thought his skinny body could tear clean in half at any moment, that he could die right there face down in a steamy pile of his own internal organs. It hurt, it damn well hurt bad, and as Caudill pushed him out of the Bears Den and into the cool autumn night, it occurred to Jimmy that high on pills though he might be, this was the first real pain he'd felt in probably six months.

OUTSIDE

Deputy Caudill pushed Jimmy out the door and into the crisp Kentucky air. They shuffled across the gravel parking lot in a funky stride that didn't break until they reached Caudill's gray police cruiser which had SEWARD COUNTY SHERIFF blazed in high red italics across both sides.

As soon as they got to the car, the deputy gave Jimmy a shove in the back, sending him flying forward. Jimmy stuck his hands out but it was too late. He knocked his skull against the steel of the cruiser's door frame; a sound echoed across the parking lot, not unlike that of a watermelon being struck with a tobacco stick. Two seconds later, blood poured out of a new gash in Jimmy's scalp.

"You should have gone home, Jimmy," said the deputy, holding his quarry fast against the patrol car. "Why's it always got to be like this with you? You actually like gettin' your ass beat on a regular basis?"

"Can't be no other way," Jimmy muttered.

Speech was difficult, the world hazy, heat rising from asphalt. Blood ran down from the cut in his scalp and mixed with the snot that poured out of his broken nose. He spit a thick reddish mixture on the ground.

"Sure it can," said Caudill.

Then he reared back and buried his fist in Jimmy's gut.

Jimmy howled, fell to his knees, chunked nasty body fluids all over the gravel. Scarlets and creams and grays and purples.

"Sooner or later you got to figure this shit out," Caudill kept going. "And if you can't, I'm gonna have to figure it out for you. You know what I mean?"

Jimmy hacked up pieces of his insides. "I guess… guess I do know what you mean."

Slow, unsure, he climbed back to his feet. He could barely see anything through the blood, the alcohol, and the pills. He wiped the mess off his face and gradually brought the deputy into some measure of focus.

He said with defiance, "You a dumb ass motherfucker."

"What was that?" spouted Caudill. He puffed out his chest and got ready to whip ass.

Jimmy staggered forward with a wild swing at his head that didn't come close to landing, much less to doing any damage. Caudill grabbed the arm mid swing and slung Jimmy face-first into the side of the cruiser again. Jimmy felt two of his teeth shatter as they met window glass, followed by the hot wet splatter of his own blood across his lips and cheek.

Right after that, Caudill's knee ground into his liver.

"You want to finish this here, or down at the jail?" the deputy sneered.

"Turn me around and find out," came Jimmy's answer, tough words through a pained and shaky voice.

The deputy shook his head and muttered, "All right, have it your way, dickhead." He spun Jimmy by the shoulders so they faced each other. Before Jimmy was all the way around, Caudill drew back his fist to deliver what he knew would be the blow that would end it, the final blow that would break the fucker's jaw, knock him out cold, kill him, whatever.

But not this time.

This time, Jimmy was quicker.

As Caudill spun him, Jimmy found his opening. He jumped forward, and drove his shoulder into the blue uniform shirt, up under the lawman's incoming fist. Both men sprawled backwards. Jimmy drilled his shoulder home as Caudill's back hit the sharp gravel and absorbed the force of landing. The air blew out of the deputy's lungs at the same time his neck snapped backward, and the rest of the world went bright white for a second.

Now Caudill looked vulnerable. Adrenaline shot through Jimmy. In a desperate moment, a frantic moment, a moment of preservation, he clawed his way across the deputy's blue paramilitary outfit, and with every last bit of wiry strength he could muster, he commenced pummeling the deputy.

Bone crunched. Cartilage shattered. Blood painted the grey gravel. Jimmy's fists pounded the big deputy's face like pistons hammering through a dry engine block until most of his visage was hamburger.

When the beating was over and Jimmy was satisfied that Caudill wouldn't be moving any time soon, he reached down and took the deputy's .38 out of the holster. He stared at the black barrel. It occurred to him that everything had blown out of his system – the whiskey, the drugs, the pain. All gone, swept away by a storm surge of fear and adrenaline, leaving behind only the taste of his own blood. It tasted like an old fork: bitter, metallic, awful. He swallowed it anyway.

After that, Jimmy bent down and poked the gun barrel under Caudill's chin.

"I'd be careful with that if I were you," growled a deep voice, from the other side of the cruiser.

SHERIFF

Jimmy knew that growl far too well to suit his own tastes. He associated it with the business end of a retractable baton, raining blows down on his back and shoulders. He had faced the growl and the baton at the end of many a drunken night in Sewardville. They were the first steps in a spiral that always ended on the cold concrete floor of the Seward County drunk tank.

The growl's owner stepped out from the driver's side of the shiny gray police car. The sheriff.

Jimmy's guts dried up in his belly. Deputy Caudill was more than a handful in his own right. But now, here stood Sheriff John Slone, tall and muscular, clean shaven, with a tough, sharp face that could have been sculpted out of sandstone. Another beast in a blue paramilitary uniform with a gold badge stuck to his chest.

He was Walt Slone's son, every bit of it. He had one hand tucked into the side of his pants, and the other flexed carefully above his unbuttoned gun holster. A Beretta 9mm pistol hung at his fingertips, ready to draw, with a custom Confederate flag inlay on each side of the grip.

The sheriff smiled, ran his thumb across the stars and bars. Jimmy never liked to see John Slone smile. When John Slone smiled, bad things happened.

From his knees, Jimmy jerked and turned Caudill's gun on the sheriff.

Slone pulled his hand away from his holster and stopped where he stood. "Okay now, just hold up, budrow," he said, without even the slightest hint of nervousness despite the gun pointed at his face.

"What the fuck are you doing here?" barked Jimmy.

"Why don't you put the gun down."

"*What the fuck are you doing here?*" Jimmy screamed even louder, as if it might make any dent in John Slone's cool exterior.

The sheriff shrugged. "I'm workin'," he said. "What are you doing here?"

Jimmy squirted to his feet, with the .38 still trained on Slone.

"Tell me you didn't just kill an officer of the law," said the sheriff. His voice was calm, smooth, a cemetery wind.

Jimmy shrugged. "So what if I did?"

Slone nodded slowly. He didn't answer; they both knew what would happen to Jimmy if Caudill was dead.

For his own reassurance, Jimmy kicked Caudill in the side. A weak groan came out of the deputy's mouth. He was alive.

-click—

Jimmy pulled back the hammer on the .38 and pointed it at Slone's chest. "I'm gonna ask you again," he said. His heart beat so much faster now. "What the fuck are you doing here, sheriff?"

"I told you why I'm here," Slone answered.

"Why's that?"

"You know."

Of course Jimmy knew. It wasn't dumb luck that had put the Sheriff in that place at that time. Walt Slone had told his son to get out there and find Jimmy, and of course there was really only one place to look. He knew Jimmy was at the Bears Den that night, because Jimmy was at the Bears Den just about *every* damn night for the last twenty years.

"You tell Walt that I ain't got any money." Jimmy said. His hand shook slightly. "I ain't got no money today, didn't have no money yesterday, and ain't gonna have no fuckin' money tomorrow. How about you tell that to Walt?"

"I ain't here for your money," said Slone. "But what I *am* gonna do is take two step towards you. I won't touch my gun. Just two steps up. Okay? Then we'll talk about this."

Jimmy said nothing. He didn't move.

"Okay, then," the sheriff said, and then he took two steps forward, just as he'd promised.

When John Slone came forward, Jimmy stepped back. His heart beat a little faster, his hand shook a little more, but not so much that he couldn't hold the gun up.

"Stop right there!" Jimmy yelled.

"Hold on, punk."

KRAKK!

Jimmy fired a shot into the air and then just as quick, he had the gun back on Slone again. "Don't come any closer, John," he said. "We already got one dead. You take one more step and there'll be another body to clean up."

Slone stepped forward anyway. He held his hand out, palms down, like keeping a sick dog at bay.

KRAKK!

This time, the bullet tore into Deputy Caudill, right under his chin, spinning out the back of his neck in a crimson splat.

The sheriff lunged at him, fully intending to grab the .38, stick it in Jimmy's ear, pull the trigger and get rid of him once and for all. But when the sheriff lunged, his boot slid on the gravel.

Jimmy heard the loose rocks shifting on the ground and knew what the sound meant. He turned back to see Slone, just as the sheriff regained his balance.

And that was when Jimmy pulled the trigger again

KRAKK!

Again

KRAKK! Again *KRAKK!* Again *KRAKK!*

Before the echoes faded from the last shot, Sheriff Slone fell to the ground. A circle of blood already expanded across his shirt. His eyes rolled halfway back in his head, and his legs went useless.

In and around the Bears Den, chaos erupted. Lorna came running outside with a couple of truckers right behind her. As they streamed outside to help, someone screamed "Call 9-1-1!" not realizing that the only officers on duty that night were lying bloody right there in the parking lot.

Jimmy tossed the pistol to the ground. His brain flashed with a million different images at once but none of them made any sense. In that moment, only one notion made sense. Only one.

This shit just got bad, that was what made sense. *This shit just got real goddamn BAD. GET OUT NOW RIGHT NOW RIGHT NOW*

He entered the woods on a dead run.

Thin whippet limbs slapped at his face and ears, bare of leaves only recently turned color and fallen, but he tore through them without really feeling anything. Although he was rapidly putting distance between himself and the Bears Den, he still heard Lorna's voice behind him. He could make out what she was saying, just barely, "He's alive! The sheriff's alive! The sheriff's still breathing!" something like that. Something terrible like that, sickening words that put rocks in Jimmy's stomach.

He knew that Walt Slone would soon get word about this whole debacle, and as soon as Walt knew that Jimmy was on the run, that would be when the shit got real. Oh, sure, the shit was real now. No question. Jimmy Sumner had just shot two police officers and people in Sewardville tend not to care much for that sort of thing. Goddamn right the shit was real. But soon, Walt Slone would be involved, and when Walt Slone got involved, he would bring all hell to bear. It was his way. And when that happened, that's when the shit would get REALLY real.

Another million mixed-up thoughts blasted scattershot in Jimmy's mind. Then somehow, his legs found another gear, and one notion overcame all others, blaring:

RUN! RUN YOU MOTHERFUCKER!

and then after that

better find your brother
find Boone
(before he finds you)

RUN

An hour passed. Two hours. Three hours.

The clock spun past midnight, towards morning. In all that time, Jimmy barely stopped running. A second here and there, a breath, a wipe of spit from his lips, nothing more. Time was not his luxury. The briars ripped at his shins and the bitter autumn midnight chapped his face, but Jimmy never stopped. He just ran.

He heard the snap of branches behind him, trampled underfoot by those angry people at his heels, but still he ran. Flashlight beams danced at his back, ten, twenty, maybe more of them chasing. But the further he ran the more they fell behind, and thirty lights soon became twenty, and twenty became twelve, and twelve became four, and four became one, and finally the lights and the angry voices faded back into the darkness. By then, all Jimmy heard was his own heart sledgehammering in his throat; all he saw was blood spilled on a gravel parking lot; all he felt was the world crumbling. So, he ran.

ALMOST

Jimmy stumbled out of the woods just after three in the morning. He knew well the wilds of Seward County, and he knew exactly where he had to go, knew it from the moment the pistol went off and the scarlet stain started spreading across the chest of Sheriff Slone. For Jimmy Sumner there was only one destination, sure as the whole damn world.

Mama's.

When he came out of the woods, Jimmy saw his mother's house sitting a few yards away. He looked at the dark, peeling old structure from the edge of the backyard. The kitchen light shone an electric yellow beacon in the morning dim, and he could see Mama inside, sitting at the table, both hands around her coffee cup. Alone.

Then he saw Boone's truck, parked in the grass with wet tire tracks running through the yard behind it.

Jimmy's steps were slow, careful as he walked towards Mama's house. Frosty grass crackled beneath him, sending shivers up his legs. He half-expected Boone to hear him coming, and shoot him dead right there in the grass. That was why Boone was there, after all. Part of Jimmy hoped that his little brother had shown up there at Mama's house to finally make things right between them, to spirit him away from Sewerville once and forever, but that was only a small part.

The rest of Jimmy knew that Walt Slone sent Boone there to kill him.

As he came around towards the edge of the house, Jimmy noticed the rifle rack hanging in the back window of Boone's truck. Only there was no rifle on it. Bad sign.

"Goddamn it, Boone," Jimmy said out loud. He wasn't surprised to see his younger brother there – Walt Slone always sent Boone out for the dirtiest work – but not being surprised and not being disappointed were two different feelings altogether.

He stopped in the yard and thought about what to do next. He couldn't go in the house. Might as well put the gun to his head himself.

Before he reached a new course of action, Jimmy heard heavy steps behind him. Someone - Boone goddammit! - said, "Hey!" and before Jimmy could even turn around, he felt a hammer-blow on top of his head, and then his world began a fade to black.

A cold drizzle blew down from the night sky, the last thing he knew before unconsciousness took him.

GRAY

Jimmy woke up slowly, clouds in his brain, his head bouncing against a rain-flecked vehicle window. Whose vehicle? He didn't know. A steady shower had set in while he'd been unconscious. Early morning had passed to mid.

He watched the water droplets roll down the glass and slowly, he regained himself. The first thing he realized was that duct tape bound his hands together at the wrists. The second thing was that he was in the woods again, only this time he wasn't running, he was riding, in Boone's truck. And Boone was driving. His little brother. Short black haircut, clenched jaw, straight ahead gaze. Boone.

"Boone?" He struggled for clarity. "What is this? What's goin' on?"

"Welcome back, beautiful," Boone growled, in a voice that had been aged by too many cheap cigarettes and too much cheap whiskey. "You really fucked up this time, didncha?"

Jimmy said nothing.

Boone tried again. "Guess you know where we're goin', huh?"

Still, Jimmy said nothing. He rolled his head over and watched the steady pour of water down the truck's window. He didn't know where the two of them were going, but didn't feel the need to know, either. He knew what was going to happen when they got there. That was enough.

RAIN

When they got to Coppers Creek, the storm kicked up. Rain broke through the opaque surface of the muddy water like buckshot.

It was a miserable rain, pounding at the core of Jimmy's soul. He hated few things in more than a cold steady rain. He thought it the worst weather imaginable. Worse than a hail storm, worse than a blizzard, worse than a tornado, worse than a hurricane. He'd never experienced a hurricane but he imagined no hurricane could be worse than the chill rains that often drenched Kentucky in October.

Boone pulled the truck down to the water's muddy, storm-broiled edge. The vehicle's front tires sank two inches into the soft gravel bank. He opened the door, grabbed Jimmy by the jacket collar, and tossed him out on the wet ground. Jimmy never said a word, nothing, as he flopped to the ground with his bound hands unable to steady him. His face landed in the shallows of the creek.

Rank water flooded Jimmy's nose and throat. A heavy pain thumped in his temple; he saw blood mixing into the creek, and knew it belonged to him.

From the bank, Boone stared down the cold barrel of his thirty-ought-six rifle, one hand at the trigger, the other firm under the stock. He kept the gun pointed at the back of Jimmy's head and watched water and yellow muck foam around his brother's earlobes.

"So, now what?" he asked.

"Don't know," said Jimmy, raising his head. He spit out water, and also something not entirely water. "You tell me."

"I guess you know, Walt sent me after you."

"Sure he did. Course he did. Mother *fuck*. How about you let me on up from here?"

"Can't do that."

"Sure you can."

Boone tightened his grip on the rifle. "Jimmy, I'm sorry, but you know what's gotta happen," he said.

"No. No, fuck no!" Jimmy screamed.

Jimmy struggled to sit up, fought the duct tape. He flopped over on his back, in the water again. "Maybe we oughtta talk about this a little more, the two of us," he stammered. "Maybe you could let me up from here and we could figure out a better way to take care of this. Ain't nobody here but us."

"There's nothin' to talk about, Jimmy."

Boone's stillness gave Jimmy pause. Neither man moved for a long moment.

"Okay, fine, we don't have to talk about nothin'," Jimmy said finally. "You just let me up and I'll be out of here, and nobody has to know a goddamn thing."

"I can't do that. You know I can't do that."

Jimmy stared at Boone. "Sure you can, you can let me up!" said Jimmy. His voice heightened, wavering. He talked faster, words tumbling out of his mouth, not fully formed and barely more than thought. It was how Jimmy spoke when cornered, too scared to think things through.

He said, "You can let me on up and then both of us get the hell out of here. You can tell 'em I got the drop on you, knocked you in the creek, ran off before you could get out of the storm. They'll believe that."

"Ain't nobody gonna believe that," said Boone.

"It's a helluva storm," said Jimmy. "They'll believe that! Shit, anything could happen in a storm like this, you know? Then after a couple of weeks, they'll forget about me."

Boone tightened his left hand around the rifle's stock. "These ain't forgetful people, Jimmy," he said. "Walt Slone don't forget nothin' or nobody. You know that."

"He'll forget me."

Boone spit in the creek. "You really believe that?"

"Yeah."

"Goddammit. You know better."

Jimmy took a deep breath and swallowed some more of his own blood. Of course he knew better. He considered the weight of his predicament for a good three minutes. The rain pelted the back of his neck, down his shirt, into the waist of his pants, but he barely felt it.

"Oh well," he finally whispered. "Fuck it, then."

They stayed there, wondering what came next.

Rain fell, and memories rolled in for both of them.

1984. Summer. Bright hot inviting thrilling summer. No rain in the forecast, just sunshine, warm air, and still water.

The dark blue Folger's coffee can sits on the ground next to the stillness of Coppers Creek, filled with dirt and a few dozen nightcrawlers. Jimmy, in the sunshine of boyhood, reaches into the can, sifts through the dirt and finally pulls out a nice fat one.

Put this on your hook, he says.

You do it, Boone says.

Jimmy laughs. *You're seven years old. Seven years old! Plenty old enough to put a worm on a hook. Come on now, it ain't gonna hurt.*

I don't wanna, Boone says. *I hate worms. You know that, Jimmy.*

Put the damn worm on the damn hook, Jimmy says.

Boone looks in the coffee can and sees nothing but gray parched earth, but he knows that underneath it, there must be at least one worm in there somewhere. And he hates worms.

His stomach knots. Sweat gilds his fingertips. He pushes his tongue between the teeth and upper lip, and finds his mouth as arid as the dirt in the can. Boone changes his mind, wonders, how can any nightcrawler possibly live in that can? He imagines what it must look like beneath the dead dirt: the rusty can bottom must be covered with a hundred dead worms, piled on top of each other in a shriveled dead mass. Dead worms in dead dirt in a dead coffee can.

Jimmy says Boone has to put the damn worm on the damn hook. Jimmy is five years older, Jimmy always knows what's right. Always. Jimmy always knows what's right because Jimmy is the older brother, and older brothers always look out for younger brothers. That's why they call them older brothers, right?

Boone takes a deep breath and reaches into the coffee can.

He digs in the dirt.

It surprises him to find that beneath the sun-baked surface, the dirt in the can is not dead, but cool and moist, alive. He finds a fat nightcrawler, slick and also alive, not shriveled at all. As it slimes across Boone's seven-year-old fingers, his seven-year-old stomach tightens up again.

I hate worms, Boone says.

Bait the hook, Jimmy says.

Boone closes his grip around the nightcrawler, pulls it out of the dirt, threads the hook through what he guesses is the head and pushes the fat worm up until it sticks firm on the metal barb.

As Boone does that, Jimmy chuckles out loud. He says, *Atta boy, I knew you could do it.*

Boone feels his older brother's hand smack him gently, playfully on the back of the head, like he always does when Boone makes him proud. Boone likes to make his older brother proud.

Brothers. Cut-off jeans and tank top shirts. The sunshine of their youth.

Still water.

Dead worms.

Digging in the dirt.

Knew you could do it.

The rain poured now, as the storm became a real gully-washer.

Jimmy held his eyes shut tight. Water crashed around him; blood thundered in his head. He didn't move.

Boone said, "I guess you need to be gettin' up now."

Jimmy didn't move. He just lay there in the mud. He knew the inevitable would come, but he would not go to it.

Aggravated, Boone picked his brother up by the shirt collar, slung Jimmy a good six feet out into Coppers Creek, and waded in after.

Jimmy staggered into the swirling, filthy water. His arms were no use, tied behind him. He quickly lost his balance and went down to his knees for several seconds before he could finally get back up again.

"Hang on, little brother!" he shouted over the creek's roar. "Hang on just a goddamn minute now. You don't really want to do this, do you? Kill me like this?"

Boone raised the rifle to his shoulder again. This time, he sighted in towards the center of Jimmy's face. "Wantin' don't come into this, Jimmy," he said. "I wasn't the one that put you here. You put you here. I'm just the one pullin' the trigger."

"You doin' what Walt Slone told you to do, is that what this is?" Jimmy shot back. "Fuck Walt Slone. Fuck him. Fuck him, you hear me?"

I only do what I'm told, Boone thought. The earth might split open and the trailers and shotgun shacks of Sewardville, Kentucky might eventually tumble into the fires of Hell, but that wouldn't be Boone's fault. He just drove his truck around. Pick up and delivery.

Besides, this was Jimmy's fault. Jimmy couldn't leave well enough alone, Jimmy wasted plenty of chances and now all his chances were gone. Boone didn't put Jimmy here, Jimmy put Jimmy here. Boone was just the one pulling the trigger.

Boone said, "I'm sorry, Jimmy. Walt Slone says you got to disappear."

"I can disappear! I can disappear just fine!" said Jimmy. "I can go up to Gallatin and disappear just fine. We can take care of it that way. Won't nobody ever know any different."

For a moment, Boone listened. He wanted to believe his older sibling. He looked at Jimmy's face - the hair that went gray too soon, the deep-set eyes that fell empty too early, the craggy face, wrinkled and pockmarked. He wanted to believe him more than he had ever wanted to believe anything else in the whole shitty world. Maybe Jimmy could run away. Maybe Boone could let him go. Maybe Walt Slone would forget. Maybe everyone could just pretend that the whole nightmare had never happened. Maybe maybe maybe maybe maybe.

"I can disappear, Boone."

"You can't just disappear, Jimmy!" Boone snapped, suddenly angry at both Jimmy for talking, and himself for listening. "If they catch wind you're still around, it's all over for both of us. They'll find you later, then they'll kill you, and then they'll kill me, too."

"No. No! They won't catch wind of shit," answered Jimmy. "And even if they do catch wind, it'll be so long that they won't care no more. I'm tellin' you, they won't care!"

"They'll always care."

"Fuck 'em Boone. Both of us can get out of this. They'll forget, they always forget."

The bitter rain poured down in thick wet drops that hammered the land harder than ever.

With one soggy sleeve, Jimmy cleared his vision as best he could. He was soaked; Boone was soaked; they were soaked; every goddamn thing was soaked. The creek filled quickly. Soon the water lashed at its banks, sometimes over them, mocking the land that could not hold its fury.

Let us bow our heads, says Mama.

Mama bows her head and thanks the Lord for their daily bread. Jimmy and Boone just look at each other. They try not to laugh. Boone steadies a load of mashed potatoes on his fork, pulls it back as if he might launch at any moment. Jimmy picks up a bread roll and cocks his hand back like Nolan Ryan, ready to unleash a bread-roll fastball at a moment's notice. If Boone launches the potatoes, Jimmy will respond. Boone does not launch the mashed potatoes.

Mama finishes the prayer. The boys lower their weapons.

How was your day at school? she asks.

Fine, they answer together.

Are those boys still giving you trouble, Boone?

Boone gazes at the mashed potatoes on his fork.

Are these boys still giving you trouble, Boone?

Not anymore, Mama, says Jimmy.

What happened?

Jimmy shrugs. *We took care of 'em.*

Took care of them how? asks Mama.

Jimmy doesn't say. He looks at Boone, narrows his eyes, and nods, slowly, like he always does when Boone makes him proud. Jimmy slaps his hand on the table and breaks into long, loud laughter. Mama slices him with a razor stare. Yeah, yeah, that stare draws blood.

Boone wants no part of that stare. Instead, he watches the mashed potatoes for a few more seconds, then takes a long drink of milk, winks at his brother and does his best not to laugh in front of Mama.

Jimmy stumbled backwards, the creek water swirling up past his knees now. Boone waded in with him, holding the rifle above his head, well aware that if he dropped his gun he'd lose it for sure in the increasingly swift currents.

"No! No! Fuck this! I'm gettin' out of here!" Jimmy cried. He turned his back, tried to run away, as if there were somewhere else he might go.

No sooner had Jimmy spun away than Boone caught him. Boone grabbed his older brother by the back of the shirt - the shirt was heavy with rain water, and slick, but not so heavy and not so slick that Boone couldn't get a firm handful of cloth - and slung him down.

"The hell with you, Boone! Goddamn you!" Jimmy screamed, his mouth filled with creek water. He struggled to regain his footing, kept screaming, "Goddamn you, goddamn Walt Slone, goddamn this whole place!"

"Goddamn *you*, Jimmy!" Boone exploded. "I don't wanna hear another word about it!"

Jimmy went silent.

Boone watched him.

It rained.

Jimmy's shoulders moved up, down, up, down as he heaved for air. Rain cascaded around his chin and shoulders. Again, Boone lifted the rifle to his shoulders, wrapped his right hand around the wooden stock. He fingered the trigger, sighted his shot straight into Jimmy's head.

The only sounds were the sounds around them: the machine-gun fire of the rain, the thunder of the creek. It seemed that way for twenty years, but in fact it was that way for just three minutes.

Finally, Jimmy sloshed forward two steps. He bent down and pressed the top of his head firmly against the end of Boone's rifle barrel.

"Go ahead and do it then," he said. "Let's get this over with."

"You know I never wanted it to be this way," said Boone.

"You're my brother, dammit. You're family."

Jimmy stood still. "I guess family don't matter anymore, huh, Boone?"

"It ain't like that. You know it ain't like that."

"It's like that," Jimmy said. "If family mattered, I wouldn't be here in this creek with your gun in my face, now would I?"

Another long silence came between them. Jimmy looked up, first into the certain death of the rifle's black barrel, and then past the cold steel, directly into Boone's eyes.

"Time's a-wastin', Boone," he said. "Get it over with."

"I'm sorry, brother," Boone said. "You know I don't want it this way."

"There ain't no time for wantin'. Do what you have to do."

One more time, Jimmy looked down. One more time, he pressed the top of his head against the cold steel and waited for the end of everything. He began singing, an old Merle Haggard song they'd known since childhood. *"Mama tried to raise me better, but her pleading, I denied. That leaves only me to blame 'cause Mama tried..."*

Boone felt a pull in his throat as his brother looked up at him with the cold, hurting eyes.

"Well now, Boone," Jimmy said. "Here we are. Mama always said we were her pride and joy. So which one do you think I was?"

Boone didn't answer.

Jimmy closed his eyes and gave up. "Come on. Let's do this."

A chill shimmied up Boone's spine, a chill that had nothing to do with the autumn rain or the angry floodwaters in which he stood.

He wished Jimmy would look at him one more time. Just one more time. It didn't happen. In the weeks and months to come, Boone would actually be glad that his older brother refused to look up in his final moments, but now, he just wanted to look into Jimmy's face one last time, only to apologize to him, to say he was sorry one last time, he wished it didn't have to be this way, he was only doing what he was told, if there was anything else he could do he would do it, he would do it, he would do it, he would do it.

But there was nothing else to do.

Jimmy pressed his skull harder against the rifle barrel.

Thunder and lightning ripped the dark sky above, as the uncommonly strong autumnal storm bloomed. Underneath the atmosphere, a few feet out into Coppers Creek, a loud, sharp crack ripped through the October air, blasted from an unforgiving metal barrel. A quick flame burst in the night, followed by a soft splash. Jimmy fell into the creek and sank beneath the surface of the waters. And then, nothing else but the rain.

Hey Boone, Jimmy says. *I came by your house last night. You weren't home. Were you out with Karen again?*

Yeah, we were out, says Boone.

Jimmy smiles and says, *Walt Slone's got somethin' he wants us to do.*

Will he pay? asks Boone.

You know Walt Slone always pays, says Jimmy. *He runs everything. He's got the money.*

How much?

Two thousand.

Two thousand! What's he want? asks Boone.

Get your pistol and we can talk about it in the truck, says Jimmy.

Boone's heart sinks. He could use the money, but not that badly. He doubted he would ever need Walt Slone's dirty money that badly. But, then again, two thousand dollars was a lot of money for an eighteen-year-old. Two thousand dollars was a lot of money for just about anybody in Sewerville. A man could do a lot with two thousand dollars. And besides, they could do just this one thing, Jimmy and he could do just this one thing and then get the hell out and never have to worry about Walt Slone or his gang again.

Just this one thing, Boone tells himself. How bad could it be? Two thousand dollars is a lot of money. A man could do a lot with two thousand dollars. And it's just this one thing...

HOME

An hour after Boone took care of his only brother, the rain disappeared from the valley. It would return soon enough.

BOONE

It was the worst of times, and it was the worst of times. It was the worst of the worst times.

Boone Sumner woke up the next morning feeling like he might throw up. The window by the bed hung open. The room was so cold that a thin frost glazed his blanket. His throat was sore and scratchy from sleeping under the chill. He rolled over, but found the other side of the bed empty, just as cold as the air in the room. Through the fog of half-sleep he remembered a fight with Karen the night before, something her daddy wanted, the usual shit.

Quickly Boone let it go. No doubt they would take it up again later. They always took it up later. These days their fights were interminable, peaks and valleys.

Visions of his brother clanged in his eyes. He wanted no part of them.

He looked over at the night stand and picked up the green picture frame which contained a photo of his five-year-old daughter. Samantha. This was the perfect gift for him whenever he found it upon waking – her perfect smile forever captured, her gossamer curls forever spilling down across her forehead. He wasn't sure when or where the picture was taken, but felt that, judging from her size, it must have been recently.

He looked at the picture for a solid minute, thinking. Samantha. He went through peaks and valleys with Karen, a lot of pain and doubt and who-knows-what, but never with Samantha. With Samantha, there were no valleys.

He put the picture back on the night stand, gathered himself up, and headed for the shower.

In the bathroom, he glimpsed his thirty-four-year old face in the mirror. A six-day beard made a thin blanket on his jaw line; it had started out dark, matching the short black hair on his head, but now turned the color of rust. It always went that way when Boone went too long without shaving. Another thing: his jawline was normally clean, and firm, but this morning, the beard softened it. Boone didn't like that, but he didn't really feel like doing anything about it, either.

HELL

The sun dared show itself again just past six-thirty that morning. An angry wind screamed out of the valley, whooshing all the tree limbs on all the hillsides at once, sighing in unison, helpless against the whims of the breeze. Dead leaves and dusty dead-leaf pieces fluttered in the air, the last remnants of summer in their annual dive towards nothingness. Heavy gray thunderclouds rolled over the ridge; already, another storm growled near.

Boone watched all of this from his truck, which was parked right back where it had started the night before: in Walt Slone's driveway. He hadn't even begun to think about sleep.

Finally he got out and went back to the front door. He knocked, and waited for the old man to answer. He waited, and waited. Walt Slone did whatever he wanted, whenever he wanted; he lived on his own time and didn't care about anyone else's. Certainly not Boone's time. Even if Boone was his son-in-law, that didn't move him up any higher on Walt Slone's priority list.

So, Boone waited. The damp, unseasonably cold air lingered around his ears, and he pulled his collar up, and he waited. He buried his hands in his jacket pocket and waited.

No one came. He turned and looked down the hillside. From the doorstep, even in the gray mist that hung around this close to dawn, Boone could see all of Sewardville in the valley below.

He closed his eyes and envisioned something else.

In his mind, Boone saw a nightmare version of the valley. Highway 213 snaked through from bottom to top, pock-marked with potholes and crumbling shoulders. In the brush near the road loomed rusty old dinosaur farm equipment: tractors, hay beds, belt feeders, combines, spreaders, junk. Beyond the dinosaurs stood shoddy mobile homes, shouldered together one after the other like old men in a soup line, with their walls buckling under the twin strains of time and poverty. Past the mobile homes, way down the road, way down in the valley, was a little town. Gas stations filled the town, along with churches, secondhand furniture stores, and fast-food restaurants. A school stood on one end of town, so children could get away from their families. A jail stood on the other end of town, so that families could get away from the school. It rained a lot.

Images rushed at Boone, as if he were looking through a telescope and jerking from side to side at the same time. A Baptist church here. A Methodist church there. A BP station on one corner. A Chevron on the other. A McDonald's to the east, a Taco Bell to the west. A logging truck. A school bus. Children. Old people. A pharmacy. A meth lab. A dealer. An addict. A blonde. A cheerleader. A cross. A coffin.

Boone felt sick.

The pictures in his mind shifted. He imagined everything in Sewardville sliding into the very bottom of the valley. The churches and the gas stations and the fast food restaurants piled on top of one another - sinking, sinking, sunk - as the earth crumbled beneath them. Everything went down, down, down to the bottom of the pit. The rusty machinery slid a little further down the valley, creeping closer towards the mobile homes. The mobile homes sank down the hillsides, headed towards town. The town sank into a black pit, headed towards oblivion, and Boone could do nothing but stand there and watch them go.

But, then, the vision went away.

Boone chased it all away with the thought of his daughter. Samantha. Nowadays, she spent most of her time in this house on the hill overlooking Sewardville, with her mother and her grandfather. Boone didn't want that, but that seemed to be more and more the reality of the situation. His little girl was growing up while he spent his days and nights at Walt Slone's beck and call, chasing people through the woods and collecting money from low-rent gamblers or hawkers of illegal cigarettes. While Boone stood on one side of Walt Slone's closed door, Samantha spent too much of her time away from him, on the other side of that door. And the further they went, the less Boone saw that door opening.

He couldn't escape the frightful thought that one day he'd look down into the valley and see her tumbling away from him for good, down there with the whores and the pill heads and the methamphetamine monsters.

Boone opened his eyes. Real sight returned. He looked down into the real valley beneath Walt Slone's real brick mansion, and saw the town, saw the churches, saw the gas stations. He did not see a sinkhole. He did not see flames or a pillar of black dust. The combines stood there, rotting beside the roads. The mobile homes were still, the meth heads were safe, the fast-food restaurant signs still glowed in the early morning light.

The world was right. Right as could be, anyway.

So, Boone waited for Walt to answer the door. He waited. And waited.

Finally, Walt opened the door. He did not say hello. He did not say anything. Boone offered him a thirty-ought-six rifle and a case of bullets to go with it.

The two men exchanged no words at all. Finally, after what seemed like hours but was really only two minutes, Walt accepted the gun and ammunition.

"What about it," said the old man, flatly.

"Dunno. What about it," said Boone.

Now they would talk.

WALT

Walt Slone stood six foot four, with white hair as close-cropped as it had been ever since he joined the U.S. Marine Corps in 1962. His head was almost too small for his body. His skin was tanned deep from all the time he'd spent fishing all the best spots from one end of the country to the other, but especially down in Lake Cumberland, where he'd built the lake house as soon as he had his first million in the bank. Wrinkles dug deep all around his gray eyes. A smooth pink scar went from the edge of his right temple down his face to just under the ear, a trophy won in a fight at the Bears Den four decades ago.

He said, "Good morning," in a voice that sounded like skinned knees dragged across concrete.

"Morning," said Boone.

"You got somethin' to show me?"

"Sure I got something to show you." Boone pulled a plain brown paper bag out of his pocket and gave it to Walt. Walt nodded and took the offering. He looked at the bag for a moment, opened it, checked inside.

There were three spent rifle casings in the bag. Walt bounced the bag around, and soon found two bloody human fingers jumbled with the shells. Jimmy's fingers.

"That work for you?" asked Boone.

"Is that brother of yours dead, or ain't he?" Walt asked flatly, just like he was asking for the price of gasoline at the corner store.

"He's dead alright."

Walt rolled up the paper bag and handed it back. "Works for me. I know it's gotta be eatin' you up, but you did the right thing. Don't you worry about that. I know he was your brother and all, but you did the right thing, Boone. We'll have us a funeral, let Harley Faulkner handle the body just like usual, and that oughtta be that. You go see Harley this mornin' and he'll take care of us. What about that?"

Boone pursed his lips.

"Well huh," said Walt, more or less to himself. "Anyway, I knew I could count on you. Now I need you to go check on them whores."

"What makes you so sure?" Boone interrupted.

"'Cause they're whores. *Somebody's* gotta check on 'em."

"That's not what I mean."

"What the hell are you talkin' about?"

"I'm talkin' about you and me," said Boone. "What makes you so sure you can count on me?"

"You saying I ought not be so sure?"

"No, I'm asking why are you."

"There ain't no why. I just am. Now all of a sudden you got to get philosophical? You got to question what I say, is that how this is?"

Boone shrugged. They eyed each other a moment longer, before Walt opened the door and stepped aside. Boone didn't want to go into the house – these days he never wanted to go into that damned house - but he did anyway.

By the time Boone entered the foyer, Walt stood in the living room, with his weathered brow furrowed even deeper with irritation. Boone saw the old man there and followed in no hurry at all, his boots creating lonely echoes on the solid hardwood floors as he walked.

The house impressed Boone, the same way it had the first time he entered, well over a decade ago. It did more than impress him – it imposed its will down upon him. Clean lines, cold steel everywhere. Imported Italian tile and fine cherry hardwood made the floors more valuable than any other five whole homes in Sewardville combined. In every room, heavy glass cases protected the prized artifacts of Walt's passionate Civil War collection. Letters, uniforms, flags, guns, bullets, the finest collection anywhere in the United States not named the Smithsonian Museum. Cool solid colors painted the walls, dark reds and earthy browns and greens.

The Slone house was money, real money, not what some of the locals referred to as "holler fabulous." Folks back in the hollers thought they were high on the hog if they got a new above-ground swimming pool or drank Crown Royal whiskey or maxed out their credit cards on Ralph Lauren shirts from Macy's or Dillard's in the biggest Lexington shopping malls. But what was fabulous in the hollows of Seward County was pocket lint for Walt Slone.

"Karen and Samantha, are they still in bed?" Boone asked.

Walt snorted, and stared at Boone without answering. He waved his hand as if to dissipate the question.

Boone entered the living room with the serious concern that Walt would punch him in the face at any moment. But Walt didn't punch him in the face.

"They had to fly the sheriff to Lexington, take him to university hospital," the old man said, almost to himself. "Worked on him all night.

Looks like he's gonna pull through, though. Sure as shit. It'll take a hell of a lot more than one shot to put Johnny Slone down, that's one thing he got from me."

"What about Caudill?"

"Not so much," said Walt.

Boone walked over by the gigantic living room window and stared across the dewy grass. "Jesus."

"Jesus is right. That little shitass brother of yours done it up right this time."

That little shitass brother of yours. Boone hated the way that sounded, but knew the words carried truth. Jimmy definitely done it up right this time.

"Ain't really too much to talk about now," said Walt. "The shit is totally fucked. You hear? Tee totally fucked. Your brother Jimmy made us one hell of a mess, Boone. He really done it up right this time and now we gotta figure out what to do about it." White saliva jumped from the corners of his mouth when he spoke.

"Fine," Boone said.

Walt tipped his head back, pursed his lips. "It ain't fine. It's damn far from fine," he said. "Jimmy shot himself a couple of police officers. Killed one deader'n four o'clock and left the other knockin' on the door. He ain't been shit his whole life, but here he is, a cop killer now. Cop killers make news. News makes it hard to handle things ourselves, you hear?"

"Yeah."

"I hate the fuckin' TV news. Cameras and shit, sideways up a horse's ass, that's what I say about the news."

"You think they'll come?"

"Hell yeah they'll come. The news people always come for shit like this. Prob'ly they're already here."

"Prob'ly they are." Boone nodded, looking at the dew glistening off the manicured lawn. He walked slowly back and forth, from one end of the window to the other, with his arms crossed.

He didn't much like the TV news, either. He felt like the network stations from Lexington spent too much time pretending they broadcast from a big city. Lexington was what, two hundred thousand people? Three at the most? Barely a city at all. Take out the big state university, and there wasn't much left to brag about; yet, they were so quick to grab their cameras and jump in their news vans and rush out into rural Kentucky at the first word of a toothless robbery victim or a high-school dropout with a bone to pick. Boone couldn't stand it. He hated the TV news as much as anybody, maybe more.

Walt clicked some spit around his gums. "Gonna get bad," he said. "Bad with a capital B."

"It's already bad," Boone corrected.

"Some things might come to light," Walt continued. "We might have to run our business a little differently until all this blows over, you know?"

Boone shrugged. Nodded.

Walt ran his hand over his short white hair and took a deep breath. "You ain't seen Bad," he said. "Maybe you think you have, but you ain't. You will, though. Things will have to be done, they'll be Bad, and you'll see what I mean. You gonna have a problem with this?"

They looked at each other. Walt waited for an answer, but Boone said nothing.

He didn't know what he *could* say. Contrary to Walt's thinking, Boone had seen Bad in his life, plenty of it, more than enough to know where this mess with Jimmy and Sheriff Slone stood in the great pantheon of Sewardville Bad Shit, which was: pretty goddamn bad.

It was a mess now, but it would be an even bigger mess in the next few days. The news people from Louisville and Lexington would descend on Sewardville, the city reporters with their big voices and righteous sympathy. He only hoped they would quickly get bored with the story and get back in their news vans. Just leave Sewardville to Walt Slone and let things get back to normal. Don't stir up too much from the bottom of the soup. Let things go. Let Sewardville be.

"Boone?" said Walt.

"What?" Boone realized that he'd drifted away.

"You're not gonna have a problem with this, are you?" Walt said. "'Cause if you're gonna have a problem, if you don't think you can stick in there with us..." He trailed off, came back. "Anyway. You're supposed to be the bad ass. Show me you still got somethin' in your nutsack."

"I'll be fine."

Walt popped his neck. For a moment, he let the conversation hang there. It contented him if conversations stuck at odd points, because when that happened it always made the other guy uncomfortable. He liked it when the other guy felt uncomfortable.

"Go down to the Bears Den, clean out the quarter machines," he finally said. "Put the quarter machines and the video poker in the supply room. The reporters will be there later, count on that. The TV people. We can't have all that shit out in the open, they'll put it on TV for the whole goddamned world, some dumbass state senator'll see our machines in the background and there we'll be with our dicks in the whiskey."

"Okay," said Boone.

"Good," said Walt. "After everything else around here, I'd hate for us to go down over a goddamn quarter machine."

Boone took a breath. He didn't feel like talking anymore. It was obvious that Walt would not let him see Samantha or even Karen, which was also Bad, but hardly a surprise. Things went that way sometimes. Nothing could be done about it.

Resigned to his lot in Walt Slone's world, he walked back through the foyer, and out the front door, closing it quietly behind him. He descended the porch steps, ready now to get the hell out of there.

When he reached his truck, he threw the rifle in the cab and got in behind the wheel. He thought again about his older brother Jimmy. Jimmy, the little shitass. Jimmy, who'd finally done it up right this time. Jimmy, whose two severed fingers now rested inside a little paper bag with some used rifle casings.

Boone started the engine and as he drove off, familiar images visited his weary mind: rusty machinery, crumbling earth, pillars of smoke and fire, blood. He imagined again that somewhere, a shoddy mobile home slid a little bit deeper into the valley. A tight knot formed in his stomach; it didn't matter.

MAMA

On the way to the Bears Den, Boone took a detour away from his duties as an acolyte of Walt Slone, and headed for his mother's house. He had to tell her about Jimmy. She shouldn't hear from a stranger.

His pickup truck bounced up the gravel drive. The house where he'd grown up loomed at the end of this short, weed-infested drive, and now he off-roaded his way back there. Oak limbs hung over the road from both sides, dotted with orange leaves that hung on to the branches for dear life. A graying wooden fence lined both sides of the driveway, with blackberry bushes poking through the rails in several spots.

Several yards out in the field beyond the fence stood a tattered red mare. The animal watched Boone come in and chewed dead weeds as the black truck bounced past, not all that interested in much else.

Boone glimpsed the horse through the trees and wondered where it came from. As far as he knew, Mama hadn't done anything on the farm since Boone's daddy drew the ace-deuce two decades earlier. Maybe the mare wandered over from a neighbor's pasture. Maybe not.

Boone pulled into the ragged yard, just a few feet from the front door. He shut off the engine and gazed out the windshield at the fading old house wall. The place was buckling under its own weight, much like Boone's memories of the childhood spent there. He felt sympathy for this house. And empathy.

An awful dread sunk in his heart like a poisoned arrow. He did not want to go in, did not want to tell Mama that her eldest son was dead.

Maybe Mama wouldn't answer the door. The last time Boone had seen his mother, she'd sworn that her house would never be open to either of her sons again. She had kept that promise, too, and at the moment Boone hoped she would still keep it.

Through the front window, he saw her. The sun-bleached yellow curtains were tied back and there she was, sitting in the kitchen where the family had once spent so many breakfasts, lunches, and dinners together. She had her silver hair pulled into a graceful bun atop her head, and a lacy yellow apron tied around her thin body. She sat alone at the kitchen table, which looked much too big for only one person.

Her Bible lay open in front of her, the same Bible with the black leather cover that Boone remembered her reading when he was younger.

He recalled that this Bible had been a gift from her own mother, who died a decade before Boone was even born. As she read, Mama's lips moved along with the words, though no sound escaped from them; that was her way. She liked to read with the gentle whispers of her own breath for company. He guessed she'd read the whole book a hundred times and knew it by heart.

Boone realized his mother could see him through the kitchen window, just like he could see her. It occurred to him that she must have heard his truck. How stupid, to think she wouldn't hear the truck. Mama always heard everything.

Now she stared at Boone through the square kitchen window. It was so hard to not look her in the eye. Instead he focused on other things: the light glinting off her silver hair, the pink skin on the back of her hand, the lines of worry around her mouth that her sons helped put there. Her wrinkled face was utterly without expression, her mouth drawn tight, her eyes open and looking at Boone, but also not open and not looking at him.

Suddenly Boone wanted to leave.

Jimmy was dead and that was that and why should he be the one to tell her? She could see it on TV or read it in the paper just like everyone else. Maybe that was cold but hell, the world was cold.

Boone picked up his cell phone and dialed her number, the number she often threatened to change but never did. He watched her answer the call after four rings. She turned her back to him as she spoke.

"Hello?"

"Mama, it's me."

"Who is this?"

"Boone. I'm out in the driveway."

"I know." Of course she knew. "I saw you out there." She paused, let him think about that, and then said, "You stay out there, too, you hear?"

"Mama -"

She spoke louder now. "Stay out there now, you here? I told you not to come around this house. You come here this morning and brought your wicked ways with you, now you and your brother run off into more wickedness. Wickedness, you hear? You got the devil in you, boy. What is it that makes you think I want your wickedness come near me?"

His heart flipped in his chest as he thought of the awful news he had – had – to share. He decided to keep the news from her just a little longer.

Boone took a deep breath. A long moment passed, until he said, "It's Jimmy, Mama. Something's happened. I need to tell you -"

"More trouble. Lord knows you all need more trouble in your lives."

"It's something like trouble, yeah."

"I ain't surprised," she said. "Sometimes I think you don't know nothin' but for trouble. Trouble and wickedness, that's all you got. You know what I think? You ain't got the devil in you, son, you're the devil in himself. That's all there is to it," she said. Her words came out plain, short, calm even, just like she was reading from a cake recipe.

Then, she hung up. Boone saw her throw the phone across the kitchen, and walk into the other room without turning to face him again.

Boone sat in the truck for a few more minutes and waited for her to come back, but she never did. Now he wanted to run away. He couldn't tell her, not now, not after that exchange. How could he tell her? He couldn't tell her.

He had to tell her.

Mama, I'm so sorry, he thought. He opened the truck door and got out, then walked towards the house, watching through the window with every step.

He ambled up the front porch and knocked on the door. "Mama?" he said, hoping she would not answer.

She did not answer.

Boone knocked again.

"Mama? You in there?" Of course she was in there. He knew she knew that he knew she was in there. Still, Mama didn't answer the door. He allowed that really, it was good that she didn't answer, because if she answered the door, how would he say what he had to say? But she wouldn't answer the door. Or, she might.

If Mama did answer the door, what would he say? Something. Somehow.

Jimmy was dead and Mama would hear the bad news from someone, eventually, yes, but Boone knew what was right: he should tell her. He needed to be the one, as though it might somehow sweep away the ash from his heart. The need to tell Mama that her oldest son was dead - that heavy need kept Boone on the porch. He was a bastard but he wasn't a piece of shit.

Boone knocked on the door one more time.

"Mama? Mama, you in there?" he said one more time.

The door stayed closed. Mama being Mama, Boone being Boone, the door stayed close. But Boone had prepared for this moment. He knew she wouldn't answer the door, so this morning, when he got back from Coppers Creek, he'd written his mother a note. The least he could do.

Now Boone took the note out of his inside jacket pocket, just four ragged black words scrawled on a brown paper scrap of grocery bag, the same grocery bag that he'd filled with rifle casings and his brother's severed fingers. The only thing in the truck that he could find to write on.

The note said, "Jimmy's dead. I'm sorry."

That was all.

He folded the wrinkled paper twice. His head hurt now. He took a deep breath and thought one more time about running away. He thought about Jimmy. He thought about fishing worms, sunshine, rain. He pressed the note between his palms, and brought it to his lips, then finally kissed the piece of paper and slid it under the door. He hoped Mama might read it soon. He didn't really expect that she would, though.

DEVIL

Inside the house, Mama saw the note on her kitchen floor. She picked up the note, and she read the note.

"Jimmy's dead.," it announced, plain. "I'm Sorry."

After Mama read the note - the note that her son had written in blurry black ink on a torn piece of grocery sack - she stared at the kitchen door and battled back tears. She tried to be strong, tried to be quiet so that Boone wouldn't hear. She didn't want him to hear. He was a bastard. He wasn't her son anymore. He was a bastard, a bastard that had fallen in with the awful likes of Walt Slone and John Slone and gotten into wickedness, drugs and gambling and killing and hatefulness and sin, and now all that wickedness had finally got somebody killed, finally got her Jimmy killed. She always said this would happen, back in the days when she still talked to her two sons, when she still saw them every Sunday for dinner. And now, it had happened.

Evil awful hatefulness. Wickedness. Sin. Bastard. The devil in himself.

That wicked Walt Slone. This was all his doing. Walt Slone took her boys away from her. Walt Slone brought the silence between her and her sons. They were such good little boys. Her home had been filled with joy and love and the bright chatter of hope and harmony. But then her boys fell in with Walt, and Walt brought the silence into her home and wedged it between Mama and her sons.

She thought of it all, and it all came down on her heart, heavy, heavy, heavy in a way she never imagined. And she stopped trying to be quiet.

She didn't care what Boone heard.

She put her hands to her face and the tears stormed free, down her face, onto her hands, onto the kitchen floor.

Those tears flowed for Jimmy, her oldest son, her dead son. They flowed for Boone, her baby, the only baby she had left. And they flowed for her, too. The tears poured forth and Mama's head hurt, and her eyes hurt, and her heart hurt; and she screamed the name of one son, and then the other; and she screamed for Heaven and she screamed for Hell, and she fell to the floor and she kept screaming; and she kept crying; and she hated Walt Slone; and she hated this place; and she hated Boone. She hated Sewardville. She hated all of it.

But by the time Mama screamed Boone's name, he was already gone; and he was on his way back to Walt's place; and he didn't hear anything. Still, he knew what his mother thought about him.

WALT

After Boone left, Walt sat down in the living room, comfortably in the center of his expensive leather sectional. He put one hand on each knee and silently watched through the tall front windows of the house as the gray dawn mists slowly burned away. He was alone now; he liked to be alone in the mornings. The house was quiet, the world was quiet, and he could think.

So Jimmy was dead.

It almost didn't seem real. When Walt had called Boone the night before, to tell him the sheriff was shot and Boone had to find his brother, he had expected a long conversation, lots of grief, lots of bullshit. Boone did what was asked most times, but asking a man to go after his own brother, that was different. Then again, if there was one thing Walt had figured out over the course of his years, it was that people would do just about anything if you asked them the right way.

Or told them.

When it came to favors owed, Walt had Boone by the short curlies. He could call in any favor, anytime. And with Boone, if the favors ever ran out – and that wasn't happening anytime soon – he could get to him through Karen. If he couldn't get to him through Karen, he could go through Samantha. But there was plenty enough he could hold over Boone's head that he didn't have to resort to playing family games very often. When a man shovels your dirt for nearly two decades, he doesn't end up too clean himself.

Of course, Boone Sumner wasn't alone in his position. Walt had spent his life building up favors that he could leverage for the maximum benefit of the Slone empire. It took more than hard work to rise up from the four-room clapboard house where Walt's tobacco farming parents raised him.

Even back to his early days running illegal fireworks into the foothills of Kentucky and West Virginia, he'd always been able to make shrewd connections that paid off later. He'd pay a teenager to deliver a few hundred Roman candles, and if the kid wanted a couple bottles of Kessler whiskey for the weekend, Walt threw those in for free. If somebody's parents needed a good word to put them over the top for that bank loan that would net them a new Chevrolet, Walt called the loan officer and just like that he was a hero to the parents *and* the kid. A few extra dollars here, some cheap guns there, some free girls over there, and it didn't take long before he had a lot of friends around town. Nor did it take long for Walt to realize that friends vote, and a lot of friends meant a lot of votes, and a lot of votes meant he could get himself a pretty big chair in the courthouse. And big chairs made it easier to do big things.

But even with his big chair and all his friends and favors, Walt Slone couldn't control everything that happened in Sewardville. Jimmy shot the sheriff, and as far as the rest of the world knew right now, the shooter still ran free. That was news, big news.

Reporters and probably even Kentucky State Police would be descending on the county soon if they hadn't gotten there already. The KSP he could handle; he had people he could call that could keep any heat off. The reporters were a different story, though. There were no friends or favors there, only a deep rooted preference on Walt's part that every news van and mobile satellite stay the hell in the big cities where they belonged. Reporters brought overblown interviews, sensational ratings ploys, film-at-eleven network wannabe bullshit.

Walt didn't need any bullshit right now. What he needed was for everything to blow over. He needed the sheriff to get back on his feet, Harley to take care of Jimmy's funeral and if need be his body, too, and Boone to keep his shit together long enough that he didn't fuck things up any worse. He needed the smoke to keep smoking, the pills to keep popping, and the whores to keep whoring. He needed the green to keep rolling in. He needed the numbers to be up again.

He thought about the first man he'd ever shot. Moments like these, he often thought of that man. Anthony Epperson, a chicken fighter out of West Liberty. They'd gotten into an argument at the chicken pit because Walt thought Anthony was spiking some of the bird food, making some of the roosters sick so his own animal wouldn't have any trouble shredding them in the fights. There had to be some reason that Walt had lost six straight cockfights to the guy, and that seemed as likely a reason as any.

So, after the matches one Saturday, Walt cornered Anthony Epperson of West Liberty behind the barn. It quickly escalated into shouting. Walt had a gripe. The other guy didn't want to hear it. Before long, weapons were drawn and Walt fired the first and only shot. He hadn't killed his man – the bullet grazed Epperson's right temple and ripped off into the barn wood – but the message went through just the same. Walt Slone was not to be fucked with.

Over the years, Walt would say that he'd missed intentionally, and just wanted to scare the shit out of the guy. It didn't really matter. The story was the story. Besides that, a couple years later, Walt and Anthony had another run-in, this time over a few cases of Walt's whiskey that had turned up missing, and that time the gunshot didn't go awry.

Walt noted the symmetry. That was the first body Harley Faulkner had ever disappeared for him, and here it was decades later and Harley was still disappearing them. He'd get another body today, if Boone did what he was told.

The old man closed his eyes. He rubbed his head gently and cast those thoughts away. Then he stood up and headed into the kitchen.

KAREN

Karen Sumner, Boone's wife and Walt's daughter though not necessarily in that order, woke up shivering. She was in one of the spare bedrooms, just down the hallway from where her father normally slept. The second-story window hung open, where she'd left it when she drifted into sleep. Her five-year-old daughter Samantha lay beside her, also shivering. Chilled fog puffed from both their mouths.

Karen sat up in bed, pushed the blankets closer to the little girl's chin, and then swung her own bare feet around to the floor. The lacquered pine hardwood felt cold, almost wet on the soles of her feet, a sensation Karen found more than unpleasant. She recoiled, jumped back into the sheets.

The movement woke up Samantha. "Is Daddy home?" she asked, wiping the night from her eyes.

"No, Daddy's not home yet," her mother answered. "Daddy's still at work."

"It's cold in here," said Samantha.

"I know. I'm sorry, honey," said Karen.

"Where's Daddy?"

"I don't know."

"I heard his truck —"

"He's not here."

"But I heard him, Mommy," Samantha muttered. "I heard him outside." She slipped back into slumber.

Karen loved watching her daughter sleep. Thick blond curls framed the child's soft face, a gift from God and the Slone family gene pool. These gorgeous ringlets normally brought compliments from friends and strangers alike, and Karen proudly noted that she'd had the same ethereal curls when she was that age.

Samantha yawned, not asleep after all. "Where's Daddy?" she asked again. Her eyes stayed shut.

"Daddy's not home right now."

"Where is he?"

"He's at work," said Karen. She reached for the girl's shoulder, but Sam pulled away.

"Is this going to be one of *those* mornings?" asked Karen.

"Mmmm-hmmm," nodded Samantha.

Every time Samantha woke up and her daddy wasn't there, it became one of *those* mornings. For Karen's money *those* mornings happened far too often these days.

How she wished Boone could be there to see their daughter this way, to actually feel for once the brunt of the child's disappointment. How she wished she could grab him by the throat and say *Look, look at this, this is what you've done.*

But in her most honest moments, Karen admitted that only part of her wished she could say that. The smallest part of her. The part that still ran to the window every late night when headlights appeared coming up the driveway, casting starburst in the sparkling glass. That part of her still cared.

There were other parts of her, though.

The mother and daughter conversation faded away like mist in the morning sun. The child turned over and pulled the covers tight around her, and a few minutes later, she was asleep again, this time for real. Karen got out of bed and went to the window, pulled it down and locked it, then walked across the room and set the thermostat to seventy degrees. The heat kicked on.

From there, she went into the expansive hallway and quietly closed the bedroom door behind her. The hardwood was cold here, maybe colder than it had been in the bedroom. She hustled towards the bathroom, but found the tile there even colder.

A morning shiver rolled up her legs. The house stayed cold, no matter the setting on the thermostat, and she couldn't get used to that cold, no matter how many years she spent here. Cold in the spring, cold in the summer, colder than cold in the fall, colder than all hell in the wintertime. She was thirty now, and still she thought she would never get used to that damn cold.

As a child she believed the house was too big, that she might get lost in it and never found. It felt even bigger, more vast and empty and echo-filled, when her mother died, and still more vast and more empty after Karen moved back in there with Boone, as a way of keeping an eye on her father. Just in case. Just because you never know. But even with the three of them, and then later with Samantha, the house was too big, and eventually they'd moved back to their own house on the edge of town. But they still stayed here at least once a week. Boone didn't care for that arrangement, not that it really mattered what Boone thought.

Too big. Thirty-two rooms sprawled about the loose floor plan. Too big. Even though she'd spent nearly all her life here, she was certain she'd never done more than walk through most of those rooms. Her mind barely registered the contents of the home around her - antique chairs, expensive fabrics, ten thousand dollar imported rugs, heavy furniture, art on the walls, her father's Civil War collection, stuff. None of it meant much to Karen. Not as a child and not now. Stuff. Just stuff.

She had her comfortable corners: her bedroom, her living room, her kitchen, her bathroom, and she knew those and that was enough. The rest was just too much. Too big and too quiet, incapable of bringing comfort. She always felt a constant wind skirling through the house, rustling curtains and whispering old names. The family that raised her and the family she herself now raised echoed together in the same deep spaces, haunting this great Xanadu of the eastern Kentucky hills.

Karen flipped on the bathroom light, looked at herself, thought about Boone. The truth was, she'd heard him come in that morning, after all. But he hadn't stayed long. That was why she lied to Samantha. She felt guilty for it, but lying was just so much easier. How could she explain to a little girl that her Daddy came to the house but didn't come up to see his only daughter?

One day there would be explanations and truths, but for now there were lies, and lies did the job. Lies got everybody through the empty mornings.

Daddy's still at work. Those were the words Karen knew by heart, the words to which she usually turned when she needed a bandage for Samantha's wounded soul. They were a lie; they weren't a lie; they both were and were not a lie. For them, Boone often existed in a liminal space, neither here nor there, somewhere in between. And sometimes his wife wondered if he would exist there for the rest of their time together.

All Karen knew for sure was that whether they were a lie or not, the words worked. *Daddy's still at work.* She understood this from her own experience as a mother and more importantly, as a daughter. They were the words her own mother had said, so many mornings like this when Daddy came to the front door but didn't come up the stairs, didn't come to see his little girl. They were the words she knew by heart, those empty comforts for little girls who wondered why their fathers spent so much time away from home.

But she didn't really want to think about such murky topics now. Later. There was always later. Maybe even today she would talk to Boone a little bit.

She opened the glass shower door, reached in for the expensive handle, and started the water. It heated quickly; she tested with her hand until the temperature got to the perfect degree, which for her meant just barely less than scalding. Steam quickly surrounded her; she took off her nightshirt and stepped into the cascade, gratified, warm at last.

FAMILY

Downstairs, in the kitchen, Walt poured his morning coffee. He leaned against the black granite counter and turned on the HDTV that hung from a brushed-chrome arm underneath the dish cabinet. The morning news out of Lexington came on and quickly faded into background noise. A weather report. A drug arrest. Somebody overdosed on Lortabs. A car drove off a bridge. Somebody overdosed on Oxycontin. A University of Kentucky basketball game went into overtime. More rain for the weekend.

Walt picked up his coffee, and just as he turned around was surprised to find Karen standing there, looking at him. Her hair was still wet, and she was wide awake.

"I told you, if you don't dry your hair you'll get sick. House this big always has a draft," Walt said.

"I'm used to it," she said, even though she wasn't.

"Suit yourself," he smiled, and drank from his steaming cup.

Karen went to the cabinet above the dishwasher and pulled down a ceramic mug of her own, one that was adorned with a picture of four playing cards, the Ace and the Eight of spades on one side, the Ace and the Eight of clubs on the other. While she filled it with coffee, she asked, "You had Boone out workin' late again?"

Walt shrugged. "Nah, he came in."

"I know he came in. I heard him this morning," she said. "But he didn't come up. Samantha's not real happy about that, you know."

"I needed him to move the quarter machines down at the Bears Den."

"Why?"

"The TV people will be there sooner or later," said Walt. "You know they will, after everything that happened last night."

"I don't think they care about the quarter machine. Why would the TV people be at the Bears Den, anyway?"

"They like to stir shit up. You know how that is, honey."

Karen leaned against the counter, waited a moment then pressed on. "So do you know where Boone is now? It's been a couple of hours since he left here. It doesn't take that long to move a quarter machine."

Walt sighed. He looked askance at his daughter. "Yeah, I know where Boone is," he said with a shrug, holding the coffee against his chest. "He's workin'."

"Workin'?"

"Yeah."

"What's he doing?"

Walt shrugged again. "He's workin', that's all," he said. "You know how that is."

She did - she knew how that was. It was not to be discussed any further that morning, not between Karen and her father, anyway. She knew the old man's business, knew it well, ran all the books and understood the numbers and what went behind the numbers. She also knew that if he wanted to talk about it, he talked about it. If he didn't, he didn't, and clearly this morning he didn't. Instead, he went to the little breakfast table beside the window and sat down.

And so. The world was still and there they were, just the two of them, father and daughter.

The empty drone of local news drifted through the room and then went away without consequence, a weather report, a basketball game, murder, suicide, fog, basketball, rain, something, nothing.

But then one story caught Karen's attention.

"We have a reporter en route to Seward County, where Sheriff John Slone has been hospitalized following a shooting last night that left one of his deputies dead and the gunman on the loose."

"Oh my God," she put her hand to her mouth, and spoke into her fingertips.

"Yeah," said Walt.

"Jesus! Why didn't you tell me?"

Walt shrugged, drank his coffee. "I didn't think nothin' about it."

Suddenly Karen felt like she might vomit. "John got shot last night and you didn't I needed to know?"

"He ain't in too bad a way," said Walt. "I'd have told you if the doctors said he was in any serious trouble. We can go see him later, if you want."

"If I want?"

"Yeah. If you want."

She put her hand over her mouth, processed a thousand ugly thoughts at once. *How could you not tell me? When were you going to tell me? Who do you think I am, not to wake me up in the middle of the night when my own brother's been shot?*

"Don't worry about it. He's gonna pull through just fine," said her father, in the same easy tone he might employ if he were talking about some random victim from the local news. "He's a tough bastard. He's one of us, idn't he?" He took his coffee cup and headed out of the kitchen.

"Who do they think did it?" Karen yelled after him.

"They don't think nothin'," Walt answered as he left the room. "They know damn well who did it. Jimmy Sumner. Lorna came out of the parking lot and saw him runnin' off into the woods. He can't run forever, though. You know how that is."

Now, everything made sense to Karen.

Now, she knew Boone's whereabouts. Working, indeed.

No more questions were necessary. Her brother would pull through, that was what mattered – if it looked that bad, they would already be at the side of John Slone's hospital bed – and as for his assailant, Lorna saw Jimmy Sumner running away and Boone had work to do. Things would get straight.

She said, "We should go to the hospital."

Walt shook his head. "Not now. We'll go later."

"Later? Are you serious?"

"Doc has him. He'll be all right. There ain't anything we can do to make it better or worse. You know how that is. What do you want to do, go down to the hospital, go see your brother, and sit there to watch the ventilator work?"

She didn't answer.

Karen followed her father into the living room. He sat down in the middle of his ten thousand dollar, chocolate leather couch and she sat on the end.

He grabbed the remote and turned on the sixty inch LED screen. The morning news on WTVL On Your Side took their attention for the moment. Iraq, Afghanistan, scary people with big guns, the weather. Politics as usual, grown men hurling schoolyard insults. What this is about is freedom and liberty, your unfettered right to kill yourself in the manner of your choosing. This is the greatest country on Earth. Mumble mumble. Walt watched and shook his head at the same old back and forth. Nobody added much of anything new to the argument these days. It was all just so much background noise. He didn't really give a damn.

Karen sat down on the other end of the couch and watched her father watching the news. A couple of minutes passed between them.

Finally, she said, "So where's Boone now?"

"I already told you where he is," said Walt. He shrugged, lifted his coffee, held it in mid-air. "He's workin'."

"Working?"

"Yeah."

"What's he doing?"

Walt brought the coffee back down and sipped from the cup. "He's workin', that's all, Karen," he said. "I told you. You know how that is."

The news show morphed into a chirpy commercial for laundry detergent.

"Look. Don't worry about it," Walt said, hoping to wrap up the conversation. "Boone's been out working but he's fine. John'll be up and walkin' around soon enough. We'll get back to normal."

Karen stood back up, wandered over towards the window. She looked out towards the edge of the yard, at the chest high wrought-iron fence that had been erected where the lawn ran up against the tree line. Forty clean black spikes ran in an elegant square, fifteen feet on a side. It was pretty, like something from a 1950's television show.

It was also a grave.

Ellen Slone, wife of Walt, mother of Karen, mother-in-law of Boone, slept her forever sleep beneath a black granite tombstone at the edge of her family's lawn, the most expensive tombstone that could be bought in the state of Kentucky, with a nice portrait of the deceased etched on the side facing the house and a simple name sprawled across the back side, etched in pretty, looping letters meant to look like the lady's signature, reminding the woods just who lay at their edge. Under the signature were the dates of necessity, 1944 - 1999, and under those dates the only other writing on the tombstone, in two-inch classic Roman lettering:

ELLEN SLONE
WIFE. MOTHER. FRIEND.
WE WILL SEE YOU SOON.

Two short marble vases held flowers on each side of the stone, usually orchids in one variety or another. Karen's mother loved orchids. Yellow orchids, blue orchids, and especially white orchids. White orchids were her favorite. And also Mountain orchids, any color, thought not because Mountain orchids were especially pretty, but more because they grew only on the hills around Sewardville.

Three distinct species of flower grew no other place on Earth but the hillsides and creek beds of Seward County, Kentucky, and as far as anyone could tell, those three flowers had *never* grown anywhere else. *Rosa vanglorious,* and *cannabis exultae,* and *Orchistradae Mountain* – the Mountain orchid, whose long white petals drooped downward and came together at the ends like tiny hands clasped in prayer.

Karen noticed that some of the flowers had blown off in the night, and lay strewn around the base of the headstone. Daddy would want those replaced that day. She made a note to drop by the florist shop when she was in town later that morning. And while she was there, she would get something for her brother.

"We should go to the hospital," she said again.

"Later," Walt reaffirmed. "He ain't going anywhere, not in the meantime."

She found her father's stance on the issue ridiculous. Did he really not want to go see his son in the hospital? His son, the sheriff, who'd been shot in the line of duty just a few short hours ago? What sort of tough-old-bastard horse shit was this?

But ridiculous as that seemed, it was clear that they were not going to the hospital any time soon. Not together, anyway.

Karen moved away from the window, back towards the couch, but this time didn't sit down. Instead she stood behind her father, with her hand on his shoulder. The world was still and there they were, just the two of them, the father and the daughter.

The empty drone of world news drifted through the room and then went away without consequence. Free elections in Afghanistan, a test for democracy. The elderly will face two choices: government-mandated euthanasia, or higher income taxes, whichever seems more economically feasible at the time. America is the light of the free world. Crazy people roam free in rural areas with machine guns in their hands and tree branches in their hair. Thirty-seven percent of Republicans in North Carolina believe that Hawaii is not part of the United States. Eighty percent of Democrats believe Ronald Reagan started the downfall of America. Tomorrow, sun. Day after tomorrow, rain.

Walt sipped his coffee and kept his eyes on the television. He listened, he watched, and he waited, hypnotized by the background noise that emanated from the rest of the world. Karen watched along with her father until she had her fill of world events, and went upstairs to get Samantha out of bed.

SEWERVILLE

An hour and a half later, Karen was headed for the hospital without her father. She drove Walt's black Cadillac Escalade down the main drag of Sewardville, with Samantha riding shotgun.

Rain fell once more, big heavy drops. Through the windshield of the Escalade, Karen saw nothing new. The town existed as a still photograph in her mind, unchanged from her teenage years. The street retained a certain ramshackle quaintness, lined with run down gas stations and consignment shops, the very same old buildings that had been there since the days when she'd been in high school cruising their parking lots, looking for boys who might give her a cheap beer and maybe a little more if she played them the right way. Some of the occupants may have changed, but the blighted view never really felt that different. Once a gas station, now a Dairy Freeze, once a used-clothing store, now a HUD-backed apartment building – but the blighted view never really felt that different.

Up ahead, just past the Kwik Mart, she could see foreign shapes blocking the pavement. Probably a wreck. Karen strained to see what was going on, and as she got closer she made out more of the picture. It was not an accident. Something big lay in the road, the size of at least two people, under a heavy tarp. No wait, there was no tarp, just something… big. There were hooves. An animal. A deer. No, wait. A cow.

A cow?

There was a dead cow in the road, lying on its side with its eyes closed and its thick tongue laid limp from its half-open mouth.

Right there, in the middle of Sewardville.

"You've got to be kidding me," she said to nobody in particular.

"It looks like a cow," said Samantha.

"I see that."

"Is that a cow, Mommy?"

"Yes. It's a cow."

"What happened?"

"I don't know, Samantha. Something."

Karen rolled the Escalade to a stop a few yards from the carcass. In her rearview mirror, she saw a police cruiser come up behind, but it cut into the other lane and went around the scene without much more than a look sideways. Where was he going? Was he just leaving this dead thing here? Who knew.

Then again, she did not know if there was any sort of protocol for dead-bovine removal. She had seen many odd small-town things in her life, but this was the first time she had seen a deceased cow laid down across one full lane of Church Street.

She wondered how it got there. Maybe it fell off a truck and the driver didn't notice. Maybe it wandered in from one of the farms outside of town and got hit by a car. Maybe it had a heart attack. Who knew. How long had this dead cow laid there in the middle of the main road through town?

Karen's vehicle idled close enough that she could see a small pool of rainwater built up on the side of the animal. She could also see a number of tracks in the wet road, where others had gone around just like the sheriff's deputy. One of the front legs had been torn off, whether by impact or scavenger, she didn't know.

Based on the evidence, Karen Sumner reasoned that this road kill had been there at least a little while, plenty long enough to have drawn the attention of some official or another.

It seemed only logical that somebody would notice there was a damn dead cow right there in the damn middle of town. You would think they would do something about that. You would think.

She sat there for another minute, hands rested on top of the steering wheel. No Sewardville official came by, which was not really a surprise. The sheriff's department operated on its own schedule, Karen knew that as well as or better than anyone. That schedule was never exactly tight to begin with and surely even more out of whack with Sheriff Slone laid up in the hospital. Hell, half the whole town operated at the whims of her father as much as anything else.

Something needed to be done, though, so she picked up her cell phone and dialed the county dispatch.

"Seward County Dispatch," answered a slow drawl of a voice. "What's your emergency?" A nasally banjo twang, like something out of an old hillbilly radio comedy, *Swampgrass* or *Lum and Abner*. It belonged to Lou Clark, the oldest deputy in the department, who served under the last six sheriffs. He was five foot five and a hundred and forty pounds. The voice fit him.

"Lou? It's Karen."

"Hey there. How's your brother?"

"Dad says he's fine. I'm on my way to see him now. Lou, there's a dead cow on Church Street."

Silence. She pictured the dispatcher sliding his mesh baseball cap back, scratching his head, thinking about it. She thought she heard him chuckle, but wasn't completely sure.

"Lou?"

"A dead cow. Really?" He didn't believe her. How could he not believe her? Had nobody reported this already?

"Yeah. Really."

"How dead, do ya think?"

"Pretty dead, Lou."

"Well, huh. What about that."

She rolled her eyes. "You think you could send somebody out here to do something about this?"

"Well, I guess so."

Karen heard Lou take a long, slow breath and imagined him thumbing through a departmental procedure manual. A few more empty seconds passed.

"Where abouts exactly is this cow?" he said, finally.

"Near the Kwik Mart," Karen said. "Just send somebody. There's a dead cow on Church Street. It's pretty hard to miss."

She hung up without waiting for him to answer. She shoved the Escalade into gear and drove around the animal, as everyone else had apparently done before her. Surely they could get that cleaned up now. She'd done her part, made them aware.

Samantha shifted in the seat and looked over at her mother. "What happened to that cow?" she asked again.

"Somebody ran over it," said Karen.

"With a truck?"

"Maybe."

"Or a car?"

"Maybe a truck, maybe a car. I can't really tell. Are you ready to get some flowers now?" Soon they were headed to the local florist, and the cow was a memory.

THE NEWS PEOPLE

Put the quarter machines and the video poker in the supply room. The reporters will be there. The TV people. After everything else, I'd hate for us to go down over a goddamn quarter machine.

Walt's words rang shrill in the dingy air, as Boone sat in his truck staring at the concrete blocks of the Bears Den. This was the menial reality of his day, no matter what happened, even the day after he shot his own brother at the behest of Walt Slone.

Jimmy loved the quarter machines, Boone recalled. He'd put at least ten dollars a day into the one at the Bears Den.

Boone got out of his vehicle and slammed the door shut. Yellow police tape still ringed the parking lot of the Bears Den, further separating the gravel area where Jimmy shot Sheriff Slone and Deputy Caudill. A white news van from WTVL-TV Live on Your Side sat near the building's front door, which hung open enough that Boone saw a young lady reporter interviewing Lorna near the corner of the bar. A tall, fat guy with a black mustache and a University of Kentucky baseball cap manned the video camera. The reporter wore a navy pantsuit and matching high heels from her favorite mall department store, and the thought crossed Boone's mind that she had bought the outfit especially for this occasion. Her long blonde tresses seemed especially well-coiffed, too.

Boone walked up the lot, into the Den, his eyes trained on the reporter. His mind ticked back and forth, back and forth.

He pivoted towards the reporter. "Excuse me, ma'am."

"I'm sorry, we're doing an interview," she said, looking like she expected that Boone would simply walk away. But instead, he grabbed her microphone and slammed it to the ground, fast and angry, like he was pulling a viper from a demon's hand.

"I don't give a good goddamn about your interview!" Boone snapped. "What's your name?"

"I'm with WTVL, from Lexington."

"I didn't ask who you were with," Boone said flatly. "I asked who you are."

No answer. The reporter stared at the microphone, and at her cameraman, who just stood there in no hurry to do anything.

"What's your name, lady?" Boone asked again.

The reporter kept quiet, blinked at the cameraman in such a way that said she clearly wanted him to keep quiet, as well.

Boone glared at her. He knew plenty enough about her already, having seen her live reports on a nightly basis. Her name was Carla Haney, and she was a reporter from WTVL-TV, the NBC affiliate from Lexington. In fact, their paths crossed on occasion; Boone firmly believed that WTVL kept Carla Haney and her news van on call, just in case something newsworthy happened in Sewardville. Sometimes it was big news – one night a robbery, one night a warehouse fire, one night a busted prostitution ring. Sometimes it was not such big news. Whatever, whatever.

Boone had the general impression that she enjoyed sharing their bad news. Every time any scrap of a news story appeared in Seward County, she buzzed into town and flitted about like a prom queen candidate. Boone guessed that it must have taken her about four and a half seconds to get across the county line once news got out that two local police officers had been shot.

He snapped his fingers in front of the girl's face. "I said, what's your name?"

She pointed at the camera and told the man working with her, "Turn it off."

Lorna frowned, and slunk away, back to cleaning beer mugs.

Carla Haney, WTVL Live On Your Side picked her microphone up. Hot blood flashed behind her eyes. A sense of bold indignation reared up in her chest. "You'd better hope this still works," she said to Boone. "Because if it doesn't, your little act will cost you about three hundred bucks."

"Fuck you and fuck your three hundred bucks. How about that?" Boone shrugged.

The camera man tugged at the bill of his cap and looked for a second like he might take a step towards Boone, but Carla Haney, WTVL Live On Your Side held up one hand and stopped him.

"Get in the van, Bruce," she said.

Bruce the camera man took on a cloudy, confused look. "What are you talking about? Who is this asshole?"

"I said, get in the van, Bruce," she repeated.

"Yeah. Get in the fuckin' van, Bruce," said Boone.

Bruce lowered his camera, still confused, and now more than just a bit embarrassed. But he didn't say anything else. The way Boone cocked his head just a certain way told Bruce the camera man he should shut his mouth and walk away. And walk away Bruce did, towards the white news van with the big red-and-blue station logo painted on both sides.

Carla Haney crossed her arms, patiently awaited Boone's next words. He didn't immediately offer any. Instead, he let the uncomfortable moment sink into her skin. She fidgeted, anticipating more confrontation, and he enjoyed that. One thing he knew about all the reporters that came from Lexington and Louisville, with their satellite trucks and their cameras and their microphones and their cheap Macy's suits and their wannabe stylish hair and their sense of utter snot superiority: these people felt like they walked above the simple folk of Sewardville.

Boone looked down at these reporters the way they looked down at him. Their diplomas and white-collar jobs and big fancy subdivision might hold sway at the country clubs, but meant nothing east of Interstate 64.

"I'm surprised you weren't here before they got the sheriff loaded in the ambulance," he said with a sneer. "You people never miss a good opportunity to take a swipe at mountain folks."

"You people?"

"Yeah, you people. You motherfuckers. The news. Whatever the you call yourselves. I figured soon as you caught wind there might be a dead body in Sewerville, you'd all be movin' faster than cats coverin' up shit to get up here and stick a camera in somebody's face."

Carla Haney closed her eyes, reopened them, looked away towards the open door of the Bears Den. Boone thought she might head for the safety of the news van, but she didn't. Instead she only nodded her head, carefully waiting as the proper words danced into alignment at the edge of her tongue.

"I don't know what you're talking about," she said finally.

"I'm just here to do a story on the shooting of Sheriff Slone and one of his deputies. Now, if you'll excuse me, I'd like to get back to work."

Boone swished saliva around in his mouth. He yanked the reporter's microphone away again, slammed it on the ground, and stomped on it, until the microphone broke into three distinct pieces which he angrily kicked out the door and into the gravel parking lot.

When that was done, he turned around and once more faced Carla Haney WTVL Live On Your Side. She stood there, hands balled into fists, one resting on each hip.

He said, "Fuck off."

This time, she did. Carla Haney stalked out of the Bears Den, casting a witch's stare at Boone as she went, but he couldn't care less.

When she was gone, he walked to the bar, sat down on exactly the same stool where his brother had been just the night before, and stared at the little television that rested to the left of the liquor shelves.

Lorna came over and poured Boone a pint of Budweiser. "You handled that awful well," she said.

"Thanks," said Boone. He gripped the cold glass, turned it in his hand, but didn't lift it off the bar. The only thing that came to mind was, "They see the quarter machines?"

"Nah," said Lorna. "Those people come in from Lexington, they think they own the town, you know?"

"I guess so," said Boone.

"Don't think she'll be back for a while, though."

"I guess not."

Lorna reached under the bar, got a towel, wiped down the wood surface. Boone finished his beer, then went into the supply closet and emptied the three quarter machines of everything they had, which as it turned out, meant two hundred and twelve quarters, four Canadian nickels, and some burnt-out marijuana roaches that somebody stuffed in the catch basin. He put the money in a plastic bag, threw the roaches in the trash.

When Karen got back to the great Slone house on the hill, she found her father out back. Walt stood at the border of the little cemetery, a solitary figure in the wet grass. He leaned against the white pickets, and gazed at the black marble monolith that was his wife's headstone. He didn't look sad, he didn't look contemplative. He looked like he was there. Just there.

Karen had watched her father visit the grave almost every morning since her mother died, had even joined him on many of those mornings, and never once had she heard him say a single word. Instead, the whole time, he stood there, and stared at the smooth black marble marker of his beloved. Sometimes they would be there for a few minutes, sometimes for an hour, sometimes for even longer. And no matter how long he stood, Karen never said a word.

And he stood there now.

Karen figured he'd come out here soon after she pulled out of the driveway that morning. She approached the gravesite, carrying a new bouquet of white Mountain orchids, the beautiful flowers that grew only on the hillsides of Seward County, whose long white petals drooped downward and came together at the ends like tiny hands clasped in prayer. Little Samantha carried a bouquet, too.

The mother and the daughter opened the wrought-iron gate, walked to the headstone, and put the flowers in the round vase at the bottom of the stone, carved from the same piece of marble.

"Where you been?" Walt said.

"I told you, I was going to get some orchids for Mom."

"Well, yeah. I see you did. They look fine, mighty fine."

"Mom loves them."

"Yes, she does."

He bit his lip. The wind blew.

"Did you see Boone?" he said, from the bottom of his mouth like it was an afterthought.

Karen stood up straighter, surprised. "No. Should I have seen Boone?"

"I told him to go move the quarter machines at the Bears Den. The news is in town. I told you they'd come. If they saw those quarter machines, we're fucked."

"They won't see the quarter machines."

"Those news people, they look for stuff like that."

"They got bigger things on their mind, Dad."

"You say that." He turned and spit across the fence, back into the yard. Not near his wife's grave. "All I'm saying is, we got to be careful with people from the TV running around. You know how that is."

"I do know how that is," she said.

He nodded in agreement, with her and with himself.

It seemed like a good time to change the subject. "I got some flowers for John, too," she said. "We can go see him in a little while."

"Don't want to," said Walt. "Not until he wakes up. There's no point going down to that hospital until he wakes up."

Karen patted her father on the back and kissed his cheek. "We're going back in the house," she said, and picked up Samantha so the girl could hug her grandfather. When the hug was delivered and the child's feet were back on the ground, the three of them stood still, looking at their reflections in the polished black marble of Ellen Slone's headstone. Her headstone, which cost more than many houses in Seward County.

Walt's gaze shifted a few times – the stone, the flowers, the dewy ground, Samantha – and then settled on Karen again.

The daughter and the granddaughter waited for a few seconds to see if he would leave with them. When they realized he wasn't leaving the gravesite just yet, Karen and Samantha walked back out through the gate and headed up the hill. Samantha bounded ahead with a playful laugh, and her mother let her go.

DEATH

Boone left the Bears Den with a sack full of quarters. From there, he headed for the Faulkner Brothers Funeral Home, the only funeral home in Sewardville. He'd said good-bye to all four of his grandparents there, his father, too, and now he had another family member that required a final sermon. Harley Faulkner ran the place now. He did a lot of work for Walt, too.

Not feeling very comfortable, Boone wandered in the front door. He never felt comfortable here, whether Harley had someone out for showing or not.

The parlor stood empty, an eerie sight, given that Boone normally experienced it filled with mourners and floral arrangements. The small room with pink pastel walls looked ready to go, just waiting for the next unfortunate soul that came through the doors ready for their final send-off into the great Who Knows.

A worrisome notion kicked around in Boone that he might actually be the one next in line, that he'd arrived just a bit too early, like coming in on a surprise birthday party while the guests were still blowing up balloons. Maybe the surprise would be his; maybe ol' Harley was getting ready for a funeral all right – Boone's.

A wicked shudder knifed up his back; he glanced over his shoulder, looking for men with weapons who might jump him. But he saw nothing.

Boone descended a flight of creaky wooden stairs, into the basement. There he found a tall, lithe man with wild white hair down to his shoulders. Harley Faulkner, the chief mortician and last of the original Faulkner brothers, bent over in quiet preparation for his next funeral service. His muscles clung tight to the skeleton underneath, even in middle age. He wore khaki slacks and golf shirts every day, except when meeting families of the deceased and during the actual funeral proceedings – in those times, he wore either a blue or a brown suit, but never a black one. Never, unless his own family member lay in their final repose. Harley deemed the wearing of black at funerals appropriate only for friends and family of the dear departed; for everyone else, it was bad luck. Better to wear another color than to test all fate and superstition.

Hearing someone on the steps, Harley called out, "Who is it?"

"It's just me," said Boone.

Harley said, "You ain't supposed to be here while I'm working. Only people can be down here when I'm working are me and the goner."

He always called it a "goner" when in familiar company. Not the corpse, not the body, not the dead, not the departed. The goner. Total detachment from human tragedy was a requirement of the job.

A seventeen year old girl lay on the steel slab, covered in a white sheet from the neck down; the skin that was visible looked gray as rainclouds. Her waxy hair, long and straight, spilled over the table's edge, the dingy color of river mud. Boone noted with mild amusement that she'd dyed a pink streak in the front, centered above her forehead. She had two noticeable bald spots – one behind her right ear, one at the crown of her head – as though she'd yanked her own hair out in an angry fit. Her right arm was exposed, also hanging over, pockmarked with sores.

He saw nothing in the girl's face that lit any flames of recognition. She just laid there, the goner of the day.

"Who is this?" Boone asked, on the approach.

"Shelley Coldiron," Harley muttered, without looking up from his business. He wore latex gloves, adjusted the fit while he trimmed her fingernails.

"What got her?"

"What gets all the kids around here these days?"

"Meth, I suppose," said Boone.

"Mmmm-hmmm," said Harley. It was an unemotional response, like they were talking about basketball statistics or World War II history. Then the mortician said, "You're welcome to have a seat. I need to finish up, so I got time to put my suit on. Her parents will be here in a couple of hours."

Boone eyed the body, wondering if he had ever known this Shelley Coldiron. "Who're her parents?"

"Ray and Jeannie Kinser. They live up on Happy Top. She teaches fourth grade. Actually Ray is the stepfather, as you might surmise by the different last names. Her real Daddy got killed a few years ago, drunk driving. I sewed him up right here."

"What about it," said Boone.

"Uh-huh. What about it," said Harley. He clipped another of the girl's fingernails. "By the way, you need to wash your hands if you're gonna be down here."

Boone walked over to the sink on the other side of the metal table. As he ran the warm water over his hands, a heavy silence blanketed the men. Small talk felt so unnecessary with a dead teenager nearby.

The girl lay on the slab, still quite dead indeed, impossible to ignore or talk around.

Boone turned off the water. The room went mostly quiet while Harley Faulkner plied his trade, a black stillness broken only by the fluorescent murmur of the light above their heads, punctuated by the occasional clack of fingernails being clipped.

While Harley worked, Boone studied the girl further. He began to see the story that meth had written for her. The funereal makeup lent her cheeks a generous pink, an unreal tone in decided contrast with the death pall that the chalky white powder applied left on the rest of her skin. Even through the makeup, he could still see dark circles beneath her eyes. Nor could the ghastly makeup hide the skeletal hollows in the girl's face, or the bubbly red chemical sores that so destroyed what might have one been a pretty visage. She might have been pretty once. Boone couldn't really tell.

Shelley Coldiron could not have been dead more than a couple of days but already she looked like she'd been buried a month.

Boone knew that look all too well. The girls that worked for Walt down at the tanning salon had it. The teenagers that hung out in the Sewardville Bank parking lot on Friday nights, they had it, too. So did the junkies down at the pool hall, and the drunks wandering in and out of the Bears Den. It was the grim visage of the lost, the self-medicated, the takers of pills, those empty souls who floated in the margins in the cold liminal spaces of humanity. There they all shuffled, from one squalid station to another, looking for any comfort that could be injected, or swallowed, or smoked.

Boone allowed himself the thought that if anyone could make her presentable in death, it was Harley Faulkner. God knew Sewerville gave him enough practice on just this type of case.

"They snort bath salts now," Boone said.

"Huh?" said Harley.

"Yeah. I heard it on TV. The pills and the meth ain't enough, so now you got some kids that get bath salts and blow 'em up their nose for a high. And if the snort's not enough then they'll shoot the salts straight into their veins. Wham. Right in. What the fuck is that all about?"

"I hate to guess," said Harley.

"You think it was bath salts that got Shelley Coldiron?"

Harley stood, set the fingernail clippers on the edge of the steel table. "Prob'ly not. No, I'd say not. Meth for sure." He popped his neck, picked the clippers back up, continued preparing the body. "Seventeen year old girl, arms and legs like sticks, looks like she rubbed charcoal under her eyes. They found her out by the mailbox. Dad came home from work and right there she was. Deader'n four o'clock.

"He told me she used to be a cheerleader, straight A's, boyfriends, Miss Popularity, the whole deal. Then she fell in with Elmer Canifax and his crowd, and that, as they say, was that. Toxicology will be back in a week or two, but that's just nailin' down specifics. We don't need the damn C.S.I. to tell us this ain't exactly natural causes."

Fell in with Elmer Canifax. Why, sure she did.

Boone started pacing, moving about the room absently, his feet moving on their own while his mind formulated the conversation.

Harley could tell that his visitor wanted words, but he didn't push the issue. Instead he contented himself with the dead girl's final manicure. When he finished with the right hand, he tucked it back under the sheet then began on the left one. Harley clipped the nails on the other hand, perfectly straight, equal lengths, and when he was done he tucked that hand under the sheet, too.

Boone walked over to the corner and stood there, facing the wall.

The mortician tucked Shelley Coldiron's dead gray hand under the sheet.

"I need a little help, Harley," Boone said, turning back around.

Harley shrugged. "With what?"

Boone stepped back out of the corner. "Walt says you'll help me. Need to get rid of something, if you know what I mean. It's been a shitty goddamn day, I'd 'preciate it if you not give me a hard time."

He stopped, in the middle of the floor, looked down again at Shelley Coldiron. Between her lips he could see that two of her front teeth were nothing but brownish gray nubs, completely rotted out. He recognized the dental work immediately as one of the finest hallmarks of meth use, just like her sallow flesh and the bald spots on her head.

"I don't know, I got this funeral to do," Harley began.

"I'm telling you, I got to get rid of one," said Boone.

"It'd mean a lot to Walt." He tossed in those last words just in case the mortician was thinking he might actually turn down this request.

Harley sucked in air. Shook his head slowly, then exhaled. Of course he could not turn down the request. He knew too well that it really was no request all; it was a specific direction, straight from the mouth of Walt Slone. He had been "getting rid of" ones for Walt and his crew for going on twenty years. The fact was, over the years Walt encountered a number of people in his path, people that had to be gotten around or moved through or run over, and almost every one of those people sooner or later turned up in the woods of Seward County with their face caved in or their windpipe collapsed or their throat slashed or a bullet in the back of their head.

Miscreants, vagabonds, thugs, drifters, rivals all, not necessarily people that would be sorely missed by the community at large. Foul play suspected but then again you never know. Whatever. But sooner or later an SUV would pull up to the Faulkner Brothers Funeral Home around two o'clock in the morning. A dead body appeared, several hundred-dollar bills changed hands, the cremator furnace fired up to the required nine hundred and twenty degrees Fahrenheit, and in that body went. There was a corpse, then there was no corpse. Problem solved.

So, Harley Faulkner considered himself a solver of particular problems, those occasional little quandaries involving bodies whose spirit had vacated under less than natural circumstances, and in particular the quiet disposal thereof. Grisly work, and sometimes he felt uneasy, but what could you do? It paid well.

"Okay. Tell me what you got."

"It's Jimmy," Boone said without hesitation. He wanted the words out there quick, before they could be reconsidered. Harley frowned. "Jimmy?"

Boone stared at him.

Deep wrinkles creased Harley's forehead; comprehension came slow. "Sumner?"

Boone leaned forward, his eyebrows arched suggestively as he ran his fingers through his hair and hoped like hell he wouldn't have to explain the situation any further. Harley was usually good about not asking for details, not requiring a back story for every dead body that came to his funeral home for disposal – he was on a need to know basis, and if it were up to him he would *never* need to know – but Boone knew that if any scenario could inspire a request for further information, this one could. He had his own brother's remains, needed to get rid of them, needed assurance that his brother's funeral would have no body for viewing. How could he explain that? He couldn't explain it.

"Jimmy Sumner?" asked the mortician.

"Yeah," said Boone. "Jimmy."

"Your brother."

"Yeah." Boone's heart fluttered into his throat. He really did not want to talk this through.

Before any awful questions came, Harley peeled off his latex gloves, threw them in the sink, and only said, "Where is he?"

"I'll go get him," said Boone.

A stark, sudden terror leapt into Harley's face. His eyes grew wide as silver dollars.

"You brought him with you?" he asked, incredulous. "Jesus, Boone, it's light out! The middle of the damn day! What if somebody saw you, did you even stop to think for a minute that somebody might see you?"

"Nobody saw me."

"Awful damn confident, aren't you? If anybody saw it and saw you come here, we're both in deep shit."

"Nobody saw."

Harley didn't believe him. That much shone clear in the mortician's horrified expression. He watched Boone exit back out of the basement, heard his heavy steps even through the funeral parlor's thick carpeted floors, then heard the building's back door open, then close. A few minutes went by. The back door opened and closed again, and then he heard what seemed to be something heavy being pulled across the floor.

In a few minutes Boone returned downstairs. He brought with him what was clearly a body, wrapped in black plastic. Boone strained, groaned, and pulled his grim package across the concrete floor until he got all the way to the steel table that held the meth-ridden corpse of Shelly Coldiron.

"You're serious," said Harley.

"Of course I'm serious," said Boone, as he let the body drop with a sick thud. "When the fuck am I not serious?" He wiped his hands on his pants.

Warm aggravation flooded Harley's gaunt face. "I'm supposed to believe that you came down in the middle of the day, drove all the way through town with a dead body in the back of your truck, brought it in here, and now you want me to take care of it for you?"

"Yeah."

"I don't know if I *can* believe that."

Boone reached for his wallet and pulled out five thousand dollars in clean, nonsequential twenties and hundreds. "I don't want you to do anything for me," Boone. "Think of it as another favor for Walt Slone."

Harley Faulkner had seen a lot of things in his years as a solver of particular problems for Walt Slone's criminal empire. He'd followed through on more than one task that put him at odds with his own good conscience, but he was sure he had never seen something like this. Here was a man bringing him the lifeless body of his own brother and asking that it be made to disappear, leaving very little doubt that the living brother had somehow been involved with the demise of the deceased one.

"Jesus. Are you sure?" the coroner shuddered.

"Burn it," said Boone. "Same as always."

FAMILY

That night, Boone returned to his own home for the first time in what felt like a month but had actually been just over one day. The two-story light brick dwelling he shared with Karen and Samantha was on the opposite side of Sewardville, five miles as the crow flies from Walt Slone's house on the hill. Though Boone liked many things about his home, he liked the distance it gave between him and Walt most of all. Even if it was only five miles.

He pulled the car into the garage and entered the house from there. The garage connected to the kitchen; when he flipped on the light, Boone saw dishes in the sink from a meal he could not remember eating.

From there he went into the living room, then down the hallway and to his bedroom. The further he went, the darker his path got, lit only by the same kitchen light he'd turned on coming in from the garage. He was too tired to reach for any more light switches, too tired to care whether he bumped into walls or furniture, too tired to do anything at all except stumble through the darkness, on a collision course with the bed where he could finally collapse into deep slumber.

When he got to that bed, he closed his eyes, lurched forward onto the mattress. and let the silence take him.

But his thoughts kept him awake.

After leaving Harley Faulkner's funeral home, he'd visited Mama again.

Not with any clear purpose – no sudden realization of words unsaid, no lingering need for closure, nothing more, really, than a heavy sense inside that he just *should* go back there. He had no idea what he might say or do when he got to Mama's house; he knew only that he needed to try again. He could figure out the details when he got there. So Boone went to Mama's house and knocked on the front door, just as he had that morning, hoping that this time he might find more to offer yet also completely unsure if there was anything that he could give to justify his presence in that time, that place.

It went badly. When Boone approached the house, his mother met him on the front porch. She refused to let him come any closer. He tried to explain, pleaded with her, but Mama wanted none of it. He'd driven there, looking for one glimmer of forgiveness, a moment to sit with her and be mother and son once again. He harbored no expectation that he could be blessed with total forgiveness; he didn't deserve her forgiveness, would never even ask for it. He just wanted some time with her, time to explain, to soothe, to feel better. Time, and time, and time.

But Mama had no time for Boone.

He was there ten minutes. Mama never said a word. She hardly even made contact with him, only held up her brittle hand and pushed him backwards. Large men had pushed Boone before, men with guns, thick-necked goons, but he had never felt a shove like the one his own mother gave him that day. He fell backwards off the porch and retreated in utter defeat.

From there, Boone found his way back to his daily routine, not out of any sense of responsibility to Walt's business, more as a way to occupy his brain and not think about Jimmy or Mama or Karen or anything. He charged on in the face of his own misdeeds, throwing up emotional drywall between himself and the conflict that surrounded him, but soon found that his most stubborn efforts provided no insulation from reality.

He collected money from the bookies, but as they counted out the cash Boone thought only of Coppers Creek. He went by the tanning salon and emptied the cash register, but saw only Jimmy's face, disappearing beneath the turbulent water. He took the money from the whores at the salon, and still he thought only of Jimmy. He'd even gone back to the Bears Den one more time to get Walt's weekly cut from Lorna, but by then he could barely even get out of the truck.

Somewhere along the way, the memories overwhelmed everything else. When that moment came, Boone gave up for the day, shut down and headed for the house.

Now he lay in the dark. He thought only of Jimmy. The bedroom darkness seemed like a living force, coming for Boone, a collapsing black hole that would suck him down to hell.

He figured that if the darkness wanted him, it could have him.

He lay there thirty minutes, an hour, two hours. He never changed position, just stared at the ceiling. He saw his brother's face up there. He saw Karen again, and Samantha. He saw mobile homes, and farm equipment, the world falling into a pit of smoke and flame.

When it felt like enough, Boone sat up. He walked over to the bedroom closet, opened the door, flicked on the overhead light. The closet was full of things to which he hadn't paid much attention in years – jackets, pants, blouses, dress shoes, golf clubs, stuff.

On a top shelf littered with haphazard stacks of clothes, he found a thick photo album, its soft, vinyl cover peeling at the corners, barely intact. He pulled the book down, and sat on the floor in the middle of the closet. Surrounded by his and Karen's junk, Boone flipped through the pictures of everyone he loved or used to love – school, church, reunions, happy times – until he came to one photo in particular, a 3 x 5 snapshot held fast in the center of the last page by a piece of scotch tape.

When he saw the picture, the world came to a halt.

Boone lightly traced the picture's upraised edges through the clear cellophane page cover. It showed Boone, and Jimmy, and John Slone standing in the high school gymnasium, all with late-1980's feathered hair and mustaches. They stood dressed in white basketball uniforms with red piping and a red SEWARDVILLE emblazoned on the chest. They were all mid-laugh. Boone couldn't remember the joke now almost thirty years later, but he didn't really need to remember it. The laughter was what mattered.

There had been no laughter that day and Boone wondered if there might be any ever again. Jimmy was gone; John Slone was in the hospital. Karen and Samantha were in the house on the hill. Mama was lost. The machinery was sliding into the fiery pit, and the whole goddamn world would no doubt follow.

Boone sat cross-legged in his closet, gazing at the picture of a distant, impossible youth. Soon he felt the warm salt of his own tears, gentle on his face. They slipped down his cheeks and disappeared into the darkness, the way his own better memories had slipped into the cold past, never to be re-lived, but never to be forgotten, either.

Boone wiped his face, stood up and put the photo album back on the shelf with all the other junk. A few minutes later he was in bed again, but it would be three more hours before he finally fell asleep.

DREAMS

Mama, where did Daddy go?

He went away before you were born, Boone. God came down and took him up to Heaven. You know that.

I know, Mama. I was just thinking about it. Me and Jimmy were talking about it, that's all. How come God did that? How come he came down and took Daddy before I was born?

Because he needed your Daddy. Sometimes God needs people and when he needs them, we have to let them go. It hurts but we have to let them go. Why are you asking, Boone?

I was just thinking about it, Mama. I'm sorry. I promise, I won't ask you again, I was just thinking about Daddy because sometimes I do that.

Don't be sorry, Boone. I think about your Daddy all the time. We all do. And we all should.

The funeral was nice. Was Daddy's funeral this nice? Maybe Jimmy's funeral could be that nice. There sure are a lot of flowers here. What are the names of all these flowers? Those are orchids. Mountain orchids. Speaking of Mountain orchids, I wonder where Karen Slone is now? She was the prettiest girl I ever saw. She thought I was dumb, but I wasn't really dumb, I just didn't know much about flowers. Karen did though. God, she was the prettiest girl I ever saw.

Jimmy and Boone always share a seat on the school bus. A lot of brothers on the bus, they don't share a seat, and Boone doesn't really understand that. Brothers should share a seat. Yet, some brothers don't like sharing. Some brothers shove each other out of the way and punch each other in the back and yell *Eat my* ass and fight to be the one to sit next to pretty blonde Karen Slone, even though she just smiles and turns them all away.

But Jimmy and Boone don't worry about Karen Slone. They worry about what Mama would say if she found out they didn't look out for each other. So, they sit together in the back seat and watch the trees go by and talk about whatever they feel like. Usually only big kids sit in the back seat, but nobody says anything to Boone because Jimmy won't let them say anything bad to Boone. Not without saying something to him, too, which nobody ever does. Nobody ever says anything bad to Jimmy.

The bus bounces along the road, rolls over loose gravel and fallen hazel nuts and jumps with anger every time it comes across a pothole, which is fairly often, because these roads need a lot of work.

Jimmy? asks Boone. *Do you remember Daddy?*

Course I do, says Jimmy.

Do I look like him? asks Boone.

Why?

I was just wondering, says Boone.

Boone often asks if he looks like his father. He sees the pictures of Daddy that Mama keeps around the house, but they don't tell him anything. That person in the pictures doesn't even seem real. His wide, easy grin and shiny eyes that almost look silver don't seem real. The person in the pictures that Mama and Jimmy call Daddy could be anybody; Boone doesn't think they would lie to him, but you never know.

Why were you wondering? Jimmy asks.

The sun beats hot through the bus window.

Boone shrugs. *I don't know,* he says. *Don't you ever think about Daddy?*

Sure I do, says Jimmy. *I think about him every day. I think about him as much as you do, Boone.*

So do I look like him?

Jimmy stares out the window. *Haven't you ever seen the pictures?* he says.

Yeah, but the pictures are different, says Boone. *I want to know what he really looked like. Did he look like me, Jimmy?*

I guess so, says Jimmy.

The school bus hits another hole in the asphalt, bounces hard. These roads need a lot of work. When the bus pops out of the hole, Boone's books fly into the aisle, spread open and lay there dead, but he doesn't care much about the books right now and he just lets them be dead. In the seat up ahead, Mike Powell laughs and taps Karen Slone on the shoulder to get her attention; but when Mike taps her on the shoulder, Karen does like she always does - she turns around, smiles, and says nothing.

Hey, Karen.

Hey, Boone.

Jimmy said I could borrow his car this weekend, says Boone. *He just got a new one. It's a Chevy.*

I don't know much about cars, says Karen.

Me neither, says Boone. *But Jimmy likes Chevy so I guess they're pretty good. What are you doing Friday night?*

I don't know yet, says Karen.

Want to go to the drive-in? asks Boone. *They're showing that new Arnold Schwarzennegger movie with the robots and the guy that turns into aluminum foil,* Terminator 2, *I'll be bock, you know.*

He's a robot, says Karen.

Right. Sorry, says Boone, *I ain't much on robots. Anyway, what are you doing Friday night?*

I told you. I don't know yet, says Karen.

Want to go to the drive-in?

Not really.

How come?

I don't really like the drive-in, says Karen.

I thought everybody liked the drive-in, says Boone. *Well, maybe we can go somewhere else. Do you like anywhere else?*

Not really, says Karen.

We just gotta do this one thing, says Jimmy. *One thing and then we're done.*

I don't want to do this, says Boone.

We already said we would, says Jimmy. *Walt expects us to do it and we gotta do it. Jesus, we already got half the money.*

Let's give him the money back, says Boone.

We can't do that, says Jimmy.

Sure we can! says Boone, frustrated and scared now. *Just give it back to him and tell him we're out. We can't do this, Jimmy. Why did we think we could do this? This is way, way over our heads. He can get his own son to do this. Let John do it. We are such dumb boys.*

Jimmy stands there, shaking his head. Boone can tell his brother is pissed now. He knows he's let Jimmy down, and he's sorry for that, but he just doesn't think he can do Walt Slone's kind of business. It's a bad business. Two thousand dollars seems like a lot of money when somebody offers it to you, but when you find out what it actually is that you have to do to earn that money, two thousand dollars isn't very much at all. Maybe Jimmy can do Walt Slone's kind of business for two thousand dollars, but Boone can't. Won't.

We ain't got a choice now, Jimmy finally says in a low voice. *We have to do it. There's no backing out. You know who we're dealing with here, Boone. I know you're scared and hell I'm scared, too, but this shit is real. This shit that we're dealing with here is real, brother, and we got to do it. It's just that plain and simple. Now, go to the car and get the stuff and let's just get this over with.*

But Boone isn't listening anymore. Jimmy's voice fades into a dull hum, shapeless and wordless. It's cold out tonight, especially cold for this early in the autumn, the weather man said the temperature would get down into the thirties but the thermometer on the bank clock said it was actually twenty-seven. There's a frost on the ground already.

Is it too cold for Mountain orchids? Probably. When do they bloom? No idea. But whenever Mountain orchids do bloom, they look like tiny hands, clasped in prayer. That is the truth.

Boone says, *Did you know that Mountain orchids only grow in Seward County, and nowhere else in the world? It's an amazing place that we live in.*

Go get the guns, says Jimmy.

Boone collapses backward, falls, sits. The frost crunches beneath his body. The gun in his hand feels cold as the ground beneath him.

He stares at the dead body in front of him and thinks strange, distant thoughts, thoughts that don't seem to be really bouncing about inside his own brain. He thinks that in real life, a dead body does not live up to expectation. A dead body does not look scary. A dead body does not look disgusting. A dead body kind of looks like a person, but it doesn't really look like a person, either. It just looks like a dead body.

Boone wonders what his Daddy looked like when he was a dead body.

It's hard to look at a dead body and see much of anything. Even if you knew the person that the dead body used to be, it's still hard to see that person in there because really, they're not in there. They're not in there.

Even when the dead body lays on the ground only five feet away from your right leg, even when you try to look away but it won't let you look away, even when the dead body is facing you and even when the dead body has its eyes open and stares at you and judges you and seems to say *Look at me, Look at what you did to me, Look at what you've become you dumb little boy* you still look at the dead body and you don't see an actual person. At least, you try not to.

Hey Boone can I borrow some money? says Jimmy.

What for?

I wanna build us a cabin.

What are we gonna do with a cabin?

We'll have us a place, says Jimmy. *A place we can go won't nobody know about. Somewhere we can get away from the shit.*

I ain't got no money, says Boone.

Bull fuck! says Jimmy, and he laughs.
Not for no cabin, anyways, says Boone.

The funeral was nice. There were a lot of orchids, orchids of all colors and varieties, blue and yellow and red and pink, some sturdy, some weak, some upright and proud, some bent to the earth. Most especially, there were Mountain orchids, plenty of gorgeous white Mountain orchids.

Boone showed up late to the chapel. He sat with Walt and Karen, and he held Karen's hand and she cried into his shoulder and in one way, that was really nice because it made him feel closer to her than he'd ever felt before, but in another way, it wasn't so nice, either.

Karen, do you like orchids?
Yeah.
These are called Mountain orchids. The old lady at the florist shop said these only grow in Seward County and nowhere else in the world. Have you heard that?
Yeah, I've heard that. They're my mom's favorite.
What are you doing Saturday?
Nothing.
Want to go somewhere with me?
No. Sorry, Boone. I can't.
Why not?
You're just a dumb boy.
Oh. Right. Yeah, I guess I am just a dumb boy.

You boys did a good job, Walt says. *It had to be tough for you, but you did a hell of a good job.*

Look what you got yourself into, dumb boy.

Walt hands Jimmy an envelope of cash. Jimmy takes it, counts it, and immediately gives Boone his half.

Boone accepts the money. As he puts it in his pocket he feels like he might throw up. But he doesn't throw up.

Walt says, *Jimmy, give me and your brother here a few minutes.*

Jimmy looks at Boone, tilts his head like a curious hound. He counts his share of the money again - Boone has no idea why Jimmy did that - and then he walks away to the car.

With Jimmy gone, Walt talks in a more serious tone. *I know you didn't want to do that, Boone,* he says. *I can't imagine how tough it was for you. But it was tough for all of us, something like that is always tough. It don't come easy but sometimes, you know, it just has to be done. Sometimes bad things have to be done. I wish there was another way but there just isn't. But now that you've gone through it, Boone, I want to tell you, you can really go far with me. And if you can go far with me, you can go far with Karen, too. She's a good girl, Boone. I don't want her with just any man, I want her with somebody that can go far. You know what I'm saying, son?*

Boone doesn't answer. Walt asks him again - *you do know what I'm saying son, don't you?* - but Boone doesn't hear him now. One more time, he feels vomit rising in his throat. Rocks hammering his ears. Gauze in his eyes. Hot hot hot, everything is so hot.

But he doesn't throw up.

He stops listening and pretends he is standing somewhere else, talking about something else, talking to someone else. He imagines that he's talking to his Daddy, looking at Daddy's easy grin and shiny eyes that were almost like silver, at least they looked that way in the pictures Mama kept around the house, which was all Boone had to go by since God came down and took Daddy before Boone was even born.

He wonders if he looks like his Daddy.

He wishes he had a cabin.

He wishes he had a place they can get away, a place nobody knows about, a place where all this shit don't matter.

He wishes Jimmy was here with him now.

He wishes he never met Walt Slone.

He thinks about orchids and also about Karen Slone. She knew about robots. She knew about orchids. She knew about everything. All the boys tried to talk to her and she just smiled and turned them all away. She was so pretty. The prettiest girl Boone ever saw. Why did she think he was such a dumb boy? Maybe she was right.

BUSINESS

While Boone slept his fitful sleep, life in Sewardville went on unimpeded by the previous night's tragedy. People wondered and whispered and dramatized their own theories about Jimmy Sumner, the damn sonofabitch that shot Sheriff Slone and Deputy Caudill. The cops would catch up to him soon enough, or the state police, or the FBI, somebody. Roadblocks were in order, with plenty of heavy artillery and of course those spiky metal chains strung out across the road. Helicopters, SWAT teams, the National Guard. A swift trial, then Death Row for sure. Hell what do they need a trial for, he did it right there in front of God and everybody. Give the fucker the electric chair. No wait, now they just give injections. Whatever. Shove a rubber hose up his ass and get it over with. He's going down.

Rumors and conjecture spread throughout the community.

The day moved on. The gas stations and fast food restaurants served their customers with great aplomb, as did the pharmacies, the churches, and the second-hand clothing stores.

Walt Slone's business interests maintained their routine, even without Boone or the sheriff to help them along. After closing time, the daily receipts were totaled and the cash wrapped neatly with rubber bands. Then the bag men arrived, some in pickup trucks, some in old sports cars, one still in his off-duty sheriff's department cruiser. The receipts and the cash got collected. Deliveries were made to the house on the hill that overlooked the town. There, the cash was counted, the figures reconciled.

The father and the daughter sat at the kitchen table that night, same as they did every night. The ledgers were open in front of them, stacked six high on the flat wooden surface.

He knew the ledgers were archaic, dusty remnants of business long usurped in the technological age, but he liked them precisely for that reason. The small notebooks with red binding and green cloth covers gave him comfort; he thought them solid, dependable, always there when needed. The papers did not require broadband connectivity, or flash drives, or terabyte hard drives - they required only sharp pencils and basic mathematical abilities.

He provided certain pencils, but he trusted her with the mathematics. While she worked, he stayed quiet, and leaned back in his chair with his meaty, weathered hands folded in his lap.

Across the table, she punched numbers into the calculator and scribbled figures on lined paper.

Samantha slept upstairs, which made things easier, and was another reason they preferred to crunch the numbers late at night.

"How's the store doing?" he asked.

"Fifty-eight hundred and change yesterday," she said.

"What about the girls?"

"Fifteen thousand this week."

"Is that all?"

"Flu's going around, I guess. A couple of the girls caught it."

He grinned. "I hope that's all they caught," he said.

She closed one ledger and opened another. "That truck from New York ought to put us over a hundred grand for the month. Did you talk to the guy?"

"Yeah, I talked to the guy. He's running late but it will still be here tonight. Might be midnight, but it'll be here."

"Who do you want to meet it, now that John's out for a while?"

"Send Boone."

"Okay." She hesitated. "Do you think you can call him?"

He knew what she meant, and nodded his head in agreement. She didn't want to talk to Boone herself. He considered for a moment longer and then offered a compromise. "Send another one of the deputies. Rogers."

She scribbled down a note to do that.

They went through a few more figures. The renters, the cigarette store, the weed, the poker game, the quarter machines, the damn thieving bookies. She scrawled down the final figure and handed it to him.

The numbers were still down.

He studied the number carefully, but it did not change. The handwritten digits sat there in front of him, an insult to all his work done over the years. Frustration boiled in his stomach, up his throat. He ripped the paper in half and threw it in the floor. He smacked his palm on the table so hard that it sounded like a tire blowout, echoing around the expensive hardwood.

They sat there, as the smack faded.

She decided to change the subject. "You'll be glad to know, I got the election signs ordered today."

He brightened. "What color this year?"

"Same colors as every other election. Red, white, and blue, just the way you like it. The proofs will be in next week, and once you give the go ahead on those, they can start printing. We should have everything ready in time for the primary. Come spring."

He liked thinking about elections. They warmed him. The numbers were down, the ledgers much lighter than he preferred, but the primary loomed just a few months away and that warmed him up just right.

"Anybody running against me this time?" he asked with a chuckle.

"Does it matter?" she shrugged

Someone would run against him. Someone always ran against him, just for appearances if nothing else. Of course it didn't matter. The signs were red, white, and blue.

The telephone rang.

It was odd for a call to come in so late, and she could tell that the call annoyed him. When she moved to answer, he waved her off and took it himself.

He said his hello into the receiver, then listened for several moments, nodding his head, asking only vague, occasional questions.

"What time?"

"When?"

"How long?"

Soon enough, he hung up the phone. Before she could ask about the caller's identity, he said, "That was the hospital."

She sat up. "Is it John?"

"Yeah."

"Is he all right?"

"He's awake."

She jumped out of her chair and ran up the steps to get her sleeping child. He walked briskly across the kitchen, towards his car keys, which hung on the hooked board plaque by the door.

HOSPITAL

Twenty minutes later, they parked beneath a street light in the lot of the Sewardville Medical Center. They got out and hurried into the building, with the mother carrying the sleeping little one in her arms.

The Sewardville Medical Center occupied the old middle school building that stood alongside Highway 213 in the western corner of Seward County, a mile or so outside of Sewardville proper and not far from the East Kentucky Parkway westbound exit, ideally situated both for quality medical care and also quick transfers to the larger hospitals up the road in Winchester and Lexington.

On the exterior, the structure itself looked straight out of the nineteen sixties, red brick and white cement, green gutters, simple rectangles. The interior, however, was a complete contrast. The building had been refitted with the most modern office furniture and medical technology that a few million dollars' worth of rerouted state infrastructure funds could buy. Sleek modern stainless steel and ceramic and high-dollar electronic displays. The place still smelled new.

The center consisted of only two floors, but the small town only needed two floors. The first floor housed the emergency room, and the X-ray machines, and the CRT tubes, everything needed for the quick ins and outs. Twenty-four proper rooms waited for admitted patients on the second floor, with calm pastel walls and the omnipresent odors of disinfectant and unnamed body fluids.

They entered the elevator and went up to the second level, with the little one still asleep, head resting on her mother's shoulders.

At night, the hospital was quiet, empty of non-medical personnel, the silence penetrated only by the dull electronic hum of the lights overhead.

For most people, visiting hours were closed. For most people.

They walked past the nurses' station, and the nurse on duty didn't even look up. They moved on down the hallway, to the room at the end of the corridor. There they stood in the doorway and peered at the room's lone occupant: Sheriff John Slone.

He lay in bed with his upper body raised at a slight angle, hooked up to three separate intravenous tubes, his head resting on thick white pillows. An EKG beeped in steady rhythm with his heartbeat. His breath was shallow, but steady. His head turned to one side, facing them. His eyes were closed.

"I thought he was awake?" she said.

"That's what the doctor told me," he answered.

He left her there to watch the sheriff and went in search of the doctor. Soon he found him, Doctor Hall, a short bald man with olive skin, the only doctor on shift. At night, Sewardville needed but one doctor.

"You said my son was awake," he said to the doctor.

The doctor stiffened. "I told you not to come down here tonight."

"You know better," the father said. "Go check him again."

The doctor sighed, shook his head the way doctors shake their head when faced with stubborn human beings who have no concern for medical reality, only for their own emotional reactions.

Doc Hall and the father walked back to the doorway where the daughter stood watch over her brother. "The guy took a gunshot to the chest last night," said the doctor, while they stood there. "He's not ready for visitors. He was awake, yes, for a moment, but it will be a couple of days before he can see anybody. He's a strong man, but it will take time."

She looked at her father. The expression in his eyes - the lack of expression – brought her no comfort. Why had the doctor called them if John wasn't awake?

Suddenly, she felt she couldn't stand there in the doorway any longer. Over the doctor's objections, she handed the child to her grandfather, went in to the hospital room, approached her brother's side. She touched his hand, felt his warmth, then turned back and faced the men at the door.

"It won't be long," she said. "He'll be awake soon. Tonight."

The men at the door shrugged. They nodded slowly, just being polite. Arguing with her served no purpose.

She turned back to the sheriff, touched her hand lightly against his forehead. "It won't be long at all," she whispered to herself, to them, to him. She held her brother's hand and she wanted to cry, but she didn't cry. She stood by his bed. Exactly three hours later – to the second – Sheriff John Slone opened his eyes, and when he did, his sister Karen was still standing there.

PART THREE
DUMB BOY

In the early 1900's, a passenger train route went right through the middle of Sewardville. The town was widely held as a thriving industrial and cultural center of Appalachia.

In 2009, only fourteen percent of Sewardville households had a car that was less than 5 years old.

On the last United States census report, the median household income in Sewardville, Kentucky stood at $19,347. If Mayor Slone and his family were removed from the equation, the number dropped down to $13,243. The public school system was the number one employer in town. The Department of Sanitation was second.

Three 80mg OxyContin pills might cost a hundred and fifty dollars on the street in Sewardville.

Per capita, more people died every year as a result of prescription-drug overdoses in Sewardville than in Los Angeles, Chicago, Seattle, Boston, and San Francisco combined.

TIME

Two weeks after Sherriff John Slone awoke in the hospital, he was discharged and sent home, where he finished his recuperation without much incident. He was working again by Thanksgiving, against Doctor Hall's best advice, though he did promise Doc that he'd stay behind a desk until spring.

The Sewardville *Times* ran a full-page photo welcoming him back to work.

At first, the courthouse employees kept their respectful distance, figuring John would not appreciate bombardment with questions about that traumatic night at the Bears Den. But soon enough, the ladies in the building found entertainment in asking the sheriff to show them his bullet wounds, and John Slone found entertainment in obliging them, always unbuttoning his shirt and pulling it down far enough to show them his quarter-sized pink scars.

Jimmy Sumner's memorial went about as well as anyone might have expected. The short service took place on the edge of the woods behind their mother's house. She allowed them that. No one attended except for Boone, Harley Faulkner, and Brother Wayne, the pastor at Presbyterian. Brother Wayne said a few words and recited a passage from the Bible, which Boone didn't recognize. After that Boone said a few words himself. They didn't have a coffin, or a body, since Jimmy hadn't been found yet. But they had a funeral.

The entire time, Mama stayed inside the home, and watched through the kitchen window. Boone understood.

Six long months rolled off the calendar.

Autumn passed into winter, a pitiless season for Sewardville, Kentucky. Mother Nature blasted the area with three separate snowfalls of at least eight inches' depth, and an average temperature for the season of twenty-one degrees Fahrenheit, well below the norm. Between December 15 and February 1, at least one inch of snow covered the ground for all but two days. In that same period, the children went to school exactly six days total, and not at all between Christmas and January 20. Twice, the county exhausted their stockpile of road salt and Walt Slone put in a personal call to the governor to get the supply replenished. Even worse than the snow and cold, two ice storms roared through the latter days of January, and the weight of the falling ice splintered so many trees and utility poles that it looked like an air force squadron cluster bombed Seward County.

By the end of winter, Seward County saw its population dwindle by twelve people: five killed in traffic accidents, three frozen to death during power outages, one in an electrical fire, and the other three cooked in a meth lab explosion. After a short investigation, the meth lab explosion was not attributed to the weather.

Eventually, though, the bitter temperatures gave way to spring warmth.

Treetops enshrouded in winter's gray blossomed lush green under azure skies. The Mountain orchids bloomed full, yellow, pink, red, and especially white, clean sparkling white, the favorite color of Ellen Slone. Children played in freshly-cut backyards. Laughter again echoed throughout the valley.

Construction went quick on a new Shell gas station and convenience store, out by the East Kentucky Parkway, not far from the medical center. A front page story in the *Times* heralded the coming of a Taco Bell to the corner of Second Street and College Avenue, and when it opened for business, four hundred cars went through the drive-in window the first day alone.

So spring sprung, bringing rebirth with it. Life returned to the area, and the people welcomed it with open hearts.

As the garden flowers unfurled their new petals, everyone in town looked forward to the Orchid Festival, the town's annual spring celebration. It happened the final weekend of every April, and this year was no different. City workmen readied the Sewardville City Park for the occasion; they carefully trimmed the grass, picked up the branches that fell during winter, and between the trees hung white vinyl banners that were ten feet long. Anticipation sparked in the air. Folks looked forward to the festivities: the car show, the Miss Orchid Pageant, the concerts. The annual caravan of vendors would come from across the commonwealth, offering rides and hobby crafts and food of all sorts. The funnel cakes, the gyros, the corn dogs, the candy apples. Patrons would come from all corners of Seward County and the counties surrounding, intent on riding the rides, sampling the food, seeing all the sights.

Great days lay ahead, the best days of the year for the people of Sewerville. They would celebrate the flower of their home, the flower that grew no place else on Earth but the green hills of Seward County, Kentucky. *Orchistradae Mountain,* the Mountain orchid, whose long white petals drooped down and came together at the ends like tiny hands clasped in prayer.

MAMA

On the Tuesday before the Orchid Festival, Boone went back to Mama's house. He hadn't seen her since Jimmy's memorial, and that had only been through the kitchen window. Many times since then, he'd considered a visit, but never had he actually worked up the guts to do it. Until now.

He scaled his way up the rickety front porch, which was only three feet off the ground but which also in this moment seemed high as Kilimanjaro. He paused to gather himself, knocked on the door. Soft, ever so soft, just soft enough that maybe she couldn't hear.

But he knew she could hear.

"Mama?"

She did not answer. Boone knocked again.

"Mama? You in there?"

Still no answer.

He knew she was in there. He knew she knew that he knew she was in there. Regardless, Mama didn't come to the door, and as Boone stood there he thought that didn't really surprise him. He wondered: maybe it was a good thing that she didn't answer. A blessing of sorts. After all, if she had answered the door, what would he say? He hadn't thought that far ahead. He didn't know what he would say if she answered.

But she wouldn't answer the door.

So Boone waited. He owed it to himself, he owed it to Jimmy, he even owed it to Mama not to run away anymore.

Soon enough he heard a miracle from inside the house: the creak of her walk across the old wooden floor. She was coming, she was coming. She was coming. He stepped back from the door to give her a little room, so she could swing the door open wide and see him standing there.

He didn't know what he would say when she answered. But he would say something.

A minute later, the old door slipped ajar. She didn't swing it wide at all. Instead, Mama popped her head out in the narrow space between the open door and the frame. She set her jaw firm, squinted, and looked Boone square.

"Go away," she said. Then she slammed the door in his face, and they were done.

ELMER

Later that week. Friday.

From where Elmer Canifax stood, the naked girl on his bathroom floor looked awfully pretty. She was the kind of pretty and young that often graced his bathroom floor in the morning hours following one of his famous soirees on the distant outskirts of Seward County.

Her skin was smooth and white as the bathroom tile beneath her. No traces of meth use yet. The meth wracked those young nubile bodies. That made Elmer sad. Goodness gone to waste, that's all it was, and no matter how many times he saw it happen it still kicked him in the gut. Beautiful youth turned into staggering meth monsters, all rotted teeth and infected skin. How far and fast they fell. It broke his heart, even if he *was* usually the one selling them that meth.

Elmer watched the girl for a moment, waiting for her to breathe, or move, or make a sound. Anything that would show she was alive. The last thing he needed was a dead teenager sprawled out on his bathroom tile. But a few seconds later, her chest expanded and gently dropped again, and that was the proof he needed.

He leaned back against the bathroom sink and lit a cigarette. This had become part of his morning routine, this sweep through the house each morning, exploring all rooms for remnants of the previous night's party so he could get them up and out of there before any upset boyfriends or girlfriends (or worst of all, parents) showed up and raised hell. There was nothing worse for Elmer than hell being raised in his face when he stood in the vapors of a hangover. He hated that.

So, he explored every morning in the party aftermath, and when he did, he often found pretty young things like this one.

And even though he was glad he found them before their parents/boyfriends/girlfriends found them, he was too often faced with another discomfort when, in the clearer wisps of morning light, some of the girls just looked a little bit younger than maybe they did the hazy night before. When the booze and the drugs and the love flowed freely, it was just so much easier to believe them when they said they were eighteen.

He realized that he couldn't remember her name. That didn't surprise him. Elmer Canifax threw a hell of a lot of parties, and there

116

were a hell of a lot of pretty girls at those parties. He'd long ago given up knowing them all on a first name basis.

A few different names rolled through his mental catalogue. Jessica? Jennifer? Lisa? Lana? Whothefuckknows. Whatshername. He hoped she was eighteen, at least. If she was eighteen – *really* eighteen - then everything would be fine.

Elmer prodded whatshername with his foot. "Hey. Hey, you. Girl. Wake up. "

The girl sighed and rolled over onto her side, away from him. "What time is it?" she murmured, not really awake.

He said, "How old are you?"

"Eighteen," she said with her eyes still closed. "Why?"

Relief waved over Elmer. In his experience, the wily female brain produced most of its truths when just humming into consciousness, or when it floated halfway between awake and asleep, a magical place where there was no need to scheme, lie, or otherwise make shit up. If this girl said she was eighteen now, still fully under sleep's control, then she likely wasn't bullshitting. That made him feel much better.

What was her name?

What was her name?

What was her name? Whothefuckknows. Whothefuckcares.

He took some time to appreciate her a bit more. Whatever her name, she was a real beauty: tall and lithe, with long black eyelashes, curly auburn hair six inches past her shoulders. Smooth clean tanned body. Perfect C-cup tits. oh, how Elmer loved those perfect tits, nipples the size of quarters, drawn up tight, hard against the cold tile, the expensive tile.

He pulled a navy blue bath towel from the towel rack next to the sink and tossed to the naked girl on the tile. "Rise and shine, honey pot."

He turned his attention elsewhere. Another girl slept in the bathub, a blonde. She wore one of Elmer's white Hanes undershirts, and nothing else. He wondered how she got that piece of clothing, but after considering the hows and whys for a moment he decided that maybe he didn't want to know after all.

Unlike the beautiful creature on the tile, the one in the bathtub wasn't much to look at. The meth had taken this one. Her face was sallow, washed out like old newspaper left too long in the sun, and cratered with deep sores and pockmarks. Sick bruised bags gathered under her eyes. She had brittle blonde hair, with two little ragged patches noticeable in their absence. Each was about the size of a nickel, one just below the crown of her head and the other behind her right ear.

The meth girl rested against the tile shower wall, the same tile covering the floor. She splayed one bony leg over the side of the tub, while the other stretched out in the bottom of the tub. She was wide open, for anybody that wanted to see.

Elmer gawked at her and tried not to look at her chemical-burn face. She probably had a name, just like her friend, but he couldn't remember this one, either. Susan? Allison? Stacy? Whothefuckknows? Whatshername.

He surely had been introduced to both of these girls last night, but that was information meant for last night and last night was long gone. In the corner behind the door, he could see two black-and-red Sewardville High cheerleaders' uniforms laying in a loose pile, with two pairs of lacy panties (one black, one lavender) thrown haphazardly atop them.

Elmer stepped towards the girl in the bathtub, tapped her lightly on the chin. "Time to get up," he whispered.

Behind him, Tile Girl sat up slowly.

"Morning, sunshine," he said.

"That was a hell of a party," she answered.

Elmer smiled back at her. "Thank you," he said. "But unfortunately, now back to reality." He decided to take a stab at her name. "You ready to go, Shana?"

Instantly, the sunshine in the girl's face clouded over. "My name's not Shana, asshole."

"Really?"

"Yeah, really."

"You sure about that?"

"Yeah. I'm pretty damn sure."

"What is it, then?"

"Fuck you, Elmer."

Tile Girl pulled the bath towel around her and rose to her feet. So did Elmer. "Sorry about that," he said. "I was just kidding."

The cheerleader sarcastically rolled her eyes back in her head, but said nothing. She glanced around the room and finally found her panties in the corner. Elmer noted with surprise that the lavender pair was hers; he'd already pegged those as belonging to the blonde in the bathtub. He had a longstanding theory that blondes *always* preferred lavender-colored panties. Actually that was not so much a theory as an oft-observed tendency.

Tile Girl slid her panties on. She tied the towel around her side, then began the tough task of rousing her blonde friend out of the bathtub.

"Don't you guys have school today or something?" Elmer asked.

"I think so," Tile Girl answered.

"You think so?"

"Yeah. I'm not sure. What is today?"

"Oh. Right," said Elmer. The calendar. An inconvenience. "I think it's Sunday," he offered, not sure at all if it was Sunday or if it wasn't.

Tile Girl stood up. "I gotta go to church," she said.

Now the blonde zombie stirred in the bathtub, moaning in anger at being awakened. "It ain't Sunday. It's Friday, goddammit," she said.

Elmer stood up and looked at himself in the mirror. He raked his fingers across the length of his clean-shaven head, front to back. He had a handsome symmetrical dome that he'd been shaving since he was twenty-four. Three days' worth of black stubble dotted his angular, ratchet face. He thought he might grow his beard out longer, see how that looked, try the whole Jesus look of which all the Brit rockers in *Q* magazine seemed so fond those days.

He had a thin body, but muscular and well-defined. He couldn't really explain why he looked in such good shape, of course. He never exercised and didn't give half a shit about what he ate. Probably ten years from now his body would fall apart and he'd look like every other middle-aged guy in Sewerville, but until then he'd go with what he had.

There was also a tattoo, maybe six inches wide, screaming out from the right side of his arm - a demonic skull, with vampire fangs, and two Viking battle axes crossed behind that skull that fanned around to touch on the underside of his bicep. Bright scarlet blood dripped from the fangs. Underneath it all, in barbed-wire letters, the words "GET SOME" clearly stated Elmer's life philosophy. He was proud of the artwork. He'd designed it himself, in tenth-grade art class.

He turned to one side, pushed his chest out, admired the tattoo.

Behind him, one of the girls gagged.

Elmer looked just as Bathtub Girl leaned her head over the edge of the tub and threw up a prodigious amount of chunky orange stuff all over his nice tile.

"Aw, shit, baby!" Elmer howled. "Not on the damn tile! Fuckin' hell!" The bathroom tile. Not the bathroom tile. It cost eight thousand dollars. Nobody else in Sewardville had bathroom tile like that, not even Walt Slone.

Elmer jumped to push Bathtub Girl away before she could do any more damage. His hands landed against her shoulders and he shoved her backward, against the wall and down into the tub, where his ample experience in such matters taught him that it would be easier to clean up the puke from there because he could just turn the shower on and wash the stuff down the drain.

In the tub, the girl continued vomiting, purplish orange chunks, beer, chili, vodka and cranberry, equally across herself and the ceramic around her. A geyser. She would not stop. Her puke spread out like an alien blob, putrid, massive, more puke than Elmer had ever seen in one place.

Tile Girl slouched against the wall, staring at her sick friend, who was still throwing up all over herself.

"I got your name," Elmer said, doing his best to change the subject.

"Sure you do," said Tile Girl.

"Nah, I do. I got it. I was just fuckin' with ya earlier."

"Sure you were."

Elmer thought to himself, *little girls try to act like they don't care, but they do. They care.* "Emily, right?" he said.

Tile Girl shrugged. Better. Not the best, but better. "Yeah," she said. "Look at you, mister fucking brilliant."

"I told you," said Elmer with a gleam. "I was just kidding earlier. I knew your name." But he hadn't been kidding; the only way he knew it now was because he'd just looked in the corner of the bathroom and noticed the name on her cheerleader uniform.

"You think you're friend's gonna be all right?" he asked.

"She oughtta be okay, I guess."

"All right then, Emily," he said. "You guys go ahead and get out of here once she's finished. I'll see you tonight, right?"

"What's tonight?" Emily asked.

Elmer chuckled. "There's always something going on around these parts," he said.

SHERIFF

Sheriff John Slone sat in his police cruiser, the sun shining through the windshield, already warm on his face even though it was only a mid-spring morning. The car idled at the edge of the Seward County Bank parking lot, facing the street so he could watch the traffic. There wasn't much in the early afternoon.

Here, he felt peace. Jimmy Sumner's bullet put him in the hospital, but not in the grave, and he was back where he felt most comfortable. The agony, the physical therapy, the long moments spent deep in doubt wondering if he would ever walk normally, much less get back behind the badge again – all this vanished in the distance of memory. He belonged here. He needed to be here.

John checked himself in the rearview mirror, tucked some stray black hairs back underneath the front of his police hat, and winked at himself. Women liked him. He could see why. He had a strong jaw line that he couldn't keep clean shaven, and he filled out his Seward County Sheriff's Department uniform completely, broad and full at the shoulders and chest. There were no problems getting Sewardville's finest tramps and Bears Den ladies to head home with him before the shooting, and there were no problems with that after, either.

The sheriff had rigged an MP3 player through the cruiser's stereo. He'd filled it with all of his favorites, the soothing sounds of AC/DC, Molly Hatchet, Zeppelin, Black Sabbath, and all the other hard rock bands that he loved so much. Now he pushed a button, and Nazareth's "Hair of the Dog" burst forth with clarity.

He drummed on the dashboard, in perfect time with the song, and watched cars pass on the highway.

Now you're messin' with
A SONOFABEEYITCH
Now you're messin' with a sonofabitch

Then, behind the song, the police radio crackled to life. "Seward County one twinny eight?" said dispatcher Lou Clark, in his unmistakable country voice. "One twinny eight, come back?"

Slone stopped his drumming, turned down the Nazareth and picked up his radio. "This is Seward County one twenty-eight."

"One twinny-eight, the cawler advises that we got a ten thirty-nine in progress at four oh two Brush Creek Road. Four oh two Brush Creek Road, one twinny-eight, we have a ten thirty- nine in progress."

"It's awful early for a ten thirty nine don't you think?" asked the sheriff.

"Maybe so, one twinny-eight. But we got one."

John Slone clicked off the radio for a moment. He didn't like this at all.

The cascade of numbers was a means of disguise, an attempt to hide the nature of the call from any common citizen who might be listening in on their handy dandy police from the comfort of their own recliner. This of course never worked. All the scanner disciples were more than familiar with the different numbers and their actual meaning, having spent way more than a sufficient number of hours to have deciphered the code. As soon as word went out over the scanner that something unlawful might be going down in Seward County, telephones lit up around the area. Neighbors rushed to spread the latest gossip about the dastardly robbery/assault/car accident/drug overdose that just occurred.

Ten thirty-nine. The number gave John Slone pause, even after all his years with the sheriff's department, even after the hundreds, thousands of calls he'd taken. Ten thirty-nine was the code for a domestic violence incident. He considered that the worst sort of call. Domestic calls could go in any of several different directions, but none of those directions were any good. Emotions ran high in those cases and when emotions ran high, people often wound up hurt, or worse than hurt.

"One twinny-eight, you there?" said Lou Clark.

"I heard you the first time," said the sheriff.

"Sorry, sheriff," said Lou. "I was just tryin' to be clear. You know how that is."

The sheriff said, "I'm sitting out by Highway 213 now, but I can be on Brush Creek Road in ten minutes, Seward County," he sighed. Then he thought about it some more. "Four oh two. That Elmer's place?"

"Yeah, Sheriff, it has been indicated that there very well is somethin' of a high likelihood of that address being Elmer Canifax's address."

Of course it was Elmer Canifax. "He's probably got them cheerleaders out there again," said John.

"Caller does advise there was a suspicion of there bein' multiple females in the vuhcinty, yes. Would you like to request back up officers be en route to the scene of the altercation, Sheriff?"

"No backup needed, Seward County," the sheriff said.

He started the engine and pulled out onto the highway. As the car accelerated, Slone clicked off the police radio and raised the Nazareth's volume. He lay heavy on the gas pedal and continued south, towards Elmer Canifax's place.

John Slone knew Elmer's place well, much better than he really preferred. The Slone family had seen more than their fair share of run-ins with Elmer over the years. Now would be another. The two sides didn't share many warm feelings for each other.

Twenty minutes later, the sheriff pulled into Elmer's driveway.

ELMER'S PLACE

The farmhouse of Elmer Canifax sat safely out of sight and sound from any other residence in that remote part of the county (remote even for Seward County, Kentucky). It loomed half a mile back from the highway, at the end of a pothole-ridden gravel drive that was curvy as a rattlesnake's back. Thick trees lined the road on both sides, their limbs hanging over the road like sagging, elderly appendages.

A hundred yards from the house, the trees broke into an open field. At the center of that field stood the old house itself. It was a blanched two-story beast, and had passed to Elmer when his mother died three months after his nineteenth birthday.

Globs of white paint blotched and peeled on the structure's every side, and some of the boards near the ground showed signs of rot. Elmer paid those defects little mind. He concerned himself mainly with two things: one, his business of choice – the retail of meth, marijuana, and pain pills – and two, the constant schedule of parties which kept a stream of customers pouring through his front door practically three hundred and sixty-five days a year. Kids thought he was cool as hell.

Sheriff Slone didn't think Elmer was so cool, though. To him and the rest of the Slone family, Elmer Canifax was a rat, nipping at their business. His pain pill distribution cut into their profits, no question about it. After all, the numbers were down.

The sheriff drove his cruiser up the driveway. This morning, like most mornings at Elmer's, was accompanied by the pulsating techno music that thumped at top volume from two five-foot tall loudspeakers positioned on each corner of the front porch, and John felt the bass in his own chest. As he rolled up the drive, he found himself driving through a group of forty kids, who were standing still in the yard. Just standing there, with the morning wind skitting in their dirty hair. Blank looks hovered around their faces. They were all on the big come-down, fresh out of fuel, having burned off all the drugs they ingested the night before.

They reminded him of birds: tall, thin crows, hovering, telling fortunes of sorrow. Crows with styled hair, pale sharp faces, tattoos from a cheap strip-mall tattoo parlor, sweat-soaked t-shirts that said things like THIS IS LOVE. Dark and beautiful and ugly and alive and dead all at once, they stood there. Often, Elmer sat on the porch right behind them, in his grandfather's high-backed wooden rocking chair, between the two big speakers.

Only this time, the crows were alone. Lost in themselves. Not one of them looked up or moved as the sheriff parked his car by the house.

Then, Tile Girl/Emily came running out of the house in her cheerleader uniform, screaming.

Slone stepped up onto the porch just in time to catch the girl in his arms. The first thing he noticed was that she was incredibly fucked up, on what he didn't know.

The second thing he noticed was the blood seeping into the wool of her cheerleader's uniform, from a deep slash just below her collar.

"Whoa now. Whoa," the sheriff said in his deep, strong sheriff's voice. He put his hands on the girl's shoulders. "What's your name honey?"

"Emily," said the girl in the cheerleader uniform, as she tried to suck back her tears, at least enough to talk.

"What the hell's going on here, Emily?" the sheriff asked. "Did Elmer do this to you?" He might just have another reason to smack ol' Elmer Canifax around. Perfect.

"No, no, not Elmer," said the girl. She started sobbing again, heaving for breath, exhausting herself, making sense, not making sense. "It was my friend. My friend Lisa. She's in there. She got a knife and went after me, she went after Elmer, she was fine. She was fine when she woke up, but then she got sick and then after she got sick she just went crazy sheriff you've got to do something please sheriff do something she's got Elmer he ain't bad he ain't done nothing but she got a knife a knife on him please sheriff YOU GOTTA HELP!"

Slone opened the car door again, grabbed his police radio, called an ambulance. Then he turned back to Emily.

"You think you can wait here in the car for the ambulance?" he asked.

"You gotta go in there sheriff, you gotta go in and get her out!"

"I will," said John. "You just wait here in the car. I'll be back."

He held the car door open for the girl. Emily looked at him, then looked at the house, then back at him again. She blinked twice, wiped the tears from her face. Finally she climbed in the cruiser.

The sheriff closed the car door behind her, and walked towards the front door of the house. He creaked up the porch's old wooden steps, unfastening his gun holster as he went.

Through the screen door, he could see two blurry figures on the living room, locked in struggle. One was astride the other. Though the figures were mostly silhouette, backlit by the sunlight streaming through the house, John Slone could identify Elmer Canifax, and sensed that the other figure had to be this girl Lisa.

Lisa was the one on top. She held a butcher knife in her hand high above her head, poised for murder.

SHERIFF

"Get off me bitch!"

"Give 'em to me!"

"I ain't doing no such thing!"

"The hell you ain't!"

"The hell I ain't! You got that right you crazy cunt! I ain't giving you nothing!"

"Fuck you Elmer!"

"Fuck you bitch!"

"Fuck you!"

"Give me those pills!"

"Fuck you!"

The sheriff pulled the screen door open. What he saw there, on the dark hardwood of the living room floor, made him laugh; he couldn't help it.

Elmer lay on his back, with his plain white t-shirt ripped at the collar and a bloody gash jagging across his forehead. He was scared white as Christmas morning. His eyes looked like they'd been inflated with a bicycle pump, and the veins on his neck were banjo tight.

Lisa, one of the cheerleaders, was on top of him, all ninety pounds of her, her ass planted in the middle of his chest, her feet hooked underneath his armpits. She breathed in psychotic heaves, chunking white spit between her teeth on every ragged exhale. In her right hand, she had a death grip on the black rubber handle of a well-honed butcher knife, the nasty end of which pointed straight at the dimple in Elmer's chin.

The unease that Sheriff Slone felt at being called to this domestic incident dissipated as he stepped into the house. This wasn't so bad - he could take care of a knife. And a little girl.

"Get this bitch offa me!" Elmer screamed.

"Hold on there, Elmer," said the sheriff. "Lisa, honey. Put the knife down, careful like."

"See, Lisa, I told you," Elmer said, "I told you that somebody'd call the law on your stupid ass!"

"Shut up, Elmer," Lisa said. Spit flew.

"No, you shut up!" said Elmer. "You shut the hell up, and you get the hell off of me, before the sheriff has to take care of you himself!"

"Sheriff ain't doing anything," she said. "Are you, Sheriff?"

Slone just shrugged.

"Are you, sheriff?" Elmer said.

The sheriff stood there. He smiled, and wondered whether he should intervene or just let this scene play out to its rightful end. Either way suited him just fine, as long as Elmer Canifax got what he had coming. And he had a hell of a lot coming, as far as John Slone was concerned.

Elmer waited. Lisa waited. Nobody said anything for what felt like six years. But it was only thirteen seconds.

Finally, the sheriff stepped toward Lisa. "Come on, now. Get off of him," he said. "Throw the knife across the room. This doesn't have to be ugly. Just get on up."

"Fuck no it ain't going to be ugly!" said Elmer. "Fuck no it ain't, you wild ass crazy fuck cunt whore!"

"Shut up, Elmer!" the girl yelled.

"Shut up, Elmer!" Sheriff Slone yelled.

In response, the girl sliced the knife into Elmer's chin. A flap of skin opened across his chin. Blood flicked into the air, straight up, paint from a brush.

Elmer screamed. God, how he screamed, long and loud, like he'd just seen his own bloody ghost.

Before Elmer could finish screaming, Slone was on the girl from behind. He wrapped one arm around her waist, and yanked her up, away from Elmer. With his free hand, he ripped the knife from her hand and slung it across the room, where it stuck in the cracked drywall.

Lisa struggled against the sheriff's grip. She fought him for two solid minutes before finally giving out. After that, John dropped her to the floor, and everybody caught their breath.

"What happened?" Slone asked, looking down on her.

"Motherfucker stole my pills," Lisa said.

"Stole your pills?"

"Yeah. Stole my pills."

"What kind of pills?"

"You know." She glanced upward, caught his eyes for just a second, and then looked away again. "My pills."

John looked around the living room, ready to thrash Elmer Canifax from wall to floor to ceiling and back to the floor again.

But Elmer was gone.

The bathroom door slammed shut in the background, at the far end of a long hallway. Right after that slam came a *cha-click* as Elmer bolted the door shut.

Slone turned towards the sound, took twelve big steps, and was in front of the bathroom door almost before the lock settled into its final position. He banged on the door one, two, three, four times. His big right fist denting the door's wood.

"Elmer!" he said, banging one, two, three, four more times. "Elmer, open this goddamn door!"

From the bathroom came a weak, "Where's Lisa?"

"In the living room. Open the door," said Slone.

"Who's watching her?"

"I'm watching her. Open the door."

"Did you whip her ass, sheriff?" Elmer asked.

The sheriff moved away, into the middle of the hall. He measured the distance between the door and one full extension of his right leg. "I didn't have to whip her ass. Open the door, Elmer."

"I ain't openin' the door," said Elmer. "Not until I know that bitch got a good ass whipping out of this."

"Elmer, if this door ain't open in five seconds, I'm going to break it down," Slone said. "And if I have to break this door down, then there'll be an ass whipped. You got that?"

"I ain't openin' the door."

"You sure?"

"Hell yeah, I'm sure!"

"Okay then."

Slone's foot hit the door with every single last pound of force that he could put behind. The doorframe cracked and splinters danced in the air. The door itself flew off its hinges, into the bathroom, and blasted Elmer in the side of the head so hard that he staggered back, tripped on the toilet, and collapsed on the bathroom tile.

With scary ease, Sheriff Slone lifted Elmer off the ground and drilled his face into the bathroom mirror. The mirror shattered, but didn't break apart, held together from the weight of Elmer's left jaw pressed firm against the glass.

"You know what, Elmer?" said the sheriff, calm now. Scary calm. "I don't think I've been back here since I got out of the hospital. What about that."

He pulled Elmer's head back, looked at him, saw shreds of blood and tissue. "Aren't you glad to see me?"

"I swear to God I didn't do nothing to that bitch," Elmer said.

"Sure you didn't," said the sheriff. He shoved Elmer's face back into the mirror and ground it in the glass. Scarlet oozed into the sink below. "You mean to tell me, that pretty little lady out there just pulled that big knife and jumped on top of you for no reason at all?"

Elmer wanted to answer. Elmer didn't want to answer. Elmer couldn't answer. Elmer thought it best that he not answer.

"No reason at all, huh?" asked Slone again.

Elmer still couldn't answer.

The sheriff pulled back from the mirror. He smiled and pushed Elmer against the opposite wall, where he slid down and sat on a kaleidoscope of his own blood.

Things got quiet.

For five minutes, neither man moved. Elmer sat on the floor and whimpered and bled and cried and bled some more and cried some more. Slone just watched him. They breathed.

The sheriff bent to Elmer's ear. "You know, I don't really give a shit about that ol' girl out front," he said, slowly. "I'm just glad I got to come up here and renew our friendship like this."

Elmer tried to get some words out but couldn't, not with the pain still jagging down his face in sharp bolts. His lips parted. He tried to whisper but couldn't even do that.

Slone grinned. "Come again?"

Elmer opened his lips a little more. A thin trickle of blood fell down the side of his nose and into his mouth. He flopped his head to the other side, the best he could do at that moment.

"Here's the news, Elmer. My family's numbers are down. That's not good. And to be honest, we think you got something to do with it. In fact we're pretty goddamn positive about that. That ain't good, either, at least not for you anyways. So here's the deal. I been down a while, but I'm back now, and that means the Slone family's numbers are gonna go back up where they belong.

"You and all your parties, sellin' to the kids, all that shit's gonna slow down. Way down. You're messin' with our market, Elmer. We've put up with it for a while but we ain't puttin' up with it anymore. So back off. Back off, you hear? If you don't, I'm gonna come back and see you one more time. And if that happens, a helluva lot more than your mirror's liable to end up broken."

Elmer lay there, and bled.

Sheriff Slone looked at him for another few seconds. He gave Elmer one more kick in the ribcage, then spit on the floor by Elmer's head, and walked away.

From there, John Slone headed back into the living room. He found Lisa sitting on the couch, smoking a joint. He took the joint from her, ground it under his size twelve uniform boots, and led her outside to his cruiser. There, he threw her in the back seat and then he also retrieved her friend Emily and threw her in the back seat, too, for shits and giggles.

The sheriff slammed the cruiser door and got into the driver's seat. He started the engine. He reached over to the passenger's side, switched on the MP3 player. The Nazareth started up again.

Now you're messin' with

A SONOFABEEYITCH

Now you're messin' with a sonofabitch

Damn right. John Slone was back in the saddle. A bullet to the chest couldn't even stop him. Not then, not now, not ever.

COURTHOUSE

The Seward County courthouse was a boxy, one-story structure of dark brown brick that looked like mud. After a fire destroyed the courthouse that had stood since the early 1900's, the county built a new one in 1974 but decades later it wasn't quite so new anymore. The place still had the same black-flecked tile floors, plaid upholstered furniture, and orange curtains that were there when it first opened. The judge's chambers featured imitation oak paneling. Two ashtrays stood in every room. Folks used them liberally, since no smoking ban existed in Sewardville, and never would.

The sheriff parked his cruiser near the courthouse entrance. He got out, opened the back door of the vehicle and waited for Lisa and Emily to say something.

"Either one of you ladies thinkin' you might wanna fight with me when I pull you out of that car?" he said, smiling.

"Fuck off," Lisa shrugged.

He looked at Emily. "How about you?"

She gave no response or reaction.

The sheriff let out a bored sigh as he glanced around the parking lot. "Tell you what," he said, not looking back at them just yet. "This can go one of two ways between us. You all can come out of there on your own, nice and quiet, march yourselves into the courthouse there and on down to the sheriff's department, and we can all get about on our day. Or, if you want, y'all can fight me. If you fight, I'm still gonna pull your asses out of there and we're still goin' inside. Only difference is that if I gotta drag you out, when you get there, those pretty little faces prob'ly ain't gonna look quite as pretty as they do right now. You get me?"

The two girls thought about it, as if there really were anything to consider at all. Finally, Emily swung her legs around and exited the vehicle, though with her hands cuffed behind her, she needed the sheriff's help to gain full balance.

"That's good," Slone said.

Lisa decided she wanted to fight after all. She kicked the hell out of the seat in front of her, shook her head back and forth back and forth, and screamed animal nonsense, high shrieks that barely even passed as language.

Slone watched her, hands on his hips, unimpressed. He let her go on, hoping the tantrum would burn itself out soon enough, which happened sure enough. When she was finished, the sheriff grabbed her hair and yanked her out of the back seat, standing her up in the parking lot next to her friend.

John slammed the cruiser door shut and put one hand in the middle of each girl's back, pushing them towards the courthouse entrance and then on through it.

In the courthouse, the steps of his heavy black boots echoed on the '70's-era floor. The girls stiffened, trying to keep from moving forward, but with little effect. Sheriff Slone shoved them where he wanted them to go. He waved hello to the ladies he saw in the County Clerk's office and proceeded down the hall, towards the large open room that housed most of the Seward County Sheriff's Department.

On his way, he passed a row of photographic portraits that started on the main lobby walls and extended all the way to the back of the building, showing every one of the nineteen sheriffs to hold office in Seward County since 1880.

They found the Seward County Sheriff's Department empty and quiet except for one deputy: J.T. Rogers, a slight man with black hair, parted to the right, and a Tom Selleck mustache. He sat at his desk reading a week-old edition of the Sewardville *Times*, as he'd done most days in the nineteen years he'd been employed by the Seward County Sheriff's Department.

A wide, brown Formica counter ran at an L across the full length and breadth of the room, with a hinged door at the corner of the L that department employees could enter through and lock once inside. The two deputies' desks lined up in the middle of the room, covered in paperwork and coffee cups that might or might not get cleaned up by week's end. One of the empty desk chairs had a department windbreaker hanging on the back, and a cigarette still burning in the ashtray.

Slone pushed the girls against the wall, into a couple of brown wooden chairs that were linked by a metal bar. He walked towards the cigarette, picked it up and looked at it. "I thought I told you all, no smoking in here," he said to his deputy.

"This ain't a no-smoking establishment," said Rogers.

"I don't give a fuck what it is."

"Well, that ain't my brand."

"I don't give a fuck what brand it is, either," Slone said, as he crushed the butt in the ashtray. He gestured to Lisa and Emily. "Take those bitches over to the jail and book 'em in. I've already got tired of lookin' at 'em."

Rogers folded up the newspaper. He strolled over to the girls and pulled them upright by the shoulders, unconcerned with their comfort or physical well-being. each of the teenagers gave him a violent, squinty glare and in return, he knocked them both hard across the top of the chest, snapping their heads back hard against the wall. They yelped like kicked coyotes and muttered a few curses that the deputy neither understood nor cared to understand, but just for the shit of it, Rogers delivered a couple of well-placed forearms into their stomachs.

"You sure you want ta give me a hard time?" the deputy asked them, while they were still doubled over in pain.

Now they seemed sure that they didn't. He led them away.

While they left, Slone walked towards the doorway that stood centered in the wall behind the row of desks – the doorway to his private office. He worked out of a spare room with only a desk, a black leather chair with wheels, and a Seward County Lions Club calendar on the wall. There was another black leather chair across the desk, for visitors both welcome and unwelcome.

He found Walt Slone inside, by the window, gazing outside at the street with his back turned to the doorway.

"Hello, Mayor," said the sheriff.

"Hello, Sheriff," said the mayor.

"What are you watching out there?"

"The road."

"Anything on it?"

"Not really. A few cars."

They stood there, each waiting for the next one to speak, neither really concerned with the next step. Walt sat down in the sheriff's chair and propped his feet up on the desk and without saying a word, dared his son to say anything about it.

Instead, John quietly stepped around to the other chair, the chair for visitors, and eased himself down into it.

Seconds passed.

Two minutes.

They waited each other out.

Beyond the window, an old man strolled along the road's shoulder, pulling a tricycle behind him on a rope. Walt saw him out there, but didn't remark.

Finally, the sheriff spoke. "You're in my chair again."

"I know," said Walt. He smiled. "I like this chair."

John smiled, too. "But it's my chair," he cracked. "I don't suppose it ever crossed your mind that I might like this chair, too."

"Not really. I don't suppose it did." Walt grinned wider now, like a big Texan holding the winning poker hand. The sheriff laughed, too.

Walt swung his feet off the desk. Rather than get up he settled into the soft leather back, resting his elbows on the wooden arms of the chair. "But even if that had crossed my mind," he said, "I'd still be sittin' right here in your chair, and you'd still be sittin' right where you are."

Deputy Rogers led the two girls, Lisa and Emily, into the county jailer's office. He sat them down on a flat wooden bench with no back, just inside the glass double doors of the entrance.

He stepped up to a grimy plexiglass window that was glazed with thirty years' worth of cigarette smoke. Behind the window sat Bunny Groves, the longtime county jailer who had supplied most of that smoke himself thanks to his three-packs-a-day penchant for Marlboro unfiltereds. Bunny was sixty years old, barely the height of a refrigerator and about half as mobile. His hair stayed plastered straight back and in the last few years had taken on a yellow tinge, also thanks to the Marlboro unfiltereds. He hardly talked, mostly just hummed and smiled every now and then. Nobody in town could remember why they called him Bunny.

Rogers tapped on the plexiglass. The jailer put down his cold double cheeseburger, and looked up through thin tendrils of toxic smoke.

"Hey, Bunny," said the deputy. "Can you take care of these two fine ladies for me? Sheriff picked 'em up from Elmer Canifax's place just a little while ago."

"It's lunch time," said Bunny.

"So?"

"So I'm eatin' lunch."

JT's cell phone buzzed against his hip. He recognized the number. "I gotta take this," he said, turning for the exit. "Book these two in. Sheriff wants 'em to cool it here for a while."

"What's the charges?"

"Charges?" The deputy shrugged, and thought about it for a second. "Like I said, they come from Elmer's so I'm sure you can figure something out. I'll be back in a minute."

With that, Rogers turned his attention to his phone. He picked up the handset, and wandered outside, all the way around the far corner of the building where no one else was within earshot.

"What do you want?" he asked the caller.

"We got a problem," said the voice on the other end. It was Elmer Canifax.

Rogers let out a deep breath and said, "I told you not call me when I'm on duty. Actually, I told you it'd be best if you don't call me at all. Especially not on my damn cell phone. There's old ladies that sit up listenin' for cell phone calls to bleed through on their police scanners, you know that?"

"I don't give a shit about that right now."

"Maybe you'll give a shit if the sheriff catches wind of me and you talking. Tell me Elmer, how do you think that would turn out for us?"

"The sheriff came to see me this morning."

Rogers lost his breath. He imagined his face being crushed under one of Sheriff Slone's cement-block fists.

"I told you. We got a problem," said Elmer. "Some people around here ain't big fans of competition, if you know what I mean. When can you come up here?"

"I'm pullin' a twelve hour shift," the deputy said finally, after he'd taken a moment to settle his mind back down. "I'll come up tonight, after I get off. Don't call me again. I'll see you in a little while. Don't call me again. I ain't kiddin', Elmer." He hung up the phone, hoping their conversation went unnoticed by all the scanner radios across Sewardville.

BUSINESS

"I heard you went up to see our friend Mr. Canifax," Walt said to the sheriff.

"Mmmmm-hmmmm," said John. "Got a call that he was rough housin' with one of the local beauties. Stupid shit, nothing new."

Walt kicked back in the sheriff's seat and clasped his hands across his stomach.

"You should have taken the opportunity to kick that idiot's head in," he said. "He's a big reason that business is off for us. This ain't capitalism here. We don't need competition."

"Actually, I did give him a message while I was there."

"Really? What kind of message?"

John shrugged. "The kind that says, 'back the fuck off before I come up here and put you in a wheelchair for the rest of your little life.'"

They laughed together.

Neither of them felt anything else should be said about Elmer. It was a simple matter of fact – Elmer was hurting their business, and he would be stopped one way or another. No need to waste time worrying about it any further, at least not for now, anyway. Things stood where they stood.

Besides, there were much bigger items on the agenda than Elmer Canifax. The latest tractor-trailer from New York was due in at midnight that evening.

Life for Walt Slone had gotten much better since the trucks started rolling in from the Northeast corridor. They carried their precious cargo of both heavy and light ammunitions, pain pills, and counterfeit consumer goods (fake Nike and Ralph Lauren were especially big sellers in Walt's market). Elmer Canifax had taken a bite out of the Slone family's numbers, but the trucks from Boston and New York ensured that the cash still flowed.

The original agreement with the East Coast people held that there would be one truck a month. Business boomed, though, and soon the shipments rolled in three times more often that. It was usually some nondescript truck with a plain white trailer. Down the trucks came, on the parkways and interstates of the Northeast and through the Appalachian mountains, blowing past weight stations and bribing officials from the Department of Transportation. For camouflage, the drivers loaded a few pallets of children's toys or steel nuts and bolts on the end of their trucks, just in case the bribes didn't land where they were supposed to and the truck had to actually make a stop at one of the weigh stations en route.

Once arrived in Seward County, each truck would come off the East Kentucky Parkway and roll out Highway 213 until it came to the boarded up old Methodist Church. There, the driver could pull into a large gravel parking lot in back and wait, until Deputy Rogers showed up, and with him a couple of men with U-Haul trucks. It would take them an hour or so to unload all the wooden crates and duffle bags and transfer them into the U-Hauls. The men would whine about all the weight they lifted, but when they were done, Rogers would hand the New York driver a manila envelope stuffed with cash. They'd make jokes about each other's home states

What has twelve nipples, three teeth, and smells like dog shit? A Kentucky whorehouse.

And then they'd all be on their separate ways. By the time the empty tractor-trailer hit the Parkway, headed back up the East Coast, Walt's men were already unloading their goods to the lower-level dealers who would put them out on the street in a few short hours. Chinese assault rifles, faux Ralph Lauren jeans, 9mm handguns, tennis shoes, Coach purses that looked almost like the real deal. People in Seward County and those counties surrounding couldn't get enough. When the next truck came around two weeks later, half of it was already committed to backorders. The market showed signs that it might be bottomless.

"Truck's comin' in tonight," said Walt.

"I know," said Sheriff Slone. "Rogers said one of the guys that usually helps him is down in Florida on a pill run, so he asked if I could drive one of the U-Hauls and help unload."

Walt closed his eyes and slowly shook his head in dismay, as though he felt a sudden, deep distress. "Motherfuck," he said, low, almost to himself. "Like you got time for that. What did you tell him?"

"I said it wouldn't hurt him to get his ass up and do some real work for a change," shrugged John.

Walt smiled, a broad grin that showed all his teeth. They sat there a moment longer.

As they sat there, John noticed for the first time the old man outside with the tricycle trailing behind him. But just as Walt had done, the sheriff didn't mention it.

Finally, Walt got up from the chair and headed for the door, tapping the sheriff on the top of the head as he went by. "I ever tell you how glad this town is to have you back at work, John?" he said.

"Every day," said the sheriff, rising from the chair to follow him. "Now how about we get some lunch?"

"Yeah, we can do that," Walt replied. "After that, I promised Karen we'd come out to the city park and help 'em decorate for the Orchid Festival."

Slone grimaced. "We?"

"Of course 'we.'"

The sheriff's heart dropped somewhere around his kneecaps. Walt was always signing him up for shit like that. Community appearances, kissing babies, smiling at strangers, the sorts of things that were expected of any smalltown sheriff and community leader. He quickly flicked through several excuses in his brain that might allow him an exit out of going, then realized that no way was Walt going to let him beg out and so there wasn't any point in even trying.

Walt motioned again. "Come on now, I got to give out some election cards. You can make yourself useful."

"I hate that election shit," said John. "You *know* I hate that shit. Shakin' hands. Kissin' asses. I can't stand it. Who else are they gonna vote for, anyway, besides you?"

"Nobody. So what?" asked Walt.

He had a point.

"Raise on up. Let's git," Walt said. "The printer just dropped off a stack of election signs in my office. Go grab 'em, and I'll meet you at your cruiser." He ambled out of the room.

John stood next to his chair a bit longer, not at all anxious to follow, or go to the park, or kiss babies, or shake hands, or be in the communal spirit. He glanced out the window, again trying to come up with an excuse he could feed Walt that would get him out of that damn chore. Outside, the old man with the tricycle had circled back towards the courthouse, and no longer pulled the three-wheeler behind him. Now, he just rode it.

BOONE

Boone sat on the bed, in the room where he spent so many nights, in the house he hated more than any other. Walt Slone's house. He looked towards the bathroom door, just beyond it. His eyebrows arched as he bit his lower lip. Bored, waiting. He saw Karen as she stood in front of the sink and leaned in towards the mirror, applying makeup to her face.

Every morning he woke up in one of his father-in-law's extra bedrooms meant a morning filled with bitter, cold resentment, and this morning was no different. Up to that point, the day had passed quiet and surly between husband and wife. He didn't want to be there, she knew he didn't want to be there, and he knew she knew that he didn't want to be there.

Still, he was there.

Boone made no secret that he preferred sleeping in his own house, in his own bed. This preference had been the source of many a long, loud argument with Karen. How could she stand it, spending so many nights under her father's roof, never straying far from the hallways where she grew up, never able to take more than the smallest step beyond the shadow of Walt Slone? How could she manage only half of a life? He couldn't stand it. How could she stand it?

But he knew Karen didn't think of this as half a life. For her, this was whole, the life she wanted.

Boone felt like he spent too much of his time looking into the Sewardville valley, thinking of smoke and fire and dead people. He denied the truth the best he could, but still that truth remained, lurking in the shadows, never far away. That truth was: he lived half a life. Maybe Karen didn't, but he did. He spent his days and nights going from point to point, doing what he was told to do. He belonged to the whims of others, and whatever scraps of his soul they left behind, he claimed as his own. In the rarest moments of honesty – the deep down moments, the hard moments he did not often allow – the worst reality hit home: his was not even half a life. It was far less.

You're such a dumb boy, Boone.

He grew impatient. He felt like he'd been waiting a millennium for Karen to finish in the bathroom. He picked up the television remote and flipped on the TV that sat on the dresser. Nothing interesting came on.

"You about ready yet?" he called towards his wife.

"Nope," Karen answered.

Of course not. Boone stood up and walked into the bathroom. When he went in, Karen didn't even acknowledge he was there. Rather than force the issue any further he headed downstairs.

In the living room, he found Samantha on the couch, watching SpongeBob cartoons. He sat down beside her and they watched together.

"Where's Mommy?" his daughter asked after a few minutes.

Boone stared at the cartoons. "She's upstairs."

"Is she ready to go?"

"Not yet."

They were supposed to be headed to the Sewardville Park that afternoon, at least, Karen and Samantha were, so they could help set up for the Orchid Festival festivities. The festival commenced tomorrow, the last Saturday of April, just as it commenced every year. Samantha had looked forward to this since the moment her mother said she could help with the decorations. She'd insisted her Daddy be there, too.

After two weeks' worth of his daughter's begging, Boone had finally relented. He had no intention of sticking around long – banners and bunting were not in his field of expertise – but still he promised he'd go with them for a little while, anyway.

When it came right down to it, he really couldn't give a great fuck about anything related to the Orchid Festival. For Boone it was just another shabby community festival like all the other shabby community festivals of rural America. He could get his fill of Americana on his own with a mason jar of apple moonshine and a bag of hand-rolled cigarettes, thank you very much.

Still, regardless of his own apathy towards the festival, Boone knew that he couldn't shirk his duty completely. So he promised Karen and Samantha a ride to the Sewardville city park, where he would help hang the red and white "SEWARD COUNTY ORCHID FESTIVAL" sign over the park's main gate. But that was all; after that, he would slip away. He could pick them up later, or maybe catch them back at Walt's if either John or Walt decided they would take the girls home, which would likely be the case.

Samantha didn't like that plan. She wanted her Daddy there with her all day. But Boone got by with a "Daddy has to work, honey," and a promise that they would be together all weekend.

That wasn't good enough for Karen. Of course it wasn't good enough for Karen. In her mind Boone had broken his word to their daughter, regardless of whether the daughter felt that way or not. His little plan had caused an argument with Karen. Of course it had caused an argument with Karen. What didn't these days?

Boone thought back through the last few hours.

This morning, just as he opened his eyes to the sunlight, she hijacked him while they still lay in bed.

"That's pretty bad," she said. "I can't believe you won't even spend one entire day with your own daughter."

He'd barely felt awake and had no idea what he should say. He hated when she did that, when she took him by surprise in his slowest moments. And she did it a lot.

Karen was a master at holding in her anger for days or weeks or sometimes months at a time, letting it boil inside her until it burnt her up and finally poured out in Boone's direction. This time, he refused to answer. If he'd learned one lesson from all the times they'd lit into each other over topics both significant and not, he felt secure in the knowledge that as far as Karen believed, no matter existed in the universe on which Boone could be right, and she could be wrong.

So when she woke him with that particular loaded statement - "I can't believe you won't even spend one entire day with your own daughter" – he knew where the discussion was headed: absolutely nowhere.

So, he ignored her. "Mmmm-hmmm."

"I know you heard me," she said.

"Mmmm-hmmm."

"You're an asshole, Boone. You know that?"

Her words bounced off him and evaporated, like raindrops on summer concrete.

She sensed that he was blocking her out, having grown finely attuned to the mmmm-hmmm nature of it all.

"I know you heard me," she said.

Boone raised his eyes towards Karen and took a deep, long breath. He knew he couldn't ignore her forever. She would never allow that. He'd learned that there were times when Karen would let things drop, and then there were times where she would most certainly *not* let things drop.

This was the latter. He could tell by the way she propped herself up on one elbow, holding the side of her head in the palm of her hand, steel eyes drilling into him as though she stared down the barrel of a high-powered rifle. Boone felt the only thing he could do was flip the situation around and throw it right in her face.

"Yes. I heard you," he finally said.

Her glare narrowed.

Boone turned and looked straight at her. "Tell you what," he said, with more than a hint of sarcasm. "Why don't you go ask your Daddy why I can't spend an entire day with my own daughter? 'Cause he's the goddamn reason why. It's his damn business, that's why I can't get some real time with Samantha, because your Daddy's got me runnin' all over God's Earth emptyin' quarter machines and taking care of his shitty laundry. What about that?"

Karen didn't say anything.

She closed her eyes. Blood flushed into her cheeks and he could almost feel the anger radiate from her face. A solid little bump formed in both her jaws as she clenched down on her teeth and tried not to scream.

"So, what about that, huh, Karen?" he hissed.

She drew back, opened her mouth a little, a copperhead snake about to strike. But instead of saying anything, she jumped out of the bed, stormed into the bathroom, and slammed the door shut behind her.

Boone sat up in bed and stared at the closed door. He wondered if he should follow her, which no doubt would have turned the morning into a ten-round, knockdown drag-out heavyweight fight. After pondering that for all of one half second, Boone decided that he had zero interest in such a fight.

He crawled out from under the covers and sat up at the edge of the bed, in his silver jogging shorts and white University of Kentucky t-shirt. And there he waited, knowing that sooner or later his wife was bound to come out and smack him right in the face.

An hour and a half later, Karen still hadn't come out of the bathroom. She'd taken a shower, dried her hair, gotten dressed in some clothes from the bathroom's walk-in closet, but she hadn't come back out to the face him again. She'd cracked the door and peeked out, then left the door open just enough so he could see that she'd turned her back on him.

And that's how things stood now.

Boone sat there and waited, not impressed. This particular back had been turned on him many times before. So, he waited.

He held his ground and he waited, like a soldier hunkered down in the foxhole, hearing mortar rounds exploding in the distance and anticipating the moment when one rained down on his own head.

Finally, after he'd waited long enough, Boone went into the bathroom to give it one more shot with Karen. He pushed the door open and stood behind her, looking at her reflection. She ignored him and just kept brushing her makeup on. Briefly she made eye contact, just to let him know that she recognized he was behind her and chose not to pay him any attention.

"Perfect," he sighed. With his belief affirmed that this encounter led nowhere, he left the bathroom and went downstairs.

The telephone rang, behind him.

Boone ignored it at first, content with things as they were. But it rang again, and again, and again, and midway through the fifth ring, he picked up the cordless black handset that sat on the end table.

"Hello?"

The male voice on the other end sounded desperate, hurried, their words whirled together in a rush of wind and spit.

"Boone? Is that you?"

"Who is this?" Boone asked.

The caller paused. Boone heard him snort back hard and knew there was a crushed painkiller involved. That particular sound was unmistakable.

"Boone. Fuck. I knew you'd be there," the voice on the phone said, ramping up the anxious tone even more. "You got to help me, man."

Boone recognized the frantic voice now.

He glanced at Samantha, saw she was immersed in the SpongeBob cartoon, then walked into the kitchen. There, he dropped his voice so she couldn't hear.

"Elmer?" he whispered into the phone. "Are you out of your mind, calling me here?"

"I'm at the house. The sheriff just left. I need you to come up here right fuckin' now."

"I can't come up there," said Boone.

"COME UP HERE RIGHT FUCKING NOW!" Elmer screamed into the phone, so loud that Boone yanked the receiver away from his ear and could still clearly hear every word that came through.

"They're gonna kill me, Boone."

"What are you talking about?"

"Come up here. You gotta come up here, to the house. They're gonna kill me. I'm fucked."

Boone didn't know what to say. Sheriff Slone must have paid the man a visit and delivered a message. Elmer Canifax sounded like he'd just faced a vision of his last moments on the mortal coil.

He just couldn't figure what the fuck Elmer thought he could do about that. If Walt or the sheriff (perhaps Walt *and* the sheriff) decided that they wanted somebody dead, nobody could stand in the way of that. Not Boone, not Batman, not sweet Jesus himself.

He turned around to check Samantha again. When he did, he saw Karen standing there, in the entrance to the living room. The conversation with Elmer was over. "I'll call you back," he said, and hung up the phone.

"Who was that?" asked Karen. She pressed her hands hard on her hips, enough to turn all the tips of her fingers white.

"Nobody," said Boone.

"Nobody. Sure." She did little to hide her suspicion.

Boone didn't care about Karen's suspicions. He glanced past her, and saw his daughter still engaged in the cartoon.

He walked over to the kitchen counter and set the phone down. Before he could turn back around, Karen loomed in his face. He stared at her; she stared at him. He tried walking around but she sidestepped and blocked his path.

"I have to go," he said. He went back into the living room, kissed Samantha on the cheek. "Daddy will be back soon. Daddy will be back and we'll go to the park all day today."

Samantha's face lit up. "Really?"

"Yes, really." He kissed her one more time, then headed for the front door, leaving his wife on full steam in the kitchen.

Rage swirled into Karen's face. There was no way she could let him go that easily. "So that was nobody?" she roared.

"Yep," he said over his shoulder.

Karen blew up. "Where do you think you're going now?" She followed him towards the entrance, but couldn't beat him there.

Boone went on outside, trying to get away, but she made it onto the porch just as he reached the bottom of the steps. He didn't turn around. He heard a clatter of yelling and cursing aimed in his general direction, but he didn't dare turn around. Instead he went straight to his pick-up truck, got in, and drove away without saying another word.

BUSINESS

A tumbledown outbuilding stood behind Elmer Canifax's house. On the exterior it looked like an old Cajun fishing shack, all grey wood and rust, with mushrooms growing out of the cracks in the walls and waist-high weeds poking out around the cement foundation. Thirty feet by thirty feet of ho-hum rural neglect.

But that was just the outside.

On the inside, Elmer's shack was a mad scientist's lab in all its haphazard glory. Crooked shelves were lined with dusty glass beakers, rubber hoses, Bunsen burners, objects from high school chemistry class that no one ever thought they'd use in real life. Sundry items lifted from kitchens and bathrooms in every corner of Seward County, the most common of harmless household items that mixed together with ease for results both delightful and deadly.

Half-empty bottles of rubbing alcohol. A few cans of paint thinner. Cardboard cylinders filled with drain cleaner.

Enough cough medicine to beat down the Black Plague.

A heap of car batteries, packages of diet pills, cans of Coleman lantern fuel.

Freon jugs, Red Bull energy drink, rock salt by the gallon.

Hypodermic needles.

Light bulbs.

Bottle caps.

Elmer had his special recipes, perfected over many late night cooking sessions. Depending on the occasion – birthdays, anniversaries, Christmas, Wednesday – he carefully picked from the ingredients at his disposal and conjured the appropriate version of his exquisite meth, up here in the little edifice on the back yard's edge.

He considered himself something like a chef. A master meth chef. He offered a good product, and the market reacted in accordance. The party kids gave him a few dollars each. Some snorted his creation through empty ink pens, while those that couldn't handle the snort grabbed a needle-less syringe and shot the candy straight up their asses. Everyone laid around, fucked up on Drano and firestarter. On went their feathery lives.

*

Boone found Elmer in the shack, sitting on the picnic table amidst a scatter of chemistry equipment, wearing an industrial gas mask. When Boone came in, Elmer held his hands on his knees and looked at the dirty wooden floor, where broken glass and twisted yellow hoses intertwined in an angry mass at his feet.

"Callin' me like that probably wasn't the smartest thing you could have done, Elmer," Boone said as he closed the rickety door behind him.

Elmer lifted his head but didn't turn to face his visitor. Still, Boone could see the cuts on his face. The injuries glistened fresh, raw. A dark purplish bruise deepened in Elmer's left jaw, the same jaw that Sheriff Slone ground into the bathroom mirror just a few hours ago.

"You all right, Elmer?" said Boone.

Elmer sat up straighter, made eye contact. "Do I fuckin' look like I'm all right?"

"Not really," said Boone.

Elmer climbed down off the table. He stepped around the room, away from Boone, then back towards him, then away again. Eventually he wandered into a far corner, where he found a heavy green tarp covering a pile of old blankets. He stood there, in thought. He crossed his arms at the waist and considered the tarp and the blankets.

Boone waited.

Elmer gave off the clear impression that this pile of blankets was a matter of extreme importance. Some time passed. Boone waited. He wondered if this visit was a complete waste of time, but he also couldn't escape the nagging idea that something important would be missed if he left. So he waited.

Finally Elmer reached down and slung the tarp aside. He pushed back the blankets and revealed something else underneath: two wooden crates stacked in perfect alignment, each one six feet in length, two feet wide, and two feet high.

Elmer ran his hand over his smooth bald head. "You know, Boone, I been wanting to ask you something for a while now," he said.

"What about?"

"Just a little somethin'. I don't mean to get too personal, but hell, I been wonderin'."

Boone just looked at him.

Elmer pursed his lips, nodded slowly. "Right. Right. So is it true, about you and Ellen Slone?"

"Is what true?"

"That Walt had you kill her 'cause he was too chicken shit to do it himself."

A look came across Boone's face like he'd just drunk a gallon of gasoline. "You heard that?"

"I heard that," said Elmer.

Boone stared, dead silent. Elmer knew his comment had hit its mark. They stood there, each waiting for the other to say something, neither completely sure what that something might be.

Eventually Elmer waved off the tension and changed the subject. "Come over here, Boone," he said, as he bent over and pried open the top of the crate with his bare hands. "I got something you want to see." He found shredded newspaper and bubble wrap covering bags of white rice in the top of the crate, Rapidly he burrowed through it, as Boone obliged his request.

Boone considered that the best course of action might be to just turn around and get the hell out of there. Especially given Elmer's questions about Ellen Slone. What kind of play was that? Where had it come from? Boone didn't know and didn't really want to know.

"I'm gettin' out of here," he said, and took a step towards the door.

"Hold on, hold on now," said Elmer. "I'm sorry. The Ellen comments were too much. I was just playin'. I didn't mean nothin' by it no ways. Come over here and look at what I got. Trust me, you want to see it."

Again Boone hesitated. He couldn't see how this ended up anything but a fiasco. If Walt found out he'd visited Elmer, there would surely be a lot of questions, and Boone wouldn't have any answers. Not any that Walt Slone wanted to hear, at least.

"Come on. Come on," whispered Elmer, motioning with one hand for Boone to join him. "Tell me, you ain't afraid of ol' Walt are ya?"

"This has got nothing to do with him," said Boone, knowing that was a lie. "You're a world famous shit ass, Elmer. It ain't really in my best interest to have dealins with you."

Elmer chuckled. "Whatever."

Against his better judgment, Boone wandered over to the pile of blankets. When he arrived there, the floor around Elmer was covered with trash and bubble wrap and rice. The crate stood open, the lid swung backward as far as it would go on its hinges.

With deferential silence, the two men gazed upon the contents – the true contents – of the wooden box as if they were peering at the secrets in the fabled Ark of the Covenant.

Ten bags of marijuana.

Four plastic cases, packed full with hundreds of little pills - one case for Lortabs, one for Oxycontin, one for Xanax, one for Vicodin.

Six assault rifles: three AR-15s and three M6A2s. Four 9mm Beretta pistols. Two Remington Model 750 deer rifles. A couple of night vision scopes. Plenty of ammo to go around.

Boone picked one of the AR-15s out of the box. "Do I even want to ask where all this shit came from?" He ran his hand along the smooth barrel.

"Probably not," said Elmer. Then he snickered. "But I'd imagine you already got a pretty good idea."

Of course Boone had a pretty good idea where all that shit came from. Better than a good idea – he knew exactly. The two crates no doubt made their way to Sewardville on one of the regular truck runs that carried Walt Slone's merchandise down from New York, blowing past weigh stations and bribing DOT officials all the way.

These plain white trucks would come off the East Kentucky Parkway and roll out Highway 213, then meet Deputy Rogers in the parking of the Sewardville Methodist Church. Boone wasn't sure how, but somewhere between the eastern seaboard and the midnight rural rendezvous with Deputy Rogers and his U-haul trucks, these two containers full of drugs and guns went missing, and wonder of wonders, turned up here in Elmer Canifax's backyard building.

And if there was any place on God's green Earth that Walt Slone's merchandise did not belong, it was in Elmer's shack.

No question, Walt must have missed these two crates. Boone didn't have a guess why Walt hadn't raised holy hell to track them down, but he had no doubt that Walt knew they were missing. If something that belonged to Walt Slone went missing, the old man knew about it. Walt Slone didn't get where he was by not keeping track of his merchandise.

But, on the infinitesimal chance that Walt *had* failed to notice they were missing, then surely Karen would not have made the same mistake. After all, Walt knew the ledgers but he trusted her with the math. Between father and daughter, it seemed unlikely they could have overlooked all of this, which represented two large piles of cash for them, once everything sold on the local market. And definitely, everything *would* sell.

"Oh, yeah," Elmer said on cue. "I hear Walt and them kids of his are right pissed some of their stuff didn't make it all the way down South."

"They'll find it." Boone shook his head. "Either they find it, or they'll find out who took it. One way or the other, I wouldn't be spendin' too much time out in public if I was you."

A few other thoughts went through Boone's mind, but he didn't allow them to pass over his tongue. Like: *what the fuck are you doing you stupid little fuck? Don't you fucking understand that you're sitting here on your own fucking coffins?*

Boone saw no point in bringing them up. Elmer knew what he'd done. How could he not know? He knew.

Elmer Canifax had stuck his hand in the Slone bank account, the only place where he could actually hurt the old man. That was not an accident. It was the result of a little bravado, some careful planning, probably some blind luck somewhere along the line, and a whole hell of a lot of recklessness. There was a small part of Boone that appreciated Elmer's pulling it off.

Now he wondered: why exactly would Elmer call *him*. What did Elmer hope to accomplish by dragging *him* into this?

"I oughtta leave right now, before you say something that gets us both killed," said Boone.

"Don't you want to hear my business proposition?" Elmer answered.

Now, he paced. The more he paced, the more he talked. The more he talked, the faster the words flew out of his mouth. "It ain' no secret, how you and your father-in-law don't get along so good these days. I figured maybe you might want a chance to strike out on your own."

"Right," Boone said without any enthusiasm. "That's what I want to do. Start up a business with some guns and drugs you stole off Walt's truck. That would be smart. Why don't you just shoot me in the head now?"

"Just hear me out."

"I ain't hearin' you out, Elmer."

Elmer shook his head, rolled his eyes, kept pacing. A minute passed. He went back towards the crates and leaned against them.

"I don't know, I just figured you might be interested," he shrugged.

Boone found himself stuck in a void, unsure what to say or what not to say. The idea that Boone might be interested in this scheme hung so far out from reality that no response seemed appropriate.

"You don't even have to get your hands dirty," continued Elmer. "Just keep Walt and the sheriff off my back for a couple of weeks, enough time so I can unload all this. I'll give you half of the money it brings. Then we can all be on our merry little way."

"Our merry little way."

Elmer nodded.

"I don't think so," said Boone. "Best thing I can tell you is, you need to get all this shit back where it came from before Walt finds out it's up here. 'Cause when he finds out, you got some *real* problems on your hands."

Those last words shocked the room like hot water on cold glass. The two men stood there for several seconds, waiting to see if that ominous thought would mark the end of their conversation.

LYING

Boone left Elmer's and went straight to the Sewardville City Park. He felt sure that as soon as he'd left Walt's house, Karen would have plucked Samantha off the couch and tore off the hillside in a fit of marital frustration, spiriting her away to the city park before Boone could come back and fulfill the promise he'd made earlier that day. Karen tried to create any little advantage possible, any chance to suggest, *Look honey. Daddy runs away, Daddy can't keep his promises. Mommy will take you wherever you want to go. Who loves you more? Mommy loves you more.* He'd learned to think like his wife. Learned to anticipate.

And he'd learned well.

When Boone got to the park, he saw Karen's black Escalade in the grass, just outside of the entrance. Sheriff Slone's cruiser sat a few yards away; Boone could see a red white and blue "ELECT WALT SLONE MAYOR" sign stuck in the ground a couple of feet past the police car's front grill. There were some other vehicles, too – a couple of subcompacts, a small Chevy pickup, a 1992 Cadillac – but he didn't recognize them as belonging to anyone in particular.

Beyond the entrance, he saw a few people straggling about, but nobody seemed very busy. Then Boone caught a glimpse of Walt stepping into a little octagon-shaped brick building that was at the park's far end, just a few feet from the asphalt walkway that sidewindered through the grounds.

Less than twenty-four hours from now, the building would house the Orchid Festival's Chili Competition, which of course led right into the big chili supper, the single biggest social event on the Seward County calendar. Bigger than the county fair, bigger than the demolition derby, bigger even than the Miss Orchid Festival contest. If the Orchid Festival as a whole was Sewardville's annual crowning achievement, then surely the chili supper was the shining white diamond in the very front of the tiara.

The chili supper marked the one night of the year that folks from even the deepest hollow ventured out for fellowship. Some estimates suggested that seventy percent of the county's population attended some or all of the supper. The occasion required a hundred twelve-foot cafeteria tables, with the first fifteen or so setup inside the brick building, reserved for the community's most prominent citizens, and the rest standing in parallel rows that filled up the adjacent grass field.

At the moment, though, the room was bare, save for a few uncovered tables and some folding metal chairs. A stack of the red white and blue "VOTE WALT SLONE FOR MAYOR" signs sat in the corner. Red white and blue – the color of great Americans.

Not far from his signs, Walt stood against one wall, entertaining Samantha with a pink ball about the size of a tangerine, bouncing the sphere off the bricks and just out of the girl's reach while she yelped with innocent glee. Nearby, John Slone and Karen pulled white tablecloths out of storage boxes.

Boone approached his wife and brother-in-law. "You need some help?" he asked, hoping they would say no.

"Not really," said Karen. Her eyes stayed fixed on the tablecloth in her hands.

That response didn't bother Boone; he hadn't come there to see his wife, anyway. He'd come there for Samantha, and he went to her now.

"Karen mentioned you left the house in a hurry," said Walt. He caught the ball from Samantha, bounced it back, still not looking up towards his son-in-law. "That true?"

"Yeah," said Boone.

"Where'd you have to go that was so important?"

"Out."

"Out?"

"Yeah. Out."

"What's that supposed to mean?"

Boone took a deep breath, let it out slow, hoping he might formulate the magical answer that would both answer Walt and also avoid the issue entirely.

He came up with, "Elmer said he had some money for you. Wanted me to come get it. I reckon the sheriff scared the sh——" He looked at Samantha, stopped the curse word. "The sheriff must have scared him to death earlier."

"You think?" said Walt.

"Probl'y so," said Boone. "I guess he decided he owed it to you."

"For what?"

"Don't ask me. Maybe he's just trying to buy back your good graces."

A hacking wind caught in the back of Boone's throat and his heart quickened. He realized that, in the span of fifteen seconds, he'd just gone down what could end up being one black and awful stretch of road.

He'd lied to Walt Slone.

Boom. Snap. Just like that.

Intended or not, lying to Walt was as dumb a thing as a human being could do, and Boone knew that better than anybody. He'd broken plenty of arms and jaws of people who'd lied to Walt Slone. Despite that, like so many other moments in Boone's life, this one started without any bad intent and quickly devolved into a complete clusterfuck. The lie slipped out. The lie *was* out. And now, with the lie out in the open air, he had to be careful to maintain it, to build upon it wherever necessary, or else his world could quickly spin out of grasp and there was no telling where it all might end up.

This was about to become an exercise in improvisation. His brain ripped through potential questions – *what if he wants to see the money? What if he calls Elmer himself?* – but he figured the answers would come when he needed them.

Suddenly Boone was looking down into the valley, watching people and machines tumble into a pit of fire.

A surprised expression danced across Walt's brow, and Boone feared he'd already been busted in his lie.

Walt pushed his tongue around the inside of his upper lip, something he always did when he wasn't quite sure what to say next. This gave Boone a bare sliver of hope – maybe he wasn't quite so busted after all.

Samantha bounced the ball to him and he caught it again with ease, but this time didn't throw it back. Instead he squeezed the ball hard, until it disappeared into his grip.

"Elmer wanted you to come get the money?" asked Walt.

"Yep," said Boone. "He sounded pretty tore up about it. I figured you'd prob'ly want me to go get it before he changed his mind."

"So where is it?"

Boone recognized an opening. "I ain't got it," he said, shaking his head. A chance for a half-truth that might get him out of this. "By the time I got up there, he'd already thought better of it."

"He thought better of it?"

"I guess."

"What the fuck is that supposed to mean, Boone?"

"I don't know, Walt. He just wanted to fuck with me, I guess."

"What's he gonna gain by that?"

"Hell if I know."

At last, Walt stood up. He motioned for Samantha to come to him, then gave her the ball and stared at Boone. A deep suspicion crept into the moment. Walt's gaze burned, and again Boone felt like he wanted to punch himself in the face. Samantha stood there between them, holding her pink rubber sphere, oblivious to everything else.

But the lie was out. The lie breathed. Now Boone was forced to keep it breathing.

"Damned Elmer," Walt said, shaking his head slowly. "It just don't make any sense. Don't make any sense him calling you, and don't make any sense you going up there. Elmer thinks he's hot shit, like he's gonna make a run and push us out. He ain't gonna suddenly take a turn for charity."

"He told me he wanted to do just that," Boone shrugged. "The sheriff whipped his ass, and he wanted you all off his back. Hell, I thought you'd be happy about this, Walt."

"And you thought that made some kind of sense?"

"It seemed as good as anything."

"You're serious."

"I figured it was worth checkin' out is all."

Walt snorted hot wind out of his nostrils, irritated with Boone's answer that time. "You know, Boone," he said softly, "You might be my son-in-law, but sometimes you can be one hellacious dumb human being."

Boone dragged his fingers through the thick hair on the side of his head. He felt his mouth drying out, and swallowed the little bit of saliva he had left. He needed something to say, some perfect words that would end this conversation before it spiraled too far out of his grasp. Even if Walt couldn't be completely convinced now, if Boone could only get through this moment, then maybe he could fill in the gaps later.

"Did you really want me to not go up there if he said he had it?" he said, finally.

Walt looked at him, and didn't immediately answer. This was good. Walt Slone usually thought three steps ahead in the conversation, so if he didn't have an immediate answer it meant that Boone had the advantage, or at least more of an advantage than usual.

Boone pulled his cell phone from his jacket and handed it to Walt. "If you don't believe me, go ahead and call him."

Walt stared at the phone. He stared at Boone. He stared back at the phone. Then he pronounced, "Naw, nevermind. If you're lying, I'll find out, anyhow."

The cell phone went back into Boone's jacket pocket before Walt had a chance to change his mind. As further defense, he reached for Samantha's hand, which she gave him with a warm grin.

"You want to go take some flowers to your Mamaw?" he asked.

"Yeah!" the child cheered.

"You don't want to stay here and help decorate for the festival?" Walt said, entirely to Samantha, not at all to Boone. He smiled at the girl. "That's what you wanted to do today, right?"

"I want to go with my Daddy," she answered, simple and straight, and handed her grandfather the pink ball with which they had been playing just a few moments earlier.

SAMANTHA

Not long after that, the father and the daughter convened at the gravesite of Ellen Slone. In the spring afternoon, the sunlight rained upon them, a perfect radiance warming the backs of their necks. Their faces reflected in the black marble, clear as if they were standing in front of still water. Their eyes locked on the headstone that marked the final repose of Samantha's grandmother, or Mamaw as the child preferred calling her, even though she never knew the lady, even though Ellen had died so many years before Samantha was born.

This was one of the rare occasions when they came together, hand in hand, and a mutual silence suggested both of them recognized the profound rarity of the experience. Separately, they visited the grave often. Together, not so often.

Each held a bouquet of fresh Mountain orchids loose in one hand, their pearly white petals still damp with sprayed water from the florist's shop. The granddaughter knew her Mamaw loved the Mountain orchids. Papaw told her so.

Samantha rocked back and forth on the side of her foot, unsure what to do next. She did not often get moments like this with her Daddy, quiet moments, moments without push or pull. She did not often get moments of any kind with her Daddy. It seemed to her that even when they were together, other people were with them. With those people almost always came screaming, crying, or fighting.

But there was none of that here.

Here they let the silence linger, and enjoyed it.

She squeezed his palm and felt her tiny hand swallowed up inside his. That felt like safety.

"Do you remember her?" said Samantha.

"Sure I do," said her Daddy.

"Papaw says she was nice."

"She was. She was nice."

"And pretty, too."

"She was beautiful," Boone nodded. "You look a lot like her."

"Really?"

"Every day that passes, I see more of her in you."

Samantha turned away from the headstone and looked up at him. "I wish she was still alive when I was born," she said. "I wish she was alive right now."

The child's words were slow, straight ahead. In the moment, she didn't quite grasp her own thoughts about this woman she knew only from pictures on the mantle and stories from her Papaw and her Mommy and her Daddy. Still, some lonely something echoed inside her. She understood that lonely something. She felt it often. She wished her Mamaw was alive.

Samantha looked back towards the black marble slab. Her daddy let go of her hand and stepped forward. Briefly she reached for him, but pulled back when she realized he would not be more than a few feet away.

He took yesterday's orchids out of the vase on the left side of the headstone, and replaced them with the fresh bouquet in his hand. Samantha did the same on the right side. When she was done, she backpedaled away from the grave, and offered the old flowers to her father. He accepted them, and then shuffled his fingers through her fine blonde hair.

This moment would not last forever. The best times never did. In only her five short years on Earth, she'd learned all too well that the best moments could never last. The best moments came and went like fog rolling inland from the sea, providing brief cover for the oh so dark waters before being brushed away by the aurora's hand.

Sooner or later Mommy and Papaw would be home. Samantha knew that when they returned, she would once more feel the push and the pull at the edges of her soul. She knew: her quiet moment must eventually end.

But not now.

Now she and Daddy could have their time. Now they could be together. Now they had nothing to worry about - no argument to defuse, no drama to withstand, no reason to sit and cover her ears to keep out the grown ups' loud words. If only for this sliver of time, they were free, at the edge of the woods that loomed behind the big house on the hill.

She didn't know how much time they would have. How could she know? She didn't know. All she knew was they were there, the two of them, only the two of them, and all seemed right for once.

"Ready to go inside?" he asked.

"In a minute," she answered. "Let's stay out here a little longer."

He said nothing, only nodded. He put his hands on her shoulder and pulled her closer to him. They did stay a little longer, as long as they could, as long the world around them would allow. Then they decided not to go inside, after all.

BUSINESS

The longer the day went, the more Sewardvillians showed up at the city park to help with the Orchid Festival decorations. Folks took pride in their festival, after all; everything had to be perfect. As perfect as they could get it, anyway. More banners were hung, blue and yellow streamers tacked from tree to tree.

Even as the buzz increased around them, the Slones - Walt, Karen, John - took a break from their work in the brick octagon. They strolled out towards the back of the structure, where they could be alone save for the occasional wanderer.

"So what do you think about this whole deal with Boone and Elmer Canifax?" Walt said. His dry sarcasm made it plain that Walt wasn't buying the story.

"I don't think anything about it," John replied, shrugging it off completely. "Elmer's a dipshit. A fuckhead dipshit, you know? What did you expect, he was all of a sudden gonna get right when there ain't never been no evidence of that before now? Hell, Boone's half a dipshit himself these days. You get those two together and there ain't no tellin' what's gonna happen."

"Yeah, but it don't make sense," said Walt.

"It ain't supposed to make sense," said the sheriff. "Why would it make sense? They're fuckheads."

Walt shook his head. He took a deep breath, extended one arm and propped himself against the red brick wall. "You're half right," he said. "Elmer's a fuckhead, no doubt about it. But Boone, he ain't a fuckhead, not like this kind of a fuckhead anyway."

"I suppose that's why you got him on the quarter machines," John interjected.

"He does more than the quarter machines, from time to time."

"From time to time?" asked Karen.

"From time to time," said her father. He popped straight up, away from the wall.

Karen went quiet. So did the sheriff. Each of them pondered where the discussion might be going, while Walt walked around and batted the situation back and forth inside his head. Silence dug in and became uncomfortable, holding sway until John said, "Maybe Boone's not a total waste. But the fact remains, this don't make any sense. Why would he take off to Elmer's like that? On his own?"

Walt looked at Karen now. "I don't know. Why would he take off?"

"I told you already, I have no idea," she replied, sounding annoyed. "One minute, he's downstairs with Samantha, then of a sudden, the phone rings and he tears up and out of there like he just won the lottery or something."

"And he didn't even mention he was going to Elmer's," said John.

"No," said Karen. "Not a word."

Walt sighed. This discussion hurt his head; this discussion hurt everybody's head. It was a conversation destined for nowhere, no matter how much each of them sensed something out of whack with Boone's scenario. A riddle with no answer, at least no answer they could see yet.

The questions were unspoken, but they were the same for Karen as they were Sheriff Slone as they were for Walt. *Why leave in such a hurry? Why go to Elmer's alone, even if there really* was *money to be picked up? Why not call the sheriff,* especially *if there was money to be picked up?*

Glances bounced among the three people. Karen to Slone. Slone to Walt. Walt to Karen.

"You want me to head back up to Elmer's?" the sheriff asked, looking at Walt.

"Not right now," Walt answered immediately, as though he had already considered that option and dismissed it before the question could even be asked out loud. Then he paused, considered, and added, "Don't say anything else to Boone, either."

John took a deep breath and looked out into the park grounds.

"I know," Walt went on, sensing the sheriff's displeasure. "We ought to go see 'em both first. Find out what the hell's really going on. Maybe there's something else in play here."

Karen said, "And if there's something else going on, we can lay back and watch them, and see if it comes to light," she said.

Walt nodded, pleased with his daughter. "Exactly."

Karen nodded, pleased with herself. "Exactly."

"I don't know about that," John said. "What if we lay back, waitin' on them to do something, and wind up givin' them enough time to figure out a way around us?"

"They won't get around us."

"You sound awful sure."

"I'm sure. They won't get around us."

John nodded slowly. He puffed his cheeks out in exasperation, but otherwise did not hide the notion that he disagreed with his sister.

In his line of work, Sheriff Slone knew that people could get around you. Elmer could do it, Boone could do it, anybody could do it if you let your guard down and gave them a crack to ease through.

There had been plenty of people that he thought couldn't get around him, only to find out they could get around him quite well, indeed. All it took was one slip on the ground, one bead of sweat in the eye, one side thinking the other was too small or too slow to be much of a threat, and then a man was liable to find out just who could get around whom. John Slone didn't think Jimmy Sumner could get around him that night up at the Bears Den and how did that turn out? Five seconds and a quick trigger finger later, and Jimmy Sumner made his way around the sheriff just fine, after all. Shit happened. It just happened. No matter who was on one end holding the gun and who was on the other end staring down both barrels, sometimes... sometimes shit happened.

Sometimes shit happened that flipped those barrels right around. John knew that the view from the end of a gun barrel was a hell of a lot different than the view behind it. He also knew that he'd do anything he could to make sure that he never found himself in that position again.

"Lay back, huh?" John said after a couple of minutes. "That's about the damnedest plan I ever heard. If we think Boone's into something with Elmer and they're working against us, we ought to go smack both of 'em down right now. We let that shit rot and we'll never get the smell out of our hair again, you know?"

"Simmer down, John," Walt answered. "We got time."

"We ain't got time," said John.

"We got time," said Walt again. "You're givin' those boys too much credit. Even if they got something in the works, we got time. You get right down to it, Elmer's a dumbass, thinks he's too smart for his own shorts. He ain't worth foolin' over."

"Tell *her* Elmer ain't worth foolin' over," said John, motioning towards Karen. "She runs the books. How'd the books look before Elmer got in the market?"

"The books are fine," Karen said.

"The books ain't fine. The numbers are down. How many times have you said that. Now, Boone... whatever about Boone. Think what you want about Boone. Boone runs the quarter machines."

"He does more, from time to time," said Walt.

"No offense, but fuck Boone," the sheriff continued. "Boone's past his prime. Elmer's a different story. The numbers are down, he's why. We all know it."

Walt took another deep breath. Lately, anytime the subject turned to Boone, he felt a sorrow inside himself, a profound disappointment, a thorough loss of hope. When Karen was involved in the conversation it just made the disappointment that much worse, and that much harder to get around. He was her husband, after all. And as her husband, and a member of the Slone family, Boone had once been capable of such greatness. Now, he ran the quarter machines.

"I know you ain't worried about Boone," said Walt. "And that's my point. Was a time I would have said Boone was the one to keep your eye on, but now I ain't so sure."

"But now he ain't worth watchin'," John said.

"Maybe. I'm just sayin'," said Walt.

"You're just sayin'."

"Uh-huh."

Walt felt his son fishing for more substance, but he wouldn't bite. He once held some hope for Boone, felt thrilled when Boone got together with Karen and felt like it was a good addition to the family. But that was a long time ago. Now, the quarter machines. Karen and the sheriff knew, and Walt knew. The quarter machines.

"I'm just sayin'," Walt finally finished. "We got time, that's all I'm sayin'."

FAMILY

The afternoon slid into darkness. Walt and Karen left the city park and headed back to the Slone house. John followed right behind them, parking his cruiser in the driveway like he always did.

They came in the front door and found Boone sitting on the couch. Samantha tottered on his lap, father and daughter both involved in a live-action Disney channel sitcom that neither one could name, featuring handsome young boys and girls that smiled and tossed their shiny hair around with great frequency.

Boone didn't look up when the Slone triumvirate came in. Instead, he kissed Samantha on the cheek and kept watching the T.V. He practically dared Karen to come across the room and try to break up his father-daughter moment.

Karen knew what he was doing, too. She stood in the kitchen, and sweetly called her little girl's name. But Samantha never turned around.

Karen threw a frustrated glance at the sheriff. The sheriff knew what she wanted.

"Boone?" said John. "Ain't it about time for you to go to work?"

Boone pretended not to hear him.

"I said, Boone, ain't it about time for work?" said John. "You know. The quarter machines."

Now, Boone looked up at his brother-in-law.

Before Boone could say anything, Walt walked into the living room. He stopped in between the couch and the television, and held out his arms for Samantha. This time, she broke away from her father and slipped into the old man's grasp, where he brought her closer for a warm hug like only the best grandfathers could offer. As they embraced, Walt looked up at Boone and whispered that, indeed, the quarter machines needed tending.

BEARS DEN

When Boone arrived at the Bears Den later that evening, he found the place two-thirds full and cloaked in a cigarette haze. The usual rednecks and coal miners and loud country music kept the place at a constant buzz.

He passed through the carcinogen fog, waved hello to Lorna behind the bar, and found his way to the gambling contraptions in the back room.

Moments later, he took a hundred and twelve dollars from the first quarter machine, eighty-nine from the second, and one fifty-six from the last. The video poker game produced another good haul, two hundred and fifteen bucks. One thing was sure: no matter how lean the times got, no matter how far downhill the economy slid, the miners and the farmers and the scraps and the rabble-rousers would always have money for whiskey, and beer, and cigarettes, and the gambling machines - and Walt Slone would happily take the last coin from their pockets.

Once he was finished, Boone left the back room and closed the door behind him. He went to the bar, sat down near the end, three seats away from anybody else. He took out twenty dollars of Walt's Slone's money and set it on the bar.

"How much whiskey can a man get for twenty dollars?" he asked Lorna.

"About five shots of the rot gut," she said.

"Bring 'em to me, then," he said. "All at once."

Lorna reached onto the shelf behind her and got five shot glasses and a bottle of Maker's Mark. She sat the glasses up on the bar in front of Boone and poured his drinks. Boone grabbed the first glass and tossed the brown liquor down his throat before she finished filling the next. Then he did the same with the second one, slamming it back before Lorna poured the one after.

"Long day?" asked Lorna.

"Long day," said Boone.

An AC/DC tune rumbled up from the jukebox, late seventies era Bon Scott AC/DC, subterranean and dangerous. Boone didn't know the exact song, but he knew Sheriff Slone loved AC/DC. Boone hated the goddamn band, which was not a coincidence.

He swished the taste of bourbon around his tongue until the burn settled in the back of his mouth.

"Anybody sitting here?" A familiar woman's voice, behind him. Not pleasant, but familiar.

He turned around and saw Carla Haney, WTVL Live On Your Side but didn't immediately recognize her. She'd discarded her normal department-store reporter's outfit and now wore dark jeans, a University of Kentucky sweatshirt, had her hair pulled back casual and tied with a narrow black elastic band.

The sight of her elicited no reaction in his gut, certainly not the fireball disgust that ran him down the last time they'd been in the Bears Den together. This time, instead of that quick anger, Boone felt an underwhelming shrug of emotion. He spun back around on his stool and downed another shot of Maker's Mark.

"I didn't see your news van parked outside," he sneered.

"I didn't drive it," she said.

Boone swiveled his head on his shoulders, popped his neck. "That's too bad. 'Cause I really would have liked to take a piss on it."

Carla Haney WTVL Live On Your Side didn't let Boone's manner bother her. She stepped forward and claimed the barstool beside him. At first he ignored her, but before long it became clear that she wasn't going anywhere. It became especially clear after she took one of his remaining whiskey shots and swallowed it in a quick motion.

They sat quietly after that. Boone simmered. After a minute, he said quietly, "I paid for that you know."

"I know." She grabbed another shot, the last one, and downed it. "I guess you paid for that, too."

"Aren't you supposed to be getting' ready for the news or something?"

"The news is on at eleven. It's not even six yet."

"The news comes on at six, too."

"I'm not on the six o'clock. I'm on the eleven o'clock."

"I know that."

"You know what?"

"I know the news comes on at six and eleven, and you are usually on the eleven. I hate the news but I've seen it enough times to know a few things."

"Such as?"

"Such as I hate it."

He thought about the news van, the fat cameraman, the never-ending stream of stories about Sewerville. He said, "Surely there's a dead cow or a runaway fire truck somewhere that needs your attention," and he really meant, *how about you just go straight to hell?*

The reporter pressed her chin into her right shoulder and rocked in her seat until she figured out what to say next. Boone raised one hand, motioning for Lorna to bring four more shots. When the glasses arrived, Boone pulled them a few feet away from Carla, just in case she thought about taking any more of his bourbon.

Carla Haney WTVL Live On Your Side decided to come clean. "The eleven o'clock. You're right," she said. "I have to be back for the eleven o'clock. But I thought I'd come here and see if I could find you first."

"What the hell for?" Boone couldn't help but chuckle. "I wasn't friendly enough the last time we met?"

She laughed. "No, you were fine. But that was several months ago, and there was a lot going on around here."

Boone rolled his eyes. "And now you've got a few questions."

"Mmmm-hmmm. And now I've got a few questions."

He slumped on his seat, looked at the bar. He wondered what he should do next. Get up and leave? Stay and answer her questions? Stay and say nothing? Stay and tell her to stick everything up her Lexington reporter's ass? Whatever it was she wanted, it couldn't be good. There was an angle. There had to be an angle. Carla Haney, WTVL Live On Your Side did not come to Sewardville unless she smelled a story. She considered herself a hot shit reporter, and Boone felt sure she would be trying to do hot shit reporter things, bird dogging the big news story that would get her on the big TV news map.

He threw back another shot of bourbon. The smoky brown liquid burned a trail down his throat and lit his stomach on fire. He decided that he would play. If she was looking for a story, he could give her a story. The story he wanted her to hear.

"Ask away," he said.

"You want to talk here, in front of everyone?"

"Shit yeah. Don't you?" he smiled.

Carla passed a wan grin, not sure what to make of Boone's sudden willingness to talk. This was the guy who'd tossed her and her cameraman out of this same bar, threatened bodily harm, called each of them everything but a damn milk cow, and now he was willing to talk.

"Sure. Let's talk, then," Carla said. "And just so there's no confusion, I've got a digital recorder in my purse and I'm gonna turn it on now, if that's okay with you."

Boone laughed. Of course she had a digital recorder in her purse. Everybody hot shit reporter carried one. "Go right ahead," he said through a wide grin.

She reached into her purse, pulled out a little black apparatus that was about the size of a pack of chewing gum, and set it on the edge of the bar.

Boone looked at it. "Is it on?"

"Not yet," she said, then with her fingernail, pressed a tiny button on the recorder's side. "Now it is."

"What do you want to hear?"

"Well, I did some research," she said, "after everything went down with your brother. That must have been hard for you."

"It was," said Boone.

"You know, even after all this months, I still can't find anybody who can think of a reason why he'd do that. Why he would shoot that deputy, and the sheriff."

Boone smirked, half heartedly. "You didn't know Jimmy."

The reporter continued, "I want to hear more about what happened six months ago. I want to hear about the sheriff. And Jimmy. And Walt Slone."

Boone inhaled deeply. He motioned for Lorna to bring more shots of Maker's Mark, which she did.

When the drinks arrived, he handed one to Carla. She took the drink, they clanked their glasses together, and then threw back their liquor simultaneously. By the time his empty shot glass hit the counter, Boone was already staring at the recorder again. A red LED light blinked on the side, a hypnotic off and on that could go forever if left unattended. Around them, cigarette smoke and the hard music of AC/DC swirled together in the Bears Den atmosphere, broiling into that special Sewardville haze, the haze Boone knew so well, the haze that typified everything his life had become.

He pulled his eyes away from the flashing LED and looked at the reporter. "You better be careful," he offered, smiling.

"Why is that?"

"'Cause if you go askin' questions, you're liable to get some answers. Sometimes answers can be a lot more trouble than their worth. Least, that's my experience."

Boone pushed the recorder towards her, but she stopped him and gently edged it back in his direction. *I want the answers,* that gesture meant. The red light flashed on and off, on and off, interminable.

"Let's take a ride," he said.

ROGERS

The time logs of the Seward County sheriff's department showed only one deputy on duty that night. This was hardly uncommon; the small town of Sewardville just didn't have the necessary tax base to fund a larger force. They could afford several officers, they just couldn't afford having too many working at one time on a weeknight, when the area's rowdier elements stayed mostly quiet. Weekends, though, were a different story. On weekends, the liquor and the drugs flowed most freely across town, and on those nights more than one officer patrolled the streets.

But this was only Thursday. The weekend didn't start for another day, and so only one deputy was on duty tonight – J.T. Rogers, who sat in his cruiser, occupying the parking lot of the Sewardville Rx, faced towards the street. Eyes closed, brain waves slow and steady. Asleep.

The cell phone of Deputy Rogers rang — not really rang, just broke into a tinny recording of Conway Twitty's "Hello Darlin'." At first, the sound didn't awaken him. The song rounded through a chorus and looped across another verse before Rogers finally opened his eyes. He picked up the handset to see CALLER UNAVAILABLE on his digital screen.

Rogers answered immediately. He'd been expecting to hear from this Caller Unavailable.

"Wake your ass up," shouted the caller.

It was Elmer again.

Rogers recognized the voice immediately, despite the fact that Elmer was talking over loud music and several voices in the background. He pictured Elmer standing in the midst of a party, surrounded by writhing young bodies, smiling behind sunglasses that he would no doubt be wearing for protection against blinding strobe lights.

Again came Elmer's voice, shouting through the phone,

"We're rockin' here. Come on up!"

"I told you not call me on my cell again, you dumb son of a bitch!" Rogers yelled into the phone, hoping he could overcome the noise in the background.

"We're fuckin' rockin' up here, man!" Elmer repeated. "You coming?"

"I can't hear shit, Elmer."

"Don't worry about it. Just get up here. You're still comin', right?"

"I told you, I can't hear shit, Elmer. It sounds like fuckin' Chinese New Year up there."

Through the electronic din, Deputy Rogers thought he heard Elmer say, "Hang on a second." Then the music and the party noise faded, followed seconds later by the unmistakable sound of a door slammed shut.

"Is that better?" said Elmer. He'd locked himself in the bathroom, and his words bounced off the tile.

"Much better," the deputy said. "I can hear you now. I told you not to call me but here you are, callin' me. What's wrong with you? I told you about those old ladies and their scanners. If they hear us, we're in a shit heap. Don't that mean nothin' to you?"

"Chill," said Elmer. "Fuck them old ladies. So are you comin' up here or what?"

J.T. shook his head. It was hard to talk basic sense with Elmer Canifax. "Yeah, I'm comin'. When I get off duty."

"What time is that?"

"Eleven thirty."

"Who takes over for you?"

"The sheriff."

A pause.

"Call me when you're on your way," Elmer finally said. "I gotta get a few things ready. Like we talked about. We might have some problems with the competition, but we're still gonna do us some business, right?"

"Sure. Right."

"Then get on up here so we can take care of it."

Rogers opened his mouth to say "no problem," but before he could get the words out, the call ended. The deputy looked at his phone, confirmed that indeed Elmer had cut off the conversation, then put his phone away and waited for eleven thirty.

At eleven-thirty on the button, in the very same Sewardville Rx parking lot, J.T. Rogers handed his shift over to Sheriff Slone. The deputy reported nothing in the way of action for the night, much to the disappointment of the sheriff, though really not a surprise. Folks usually did their dirty deeds behind closed doors, up in the hollows and on the hilltops. The famous smalltown Saturday nights with high schoolers cruising bumper-to-bumper on a loop through town, and all the trouble they might bring with them, were mostly relics of the twentieth century. This was a slow evening. It wasn't Saturday anyway.

The two police cruisers sat beside each other. The sheriff's faced the back of the parking lot, while Rogers looked forward, across the road. They rolled down their driver's side windows and talked to each other from there.

"You headed home now?" asked John.

"Yeah, prob'ly," sighed the deputy, doing his best to sound tired when he was anything but. "Anything comes up, though, you just give me a call."

John Slone put his car back into gear. "Will do," he said, knowing full well that there was nothing that could come up that the sheriff couldn't handle just fine by himself.

QUESTIONS

While Deputy Rogers left the sheriff, Boone and Carla drove Boone's truck through the opposite end of Seward County, rolling along the rough road that took them away from the Bears Den and back into town.

Boone could think of about three thousand other people he'd rather share a vehicle with besides the reporter from Lexington, the reporter that WTVL kept on call at all times, just in case something newsworthy happened in Sewardville. Boone hated that about her, how she was always prepared to broadcast every last scrap of drama she could find. Folks in town got the general impression that she particularly enjoyed sharing the bad news from Sewardville. They took it personally. So did Boone.

But here they were, together in his truck, riding down the road.

You want to know about Walt Slone? Go ahead. I'll tell you a few things about Walt Slone.

Carla turned the recorder on and set it down on the seat between them.

"Tell me about your brother," she said in her reporter's voice. "Tell me about Jimmy."

Boone tightened down on the steering wheel. "What is it that you want to know about my brother?"

She let her silence answer for her.

"My brother. What about it," Boone answered, eventually. "My brother shot the sheriff. You know that old song? He did it one better. He shot the sheriff, *and* he shot the deputy. Sure as shit."

Carla nodded. "I was hoping you might tell me a little more than that." She looked away from him, out the passenger's side window.

Boone turned off the data recorder and stuck it inside his jacket pocket.

"Hey!" she protested.

"You want to hear something or not?" he said.

She shrugged, willing to wait it out. They drove on in silence. The tree-lined rural highway became Main Street, running between the faltering midget buildings of Sewerville. Through the truck window, Carla observed that the town looked worse under streetlights and shadow;

172

where darkness usually covered imperfection, in Sewerville the darkness only emphasized the squalor and decay.

The truck slowed to thirty miles per, below the speed limit.

Boone let out half a chuckle, as though he'd started to laugh and then decided against it. "Fine," he said. "With you bein' quiet like that, maybe you don't want to hear anything after all."

"I still want to hear about your brother."

Boone nodded, barely. He pursed his lips and held them that way for almost a full minute, not saying anything. The vehicle came to a stop at the first of the three red lights in town. His expression changed only when the light changed; when the light went green, it was like a switch flipped inside Boone.

"I'll tell you about my brother," he said, easing the truck back up to thirty. "He was older than me, but I took care of him. Best I could, anyway. He drank and gambled away every nickel he ever had. He hit every pothole in the road coming and going. He took pills and swallered whiskey like they were bread and water. He had a talent for crossin' the wrong people at the wrong time but he didn't really give a shit because he always figured that any man he couldn't out-talk, he could at least out-run. At least until he found one he couldn't.

"He's dead now, but you already know that. He had a funeral and three people showed up, including me and the preacher. Of course that was two more than I expected, so I guess you could say he was an overachiever in that regard."

He paused, took a breath. She shifted in her seat. He went on. "What else? He liked AC/DC, that's one thing. Another thing, Mama always liked me more than him, but that ain't really sayin' much because she'd just as soon spit as say hello for most of our grown up lives. Course you're from the news so you probably already know that too, right?"

"Yes. Most of it," she said.

Boone felt like he'd said enough. He looked over at his passenger and saw that she was staring at him without expression or judgment. He didn't know if it was what she wanted to hear, but it was exactly what he wanted to tell her. If Carla Haney WTVL Live On Your Side was digging for a story, he could lead her to one: the one he wanted her to find.

"Who was the third person?" she asked.

"Where?"

"At your brother's funeral."

"Oh. Harley Faulkner. The coroner. He doubles as the funeral director around here. Who'd you think?"

"I don't know." She stretched her legs out in the floorboard, brought her right up and folded it beneath her. "Your mother, maybe?"

"Right," Boone said, and offered another half-chuckle. "My mother. Maybe I wasn't clear about what she thought about us."

Before Carla could figure out her next question, Boone's cell phone rang. He picked it up, saw that the call came from John Slone, and let it ring three more times. "I need to take this," he said.

"No problem," said Carla.

Boone put the phone to his ear. "What can I do for you, sheriff?"

"I need you to meet me up the road."

"Where?

"Up at Elmer's place. We gotta do this one little thing."

"One little thing."

"Yeah."

Boone shook his head, frowned at Carla but kept talking to John. "When?"

"Thirty minutes. I'll see you up there."

The call ended. Boone laid the phone back on the seat of the truck, took a deep breath, stared out the windshield. Then he said to Carla, "Looks like I gotta cut this short."

"I guess you're not going to tell me why," she said.

"You guess right. Sorry."

She understood. He turned the truck around, and they headed back to the Bears Den, so Carla Hainey WTVL Live On Your Side could get in her car and drive herself home. He thought that maybe they could meet again soon, and finish this conversation – perhaps he could be her Anonymous Source, and she could run a serious expose of life in Sewerville, and the TV people could actually do some work *for* Sewardville just this once.

But coming events would prevent that from happening.

ROGERS

After he left the sheriff, Deputy J.T. Rogers changed into jeans and a green and yellow t-shirt with the John Deere logo plastered across two-thirds of his chest. He drove home and traded the sheriff's department cruiser for his white Jeep Grand Cherokee, then headed back out.

At three quarters past midnight, Highway 213 led Rogers back out of town, all the way to Brush Creek Road. There, he cut a sharp right on to the narrow two-lane road, which was barely wide enough for his Grand Cherokee by itself. He drove until he came to a gravel driveway that slanted downward so sharply that it was practically hidden from passersby unless passersby were looking for it. It went back into the woods a half-mile a pothole-ridden gravel driveway that was curvy as a rattlesnake's back, lined on both sides by thick trees whose limbs hung over the road like sagging, elderly appendages.

At the end of the driveway stood Elmer Canifax's farmhouse. The downstairs was lit up by strobe lights, just as Rogers had envisioned when Elmer called him. A steady beat of electronic dance music thumped into the deputy as he pulled up to the house, then around back.

There, the deputy parked his Jeep under a craggy old oak tree, nestled tight between a Chevy Cavalier and an old brown conversion van. If anybody unexpected showed up – say Sheriff Slone, or Walt Slone, or even Boone Sumner – they'd have to put in some real effort to find his vehicle.

Soon enough Rogers found himself wading in a sea of young humanity, across the kitchen and then through the large living room. Nearly all of the furniture in Elmer's farmhouse had been moved into back rooms so that all of the guests both expected and unexpected could be accommodated (the unexpected always outnumbered the expected at Elmer's parties). No matter. The rabble rousers still jostled against each other so closely that at times the place seemed like a single shimmering mass of wet skin and hair, dressed in clothes much too skimpy for early spring, adorned by a thin sheen of sweat and glitter. They grinded against each other in careful time with the steady beat of the electronic music, some sliding back against back, others locked eye to eye. The silver and green strobe lights added a stop-motion effect.

Rogers remembered a haunted house he'd been to in the 6th grade.

175

A young girl approached him, almost his height, with long blonde hair tossed casually to appear as if little care had gone into its style when in fact he knew she'd spent an hour making it fall just so. Dark indigo makeup in the corners of her eyes gave her a faintly Egyptian appearance. For a second Rogers wondered how old she might be, but before he could say anything, she spoke first instead, in a slight voice, unencumbered cigarettes and cheap liquor.

"Who are you?" she asked.

"I'm me," he answered. "Who are you?"

"I'm me," the girl smiled. She was thin; she swayed gently in her space, as though she might start floating at any moment. She didn't answer his question, though. Instead, she offered him her empty hand.

Rogers looked at her long, delicate fingers and saw they were frosted with glitter and white powder. He couldn't decide if the dust was cocaine, meth residue, or evidence of crushed-up pain pills. One seemed as likely as the other.

From one side, someone else took her other hand, and pulled her away. It was Elmer. He wore flip flops and a silky bathrobe the color of seaweed, and nothing else. The robe swung wide open and he didn't seem at all bothered.

"Come over here, darlin'!" he howled, drawing the vaguely Egyptian girl close, nuzzling her slender neck. After a moment, he let her go again, and again she stood there, swaying in place, smiling at the moment they shared.

Once more, Rogers found his attention drawn to the glitter and the powder on the young girl's fingers, both of which twinkled in the flashing strobe lights.

Elmer looked at the deputy. "I see you met Alice," he said, pointing at her.

Rogers checked the girl over, not finding anything that really impressed him. Then, he asked her, "What's that white stuff on your fingers?"

Alice didn't hesitate. "It's what's left of the pain pill I just snorted," she said. "Why, you want some?"

"I don't think so, honey. I'm a cop," said Rogers, hopelessly trying to project an air of authority.

"You ain't no cop," Alice giggled. "You're just some dude." She laughed. "Fuck you, dude." She laughed again.

Rogers gave no reaction.

Amused to the hilt, Elmer wrapped Alice in his arms and gave her a light kiss on the cheek. "Come with us," he said to Rogers. "Come on, deputy. Alice brought her friend, and she is *mighty* sweet. Let's make this a private party, what about it."

"Where are you going?"

"We're going upstairs," said Elmer. "I lead, all you gotta do is follow. There's two of them. There's two of us. You do know how that works, right?"

Without another word, he took Alice's hand and led her away, through the human sea and up a staircase at the other end of the living room. Halfway up the steps, he stopped, and looked back over his shoulder at the deputy, and smiled. Then he continued his ascent, with the young lady at his fingertips.

Rogers hesitated for just a second. For just a second.

Five minutes later, they were upstairs in Elmer's bedroom. Five minutes after that, Elmer had his tongue down Alice's throat and both of his hands cupped on her small naked breasts.

Nearby, Deputy Rogers sat on a small brown leather couch with Alice's friend, not quite sure what to do next. She had chemically-altered black hair just past her shoulders, with a lime green swath that started in the front and ran back behind her ear. She was tall and thin, just like Alice, and also every bit as fucked up on the same white dust. Rogers knew that because a dab of it frosted the edge of one nostril.

The girl slumped back into the corner of the couch, sat there with her arms loose at her sides and both palms up. She gazed at minor details: the dim lamp in the corner, the strands of carpet, the designs dappled into the ceiling drywall, the molecules dancing in the air.

"What's your name?" he asked the girl with black and green hair and fairy dust on her nose.

"Kristin. What's yours?" she said, again looking at the ceiling.

Rogers felt the need to tell a lie. "My name's Pablo."

"You don't look like a Pablo."

"You don't like a Kristin."

"What's a Kristin look like?"

"I dunno," he laughed. "What's a Pablo look like?"

The girl shrugged. Rogers shrugged, too, and awkwardness settled back in between them. The deputy felt the thump of dance music through the floor. Writhing bodies. Sweat. Zombies.

Before the conversation could plumb further depths, Elmer joined them, while Alice went into the bathroom. By that point, she was completely unclothed. Again, Rogers wondered about the age of these girls. The more he saw of them, the younger they looked. Twenty-one? Doubtful. Eighteen? Hopefully.

"They're nineteen, dude," said Elmer, as if he were reading the deputy's mind off of a flashing electronic cue card.

"Nineteen, huh?" Rogers said. He turned back to Kristin. "Really?"

She nodded, then laid her head over on the arm of the couch and closed her eyes.

Elmer squeezed the deputy on the shoulder and sat down on the couch between him and Kristin. "Don't worry about it, man. Every girl up here's street legal, no problem. Sit back. Pull your panties out of your crack and have a little fun."

Rogers wasn't quick to believe. "How do you know they're of age?"

"Nineteen," corrected Elmer. "I said they're nineteen. And I know because I ask them, that's how. I ask every girl that walks through that door, 'How old are you?' And they tell me the truth."

The deputy didn't believe him. "They tell you the truth."

"You bet."

"And nobody's underage?"

"Nope." Elmer winked, opened up his robe for all the world to see what he had hidden beneath it, which was only his pasty body. He lifted his balls with one hand, in the deputy's direction.

"You oughtta loosen up, J.T.," he cackled. "Hell, it don't matter how old they are, long as you're the one gettin' it. Pussy ain't red wine, you ain't gotta let the shit age 'fore you partake. Am I right or am I goddamn right?"

"I really don't know how to answer that," said Rogers.

"Aw fuck it," Elmer huffed. He waved away the doubts of his guest like he was waving away a bad smell. He poked Kristin in the side, just to see how she would react. She didn't react at all. Rogers thought for a second that she might have died on them, but soon he noticed her still breathing, which brought him some small comfort.

Elmer pulled a pipe out of his seaweed-colored robe, followed by a silver flip-top Zippo lighter and plastic bag filled with dingy, crystalline clumps.

Rogers recognized the meth immediately. "Don't smoke that shit with me here," he said.

"Why not?"

"Because I don't want to be around it, that's why."

"Okay, Mr. Clean," Elmer laughed. He filled his pipe with the drug and lit it up. After a deep draw he offered it to Rogers, who rolled his eyes and declined.

"You'd probably feel a lot better if you took a puff every once in a while," said Canifax. "What do you do for fun, anyway?"

"I ain't here to have fun," Rogers shot back.

"Then what the fuck are you here for?" said Elmer.

Rogers shook his head, and stood back up. He said, "How about you put your nutsack away and shut that damn bathrobe? I didn't come up here to smoke, I didn't come up here to get with some young girl I never met before, I didn't come up here to look at you hang your balls out. I came up here 'cause you said we was gonna do us some business. Now, you tell me. Are we gonna do us some business, or what?"

"J.T., your problem is, you ain't no goddamn fun," muttered Elmer, as he stood up to join the deputy.

About that time Alice walked out of the bathroom. She asked Elmer if he wanted the two girls to kiss each other, and without even attempting to camouflage his disappointment, Elmer shook his head and told the ladies to go back downstairs and enjoy the party.

BUSINESS

Rogers and Elmer exited the party, exchanging the strobe lights and writhing young bodies for the rickety chill of the outbuilding at the edge of the back yard. They stood on the peeling wooden floor of the meth shack, quietly pontificating amongst the Freon jugs, the cans of Red Bull energy drink, the rock salt, the hypodermics, the light bulbs and bottle caps.

Open in front of them was the crate full of drugs and weapons, still stacked on another crate full of drugs and weapons.

The same crate Boone Sumner viewed earlier that day.

The same crate that belonged to Walt Slone.

Behind them in the main house, the party raged on. White luminosity flashed in the downstairs windows, creating tangled shadows, arms and legs and heads en masse. The steady drive of bass electronica thumped so hard that Rogers and Elmer could feel it pumping against their chests, even from fifty yards away.

Elmer reached into the crate and took out a bag of OxyContin, filled with little tablets of multiple colors: blue, green, red, or orange, depending on the size of the dose.

"So when do you think Walt's gonna miss all this?" he said.

"Won't be too long now, you can count on that," said Rogers. He grabbed the bag of pills out of Elmer's hand and threw it back into the crate. The irritation he'd shown inside, with the girls, flashed again to the forefront. "I told him everything was there like it was supposed to be, same as always, but it won't take long 'fore him or the sheriff figures out that not all the deliveries got made to the dealers like they expected. When they figure it out, they're gonna come ask me what's what. Hell, they prob'ly got it figured out already. I better have a good story to tell or else we got big problems."

Elmer shrugged, walked away, knew full well that it didn't matter *when* Walt found out his merchandise was missing. Sooner or later, he'd find out, all right. And Rogers was exactly right – he and Elmer needed to be ready, needed a truth they could sell Walt Slone when the old man came looking for his goods. When Walt found out, he'd come straight to his delivery man to get the truth.

"We could always just kill the bastard," said Elmer.

"We ain't killin' nobody."

"I'm just sayin'. We could do it."

"Are you out of your fuckin' mind?"

"No."

"Killin' Walt Slone?"

"Yes."

"You're out of your fuckin' mind."

"I'm not. No, I'm not. Might make things go a little better for all of us if he weren't around. Look at it that way. Just an idea, I'm offering it up."

Rogers faded out, thought it over, came back to the conversation. "You keep goin' on with shit like that, somebody's gonna end up dead all right, only it won't be Walt Slone. Hell fire, if it gets out that you're talkin' that way, we'll both turn up in a ditch somewhere."

Elmer said nothing. The two men stared at each other, and Rogers quickly became convinced that Elmer wasn't kidding with his murder talk. More than pure hypotheticals were in play. Reality settled into the bottom of Rogers's stomach, heavy, like a medicine ball filled with foul shit. He felt a green queasiness wash across him, as he realized that Elmer was feeling him out, floating the idea to see how the deputy might react. Wondering if J.T. could be a killing partner.

Rogers wanted no part of that. He needed to physically get away from it, so he strolled across the room and sat down in a metal folding chair, a couple feet away from Walt's crate.

"Let me tell you something, Mr. Canifax," he said, with his hands folded in his lap. "You are absolutely, positively, tee totally one hundred percent out of your ever lovin' motherfuck mind, my friend."

Elmer let out a sound from the back of his throat, half laugh and half snort. "Yeah, I know. It's a beautiful thing, ain't it?"

He closed the lid on the crate, rubbed his palm across the thin sheen of stubble atop his bald head, and sat down on top of the wooden box. The box with all the guns and drugs inside it. Walt Slone's box.

For an awkward time, the two of them sat in their places, Elmer on the crate, and Rogers on the folding metal chair nearby.

"Alright," said Elmer. "Killin' Walt might be a bit much. Let's not get too far ahead of ourselves. But the fact remains, you got a problem here."

He smacked the side of the crate with his palm.

"This here crate, it belongs to Walt Slone. He paid for it, looks at it as an investment, I'm sure. And I'd imagine he expects a return on his investment. Which means if he don't get that return, he's probably gonna be a little pissed off. You and me both know what happens when Walt Slone gets pissed off."

"It ain't good," piped in Deputy Rogers. He rubbed the back of his neck, which had developed a kink during the course of the conversation. "Fuck no, it ain't good."

"Uh-huh. Fuck is right," said Elmer. "But it's hard to back out now. How you gonna explain yourself anyways, if all of a sudden this missing crate turns up, like you just accidentally forgot to unload it with the rest? Hell, J.T., you're an old pro at this, you don't make rookie mistakes. Walt knows that. This crate turns up and he'll sense the shit goin' down. Won't be long after that he'll find out you were tryin' to make a deal with me, and when that happens we're both pretty much in a shit heap."

Rogers nodded. "A shit heap. Hell yeah. So what next?"

"I'll you what next," Elmer answered. He patted the crate gently, like it was a treasure chest. "Next, we gotta take all this stuff, and run it out of town. London, Corbin, Barbourville, Hazard, Jackson, maybe Pikeville or Whitesburg. And fast."

He stopped cold.

"What?" asked Rogers, suddenly confused.

Elmer spoke towards the door. "I told you girls, you can't come back here. Didn't I tell you? What the hell do you want?"

Rogers turned towards the door and saw Alice, the skinny blonde from the party, standing in the doorway. Her eyes were big as tea cups. She was breathing heavily.

The first thing the deputy thought was, *Holy hell, somebody's O.D.'d in there.*

But the truth was much worse.

Alice lowered her voice, not far from a whisper. "The sheriff's here," she said, and pointed out the door.

They could all see the flashing blue lights from John Slone's cruiser, up near the front of the house. And right behind him was Boone Sumner.

SHERIFF

"Something I can help you with, Sheriff?" Elmer smiled. As he approached the cruiser, John Slone was just climbing out of the driver's seat. Alice and Deputy Rogers watched from their position in the outbuilding, and hoped like hell that the sheriff didn't come their way.

"I got a noise complaint," said Slone.

Elmer smirked. He stretched out his neck until it went *thawpp*, a nervous release he employed often. He tried to laugh, but nothing really came out. "We ain't bein' loud. You can hear for yourself. And who called it in, anyway, since there ain't nobody around here for five miles?"

"All I know is, we got a noise complaint," the sheriff said again.

He looked towards the windows, saw the strobe lights in the living room blink steady but with different effect now. The silhouettes inside were no longer snakes writhing; they were zombies in shadow, frozen, watching their uniformed visitor.

With John's arrival the party had shut itself down, sixty to zero on the odometer in three seconds flat. The revelers weren't bouncing up and down, weren't grinding, weren't twisting into each other like snakes in a pit. No. They were standing still. The strobe lights pulsed in metronomic intervals and the dance music thumped on, but it was all sound and fury and nothing else, white noise for the suddenly tranquil masses.

"Yep, a noise complaint," repeated Sheriff Slone. "I figured I ought to check it out." He walked up the front steps of the house, crossed the front porch, and went in through the living room door. Elmer walked alongside.

Boone followed not far behind them, catching up quickly.

Two coffee-colored leather couches normally sat at a V in the middle of the living room, but for the party they had each been pushed against the wall nearest the kitchen, creating a mostly wide-open space that served as a dance floor. Of course right now there was no dancing at all, just forty or so strung-out kids slouched and silent with their hands in their pockets, wondering what they could tell their parents during their one phone call from the Seward County jail. As the three men came inside, the partygoers stayed flat-footed, except for a whispery parting of the human sea so the visitors could get through. After that, only their eyes moved, following Slone, Elmer, and Boone as the trio passed through the living room and towards the kitchen and back into the living room.

When they came back into the living room, Slone looked down at one of the couches. A plastic Ziploc bag caught his eye, one tiny corner poking out from behind a corner cushion.

When he pulled the bag out, he found it held two eighty-milligram Oxycontin pills. "Well huh. Eighties. Them's serious. Wonder who these belong to?" the sheriff asked Elmer, holding the Ziploc at eye level.

"Somebody," Elmer answered.

"Somebody is right." John went to the person nearest him, a tall, thin young guy with shaggy brown hair busting out from beneath the tight-drawn hood of his Superman sweatshirt. "How about you? This yours?" he asked the kid.

The kid looked stupid, and said nothing.

The sheriff moved on to the next person. "You?"

Nothing.

Next. "You?"

Nothing.

Next. "You?"

Nothing.

On down the line went Sheriff Slone, holding the OC-80's up in front of ten more people. High school cheerleaders, farm boys, college students, nomads, ghosts. He asked them all the same question – "You?" – and got the same stupid non-answer every time. With each successive instance, his voice raised a few decibels in volume, trying to intimidate into copping to ownership of the drugs, but it didn't matter. Nobody was talking. This was no surprise; in Sewerville, nobody ever talked.

For the pure hell of it, John stepped back to the kid in the Superman sweatshirt and crumpled him with a big fist to the gut.

Nobody else moved.

A minute passed and it may as well have been a year. All the revelers watched in silence, not sure what to do but too nervous to move even if the thought of movement actually occurred. For the longest time, the Superman kid hacked in pain and that was the only sound in the room. The sheriff stood over him, cold glare locked in place, silently daring him to get up or even say something.

Like everyone else, Boone stood by, waiting to see how the scene might play. He'd tagged along on many of these late night ass-kicking missions with Sheriff Slone and seen how quickly things could get sideways. He didn't want to spend tonight like he spent so many other nights, dropping somebody off at the emergency room with a fractured jaw or skull.

"I'm gonna go look outside," he said, when he felt assured that the kid on the floor was at least smart enough to stay down there.

The sheriff snapped his head around, and spat out of the corner of his mouth, "What the hell for?"

"Just to see what I can find," said Boone, trying to hide a sudden queasiness. "There ain't no sense in both of us stayin' here. Besides, it looks like you pretty much got this room handled."

John offered Boone a quick shrug, like he couldn't give less of a fuck.

"Go for it," he said. Then, he turned to the rest of the partygoers, raising the baggie of pills above his head. "All right motherfuckers. These pills didn't get in that couch by themselves. At least one of you motherfuckers is the proud owner of these green babies, and that motherfucker's got sixty seconds to come get his property from me. If he don't, everybody in this room's going down to the county jail, I don't care if I gotta rent a school bus to do it."

Boone wandered away as the sheriff finished his speech. He knew full well what would happen next: John would begin a verbal countdown. After about thirty of the sixty seconds elapsed, one of the teenagers would step up and claim ownership of the pills, regardless of whether the OC-80's belonged to said teenager or not, out of some misguided belief that it was better to sacrifice oneself rather than watch all of one's friends get their heads cracked open. That this belief was misguided would then be proven when John Slone handcuffed the claimant and probably one or two of his friends, dragged them into the front yard, and beat them with his police baton until they shit their pants, which *would* happen. Boone had seen it happen. He didn't want to see it happen tonight, though. Neither did he really have any desire to search the grounds and turn up other miscreants or meth heads who might provide further fodder for Sheriff Slone's head crackin' ways.

For Boone, volunteering to check outside the house was just a chance to get away for a moment. He could poke around the yard for a minute while the sheriff finished his business in the house. If anything of note popped up outside, Boone could deal with it as he saw fit. No sheriff standing over his shoulder, no bullshit, no problem.

So, he exited the house and went back outside.

As he stepped off the porch and went around the side of the house, the outbuilding at the edge of the backyard drew his attention. The shack's windows were dark, but in the glow of the security light nearby, he saw shadows rustling inside. Two people, maybe three. Knowing that in there with those shadows was a stolen crate filled with Walt Slone's guns and drugs, Boone thought it wise to check the building out before John went and looked for himself. If the sheriff looked for himself, if he found that crate of merchandise, a shit storm would come that could not be contained. That was the last thing Boone wanted, so he headed to the edge of the yard and hoped like hell that nobody followed.

CHOICE

Nobody followed. Soon enough, Boone found himself inside the darkened shack.

Slowly his eyes adjusted around the outside security lamp's pale argon illumination, what fuzzy bit of it came through the outbuilding's dirty glass windows. He could determine a few details: glass beakers, rubber hoses, bottles of cough syrup, cleaning chemicals like Draino and Windex - the familiar junk of bathrooms and kitchens, chemistry class and meth labs.

Boone felt along the wall for a light switch, but didn't find one. "Fuck." He started a careful walk towards the back corner where he'd seen Walt's crate, holding his arms out in front of him to ward off any obstacles that might have been moved out into the floor.

Ten steps in, he heard a shuffle on the other side of the room. Someone was here with him.

"Hello?" he whispered. Complete stillness answered. Yet, Boone felt that he wasn't alone.

His heart somersaulted into the back of his mouth. He took one aching step, then another, and looked around a-jitter for more movement in the darkness. Although his eyes were better adjusted to the low light, it was still hard to make out any more than silhouettes.

A row of glass bottles in one of the window sills reminded him of a city skyline.

Halfway into another careful step, a shape moved quick in the darkness, knocked over a shelf and bolted past him, headed for the door amidst the clatter of junk.

Fuck, the sheriff'll hear that sure as shit he will –

Boone leaped backwards and managed to get his hand around a flying body part. Felt like a leg. He tumbled and took his catch down with him. They slammed to the wooden floor, well short of any escape through the door.

"Who the fuck is this?"

"Hold on!" somebody said, in a vaguely familiar whisper.

Boone stood up, but held fast on the leg, leveraging the other person down. "I'm gonna turn the light on now. I've got a gun inside my jacket.

187

You make a move and I'll blow your face out the back of your head, you hear me?"

"Hold on, Boone. Don't turn the lights on, the sheriff'll come out here."

Boone stood up straight. Now he recognized the voice, straining its volume to stay within the realm of a whisper. "That you, Rogers?"

"Yeah, dammit! Hold on!"

"What the fuck are you doing here?"

"Let me up, and we can talk about it."

Boone let loose of Roger's leg. He heard the deputy fumbling around in his own pockets, and then Rogers produced a small LED that put out just enough blue light to confirm his identity when he held it under his chin.

Boone put his hands on his knees and took a deep breath. "Fuck," he said. "Holy mother fuck. Ain't this a shit heap."

"What are you doing here, Boone?"

"What am I doing here? What the fuck are you doing here?"

"I can explain."

"Are you the only one out here?"

The LED light flashed its wispy beam to the side of the room. In the redirected glow, Boone saw a thin blonde girl, standing there with her arms folded tight around her chest and her chin buried into her collarbone. Even with her head down, he could see the girl's eyes open and wild. She was scared out of her mind, shaking like a broken washing machine.

"Who is that?" Boone asked the deputy.

"Her name's Alice," said Rogers.

"Alice who?"

"Fuck if I know."

Boone took a moment and absorbed the scene. The girl was clearly one of Elmer's crowd of partygoers. She and Deputy Rogers were out in Elmer's drug shack, probably about to get it on if not already mid-coitus when Boone found them, and since this *was* Elmer's place, they were as likely to be on meth or pills as they were to be on each other. Rogers was in his street clothes, too; that much could be seen in the pale glow of the LED. Sheriff Slone had relieved the deputy, the deputy had done a quick change out of his uniform and headed up here.

This could only be looked at one way: the deputy came for the party. It wasn't like anybody did undercover police work in Sewerville.

So. Rogers was at Elmer Canifax's party.

"I'm gonna ask you again, J.T.," said Boone calmly. "What are you doing up here?"

"Nothin'."

"Nothin'?"

"Nothin'."

The deputy climbed back to his feet, and Boone drew his pistol, in case Rogers though of escaping before Boone was ready for him to go. When he saw the gun, Rogers held both hands up and made clear that he wasn't going anywhere.

"Somehow I doubt you came all the way out here in the middle of no-goddamn-where for nothin'," said Boone, tucking his pistol back in its shoulder holster, inside his jacket. "What do you think Sheriff Slone would say if he knew you come up here to see Elmer?"

Rogers tried to laugh but didn't do a very good job of it.

"You did come up here to see Elmer, didn't you?" said Boone.

The deputy breathed in deep, blew it back out, knew he was in a bad spot. "Why don't you let the girl get on out of here?" he asked, motioning towards her with a quick nod of his head. "She don't need to get involved in this."

"Nah, she better stay," said Boone. "If she goes wanderin' back towards the house it's more likely than not that she'll tell the sheriff we're out here. Either she'll tell him, or he'll drag it out of her. I don't think either of us wants that. So she can just sit there and be quiet."

The blonde whimpered at those words. Tears dripped out of her eye sockets, then streamed in wet ribbons. Boone knew she wanted to scream, for help or some other way out, and he was surprised when somehow she managed to hold it down. Surprised, but glad.

Rogers said, "You can't tell them I was up here. Walt or the sheriff. If they found out I was here, ain't no tellin' where that might lead."

Boone sighed. "You're the second person this week that's asked me to keep a secret," he said. "And I gotta tell ya, I ain't real big on secrets."

Secrets. First Elmer, now Rogers. The outbuilding. Rogers, the party, the shack, the drugs, the guns, the crates in the corner. Of course.

Suddenly it all made sense.

The regular trucks come down from New York, full of Walt Slone's merchandise, blowing past weigh stations and bribing DOT officials all the way. They get off the East Kentucky Parkway and roll out Highway 213, then met Deputy Rogers in the parking of the Sewardville Methodist Church. Not sure how, but somewhere between the eastern seaboard and the Sewerville rendezvous with Deputy Rogers and his U-haul trucks, these two containers full of drugs and guns went missing, and wonder of wonders, Walt hadn't killed anybody over the whole deal yet.

Wonder of wonders. Walt hadn't killed anybody yet.

Yet.

Again the voice of Boone's wife echoed inside him, from a time when they barely knew each other. *You're such a dumb boy. You dumb boy. Look what you got yourself into, dumb boy.*

So Rogers took the two crates from the New York trucks and brought them here. Why, sure he did. He was in a perfect position to do it, as the man entrusted by Walt and John Slone to make the exchange with the connections from up East. He'd made the exchange all right – right off the U-haul and into Elmer's outbuilding. A bold move, no doubt. Perhaps an idiotic move, but a bold move no less.

He could hear the conversation between Walt and the sheriff.

"Who the fuck around here would be stupid enough to steal from us?"

"Well, J.T. Rogers was the one carrying the crates around the whole time –"

"Nah. Surely not J.T.. Surely he would know he'd be the first one we'd ask if somethin' turned up missin' from one of those trucks."

"I dunno. He ain't the sharpest knife in the drawer sometimes, you know? Maybe we ought to ask him."

"Nah. He may be dumb, but he ain't that fuckin' dumb."

But Rogers was that fucking dumb. Dumb boy.

Boone shone his LED straight into the deputy's eyes. J.T. recoiled, held up his hand and did a clumsy tumble backward. He flung one arm out to catch his balance but instead knocked a bottle from one of the shelves to the floor, where it cracked and bounced, but didn't shatter.

"You bring those crates up here to Elmer?" Boone asked.

Rogers hesitated. "What crates?"

"You know what crates. The ones over there in the corner, with all the merchandise in 'em."

Rogers held up his arms. He spoke louder now, straining the edges of what might be considered a whisper. "Hold on, hold on," he said, waving his hands. "Hold on a second. Alice, why don't you go ahead and hustle on out of here?"

The girl didn't move. Boone directed his light towards her. She was looking towards the door, but showed no sign of going anywhere.

"Let her go and we'll talk," said Rogers.

Boone shook his head. "I told you, she'd better stay. If she goes inside, it won't be long before she comes right back out here with the sheriff leadin' her by the hand." He motioned for Rogers to come closer.

Rogers obliged, slow and careful. When the two men stood less than a full stride away from each other, they each covered their mouths and talked in lowered tones, like baseball players hiding game signs from the other team. "I know you brought that shit up here," said Boone. "What the hell are you thinking? Soon as Walt finds out, you and Elmer both are dead as four o'clock."

"I know," the deputy answered. "You think I don't know? Of course I know. Me and Elmer got a plan."

"A plan. Right. What kind of plan?"

Rogers stared at him.

"What kind of plan, J.T.?"

"I can't tell you that."

Boone shook his head, slow, in sheer disbelief. Dumb boy. "You can't tell me?" he snapped. "Don't you understand that I'm the only thing standing between you and the grave right now? All I gotta do is walk back in that house, tell the Sheriff what's out here in this building and who brought it there, and end of story. You and Elmer... bye bye."

Rogers looked back over his shoulder at Alice, stalling.

After a full minute's consideration, he said to Boone, "We'll cut you in. With what's in those crates, there'd be plenty of money to go around. You can start puttin' yours away, in case you ever get sick of runnin' Walt's quarter machines."

Boone stiffened. "What the fuck is that supposed to mean?"

"Nothin'. Don't mean nothin'." Rogers walked his words back. "I'm just sayin', you could have somethin' of your own. That wouldn't be so bad, would it?"

"Yeah, and I'd have to worry night and day that somebody was gonna come up behind me and tie a plastic bag over my head. It ain't worth it. You guys oughtta get out of this shit right now, that's all I can say."

After that, they stood there. Nobody moved or said anything else; the only sound for the next while was the quiet whoosh of breath going in and out of their lungs.

Finally, Rogers said, "Are you gonna tell 'em or what?"

Boone still weighed his options. He could send Rogers off into the night and talk his way around Sheriff Slone, then deal with the fallout later. Eventually, Walt would realize he'd been ripped off, and just who'd done the ripping, and when he did it wouldn't take long for everything to get pieced back together and connected back to this night at Elmer's. When that happened, Boone would have some hard questions to answer, and he'd probably have to answer them while staring down the barrel of a gun.

But he had time before that happened. He could come up with a story. And meanwhile, he could get a cut with Rogers and Elmer. There was a hundred thousand dollars' worth of merchandise in the two crates, easy. His cut of a hundred grand could go a long way towards getting him and Samantha out of Sewerville.

Or, he could hand Rogers and the crates over to John Slone. That would put more blood on Boone's hands, Rogers and Elmer and no telling who else that got caught in the crossfire. And there would be no cut of one hundred thousand.

"I want half of this deal," Boone announced.

Rogers shook his head. "Half? You're fuckin' crazy."

"Half." Boone had made up his mind. He held firm. "Half, or you and Elmer can take your chances with the sheriff right here, tonight."

Rogers inhaled deep. He didn't like that deal. Half was a lot, not to mention that it only left the other half for sharing between Elmer and him. Then again, he had no real choice here. He had to agree to the deal. Elmer wouldn't like it, but Elmer didn't have any choice, either.

"How do I know you won't take your half then give us up anyway?" Rogers asked.

"You don't. But one thing you can take to the bank, if I let the word out that two of Walt Slone's treasure chests are sittin' under a tarp in Elmer Canifax's meth shack and it was one of the sheriff's favorite deputies that helped get 'em there, then about an hour after that I'll be draggin' you boys down to Harley Faulkner's funeral home to be burnt up with the garbage. And you know it, too."

Rogers did know it. He paused again, as if he was actually considering some other choice, but he knew Boone was right. There was no other choice.

"All right," he said. "It's a deal. Half, and you keep quiet about this."

"Half." Agreed Boone. Then he added, "Now, get the fuck out of here."

"What about her?" said Rogers, nodding towards Alice.

"I'll take care of that," said Boone.

The deputy looked him over, not quite sure the deal was really done. But again, Boone motioned him away, and this time Rogers did as told. He scampered out the door and soon after Boone heard the sounds of sticks and leaves underfoot as Rogers stalked away through the woods that loomed behind the outbuilding.

Boone turned back to Alice. "You're comin' with me," he said, and then he took her by the arm and pulled her along with him, out of the shack and into the backyard. As they went towards the house, he told the girl not to worry, he'd take care of this for her, and oh by the way, if she said anything about what she just saw or heard, he'd kill her. She believed him.

*

By the time Boone and Alice walked back into Elmer's house, Boone holding Alice fast by one elbow, Sheriff Slone had kicked over most of the furniture and cracked a couple of teenage skulls. When he heard them coming in – and it was easy to hear them coming in, because everyone else in the room was scared silent – the sheriff stood up straight, and blinked twice.

"Who the fuck is she?" he asked, pointing at Alice.

"She claims her name is Alice," said Boone. "I found her outside. Kicked back in her car, smokin' a cigarette."

Of course this was a lie, but Alice gave no indication of the ruse. She stood motionless with her elbow caught in Boone's grip, and stared off towards a far corner.

A look came over John Slone's face that Boone had seen far too many times in the past: a confused but irritated look of *what the fuck?*

Boone continued, before the sheriff took a notion to say anything. "She was the only person out there. I just figured you'd want to see her. Just so you could be sure and check everybody out yourself."

Slone looked the girl over, and saw nothing on the surface. Nags of suspicion still tugged at him, though, the natural side effects of his lawman ways. "Just sitting out in her car, smoking a cigarette?"

"Yeah," said Boone.

"What kind of cigarette?"

"Fuck if I know. Ask her."

The sheriff looked at Alice. "What kind of cigarette?"

For the first time since coming back into the house, she rolled her head around and made eye contact with the sheriff. "Marlboro Lights," she said.

The sheriff would not be easily convinced. "Show me."

Alice snorted with disdain, and then fished around in a small pocket on the hip of her dress. Boone held his breath and didn't let it out until she actually did produce a pack of Marlboro Lights, which she held out for Slone's satisfaction.

He took the cigarettes, held them, tossed them up and down, up and down, up and down then switched hands and tossed them up and down, up and down, up and down.

He said to Elmer, "This who you was with out there?"

Elmer arched his eyebrows and tipped his head at an angle, looking confused.

Slone's voice quickened, got louder. "Don't give me that shit, Elmer. When we pulled up, you were already outside." He paused, gave Elmer time to think about it. "Were you with this young lady, or weren't you?"

"Yeah, I was with her," Elmer said quickly. "So what? You gonna tell me it's illegal to smoke Marlboro Lights now?"

Boone didn't like how this conversation was going. Clearly the sheriff had his suspicions; it wouldn't take much more to set off all his alarms and send him out the front door, straight for the outbuilding, on an exploratory mission. If either Elmer or Alice said just the wrong word or looked even the littlest bit nervous, this would get upside down in a hurry. If things got upside down, people would get hurt.

Boone regretted the agreement he'd just made with Rogers. It was only a few minutes old and already everything relied on the ability of Elmer and his young female friend to keep their shit together on the fly. And that was a hell of a thing on which to rely.

Alice held out her hand, palm up, like she was ready to be handcuffed and led away. She said, "Unless you're gonna take me to jail, I'd appreciate my cigarettes back, sheriff."

Slone studied her wrists.

Spines and sphincters stiffened all around the room. The girl dared to show less than proper respect; this might just get nasty.

But instead, the sheriff burst out laughing.

"Sure. Take 'em," he chuckled, and tossed the Marlboro Lights at Alice. The cigarette pack bounced off her chest and hit the floor with a faint *ka-chunk;* to everyone watching, the pack fell in slow, agonizing motion, like a lit match heading towards a pool of gasoline in a television commercial. A nervous ripple shuddered through the room, as everyone in the house waited for the violence they knew would surely come at any moment.

John Slone smiled. Nobody liked it when John Slone smiled. When John Slone smiled, folks got hurt.

The sheriff looked at the pack of cigarettes on the floor. Boone waited. The kids waited. Everyone waited. The smile on Slone's face became a short smirk, then the smirk went away.

Boone's whole body tensed up because he knew – *knew* – that the sheriff was about to jack the girl's jaw. And when the sheriff got even with poor smart-ass Alice, there would be two or three or four dumbasses jump to her defense, and that meant if Boone wanted to get out of there, he'd have to brawl his way out.

But instead the sheriff just laughed.

"You better pick those up, honey," he said. "If you don't, I'm sure one of these shit-heels will. Some folks around here treat smokes like bread and water."

And with that, John Slone turned his back and walked away.

Boone stood tense as ever, certain that any second the sheriff would spin quick on one heel and drop one punk kid or another with an uppercut to the chin. Boone believed that just as sure as he stood there, and he kept on believing it even as the sheriff's footsteps clacked out the door and across the porch, headed for the front yard and the driveway beyond. In fact he didn't stop believing it several minutes later, when the engine of the sheriff's cruiser roared to life, and its tail lights disappeared down the country road. It was only when the car had been gone for several minutes, and no doubt traveled several miles down the highway back to Sewardville, that Boone believed the night had come to a close. Only then could he breathe.

WITCH

Shortly past two a.m. that same night, Boone did something that would have great consequence for many people both within the Slone family, and without it.

Boone and Karen lay in bed, she under the blankets in her favorite University of Kentucky t-shirt and shorts, he on top of the blankets and fully clothed. The night stand lamp was still on. Both of them sat upright with their neck and shoulders rested against the headboard.

"He just laughed at her?" Karen asked, incredulous after hearing the story of Sheriff Slone and Alice and what transpired between them at Elmer's earlier that evening. "She said that and he just walked away?"

"Yep," said Boone. "Basically, he walked away."

"Basically." She paused, let it sink in. "That doesn't really sound like John. When have you seen him just walk away from a fight like that?"

"I'm telling you, he walked away."

"You'd think she would know better."

"Clearly she didn't know shit. She's damn lucky he didn't jack her jaw right there."

"Yeah she is." That sank in, too. "Well, huh."

Karen couldn't believe it. Boone couldn't believe it either. They lay in bed together in their bedroom at Walt's house, and neither of them could believe it. John Slone passed on a chance to whip somebody's ass? Who would believe that? Nobody would believe that.

Boone swung his legs around. He sat at the edge of the bed, with his back to his wife and his hands underneath his legs.

"There's something else," he said.

"Like what?"

"J.T. Rogers was up there."

"With you and John?"

"No. He was already there. I found him out in Elmer's meth shack."

"Doing what?"

"He wasn't looking for a bottle opener, I can tell you that."

Karen tapped the back of her head twice against the headboard, and slid beneath the blanket until she was fully prone. Boone knew that when Karen did this, she really wanted to talk. That wasn't often of late.

Boone said, "I think I saw a couple of your daddy's crates, too. You know if anything's missing from the last shipment?"

"Daddy thinks so," she sighed. "After all, the numbers are down. Guess this is one thing that would help explain it, huh?"

"I guess so," he said.

Boone got up from the bed. He walked over to the window, leaned against the window sill, and with his finger traced an invisible pattern on the glass which resembled nothing to either of them. Then he traced it again.

In a flat voice, he said, "The numbers are down."

She rolled her eyes.

"I guess you're going to tell John about this?"

"Of course," she said.

"And your daddy?"

"Sure." Karen rolled over on her side and now it was his turn to see her back. "Don't worry about it. I'll tell them tomorrow. Of course, they'll want to know why you didn't bring it up while you were there tonight, but I'll let you figure out how to answer that. Anyway, they'll take care of Elmer and Rogers." She flipped over and faced him once more. "Daddy will appreciate you tellin' this, Boone. You were a little slow on it, but still, you really came through for the family this time."

"You think so, huh?" Boone said, without any hint of excitement or pride in his voice.

"Yeah," Karen said. "I do."

Boone didn't take that as much of a compliment, but he didn't let on that way to Karen. Neither of them said anything else for a long moment. Still Karen did not turn around to face him again. The stillness in the room pressed down on them like a cold steel beam.

Finally, she said, "Are you staying here, or going back to our house tonight?"

Boone felt no need to answer her. They both already knew where he was staying, or more accurately where he *wasn't* staying. Boone would not sleep in Walt's Slone's house on the hill. Even if he had done something that might actually please Walt for the first time in a long time, Boone still didn't want to sleep under the old man's roof. He would go home to his bed, in his house, and sleep there with his own thoughts.

He reached out and quietly traced the meaningless design on the glass again. While he did that, Karen pulled the covers up to her chin, then stuck one arm out and switched off the lamp beside her. Darkness overcame them. Silence, too.

PART FOUR
THE ORCHID FESTIVAL

DREAMS

Samantha.

Karen. What the fuck. Karen.

He finds her down on her knees in the back yard. She digs in the dirt at the edge of the grass near the woods, tending to her orchids, the Mountain orchids that she loves so much, the delicate flowers with their thin white petals drooping together at the ends like tiny hands clasped in prayer.

How are you Boone? she asks, as she digs in the dirt.

Just fine, Mrs. Slone.

Ellen Slone digs in the dirt. *Karen's not here right now.* She digs in the dirt.

That's okay, he says. *I come to see Walt.*

She digs in the dirt. She looks up at him for just a quick instant, but she does not stop digging. Even though she smiles at him while she digs, there is a distance in her warm green eyes. Boone understands this. People come to see her husband Walt often and Boone knows why they come and he figures Ellen knows why, too, and he understands that after so long it must be hard to smile at these people and the things she knows they do for her husband. Not to mention the things her husband does for them.

Walt examines Boone's pistol, a .38 special. Walt doesn't know it, but that pistol used to belong to Boone's daddy. Boone took it from the top drawer of his mother's dresser. Daddy died before Boone was born.

The old man says, *You know how to use this, right?*

Sure, says Boone. *I know how to use it.* But Boone doesn't know. It's his daddy's gun but he's never shot it before. He can figure it out, though. He can, or Jimmy can.

Walt looks him over real good. *Hope you ain't getting second thoughts on me, son -*

I ain't. Boone thinks about it. *Karen won't know about this, right?*

She won't know.

How can you be sure?

201

I'm sure, son.

Boone holds the gun in his hands, measuring its weight. This used to be his Daddy's gun. Jimmy always said Boone looked like their Daddy.

Now Boone has second thoughts. Not because he's thinking of Daddy but because this is all just wrong. It's wrong. Walt said take his word for it that Karen would never know, but Boone can't just take his word for it. This is so wrong. What if Karen found out? She could find out. What if she found out?

He can't do this.

Walt puts a hand on Boone's shoulder and says, *you really can go far with me. As far as you want to. And if you can go far with me, you can go far with Karen.*

But Boone can't do this.

Before he can give the gun back though, Jimmy yanks it out of his hand.

We ain't gettin' second thoughts, says Jimmy. *You know Walt Slone runs everything. He's got the money. We can do this.*

Easy for him to say.

We just gotta do this one thing, says Jimmy. *One thing and then we're done.*
I don't want to do this, says Boone.
We already said we would, says Jimmy. *Walt expects us to do it and we gotta do it. Jesus, we already got half the money.*
Let's give him the money back, says Boone.
We can't do that, says Jimmy.
Sure we can! says Boone. *Just give it back to him and tell him we're out. We can't do this, Jimmy. This is all wrong. Why did we think we could do this? We're in way, way over our heads. He can get his own son to do this. Let John do it. We are such dumb boys and this is all so wrong, and we can't do it. We can't do this, Jimmy.*
We have to, says his brother.

She stumbles through the bare night woods, her silver hair tied in a ponytail. Her green eyes with the soft wrinkles around them are hidden underneath a black blindfold that is wound tight around her head. Her hands are bound behind her back.

She runs the best she can run, but she is old and her best isn't good enough. Boone runs behind her. Jimmy runs right alongside him. They have their Daddy's gun. Daddy died before Boone was born.

They run and they run and they run, and then she falls. Then she cries. Then she begs.

Please don't she cries.
Please let me go please please let me go, she begs.

They can't let her go.

Boone watches her, wondering if Ellen Slone could somehow rise up and get away, wondering if they could let her. But they can't let her. She can't get away. He knows it. She knows it. She cries and she begs and he hates it but still she cries and still she begs, cries and begs, cries and begs, she wants to live, *please let me live, I won't tell anybody if you let me live.*

A gunshot cracks the chilled air.

Another.

Another.

crack crack crack one right after the other. It's Daddy's gun. It's Daddy's gun. Jimmy always says Boone looks just like their Daddy but Daddy died before Boone was born so Boone doesn't really know for sure.

Boone collapses backward, falls, sits on the dead ground. The frost crunches beneath his body and cold seeps into his backside but he doesn't think about it. He stares at the cold dead body in front of him and thinks strange, distant thoughts, thoughts that don't seem to be really bouncing about inside his own brain. A dead body does not live up to expectation. A dead body is not scary. A dead body is not disgusting. A dead body kind of looks like a person, but it doesn't really look like a person, either. It just looks like a dead body.

A dead cow lies on Church Street. A damn dead cow right there in the damn middle of the damn town. You would think they would do something about that. You would think.

She digs in the dirt.
He digs in the dirt.
They dig in the dirt.
The funeral was nice.
The orchids were nice.
The people were nice.
They dig in the dirt.
There are worms in the dirt.
Ellen is in the dirt.

Down she goes, down she goes, down she goes. Ellen Slone, down in the dirt.

There is a dead cow on Church Street. Sometimes God needs cows and when he needs them, we have to let them go. It hurts but we have to let them go.

Samantha.

Everything sinks towards the bottom of the valley. Sinking, sinking, sunk. The earth itself crumbles beneath the churches and gas stations, pulling them down into the fiery pit.   The tractors and the combines slide down the valley, creeping closer towards the mobile homes. The mobile homes and the tractors and the combines slide down the hillsides together, right on into town. The mobile homes and the tractors and the combines and the whole goddamn town sink deeper into the black steaming pit. The valley falls in on itself. Everyone tumbles into darkness. The combines and the mobile homes and the meth heads and Elmer and Karen and Jimmy and Walt and the sheriff and Mama and Daddy, they all tumble together into darkness, and Boone just stands there and watches them go.

Samantha.

FESTIVAL

The big day arrived in Sewardville, the day of the Orchid Festival, the day anticipated by Sewardvillians at-large more than any other during the year outside of Christmas and Easter Sunday. *Maybe* Christmas and Easter Sunday. It was the day the community celebrated their unique flower: the Mountain orchid, the flower that grew no place else on Earth but the green hills of Seward County, Kentucky.

Just after one o'clock of the big day, the last Saturday afternoon in April, the sun was near its pinnacle in the cloudless sky. The temperature registered a stout eighty-five degrees, unseasonably warm.

Hundreds of Orchid Festival attendees filled Sewardville City Park. Having waited another year for the festivities, the masses now poured out of the subdivisions and the rural hollows to enjoy every aspect of the spectacle: the car show, the Miss Orchid Pageant, the bluegrass and gospel concerts, the army of food vendors hawking deep fried sugar and fat. And not just from Sewardville did the patrons come, but also from the surrounding counties and beyond. All the way up to Lexington and down to London, east to Hazard and west to Frankfort, people came to ride the rides and hear the sounds and see the sights. The *Orchistradae Mountain* counted many fans, indeed.

Members of the local Lions Club guided the steady parade of incoming vehicles into neat rows that soon filled up the fifteen grassy acres that had been designated as the festival's parking area. Folks got out of their vehicles and filed into the park past a patriotic sign of red, white, and blue that read "ELECT WALT SLONE FOR MAYOR." The man himself stood next to the sign, and many of them took a moment to shake hands and say hello. Walt smiled at every potential voter he saw. Voters appreciated that, even though everyone in town knew Mayor Slone was in no danger of losing the primary election come May (or the general in November, for that matter). Regardless, he smiled, and they smiled. Everyone smiled. It was the proper thing to do.

"How ya doin'? Appreciate your vote."

"Hi. How ya doin'? Appreciate your vote."

"Hi there. Appreciate your vote."

"Appreciate your vote."

"How ya doin'?"

"Appreciate your vote."

Just inside the entrance sat the first row of food vendors, squashed against each other with almost no space in between. Corn dogs, funnel cakes, pork chop sandwiches, gyros. Beyond that sat a bank of craft tables showcasing the finest in local knitting and woodworking, including one table covered in knobby, hand-carved walking sticks that featured different animal shapes on the top end. Mostly raccoons but a few wolves and mallard ducks and elk, too.

Of course there were Mountain orchids everywhere on the grounds. Most were a pale blue color, as nine out of every ten *Orchistradae Mountain* that broke through the soil flowered the hue of an early spring sky. No one really understood — or cared - why most Mountain orchids were pale blue, but pale blue they mostly were. The remaining ten percent were white. Festival planners had tucked these blue and white flowers into every available space on the ground; garlands of them wrapped around signposts and table legs and even trees, while bouquets stood on tables and in stand-up flower pots that were dusted with gold paint. Folks could buy them for thirty dollars a dozen. A few people actually did.

So the men, women, and children of Seward County and those other counties surrounding filed into the Orchid Festival. The more people that arrived, the more the air filled with the murmur of chatterboxes and laughter. Children ran through the scene, screaming playfully. Old men and women doddered along, seemingly on a mission to inspect by hand every single art and every single craft in the whole festival.

Through it all, Walt Slone stood cheerful under his star spangled sign.

"How ya doin'? Appreciate your vote."

"How's it goin', chief? Appreciate your vote."

"Hey buddy. Appreciate your vote."

"Appreciate your vote."

"Appreciate your vote."

"Hi there. Appreciate your vote!"

Walt smiled, shook hands, played his part. The Mayor, the father, the grandfather. The man in the house on the hill.

Out in the parking area, Boone leaned against his truck and avoided going into the festival. Unlike most people in Sewardville, he never enjoyed the hubbub, or the crowds, or the bullshit. He could take the Orchid Festival or leave it, and most of the time he'd just as soon leave it. He went mostly just to satisfy family obligations, but even that was a struggle this year with all the shit that Karen had been piling on top of him.

Thoughts of fleeing the whole crowded scene jittered in his brain, when John Slone came up and surprised him from behind.

"You look goddamn excited," said the sheriff.

Boone turned and saw that John Slone was not actually wearing his sheriff's uniform, the first time in two months Boone had seen him in anything other than those dark paramilitary fatigues. Today, the sheriff wore ragged jeans and a scarlet flannel shirt.

"Should I be?" said Boone.

"You oughtta." John stepped in closer and slapped Boone on the shoulder much harder than Boone liked. "You oughtta be excited, Boone," he repeated. "After this festival bullshit's over with, we're gonna go find Elmer and Rogers and take care of some things that have been botherin' us for a while. Gonna be a good day. A real good day."

Boone looked away, squinted, did his best not to extend the exchange further towards anything that might resemble an honest-to-goodness conversation.

The sheriff continued without invitation. "It meant a lot to the family, what you told us about Elmer and Rogers," he said. "I got to be honest, we was startin' to have some doubts about whether you was dedicated to what we got goin' on here. Now, thanks to you, we can use those two shitheads as something of a... teachable moment, as they say."

"What about it," said Boone.

"Well huh," said John. "What about it."

They stood there.

"Anyway," said the sheriff eventually, "the hope is, we'll all be back on better ground soon enough. Right now, I believe I'll get me a funnel cake. Karen tells me they got chocolate in 'em this year." Boone had no response for that.

ELMER

Two hundred and fifty yards away, at the outer reaches of the parking area, up a steep hill and just off the shoulder of Highway 15, sat a white Chevrolet Cavalier. The car looked plain enough, normal enough, not unlike every other Chevrolet Cavalier in Sewardville. The driver slouched behind the wheel, trying to hide behind the steering column so not to be seen by any casual passers-by or more than casual observers within the family Slone. It was Elmer Canifax.

He was there on a mission. That last visit from Sheriff Slone had sent a message alright, though not the one the sheriff intended. John Slone might have wanted to scare Elmer away, but instead he'd just pushed him into the next stage. The shakedown - showing up at Elmer's house and trying to intimidate the shit out of the situation - had only made clear that the Slone family was only getting more suspicious, and more concerned, by the day. Why else would John have come up there?

Elmer knew: if the sheriff hadn't yet reached the correct conclusion about the stolen crates, he would soon enough. Same with the role Rogers played in the scheme — that would come to light eventually, too.

Now, Elmer and the deputy were up to their knees in shit. Pretty soon it would stink down their throats if they weren't quick about their business. Time to move. If they didn't, the Slones would.

Elmer reached over to his passenger's side seat. He lightly traced his fingers along the pistol grip of the .38 snubnose pistol that jutted out from underneath the week's edition of the Sewardville *Times*.

Out the windshield, even at this distance, he could see Sheriff Slone and Boone Sumner in deep conversation. He wondered what they might be talking about, doubted it was anything good. Just a little beyond them, Walt Slone stood at the Festival entrance, still in full electioneer mode, shaking hands and smiling at everyone that walked by.

While Elmer watched, Boone finished his discussion with the sheriff, then wandered away alone, towards the park entrance. This presented Elmer the chance he needed.

Now Boone stood at the parking lot's edge, doing nothing. He watched people move along in front of him, numb to their intentions. He

208

was not like Walt; he felt no need to speak or smile at everyone that strolled by. He waved at Harley Faulkner and Deputy Rogers as they passed separately, but other than that was content to hide in the background.

His cell phone buzzed in his pocket. He reached in, saw an unfamiliar number on the caller i.d.. The phone buzzed again, and again, and again. He let the voice mail take it.

After a few seconds, the phone started again. Boone checked the caller i.d., saw the same unfamiliar number. The first time might have been a mistake, but the second call from the same whoever-it-was meant this was no mistake at all. This time, he answered.

"Hello?"

"Boone? It's Elmer."

Boone stepped away and turned his back from the crowd, an instinct. "How'd you get this number?" he said in a low voice.

"I got ways."

"What the *hell* are you calling me for?"

"You gotta help me."

"Really?"

"The sheriff. Walt. They know about me and Rogers."

"How do you know?"

"I got wind."

"You got wind?"

"Uh-huh. I got wind."

Boone exhaled, audibly. "So?"

"So they'll kill us."

"They won't kill you, Elmer. They don't know anything about you and Rogers. They'll find out though, if you keep doing stupid shit like calling me."

"Rogers told me about the deal he made with you. Half? Holy fuck."

"Careful," Boone said. "That half's the only thing stopping me from going right to Walt to tell him what you got hiding in your outbuilding."

Immediately, Boone regretted the deal he'd made. If this was how things would go - Elmer panicking and putting them all at risk by openly badgering Boone for help - then it was only a matter of time before Walt caught on. It had been just one day since he'd found Rogers in the outbuilding and made his agreement. If Elmer's nerves were this bad after only just one day, how long could he possibly hold out before he went totally off the reservation?

Elmer snorted in the phone; Boone figured he was snorting back one pill or another. "Why should I trust you won't go to Walt, anyway?"

Boone paused, measured his words carefully. "You really don't have a choice but to trust me," he said firmly.

Elmer laughed, a dry, forced laugh. "That's all right," he said. "I got me a little something for Walt and the Sheriff. Maybe if you're not careful, I could find something for you, too."

Boone rolled his eyes. It just kept getting worse. "What are you gonna do," he said, "come after them with guns blazing, cowboy?"

"Maybe. You just watch."

"I'll do that, Elmer," said Boone. "Go right on and do that. You be careful now." Then he hung up before the conversation got any deeper or more stupid.

Elmer held the phone against his ear, even though he knew that Boone had ended the call. It was as if he thought Boone would call him right back, and they would finish their conversation in a way that made Elmer feel a little better about his situation. When that didn't happen, he angrily dropped the phone back on the seat, and laid his head on the steering wheel, and started thinking about plan B.

Before his considerations went very far, somebody tapped at the car window. Elmer shot up straight, and covered his distress with a quick plastic smile. He turned his head and saw Rogers, in uniform and on duty, bent down at the waist, with one hand on his holstered gun and the other on his belt loop. The deputy's nose hovered just a couple of inches from the car window. He stared at Elmer through dark aviator sunglasses that had been out of style for two decades.

"Whatcha doin'?" he asked through the glass. He motioned for Elmer to roll down the window, which Elmer did, just a crack.

"Nothin'," said Elmer through the crack of fresh air. "What are you doin'?"

"Not a damn thing." Rogers stood up. He nodded his head with great deliberation, and looked around for anyone who might be watching them. Then he bent back down.

"It's awful hot to be sittin' in there with all the windows closed," he said.

"I like it this way," said Elmer.

The deputy chuckled. "You look fucked up." He was right. Elmer's eyes were bloodshot. A thin layer of sweat covered his face. "Are you high?"

"Of course I'm high."

"On what?"

"Does it matter?"

Rogers let it go. Of course it didn't matter – Elmer was high more often than not, on one thing or another and when you got right down to it, high was high.

"You think it's a good idea to come here in that kind of shape?" the deputy asked.

"Sure," Elmer shrugged.

"You don't give a damn, do you now?"

"Not really."

"Mmm-hmm," Rogers nodded again. He continued, "That was a close call the other night, you know, with the sheriff comin' up to your house and everything. What about it. I don't know how we got out of that one and if Boone hadn't been with him, I don't know if we would have gotten out of it at all."

Elmer didn't look like he cared or was even listening. He reached over and opened the glove compartment; there he found a plastic sandwich baggie that was a third full of sticky marijuana, along with a pack of rolling papers. He pinched the marijuana into one of the papers and rolled a joint.

"You want some?" he offered.

"If Walt or John Slone gets word you're here, it's liable to be your ass," said Rogers.

"Yeah, but they don't know."

"But if they do. If they know, it's your ass. That's all I'm saying."

Elmer offered up the joint. Rogers shook his head. "I'm on duty."

"Suit yourself." Elmer pulled a lighter out of his shirt pocket. He looked at the joint for a second, fired it up, took a deep draw. Then he said, "Fuck Walt. Fuck the sheriff. Fuck everybody."

The deputy laughed.

Elmer threw open the car door and jumped out, calmly dropped the joint to the ground and rubbed it out with his foot the way other people rubbed out a Marlboro light. When he stepped away, Rogers moved in and kicked some loose dirt over the joint, which he felt the proper thing for a lawman to do.

By the time Rogers looked up again, Elmer was already walking down the hill, towards the Orchid Festival.

The deputy's heart quickened underneath his police fatigues. "Where do you think you're going?" he called out.

Elmer didn't even turn around. "I'm gonna go look for Walt. I've had it with this bullshit."

"You're what?"

"You heard me. I'm gonna go find Walt Slone."

"I wouldn't do that if I were you."

"Well you're not me. And I'm doin' it."

Rogers took off down the hill. "Bull shit you are," he said as he worked his way in front of Elmer. "Whatever you're smokin', it's givin' you some seriously bad ideas. You're liable to get Walt on to both of us."

"So?" Elmer sidestepped the deputy and kept going. "He's gonna get on to us sooner or later, anyway."

Again, Rogers worked his way around front. This time, he put his hands into Elmer's chest and stopped his forward momentum. Knocked backwards a step, Elmer's druggy eyes went huge wild; for one instant the deputy thought he had a fight on his hands.

It quickly passed. Elmer just kept going towards the festival. Rogers moved to follow him but soon realized that would lead to a fight, which would just call attention to them. And since attention was the last thing Rogers wanted right now, he let Elmer go, and decided it would be best to just watch him from a distance and then step in if anything started to get out of hand.

When he got past J.T. Rogers, Elmer scanned the Orchid Festival crowd for Walt or Sheriff Slone – either of which would do – but saw neither of them. So, he made a straight line for the vendor booths that were lined up beyond the food stands of the park entrance, on into the Festival itself.

The vendor booths were varied and popular, more varied and more popular even than the food booths that offered corn dogs, or funnel cakes, or pork chop sandwiches, or gyros. Folks didn't just attend the annual Sewardville Orchid Festival for the beautiful Mountain orchids or the chance to eat the bountiful and comforting food, although every year there was plenty of both. They also came to spend their money on the offerings of area artisans and sellers of sundry goods.

There was plenty of shit for sale, no doubt about it. Gingham children's dresses, dolls with corn-husk heads, sock monkeys, scented candles, hand-carved wooden walking sticks, quilts, knitted caps, watercolor portraits of hummingbirds and cardinals and killdeer and baby raccoons, photographs of dewy spider webs. These were but a few of the hundreds – hundreds! – of items available to each and every person that walked through the Festival entrance. And if human artistry was not what caught one's fancy, then there were other booths, too. The Orchid Festival provided plenty of opportunities for spending hard-earned or not-so-hard-earned cash money on items more useful than mere sock monkeys or corn husk dolls.

For those with more discerning tastes, a number of dealers aimed to please. Behind their counters could be found a wide array of knives, guns, and other assorted weaponry. Switchblades and knuckledusters, ninja throwing stars, nunchukas, knives for hunting, machetes, knives for filleting, knives for just about any purpose real or imagined. Nine millimeter Berettas, .38s, .44 Magnums. They were all there, like some Reagan-era wet dream straight out of the pages of *Soldier of Fortune* magazine. And along with all those charming toys gleamed weapons of a more modern lineage, too – fifty caliber Desert Eagle handguns, Jerichos, Glocks, sundry shotguns and assault rifles, and all the necessary ammunition to go around.

Indeed, the Orchid Festival served as a Wild West market, a full arsenal at the right price, far away from any sort of Federal regulations or prying eyes.

Elmer saw one of the gun dealers in the middle of the row, a short, round guy with a thick black beard a matching denim shirt and pants. He knew the guy a little bit – Hank Deniston was his name - and saw him at the festival every year. He'd even considered that maybe they could start doing business together.

As Elmer approached his booth, Hank the gun dealer grinned. But rather than offering any verbal greeting, he just reached back behind him, grabbed a Winchester Model 70 rifle with a scope, and held it out for Elmer to see.

"What's that?" Elmer asked.

"Something I thought you might want to see," said Hank.

Elmer took the rifle, looked it up and down. "Nice," he said. "Looks real nice. How many of these you got?"

"Just one."

"How much you want for it?"

Deniston stroked his beard. "Eight-fifty for most people, but I'd let you have it for seven hundred."

Elmer lifted the rifle to his shoulder and put his right eye against the scope. "Seven hundred. Not bad," he said, then swung the gun around, sweeping the barrel quick across the crowd.

"Careful there, friend," said Hank. Instinctively, the dealer reached to take the gun back, but Elmer stepped away just enough so he couldn't get it.

"Nothin' to be worried about, Hank," Elmer laughed. "It ain't like this thing's loaded, right?" Again, he swept the rifle across the crowd.

The dealer didn't answer.

"It ain't loaded, right?" Elmer asked again.

The dealer didn't answer. Elmer kept the rifle at his shoulder and scanned the festival attendees through the scope's magnification. Soon enough, one person caught his attention: Walt Slone.

TARGETS

Walt wandered away from the park entrance and made his way into the festival grounds, figuring he could shake a few hands and kiss a few babies there, like any good politician.

He greeted most everyone that walked by, handing out four-inch plastic buttons that featured his name in the center of a white star. When the button supply was exhausted – and they did not last long – he handed out embossed business cards. Nobody really needed a trinket to remember him, but for Walt these were the proper hallmarks of any good political season. Signs, buttons, baseball caps, business cards. Perhaps they meant nothing to his constituents, but they meant everything to him.

Each person who passed in his vicinity received the same folksy charm.

"My name's Walt Slone. How ya doin'? I'd appreciate your vote for mayor of our fine little town."

"Hi. Appreciate your vote."

"Hello there, young lady. What about it?"

"Young man, I'd really appreciate your vote."

"What about it? Appreciate your vote."

"You likin' the festival this year? It's great every year, ain't it?"

"Appreciate your vote."

"Heck of a nice day, we got here, ain't it?"

"That's a cute kid you got there. Appreciate your vote. Maybe if I'm still here when he grows up he can vote for me, too, what about it?"

The people rolled through and Walt introduced himself to every single one that came within reach. He hugged old ladies, kissed babies, and shook hands until he couldn't stand up anymore. He handed out buttons and cards, and when those ran out he went to the car and got a box of baseball caps with his name on the front. When he ran out of caps, he gave away pieces of candy. When he ran out of candy, he told folks he was sorry, he'd bring more tomorrow, and could they come see him again?

Eventually he got tired. He was an old man and he just got tired. Truth be told, the electioneering would never be done, not until the fall when the election was over, anyway, but even Walt Slone needed a break from time to time to rest his body and his heart and his mind. He sat down at a picnic table in the shade of a thirty-foot oak tree, close enough to the festival's main walkway that he could see who came and went, but far enough away that he wasn't compelled to speak to everyone who passed.

Soon after he sat down, his granddaughter wandered over, alone. She stood just a foot away, looking up at him with a little squint in the sunlight.

"Where's your mommy?" he asked Samantha.

"I don't know," she said.

"What about your Daddy?"

"I don't know."

"All right then," smiled Walt. He picked her up, sat her on his lap. "Get up here before they come looking for you." The child laughed. He rubbed her hair and laughed with her.

He had absolutely no idea they were being watched, from several yards away, through the crosshairs of a rifle scope.

Over at the gun dealer's booth, Elmer stared through the scope at Walt's magnified face, centered perfectly in the black crosshairs. He imagined it exploding like a ripe watermelon in a gruesome shower of blood, flesh, and skull fragments.

Then he saw the top of little Samantha's head bob up into his field of view. That sapped some of his violent energy. He could fantasize about killing Walt Slone and somehow that seemed okay. But he couldn't fantasize about a child caught in the bullet's path.

He lowered the Winchester rifle, popped out the clip. "He's got a fuckin' kid," he said.

"What?" asked the gun dealer.

"A kid," Elmer snorted. He sounded disappointed. "He's got a kid now. I think it's that granddaughter. Boone's daughter." He offered the empty clip. "There's nothing in here."

"No shit." Hank, the owner of the booth, laughed nervously. "You don't really think I'd be sitting here with a bunch of loaded weapons, wide open for all the world, do you?"

"Hell no," said Elmer. "But I figured I could at least buy buy some from you."

Hank looked at him, wiped sweat from his neck. "Sure you can. You got one of those Winchesters at home?" he asked.

"No, I got one right here. In my hands," said Elmer, holding up the rifle with both hands, mocking the dealer.

Hank shook his head. The last thing he needed was a ruckus raised in his gun booth. Elmer was acting unhinged, though; a ruckus could be coming. Hank looked around, wondering if anyone was watching them, but in the busy festival afternoon, it looked like nobody was paying them much attention.

He peered across the crowd, trying to see just whom Elmer had in his sights, but couldn't make out any clear sight lines.

"I don't know if that's such a good idea," Hank said.

"I didn't ask you what you thought."

"I'm just sayin'."

Elmer smiled. He removed one hand from the rifle, lifted up his shirt and revealed a filet knife hanging on his belt. "Give me some goddamn ammo," he sneered. "Give me some goddamn ammo for this rifle, or I'll split you open like a twelve-point buck right here in front of God and everybody."

Hank straightened up. A wave of nervousness slammed into his gut. "What's wrong with you, Elmer?"

"No problem. Just give me the ammo."

"I don't think so."

"Give me the fucking ammo, Hank."

Elmer was one hundred percent serious, no doubt about it. Hank felt a thin bead of sweat forming at the edge of his brow, and it wasn't from the hot sun. He pondered whether or not Elmer had gone total ape shit crazy. Sure, Elmer Canifax had always seemed to Hank like a guy who drove around with his lugnuts a little loose. But was he really so far out of his mind that he'd take a shot at somebody in broad daylight, right smack in the midst of a couple thousand men, women, and children?

Surely not.

Likely not.

Well, he didn't really know him that well -

Hank decided it wasn't worth chancing. Best to just let Elmer have what he wanted, and keep a tight eye on him. If the situation went too far south, he could grab the pistol under the counter before Elmer did any real damage.

"Okay. You got it," Hank said. He found a box of bullets for the rifle and handed them over. "Just don't get too froggy with that gun. You point it at the wrong person and they're liable to come over and shove it up your ass."

"Don't worry," Elmer said. "I aim only where I mean to." Then he opened the ammo.

Boone took a look around the festival, mostly out of boredom. His mind drifted. He thought about the telephone conversation he had with Elmer a few minutes ago. It seemed unlikely that Elmer would actually go after Walt – and even less likely that he would do it here, in the daylight of the Orchid Festival – but still, it seemed wise to take a look around just in case. You never knew.

Less than a minute later, he spotted Elmer over at Hank Deniston's gun booth.

He had a rifle in his hand.

Probably just fucking around.

But you never knew.

You never knew –

Boone traced the sight line, across the park… straight to Walt. From Boone's angle it sure looked like Elmer had that gun pointed at Walt.

And Samantha was in Walt's lap. Which meant the gun was pointed at her, too.

BULLETS

At the other end of the park, Karen looked through one of the festival's prodigious orchid display. The display in front of Karen stood almost twelve feet tall and was twice that wide, a solid wall of blues, reds, yellows, and whites, of course whites, the whites of the Mountain Orchid, which grew nowhere else but in the hills of Seward County, whose long white petals drooped downward and came together at the ends like tiny hands clasped in prayer.

"I like these," said Karen, pointing at some daises and purple crocuses that were bundled together with long grass. "How much?"

"Fifteen dollars," said the girl. She wore a bright Crayola-green tee shirt and denim skirt that barely went to the knee. Karen didn't recognize her at all, but guessed that she must be the proprietor.

Karen reached for her purse. "I'll take it."

As she took out her wallet, she looked over the crowd and saw her father, sitting at the picnic table with Samantha on his lap.

They sat together, the grandfather and the granddaughter. Walt felt that they didn't get enough moments like this, just the two of them. He smiled, tapped Samantha on the chin. She tapped him back and her face lit up with perfect innocence.

"I want a Coke," she said.

"Tell your Daddy to buy you one," he chuckled.

"I want *you* to buy me one," she said.

"I don't have any money," he said, and turned his pants pocket inside out. "See?"

She smacked him on the chest and grinned just as wide as the day was hot. "You *always* have money, Grandpa!"

Walt smiled, but didn't say anything.

Into the empty clip, Elmer slid the first bullet, then the second, then the third. With each cartridge that fell into place, the knot in Hank Deniston's throat got a little tighter. He glanced more than once at his loaded pistol that rested underneath the makeshift counter, just in case.

As Elmer grasped the fourth bullet, an unexpected visitor joined them. Boone Sumner.

"If I didn't know any better, I'd say you were loading that clip," said Boone.

"Very observant," said Elmer.

"Where I come from, you don't load a gun unless you plan to use it."

"That's right," said Elmer.

"What are you shooting at?"

"Not what. Who."

Boone laughed a nervous laugh. "Okay, who are you shooting at?"

"You know who."

Boone came around, to Elmer's front side.

"All right. Shit," Boone said. "Put the gun down, Elmer. Put it down dammit, before someone sees you."

"So what if they do?" Elmer kept the gun raised at his shoulder, sighting through the scope.

Boone followed Elmer's line of sight from the end of the gun barrel out towards the crowd. All he saw was a shapeless mass of people, making their way through the arts and crafts and flowers and sundries of the Orchid Festival. Boone couldn't tell for certain what Elmer was thinking - the gun was pointed at all of them, or none of them – but worse, he couldn't tell for sure that it *wasn't* Samantha and Walt on the other end of that rifle barrel.

One more time, Boone peered out across the festival, in a straight line away from Elmer's barrel. Like before, he could not make out the person in Elmer's sights. Then, as if parted by divine hands, the crowd opened up and Boone's heart sank. He saw the target, sitting at a picnic table: it was *Walt*, after all. And Samantha was right there.

"Goddammit!" Boone spat. He smacked the rifle downward, knocking Elmer out of place. "What the fuck are you doing here?"

Elmer staggered but regained himself. "Don't touch me," he said.

Boone steeled himself, thought Elmer might take a swing at him. But instead, Elmer jerked the rifle upward, pointed straight at Boone's chest.

Hank took a step back, visibly nervous. He stammered, "Whoa now, let's not get out of hand here," and made a slight move towards the counter, trying to reach his pistol that lay underneath.

"Hank, you go for that pistol and I'll blow your face out the back of your head," said Elmer calmly, without moving the rifle from Boone.

"Put the gun down, Elmer," said Boone, calm.

"Why should I?"

"Put it down."

"What's it like, Boone, lookin' down that end of the barrel?" said Elmer.

"Put the gun down," said Boone.

Nobody moved. The Orchid Festival bustled around them. Occasionally a clueless passer-by would glance over with a mix of curiosity and amusement, but for the most part none of the festival attendees seemed to notice what was happening in Hank Deniston's gun booth.

Boone raised his hands, cautious, not wanting to make any sudden movements that might cause Elmer to get trigger-happy. Public place or not, the guy was holding a loaded weapon and Boone had no wish to set him off. He looked over Elmer's shoulder, seventy yards across the park, and again saw Samantha on Walt's knee.

Elmer smiled. "Whatcha see over there?"

"Put the rifle down Elmer," said Boone.

One more time, a crooked smile creased the lips of Elmer Canifax. The rifle never moved.

Samantha giggled, and pinched her grandfather's nose between her delicate fingers. As she held on, Sheriff Slone joined them at the picnic table.

"You see anything interesting?" asked Walt, as he gently pushed the little hand away with a laugh of his own.

"Nah," said the sheriff. "You?"

Walt shook his head slowly, not breaking his grin. Samantha grabbed his nose again and he laughed along with her.

John Slone leaned back with his elbows behind him, rested on top of the table. He stretched his legs out straight, crossed them left over right.

Then, without any lead-in at all, he asked, "Now what do you think he's doing?"

"Who?" Walt answered without looking away from Samantha.

"Elmer."

"What are you talking about?"

John pointed across the park, towards Hank Deniston's gun booth. "I dunno," he said. "I probably need to go over there. With that rifle in his hands, it just don't look good. Aw shit, and now Boone's involved."

That got Walt's attention. His smile vanished. He looked up from Samantha and saw Elmer across the park, with a rifle in his hand, and Boone standing there at point-blank range.

Then, at almost exactly the same moment that Walt found Elmer, Elmer whacked Boone in the jaw with the butt of his rifle, whipped around in the opposite direction, and trained his sights smack in the center of Walt's forehead.

"The little shit," Walt sneered. "The little *cocksucker!*" Blood flushed into his face. The happiness he'd felt, with Samantha on his knee, vanished.

White starbursts of pain danced in Boone's eyes. He rolled around on the dirt, grabbing his jaw. He tasted warm iron and knew it was his own blood. His jaw might be broken; broken or not, it hurt like all hell.

Through the pain, he could see Walt again. He could also see that for the first time, Walt himself recognized that a gun was trained on him. Boone saw his father-in-law hand his granddaughter over to Sheriff Slone, and before anybody realized what was happening, Walt was stalking across the ground, headed right for Elmer.

Elmer showed no signs of movement.

Walt jabbed his index finger in Elmer's direction, mouthing angry, violent words that Boone couldn't quite discern through the screaming agony in his head.

Boone felt the swelling in the jaw already. Still, for all the pain it brought, he knew that the jaw was not his biggest concern. The angry old man stomping across the park grounds — that was his biggest concern. As it dawned on him what was really happening, Boone noticed that for once, the rest of the festival had come to a stop. Folks stepped aside, both to let Walt through and also to get a better view of whatever action was about to happen.

Boone struggled back to his feet. He grabbed at Elmer, hoping he could take the rifle away before Walt got there, but the blow to his jaw codded up all vision and his balance.

Still, even with the smears in his brain he knew that if Walt got there, the shit was going down. But surely Walt wouldn't get there. Elmer had the rifle. The rifle was loaded. Walt was coming, but the rifle was pointed right at him. Elmer had the rifle. Walt was headed straight at him. Elmer wouldn't let Walt get there, would he? Elmer had the rifle pointed at Walt. Elmer could shoot Walt whenever he wanted.

Oh shit.

*

The sheriff saw where Walt was headed. He set Samantha on the ground and took off after his father. "Hold on, Dad!" he yelled. "He's got a gun!"

"I know he's got a goddamn gun!" Walt yelled back. "That's why I'm going over there!"

The sheriff heard Karen behind him, as she swooped in and picked up Samantha and shouted something at his back that sounded like, "What's going on, John?"

He couldn't answer her, though; his heart thumped in his neck. He flicked out one hand behind himself – *hold* on – and kept after Walt.

"Come and get it, motherfucker," muttered Elmer, as he moved his finger to the trigger.

Walt approached faster. Boone could barely believe what he saw. Flush with hot anger, Walt had covered the distance to Elmer in just a few strides. Only ten seconds had passed from the time Walt first realized he was in Elmer's sights to now, when he was only a few feet away from them.

"Elmer, don't be a dipshit," Boone pleaded.

He saw Sheriff Slone draw a pistol of his own.

"Fuck you, Boone," said Elmer.

"FUCK YOU YOU GODDAMN MOTHER FUCKING COCKSUCKER. GODDAMN SON OF A GODDAMN WHORE MOTHERFUCKING SON OF A BITCH!" Walt screamed, as loud as he could cut loose.

When the torrent of curses flew, the gathering crowd went cold silent like they'd been covered by a blanket.

"Don't do it," Boone said to Elmer again. He saw John Slone down on one knee now, his pistol almost squared up, just about ready to blow the top of Elmer's skull into the afternoon sky.

Walt yelled, "MOTHERFUCKER YOU WANT TO GODDAMN POINT THAT MOTHERFUCKING THING AT ME MOTHERFUCKER YOU BETTER GODDAMN BE READY TO USE IT!" and he kept coming. Maybe ten feet away now.

Before Elmer could fire his rifle, Boone lunged for him.

Before Boone could get him, Elmer squeezed the trigger.

Before Boone could get in the way, Sheriff Slone got his finger on the trigger, ready to take out Elmer.

Before anybody could shoot anybody, Walt stepped to one side.

And then

CRACK!

Like a kid's gunpowder snap-pop.

CRACK! CRACK!

Chaos erupted. Hundreds of panicked festival-goers scattered in hundreds of different directions, grabbing their children, leaving behind their arts and their crafts and their gyros and their chicken sticks.

Boone jumped into Elmer, even though he knew it was too late. He got his hands around the rifle barrel, knocked it to the ground, then slammed his body into Elmer's and sent both of them flying into Hank's countertop, which collapsed like wet cardboard.

On the way to the ground, Boone turned his head for a quick look and saw Walt going down, gripping his chest –

gripping his chest –

Sheriff Slone jumped up. He holstered his pistol, clutched the microphone clipped to his shoulder and bellowed into it, "This is Sheriff Slone! We need an ambulance at the festival! We need an ambulance at the festival right now!" He pushed his way through the hellbent crowd, keeping his eye on the spot where his father went down.

Finally he found Walt, lying on the ground, gasping for air and looking up at the sky with faded eyes. The old man's right hand rested his chest; beneath the hand, a circle of blood slowly expanded across his shirt. Underneath him, more blood - thicker, redder – pooled on the ground.

"Daddyyyy!" Karen wailed. A second later she was there with them, holding Samantha in her arms.

"Hold on, dad," said John. "Hold on, the ambulance is on its way. The ambulance is on its way. The ambulance is on its way." He kept saying the line, over and over. He couldn't think of anything else.

Over at the gun booth, Boone was flush with adrenaline. His head cleared, and his legs came back. He pounced on top of Elmer, landed one two three four five six seven hard punches to the middle of his face, until Elmer was unconscious and covered in his own blood.

When the beating was over, Boone took Elmer's rifle and handed it to Hank. "Hang onto this," he said. "They'll need it for evidence."

Hank accepted the gun.

"Don't touch the trigger," said Boone.

"Okay," said Hank.

Boone looked at the gun dealer. Something wasn't right. Hank seemed unsure of something.

"What?" asked Boone.

Hank took a deep breath. "The police can take this rifle, but it ain't gonna help much," he said.

"Why is that?"

"Because."

"Goddammit it, Hank, this ain't the time—"

"I'm telling you, it ain't gonna help!" Hank yelled in Boone's face. Boone pulled back, stunned.

Hank inhaled again. "Because," he said. "I stood there and watched everything happen. And I hate to tell you this Boone, but Elmer Canifax never fired one damn shot."

PART FIVE:
HELL TO PAY

DREAMS

Boone digs in the dirt. The black dirt, the cold dirt, the dirt like metal shavings under his nails, the dirt like blood caked between his fingers. Fast and frantic, he digs in the dirt.

Hurry up, says Jimmy.

I can't go any faster, says Boone.

But he can go faster. He does go faster. The October air crackles cold in his lungs. He digs faster. His fingers cramp, his nails split and bleed, but still Boone Sumner digs faster. Without stopping, he looks over to one side and sees her body wrapped in black plastic. And he digs faster.

What are you doing, son?

Nothing, Mama.

But Mama knows he's lying. He can tell from the look on her face, the way she bites her lower lip and tightens her brow and glares at him through half-squinted eyes. Of course she knows when he's lying. She always knows.

Hey Boone, Jimmy says. *I came by your house last night. You weren't home. Were you out with Karen again?*

Yeah, we were out, says Boone.

Jimmy smiles. *Walt Slone's got somethin' he wants us to do*, he says.

Will he pay? asks Boone.

You know Walt Slone will pay, says Jimmy. *Walt Slone always pays. He runs everything. He's got the money.*

How much for this job?

Two thousand.

Two thousand? That's real *money. What's he want?*

Get your pistol and we can talk about it in the truck, says Jimmy.

Boone's heart sinks. He could use the money, but not that badly. He doubted he would ever need Walt Slone's dirty money that badly. Then again, two thousand dollars was a lot of money for an eighteen-year-old. A guy could do a lot with two thousand dollars. And besides, it was just this one thing, then they could get the hell out and never have to worry about Walt Slone or his gang again.

Just this one thing. Just this one thing. How bad could it be? Two thousand dollars is a lot of money. A man could do a lot with two thousand dollars. And it's just this one thing.

What are you doing son?
Nothing, Mama.

They stand at the edge of the woods, the woods behind the big house on top of the hill. Quietly they stare at a black marble slab. Etched in the slab are words that they read over and over and over: wife. Mother. Friend. Ellen Slone.

Do you remember her very much? says Samantha.

Sure I do, says Boone. *She was so nice, and pretty, too. You look a lot like her.*

I wish she was still alive when I was born, says Samantha.

I wish I never dug in the dirt, says Boone.

Boone wonders what his father might have said to him in that moment.

You and your brother gotta watch out for each other now, you hear?

Keep your family close as you can, Boone. Close as you can, you hear?

Walt leans out the window of his truck. He motions for Boone to come over. Boone looks back at Jimmy one more time, then steps forward.

It's just this one thing, says Walt. *You and your brother can do this one thing for me, right?*

He offers Boone an envelope. Inside the envelope, Boone finds two thousand dollars in fives, tens, and twenties. It's just this one thing.

Ellen Slone stumbles through the woods. Boone and Jimmy walk a few feet behind her, but they are in no hurry – Ellen can't get far. Her hands are duct-taped behind her back. She is blindfolded.

Boone raises his gun to shoot.

Hold on! Jimmy calls out.

Ellen stumbles. Falls.

Boone gets there first.

It's just this one thing.

It's just this one thing.

It's just this one thing.

*

Jimmy runs back to the truck and gets the plastic tarp. They will need that, to wrap up the body. In less than five minutes they have her wrapped up. A minute after that, Boone digs in the dirt. The black dirt, the cold dirt, the dirt like metal shavings under his nails, the dirt like blood caked between his fingers.

What are you doing, son?

It's just this one thing, Mama.

Soon, Jimmy joins him. Jimmy has the shovel. They dig faster now, Jimmy with the shovel, Boone with his hands.

Boone stands on Walt's front porch. He's waiting. Finally the door opens and Walt stands there.

Boone hands him a brown paper bag with two fingers in it. Walt takes the bag, looks inside, says nothing. He nods slowly at Walt, hands him back the bag. *Get rid of her,* he says.

What do you want me to do with her? asks Boone.

Go see Harley Faulkner, says Walt.

Boone turns around and looks into the valley. He sees everything sinking, sinking, sinking. The earth crumbles and opens up, spitting steam and fire. Churches and gas stations fall in. Old farm machinery falls in. Mobile homes fall in. Schools fall in. Pillheads fall in. Meth makers fall in. A dead cow falls in. Every goddamned bit of Sewardville falls in to the hissing pit.

Then, Boone feels the mountain slide beneath him. A loud CRRRAAACKKK rips through the air as Walt Slone's house splits down the middle and tumbles forward. Down. The house crashes into the pit, the house that Boone hates more than any other house in the world. The expensive wood, the Civil War relics, the patriotic election signs. And then, after all his worldly possessions, Walt Slone falls in, head over foot. Then Karen falls in. Samantha falls in. A black marble slab falls in, and Boone reads the words that are etched on it: wife, mother, friend. Mountain orchids fall in, the money falls in, the pain falls in, Mama falls in, Jimmy falls in. Boone falls in. Nothing remains.

NOW WHAT

The morning after the Orchid Festival incident, Boone woke up in a chair at Sewardville Medical Center. He was positioned awkwardly on his right side, his chin propped up by a hand that still had tiny flecks of Walt Slone's blood splattered on it. In another chair beside him slept Samantha, her little head resting against his shoulder.

Through the gauze of waking, Boone realized that they were just outside the hospital room where Walt Slone lay hooked up to a ventilator. Sheriff Slone and Karen were there, standing next to Walt's bed. The steady MEEP. MEEP. MEEP. of the electroencephalograph drummed into the hum of fluorescent lights. Slowly, a mundane tableau of dispassionate hospital surroundings drew into focus: the dull white tile, the matte grey paint on the walls, the controlled bustle of doctors and nurses in the corridors.

Boone stood, stretched his legs.

Samantha's eyes fluttered open. "Is Grandpa awake yet?" she asked, her voice still full of sleep.

Boone tousled her hair. "Not yet, baby."

"I hope he wakes up soon," she shrugged.

He smiled at her. With great love he traced his finger down her face, coming to a rest under the dimples in her chin. But he said nothing.

Samantha put her head back down against the chair's arm rest, and soon she passed back into quiet slumber. He wished he could do the same, wished he could just fall into a deep sleep, free of torment, free of the Slones, free of Sewerville, free of it all.

Karen and John exited Walt's room. They gathered with Boone a few feet away from the sleeping child and talked in low voices just to be certain she didn't hear anything.

"How's he doing?" asked Boone.

"Hard to say," said the sheriff. "Bullet lodged five millimeters from his aorta. Doctor said if anybody'd moved him at all it probably would've killed him. They got 'im through surgery, but now we just have to wait and see."

"How long?"

Karen spoke up. "He could be in the hospital a month, maybe longer. They don't know yet." Her voice was flat, shell-shocked, as though her words came from across the room by a ventriloquist.

Boone started to ask if anybody thought Walt would pull through, but he caught himself and decided against it. Truth be told, it didn't matter what anybody thought. Either Walt pulled through, or he didn't. They would all know soon enough. No point wearing out the conversation until then.

Instead, he asked, "Now what?" He didn't really expect an answer. He didn't get one, either.

The sheriff nodded his head and sat down in one of the chairs near Samantha.

Karen came over and picked up the sleeping child, and quickly mother and daughter disappeared down the corridor. She didn't want to talk about now-what. In that awful moment, as her father lay in a hospital bed with a near fatal gunshot wound to his chest, now-what was the last thing on Karen Slone's mind.

"Okay, let's try this again," Boone asked John. "Now what?"

John leaned his back against the wall, squeezed his eyes shut. "I don't know. It's a fucked up situation. What do you think we ought to do?"

Boone didn't have an immediate answer.

With his eyes still closed, the sheriff said, "Karen told me about Elmer and Rogers."

Boone tightened up.

"She said you found a crate of ours," John continued. "Up at Elmer's place, when we were there the other night. I guess I should have known. That little bastard."

Hearing this didn't surprise Boone in the least. He'd actually counted on Karen telling her brother about the scheme of Elmer and Deputy Rogers, how they'd stolen some of Walt's merchandise to kickstart their own enterprise, and how they'd tried to bring him in on the deal. Karen looked out for the family above all else. She wouldn't keep that kind of information down. That was exactly why he'd told her about it – and left out the key part of the story, that he'd actually taken them up on the offer - because she would go right to her father and her brother. He wanted to make sure that the story got out on his terms, not theirs.

But with somebody taking a shot at Walt in broad daylight, Boone had a real tightrope to walk now. If anybody found out that he was hooked into Elmer to any degree whatsoever, it would get ugly quick.

"Elmer and Rogers aren't the sharpest hooks in the tacklebox," said Boone, "but still, this is stupid, even for them."

John opened his eyes, sat back up straight. "The problem with those two," he said, "is that they ain't stupid at all. They're worse than stupid. They think they got everything figured out, think they got the plan to beat all plans. That ain't stupid, Boone. That's dangerous."

He jabbed his finger at Boone. "Hell, after Dad got shot, you rode with us when we took Elmer down to the police station. You helped beat the fuck out of him, I stood right there and watched you. What did he tell us?"

"Nothing."

"That's right. Nothing. You know why? 'Cause he thinks he's got us nailed. That rifle he picked up, it's got his fingerprints all over it, and we got two hundred people that'll sign a statement saying he pointed it right at Walt. Guess what else we got? Forensics sayin' that gun never fired a single goddamn bullet. How about that? Gonna be awful hard to match that piece of metal they took out of Walt to a rifle that's never been shot, don't you think?"

The sheriff's gaze lingered, waiting for Boone to answer, but no answer came. Eventually John stood back up. "So basically Elmer might as well have had his thumb jammed up his ass, is what I'm saying."

That stumped Boone. "Why is that?"

"Because, thumb on that rifle, or thumb up his ass, either way he's cod locked for not bein' the shooter. He knew he'd have been suspect numero uno if something happened to Walt, so he took himself out of the equation. Too bad for him, he didn't count on you telling us he had a partner in the whole deal."

Boone felt his pulse quicken in his neck. Suddenly he realized the terrible place to which this all led. He could see the future as clearly as if it were painted in blood on a canvas before him: the shot that took Walt down would not be the last shot fired. Somebody was going to end up dead. Probably more than one somebody.

"Okay," said Boone through an exhale. "So I'll ask you again. Now what?"

"Now we go after Elmer's partner, that's what," the sheriff answered.

"This soon?"

"Hell yeah, this soon!" John shot back. His face conveyed a sour mix of anger, and disbelief. "Elmer and Rogers both are goddamn lucky we didn't take their heads off five minutes after Walt went down! We need to move on Rogers now. He's bound to know we're coming for him sooner or later, and we'd better get on it before he makes a run for it. If he hasn't already."

Boone thought about it. He'd anticipated this day from the moment Rogers had shown him Walt's crate in Elmer's outbuilding. He'd thought he could play both sides against each other and come out clean on the other end. He just hadn't expected it to happen this quickly.

Now, he sensed his best opportunity at hand. No more quarter machines, no more of Walt's bullshit, no more Sewerville, no more nothing. Just maybe. Just maybe.

Still, Boone didn't want to seem *too* anxious to go after Rogers. Better to follow along rather than be out front right now.

"I just think we might want to wait a little longer. Not draw too much attention to ourselves," he said. "If a lawman gets killed, people are going to come ask questions. News people. Just like they did when you and Caudill got shot at the Bears Den. If people start taking bullets around here like this is the goddamn Wild West, it'll stir up some major shit. You know how those TV people are."

"Fuck the news," John spit out. "Fuck them to hell. Walt's shot, and we have to do something, and that's just the way it is. If I didn't know any better, I'd say maybe you weren't with us a hundred percent on this. Are you with us, or are you not, Boone?"

It was not the moment for hesitation, Boone knew. The machinery was moving now. "Don't worry, I'm with you on this," he said. "I'm a part of this family, too."

BLOOD

Boone rode with Sheriff Slone to the home of Rogers. Sharp mid-afternoon sunlight cut jags of light around the edges of the sun visor above his head.

He traced his finger along the steel barrel of a twelve gauge shotgun, and stared out the windshield with a grim look on his face. As the car bounced along the two lane road, it occurred to Boone that in all his years of working with and for the Slone family, never once had he ridden in John's cruiser, until now.

"You could have really fucked us on this deal," John said. "Say you took Elmer up on his offer. Let's just say, you fell in with him and Rogers, started working against us. You could have really burnt our asses good. You know a hell of a lot about the family business and could have used that to your advantage. We'd have got you eventually, sure. But if you wanted, you had a chance there to really fuck some shit up, you know?"

Boone circled the shotgun barrel and gripped it tight with one hand. He focused on the dotted yellow line on the two-lane road, as they passed beneath the speeding vehicle.

"But you didn't do that," said the sheriff. "I guess we all got lucky there, huh?"

"I guess so," said Boone.

They drove on.

J.T. Rogers sat on the couch, wearing the fatigues of the Seward County Sheriff's department. With Sheriff Slone stationed down at Sewardville Medical with Walt, the deputy knew he'd be pulling some extra duty hours for the next few days. Just the way it was.

On the television, the Cincinnati Reds were smacking around the St. Louis Cardinals in the seventh inning. Rogers stared in the general direction of the game, but he wasn't paying that much attention. Instead his mind followed the same track it had followed for the last twenty-four hours: he hadn't seen or heard a solitary whisper from Elmer Canifax since all that shit went down at the Orchid Festival. That made Rogers nervous.

Beyond nervous.

Even worse, he hadn't heard from John Slone or Boone Sumner. Karen, either. While part of him felt like that was just because he stayed more or less on a need-to-know basis, another, more nervous part of him thought it a good idea to sleep with a gun under his pillow.

Had Boone sold them out to Walt, or to the sheriff? The shots fired at Walt could have scared Boone into silence, or just as easily scared him into coming clean with the Slone family before he found himself on the receiving end of the next round. There was no way of knowing, not yet, but Rogers was sure that the situation would shift into focus sooner rather than later. Either Boone sold him and Elmer out, or he didn't. Elmer would turn up, or he wouldn't.

He heard a car coming up the driveway, towards the house. He looked out the living room window, and saw the sheriff's cruiser roll to a stop behind his own police car. Moments later, the sheriff stepped out in full uniform, and Rogers saw that he already had the safety strap unbuttoned from his gun holster. Even worse, after that, Boone got out of the vehicle with a shotgun in hand.

Rogers grabbed his loaded pistol from the coffee table and went to the entrance of the house. He opened the door and saw John Slone standing with his knuckles raised and ready to knock.

"Hello, Sheriff," he said, holding the weapon where the sheriff and Boone could see it.

"Hello, J.T.," the sheriff answered. He checked the gun in his deputy's hand. "You expecting some company, or what?"

Rogers walked out onto the porch, closed the door behind him. He made no effort to put the gun away. "Nah," he said. "Just going out on my shift, is all. What brings you two up here? Anything change with Walt?"

John brushed the questions aside. "Walt's fine," he said. "Let's just cut all the bullshit, shall we?"

A nervous laugh danced from the deputy's throat. He forced a smile but his eyes betrayed him, jumping skitterish from one visitor to the other. "What bullshit do you mean?" he asked.

The sheriff was unimpressed with his deputy's ignorance. "Where were you yesterday, when Walt got shot?" he asked, in a calm voice that contrasted with the obvious edginess of Rogers.

"Same place everybody else in the county was," said Rogers. "At the festival. I was on duty. You know that."

"Where at the festival?"

"What's this all about?" Rogers flexed his fingers tighter around the grip of his pistol.

"You know what this is about," John said.

"I do?"

"Sure you do. You got a rifle in your cruiser, don't you?"

Rogers just looked at him.

"I don't suppose you'd care if we sent that rifle of yours up to Frankfort and checked it out against the bullets they pulled out of Walt."

"Hell yeah I care!" Rogers blurted. Any trace of cool that he'd been attempting to show evaporated in an instant. "What the fuck, you think I shot Walt? What is this bullshit?" He paused, took a deep breath, shook his head from side to side.

"You know we talked to Elmer. Elmer gave you up pretty quick." The placid demeanor of the sheriff never wavered.

It wasn't true. Though they had talked to Elmer right after Walt's shooting, he hadn't said anything about Rogers. Karen served as their only source of knowledge about the plan of Elmer and Rogers, and of course she got her info from Boone. Not that the source mattered here; the sheriff just wanted to see if Rogers would crack if he thought Elmer had turned on him.

Then again, whether Rogers admitted anything openly or not didn't matter, either. There was only one possible outcome of this visit. It could come quickly, or it could take a little longer, but this episode ended one way and one way only. And for Rogers, it would not be a happy ending.

The deputy said, "Elmer didn't tell you shit. There's nothing to tell."

John nodded his head and let out a slow, disappointed sigh. He looked Rogers square in the face. "You sure about that? You mean to tell me there's not a crate of guns and pills in Elmer's outbuilding that belongs to Walt Slone, that you and Elmer stole so you two dumb motherfuckers could set up your own shop?"

"I don't know what you're talking about."

"Bullshit."

"Sheriff, I swear, I ain't got no part of this."

"BULLSHIT!" screamed the sheriff. He jumped forward, straight at Rogers, who in turn raised his pistol to fire at the sheriff.

Too late.

Before J.T. could get his gun even halfway to the height he needed, Boone pounced on him. With his left hand he grabbed Rogers at the wrist, behind the pistol, and brought his right fist down on the deputy's outstretched arm with such strong and sudden force that the radial bone snapped and broke through the skin, like something out of a cheap action movie.

Rogers let out a sick howl and dropped the gun. Boone landed a solid punch in the middle of his face that shattered the deputy's nose like a fortune cookie, splattering hot blood across the lower half of his face and a few flecks of red onto Boone's jacket, too.

The deputy screamed. Boone grabbed him by the chest and took him down to the porch floor, Sheriff Slone headed back to the cruiser.

Boone wondered why he'd left them, but kept that question to himself. He pinned the struggling Rogers to the creaky porch wood, and muttered, "Hold on, J.T.. Just hold the fuck on if you want to get out of this."

Rogers spat in his face. "Go to hell."

The warm saliva dripped down Boone's jaw, but he couldn't free one hand to wipe it off without risking the deputy getting the upper hand.

"You motherfucker," the deputy sneered, through the twin pains of his broken arm and busted nose. "You motherfucker, you gave us up."

"Be quiet," Boone said, trying to keep his own voice down. "I didn't give anybody up."

"You motherfucker. Motherfucker. Trying to save your own ass," Rogers spit again, his words mixed with spit, and blood, and hatred. "I should have known. Fuck." Pain radiated through his body, sapped most of his fight.

"I didn't say anything," said Boone. "Just keep your mouth shut. I'll get us out of this." He checked over his shoulder, looking for John Slone. He didn't see him, but he heard the cruiser's trunk lid creak open and then quickly slam shut again.

"What the fuck... was I thinking..." Rogers went on.

Sheriff Slone came back up on the porch now. "J.T., I gotta say, I don't know *what* the fuck you were thinking."

Boone heard the gentle slosh of liquid, and when John came back around to his front side he saw that the sheriff carried two metal gasoline cans now, one in each hand. Boone guessed from the sound of the sloshing and the tension in the sheriff's arms as he carried the weight of the cans that they were at least three-quarters full.

Boone glanced back down at the man below him. Rogers breathed in quick gasps, with most of the struggle already sapped from his broken body. Still Boone pinned him down, though, just to make sure that Rogers didn't find a second wind. That would really turn this into a shitty mess, if Rogers suddenly jumped up and started fighting again. Best if he just stayed down. Best for everybody.

The sheriff set the gas can down near his deputy's head, then bent closer to the face of Rogers, steadying himself with his hands on his thighs. "Let's try this again," he said, again speaking in that flat, calm tone.

"His arm's broken," said Boone. "Nose, too."

The sheriff smiled down at them.

In that awful moment, Rogers realized what everyone else in Sewardville knew: when John Slone smiled, bad things happened.

Boone relaxed his grip on the shoulders of Rogers, and Rogers barely moved. It was difficult for him to keep his eyes even half-open.

"I think he's had enough," said Boone. "Let's take him down to the jail and let him think about it."

"He ain't had enough," the sheriff interrupted. That flat, cold voice, just as flat and cold as the voice of a gas chamber physician. "You ain't had enough, have you, J.T.?"

Rogers blinked his eyes halfway back open, in time to see John's fist come crashing down into his pulpy broken nose. White starbursts of pain exploded in front of his face. He thrashed once more, managed a fleeting thought of escape, but Boone held him fast and fresh waves of pain crushed that notion.

"Let's try it again," the sheriff continued, as Rogers settled back down. "You know, and I know, and Boone knows, and everybody that *needs* to know, knows, that you shot Walt yesterday. I don't know how you managed to pull it off, but you did. And the truth is, right here at this very moment, I don't really give a damn about the hows and the whys."

Rogers turned his head to one side and spit out thick red chunks. He fought to speak and managed, "Sheriff, I didn't do anything."

Sheriff Slone shook his head, and smiled once more. He stood back up, and without saying another word, hauled off and kicked Rogers square in the side of the head.

"Goddammit, John!" Boone protested.

"Shut up, Boone," the sheriff said.

The next blow came so quick, the pain so sharp in his skull that all of Rogers's senses were overwhelmed at once and at first he had almost no discernible reaction. His mouth dropped open and he *looked* like he was screaming, but he didn't scream. He hurt in silence, as though the strike had rendered him incapable of crying out. Blood pounded in his brain. He recoiled to one side, but couldn't go far because he was still held fast underneath Boone. He thought he would pass out. God, how he wanted to pass out.

"Are you working with anybody else?" asked the sheriff.

Rogers could barely see, let alone formulate a cogent thought. He stammered, "N-n-no."

"ARE YOU WORKING WITH ANYBODY ELSE?" Slone roared.

Rogers hung on the precipice of unconsciousness.

When the sheriff realized that he wasn't going to get anything else, he cleared his throat, and said to Boone, "Get up."

Boone stood, and stepped back. He knew that the sheriff could explode over the edge at any moment.

Sheriff Slone extended one of the gas cans to him. "What do you want me to do with that?"

"Burn it," the sheriff responded. Cold, flat. "Burn him. Burn it all."

Boone backed away.

John looked at him in disbelief. "What, you're gettin' morals all of a sudden?"

"We can't do this," said Boone. "If a sheriff's deputy turns up dead on the heels of all the other shit that's happened around here, it'll be a bigger story than either one of us wants to deal with. Let's just turn him over to the state boys, let Walt's friends up in Frankfort deal with him. We don't need this shit."

"Is that right?" the sheriff said.

"You know it's right," said Boone.

John Slone shook his head. A sour, disappointed look drew into his face. He pulled the gas can back and stood there, thinking.

Then he tipped it up and doused Rogers in fuel.

As the hot gasoline splashed over him, and the fumes burned into his nose and throat, and into his bloody wounds, finally Rogers could make a sound. A hell scream burst from his throat, risen from the pit of his mortal soul.

The sheriff didn't care. He drew his pistol, nice and easy, and began whistling a slow version of "Hair of the Dog."

Now you're messin' with

A SONOFABEEYITCH

Now you're messin' with a sonofabitch!

Rogers shuffled to his feet, gas dripping off him. His mouth fell open and he didn't so much as speak, as the words trickled from his lips.

"Sheriff, don't... don't do this..."

"Don't do what?" mocked Slone.

Boone stepped forward, in between the hunter and his prey. "Come on, John," he said. "There's no need for this goin' down this way. Let's take him back, let him rot at the jail for a while."

The sheriff shifted his gun's aim right into Boone's forehead.

Boone froze.

"Is that what you want, Boone?" barked John. "Dad's layin' in a hospital bed, breathin' through a machine, who knows when the fuck he'll wake up, and you just want to take this piece of shit down to the jail?"

Boone stayed still. He didn't think John would shoot him, but he didn't want to test that theory, either.

Rogers slobbered, "I didn't... didn't do nothin'... to Walt..."

The sheriff turned his aim again. Without pause, he pulled the trigger and blew a fist-sized chunk out of his deputy's skull.

"Sure you didn't do nothin'," said Slone.

Boone wiped a moist piece of something from his cheek and realized it must be part of Rogers's face.

John pulled a matchbook out of his uniform pants and threw it at Boone's feet. In a brief out-of-body moment, Boone saw it was emblazoned with the University of Kentucky Wildcats logo.

"Your turn," said the Sheriff.

Boone stared at the matches.

"Pick 'em up, Boone," said John. "Unless, of course, you want me to start thinkin' you ain't as big a part of this family as you been tryin' to let on."

"I'm part of the family," said Boone. "But this... Goddamn, did it really have to go like this?"

"What did you think we came up here for?" snapped the sheriff. "This is what happens when people fuck with us. You know it same as anybody. They want to come after us, then fine. Let them. But they come after us, we go after them. The shit works that way. Always has."

He walked over to where Boone was still frozen to the porch, and picked up the book of matches that still lay where he'd thrown them. "Elmer's got an alibi. Like you said, we checked his gun and it didn't fire any shots. I bet you dollars to donuts that if we take the rifle out of J.T.'s car, it'll match the bullets from Walt."

"And that covers this up?"

There was a dull *thnnnk* as he kicked the corpse. "There ain't no cover up. Rogers here died in a good old fashioned police shootout. I came up here to question him, he pulled a gun, things went south. I shot in self-defense. He took one in the face. His house burned down. Shit happens. You know how that is."

Boone did know how that was. Such a story would even fly with the state police, who didn't give a shit what really happened, anyway. The Slone family had enough troopers and detectives on their payroll to make sure any investigation would go quickly and produce whatever results they so desired. This would get covered up, the way everything that the Slone family did in Sewardville got covered up.

She stumbles through the bare night woods
She runs the best she can
They have their Daddy's gun
She cries
She begs
She digs in the dirt
The dirt
The dirt
The dirt

"To hell with this," Boone said.

He walked off the porch, down the driveway, past the sheriff's cruiser. The sheriff yelled at him – "Where the hell are you going? Get the fuck back here!" – but Boone kept walking. He heard the cock of a pistol hammer at his back, but he kept going. With each step he considered what it might be like to take a bullet to the spine. No bullet came, though. Not even John Slone could shoot his own brother-in-law in the back and explain that to his sister and his niece. So, Boone kept walking.

Behind him, the sheriff lowered his weapon. After a moment, he opened his book of matches, struck one, and dropped it on the dead chest of his former deputy. Then, he headed back to his police cruiser.

Fire spread across the porch, into the living room, and through the rest of the house. Before long, the whole wooden structure went up in orange and black plumes. Fingers of flame licked high into the Kentucky afternoon and overwhelmed the entire scene in less than thirty minutes.

Walking away, Boone felt intense heat on the back of his neck, but he looked straight ahead and kept walking. The sheriff's car ripped by him, just a couple of feet away, close enough that it stirred a breeze in his face. Still Boone kept walking.

He wondered what he would tell Karen when he got home. How long would it be before they knew where he really stood? Not long at all. Then what? He had a plan.

HOSPITAL

Boone walked all the way back to Sewardville Medical. Scenarios ricocheted in his mind, possibilities that might confront him at the hospital, when he faced John Slone again. Would John already have told Karen everything that happened, that Rogers was dead and his house burned to the ground? And what kind of spin would the story have on it? Surely John would leave out the part where he went totally ape-shit psycho.

Rogers died in a good old fashioned police shootout. I came up here to question him, he pulled a gun, things went south. Shit happens.

It seemed a real possibility that the next time they saw each other, Boone and Sheriff Slone would come to fists. And if John convinced Karen that her husband had shown anything less than complete loyalty to the Slone cause, she'd get in a few licks of her own, too.

Boone reflected on the last few days. How foolish he had been. When Elmer had shown him Walt's crate in his outbuilding, Boone thought he could play both sides against each other and walk away free through the middle. That plan had gone straight to seed. Now, Walt teetered on the sharp edge between life and death. Rogers was dead. Elmer was missing and probably dead. The sheriff bristled with righteous anger. Time would tell what Karen thought about it all.

Instead of getting out through the middle, both sides had collapsed in on Boone, and now he had to figure an escape.

And then there was Samantha.

Samantha.

Samantha.

He reached the hospital.

Immediately he saw a small, impromptu press conference happening near the revolving entrance door. Carla Haney, WTVL-TV Live on Your Side had already sprung into action. Sheriff Slone fielded her rapid-fire questions with an expression that had all the emotion of unpainted drywall.

Boone could see Karen, too, just inside the building, watching. She looked agitated and immediately He knew that she hadn't yet spoken to her brother.

As he made his way towards the hub-bub, Boone made short eye contact with the sheriff. John squinted a little, but betrayed no other thoughts in front of the reporter.

Boone heard the questions as he entered the revolving door.

"Do you have any suspects yet, Sheriff?" Carla asked.

"No," said the sheriff.

"What about forensic evidence?"

"Some."

"What can you tell us about Mayor Slone's current condition?"

"Not a whole lot."

"Is he conscious?"

"I'm not sure."

"What about reports that witnesses saw a man pointing a rifle at Mr. Slone from a gun dealer's booth?"

"I'm not sure."

"Are you heading this investigation yourself, given your personal relationship to the victim?"

"Yes."

Inside the hospital, Boone found Karen by the window, watching the interview, in the same position as she'd been when he saw her from outside. She looked with a blank expression, showing utter disinterest in what went on outside between her brother and the reporter from Lexington.

He shot a quick glance around the room, looking for his daughter, but didn't see her. "Where's Samantha?" he asked as he stepped towards his wife.

"She's asleep," Karen said without turning towards him. "In Dad's room."

"They let her stay in there?"

"Why wouldn't they?"

"I don't know."

Finally she turned to face him. "How did it go up there?" she asked quietly.

"Up where?"

"You know where," she said. Not even a Slone could speak in public about a crime that hadn't yet become public knowledge, though with Carla Haney in town already it would no doubt become public knowledge soon.

He pulled a gun.

Things went south.

Shit happens.

"Right." Boone stalled. He felt certain that any word he spoke could be twisted back in his face by the sheriff. He couldn't give her too much information right now. Better to wait it out and let the story fall into place once Boone could get a better view of his current situation. Besides, if he was wrong - if Karen had already spoken with her brother about the events of that afternoon – then she could be feeling him out, trying to see if his story matched her brother's, thinking maybe she might catch Boone in a lie. If his facts didn't match John's, then one of them had to be lying. Period. And of course, there was no way Karen would ever believe that her brother could be the man on the wrong side of the truth.

He saw that outside, Carla Haney was exasperated, throwing up her hands as her camera man turned off the camera and took it down from his shoulder. The sidewalk press conference was over.

And John Slone was coming inside now.

It occurred to Boone that perhaps he should go and check on Samantha.

"So are you gonna tell me what happened, or not?" Karen asked. Before Boone could come up with his answer, the sheriff was in the building.

"I'll you *exactly* what happened," Karen's brother sneered, as he hurried towards them. He yanked his sunglasses off and threw them at Boone; they hit in the middle of Boone's chest with a soft thud, bounced to the floor, bent to one side now. The sheriff's anger was rising already. "You want to know what happened? This dumb fuck husband of yours happened!"

Karen stepped back and extended an arm, trying to calm her brother, with no effect. "John, I don't think we should do this here –"

The sheriff kept coming. "No, we should. We should do this here!"

Two steps later, he grabbed a tight hold on Boone's shirt collar, threw him onto the slick hospital tile, and pinned him down by the shoulders, before Boone could put up any fight.

He turned a forearm into Boone's throat, and leaned in close, almost nose to nose. "How big you feel now?" the sheriff sneered, and Boone felt his angry breath hot in his face. "How big you feel now, you stupid motherfucker?"

Karen saw that the hospital workers in the lobby were staring directly at them now. She pleaded quietly, hoping to avoid any more of a scene, "Get up, John. Get up. Get up. Get up, John."

Beads of sweat popped out on Boone's forehead, dribbled down into his eyes. His face dark and darker hues of red as the sheriff choked off his air.

"You'll kill him," said Karen to her brother.

"You think I give a fuck?" he responded.

But he did. He did give a fuck. He knew that he did and he hated that he did, but no matter. He did give a fuck. Even in the raging moment, even when such fury clouded his judgment, John Slone had enough control of his senses that regardless of whether he wanted to kill Boone, he remained aware that he couldn't do it here. Not even John Slone could get away with murder in broad white daylight, in front of a roomful of innocent bystanders. Not even in Sewerville.

He eased up with the forearm, just enough so Boone didn't suffocate.

Boone gasped, took in some air. The color in his face slowly receded back towards a lighter shade of red. He stopped, took another breath. "What the hell is wrong with you?"

The sheriff came in further and now the tip of his nose *did* brush against Boone's. As he spoke, his voice lowered, so low that it became hard for even Karen to hear and she was standing only a few feet away. He took on a calmness that to Boone was more intimidating than anything else the sheriff could show him.

"Do you know who you're talking to?" said John.

"Stop it, John," said Karen.

He didn't stop. His eyes stayed locked on Boone. "Do you know who I am? Do you know who you are?"

"Please, get off him--"

The sheriff growled, "I'm a Slone."

"John, stop," Karen begged.

The sheriff smacked the back of Boone's head against the floor. "You think you're one of us? You ain't shit."

He yanked his pistol out of its holster. Stuck the barrel in Boone's mouth. "Do you like this? Do you? Maybe you ought to be the one on the other end."

A stunned murmur shimmied through the onlookers.

"John!" Karen screamed. She didn't know what all this was about, but she'd seen all she wanted to see. She stepped forward and pushed the sheriff with both hands, hard enough to knock him off of Boone.

That gave Boone a small opening, all the opening he needed to get back up on his feet. When he did, the first thing he saw was Carla Haney, standing next to her cameraman outside the hospital's revolving door, both of them with mouths agape.

Now, it was Karen's turn. "What are you doing?" she railed at John as he stood back up. "Something's going on here. Tell me what it is."

John was still on full boil. He tucked his weapon back into the holster, jabbed one finger in the air at Boone. "He went against us." He paused. "The motherfucker went against us."

Karen looked confused. "What are you talking about?" she said, turning to Boone. "What's he talking about?"

Boone's eyes went from his wife, to her brother, and back again. But he didn't say anything. He knew it was useless to get into what happened with Rogers earlier that day; if he could just get Karen away from here for a little while, he could maybe give her the story the way he wanted her to hear it.

"Don't you fuck with me," said John, staring at Boone while Karen stood between them without a clue as to what either of them were talking about. "Don't you think you can fuck with me, you weak piece of shit. Nobody gives a damn what we do here. That's the way it works, that's the way it's worked since before you or me either one came along. This is our business. It's all there is here anymore. If you don't fucking like that or you can't fucking do it, too bad."

The sheriff's words hung in the air, and, after some agonizing moments, vanished under a descending blanket of stark silence. John, Karen, and Boone didn't move. The hospital staff stood by waiting for more action, but when nothing else happened, soon went back to their normal business.

Without saying another word, the sheriff took Karen by the arm and led her away.

Shit, thought Boone. *ShitshitshitshitSHIT.*

He'd lost his moment.

He watched them walk away, the brother and the sister, talking to each other quietly, with only occasional backward glances in his direction. Boone couldn't hear much of what they were saying, but he didn't really need to hear it. He knew: the sheriff was telling Karen what happened with Rogers. Boone would not get the chance to tell the story his way. And once John told the story from his point of view, it would be the gospel so far as Karen was concerned.

He pulled a gun.

Things went south.

Boone pussied out.

Boone went against the family.

Shit happens.

Boone Sumner found himself in a tight squeeze. Before long, Karen would be convinced that he'd acted against the family, which in the mind of the Slones was the very worst act a man could commit. There would be comeuppance, sooner rather than later. Boone had already seen the sheriff's state of mind enough today that he felt sure he didn't want to see what form that comeuppance might possibly take. So, he took the opportunity and got the hell out of there.

FAMILY

Boone didn't have much time. The sheriff's hospital outburst was only the beginning of their confrontation. When or where they would next meet, Boone could only guess, but it was certain that they *would* meet again. Somehow, somewhere, some way, the two men would settle up, now that their differences were out in the open.

By now, John would have already told Karen what happened with Rogers. Boone knew this. He also knew the rest of John's story: how Boone had tried to thwart the comeuppance of Rogers and in so doing, keep the Slone family from having its vengeance over Walt's shooting. Not exactly true, but no matter. Karen would believe that story, no questions asked. It came from her brother, didn't it? Of course she'd believe. No matter that Boone was her husband and father of her daughter; John was family. *Real* family.

Boone's plan had gone one hundred percent straight to shit. There would be no more playing the two sides – the Slones and Elmer's crew - against themselves. Driving away from the hospital, Boone realized that was a stupid dream, a fever plot from a thousand cheap crime novels. Now he had to forget the dream. Now he had to save himself. And Samantha.

And Samantha.

And Samantha.

Random, desperate thoughts crissed and crossed in his head like too many fireflies in a jar. How long before he faced John Slone again? He didn't know. How long before Karen called? He didn't know. What would he say to her? He didn't know. How could he get back to his daughter? When? He didn't know, he didn't know, he didn't know.

Where was all this headed?

That, he knew.

The sheriff suspected him now. The situation could only go one way. The longer it went the more violent that way would be, but the unpleasant reality held: there was only the one way. Violence awaited them.

Prob'ly won't be long now, Boone thought. *What about it.*

*

Night fell, but brought no comfort for Boone. The world shrieked in his ears as it crumbled down the valley. Farm machinery, mobile homes, people, life, everything.

He still felt some solid ground beneath him, but knew that it couldn't last. He wanted to go back to his own house and think his position through, but no doubt that would be the first place the sheriff would come looking for Boone. And John *would* come looking for him; the question was when, not if.

Boone understood his spot. He couldn't go home, didn't have anybody to whom he could reach out. The only people in Sewardville who might help were either already dead (Jimmy, J.T. Rogers) or about to be (Elmer). People like Harley Faulkner who had helped in the past were too close to the Slones, or too scared of them, that they would never do anything to oppose the family's interests.

Filled with nervous energy, Boone made a quick in-and-out at his house, grabbed some additional bullets for his .38. In all the uncertainties of the moment, that one thing seemed true indeed: he definitely needed more bullets.

Back at Mama's house, Boone took one more try.

Under bright moonlight, he walked up the creaky wooden steps of the front porch. The outside light was on and he knew she must be home. She was always home.

"Mama?" he said, tapping on the glass of the storm door. "Mama? It's Boone."

He saw her silhouette moving inside, cast against the living room curtains. But she seemed to be going away from the door, not towards it.

Boone rapped the glass again, longer and louder this time. "Mama?"

She didn't answer.

He tried again. "Mama, I see you in there. I need to talk to you."

Her shadow was gone now. He realized she'd retreated to the back of the house, no doubt hoping her youngest son would just go away. Still he tried again, rap-rapping even louder on the storm door with the knuckle of his forefinger. And still, Mama didn't answer. He supposed that he couldn't blame her.

*

Boone didn't know exactly where to go next, but he needed to go somewhere. Needed to get away, clear the fireflies from his mind and determine his next move. He left Mama's and hopped back on Highway 15 out to the East Kentucky Parkway, then took the parkway to I-64. He didn't stop anywhere else   until he got all the way to Owen County, which was ninety miles north of Sewardville, in between Frankfort and Louisville.

It took him an hour to get to Frankfort, and another forty minutes or so to get to Owen County. It felt like 10 seconds, so preoccupied was he with thoughts of the drama in Sewerville.

The trip to Owen County required that he actually get off the interstate at the second Frankfort exit, and follow a couple of two-lane state roads, winding through the capitol and eventually breaking out into a rural area dotted with vinyl-siding homes and mottled cow pastures. Once he reached Owen County, it was only a few more miles before he arrived in Owenton, the county seat.

Barely more than a thousand people called Owenton home, but it was still far and away the largest municipality in the county proper. Boone stayed on the main drag and drove past some familiar small-town sights: Baptist church, Taco Bell, Church of Christ, McDonald's, KFC, Christian Church, a Shell station, a BP mart. The staples of Smalltown USA. He figured the pill heads and the makers of meth must be nearby, somewhere in the shadows.

All told the jaunt required fifteen minutes, from one edge of Owenton to the other. On his way out of town Boone stopped at the last gas station, a Chevron convenience store. By then he had to take a mighty piss, so he filled the truck up with gas then went inside to use the men's facilities. He grabbed a few supplies for the road, too. Doritos, white bread, some salted peanuts, four bottles of water.

He got back in his truck, pulled out of the Chevron station, and kept going in the same northern direction. In a short moment he was completely out in the countryside again, travelling in pitch black night on a narrow two-lane highway. High old oak and maple trees whipped by on both sides of the route, their leafy limbs bowed out over the road to such a degree that at times Boone felt like he was passing through a railroad tunnel.

One mile became eight, eight miles turned into eighteen, eighteen became thirty, thirty became some number more than thirty. He lost track of the distance.

Owen County gave way to the next county north, Gallatin, which bordered the Ohio River.

Boone made a hard right turn at a flashing yellow caution light. He traded one country road for another and kept going. The highway banked left then right then left again, twisting through dips and rises, taking Boone past occasional houses and farms clustered in nameless rural communities. Soon he turned onto a rough road that had gone without maintenance for the last decade, save snaky lines of asphalt patch in its worst places.

The last sign of civilization Boone saw was a run-down trailer that sat fifty yards or so from the point where the asphalt ended and the highway became a gravel service road, running against a steep wooded slope on one side, and a grassy field on the other. The field cascaded towards yet another hill that rose a couple hundred feet high.

Boone took the service road, undaunted. This place had its dark corners, Sewerville had its dark corners, the whole damned world had its dark corners. So what.

From the driver's side window, he could see through the trees silhouetted in the moonlight that the smaller hill to his left side leveled out. But then, at its far end, the incline quickly sagged back downward into a flat plain. This told him that the river was not far away.

A half mile down the service road, Boone saw a place where the grass had been driven over and tamped down after many repeated uses, a spot worn down almost to the dirt in two tire-wide tracks. He cut the wheel at that point and headed into the field. The truck's shock absorbers got a hard workout as the vehicle bounced on the terrain but soon enough he was among the trees again, riding up the hillside on a path that was far too clear to be accidental.

He followed that path to the top of the hill, then started another descent, into a small valley with no other way in or out except for the path he'd just taken. A small brook cut a steady flow through the bottom of the hill, spurred along by the recent spring rains. An unkempt grassy field spread out from the creek bank, towards the other side of the valley.

There, just a hundred yards or so away, was a little building.

A cabin.

It was small, really just a crude shack, run down as all hell. It looked like it had been plucked straight from the 19th century American frontier. Like Honest Abe Lincoln himself might stroll out the front door any minute. Knee-high weeds whipped around the place, shooting through cracks in the concrete-block foundation. In the grayed, wooden walls opened weathered gaps that Boone saw even before his truck hit the creek's edge. Dim light flickered through the gaps, and through the small windows that sat crooked on either side of the door.

He thought it must be a candle throwing off the jittery light. Yes. A candle. That meant somebody was in there.

Boone drove his truck through the creek and geared down. Slowly he pulled up near the ramshackle structure, determined to see who was there. All the thoughts of Karen, and Walt Slone, and John Slone, and the mess in Sewardville melted away as he found a new single-mindedness of purpose.

He grabbed his .38 from its spot on the seat next to him and headed for the front door, which sat a foot or so above the ground at the top of the single concrete block that the cabin owner had placed there for a step. As he stood up on the block, he looked through the windows, but still couldn't see anyone in there yet.

He lowered his head, and knocked on the door with the butt of his handgun. "Anybody home?"

From behind the door came only silence.

Boone thought for a moment, saw the candlelight flickering underneath the door, knocked again. "Who's in there?" he said, this time in a quieter tone.

"Who you lookin' for?" snapped a voice from the other side. A man.

Boone saw a shadow shift in the candlelight. Whoever was in the cabin, they were near the door, probably right up against it. "I ain't looking for anybody," he said. "Who are you looking for?"

"I'm lookin' for Mama," said the voice.

"I'm lookin' for Mama, too," said Boone. He nodded slowly and then looked up again, staring straight at the door. A surprising confidence straightened up his spine.

"Tell me this," said the man inside the cabin. "Who's Mama's favorite?"

Boone took a deep breath and said, "The oldest son is always the favorite." He waited. "I'm gonna step back now. Don't shoot."

He moved back off the concrete block, and stood in the weeds. A metallic whine escaped from inside the structure, the result of a heavy, unoiled steel bolt wrenched backward. The door unlocked. It cracked open and hung like that for a second, then with a mighty shove swung back wide and smacked against the side of the cabin.

There stood a man.

His right hand dangled limply, showing stubs in place of two amputated fingers.

It was Jimmy. He still wore the same green army jacket he'd worn that night at Coppers Creek, all those months ago.

"You're early," Jimmy said.

"I know," said Boone. "We got problems."

Jimmy shook his head but otherwise had no reaction. Of course they had problems, it seemed like they always had nothing *but* problems. Problems followed them around the way puppy dogs followed around little children, always barking, always biting at the heels. If they'd learned anything in their lives, it was that they could deal with problems.

He moved over, and motioned Boone into the cabin.

PART SIX
VENGEANCE

Vengeance and retribution require a long time; it is the rule.
Charles Dickens, *A Tale of Two Cities*

TRUTH

After Boone came inside, he and his brother sat down at a square card table, in two plastic deck chairs that were the color of bread mold. Two slender white candles stood halfway melted in the center of the table, providing plenty of light for the two men in this small space.

A profound silence wedged between them. Boone stared at the slight flame that flicked from the candle nearest him. Jimmy stared at his little brother, waiting for the right moment to continue the conversation.

Boone tapped his knuckles on the table, once, twice, three times, while looking around the room at the creature comforts that his brother lived with for the past few months. A cot stood in the far corner, away from the windows, with several ratty quilts piled on top of it. A dented metal wastebasket sat by the door, filled with plastic food wrappers and soda bottles. Several gallon jugs of spring water lined up against the wall. Magazines and newspapers lay about haphazard, screaming outdated headlines.

"Looks like you been livin' high on the hog," said Boone.

"You bet," said Jimmy, without expression.

"That face of yours don't look too bad. When's the last time you shaved?" Boone asked.

Jimmy shrugged. "One of the neighbors lets me stop in once a week or so and take a shower, shave my face, even shit in a toilet for a change."

Boone sat up straight, agitated now. "Are you fucking kidding? We agreed on it! You wouldn't leave here until I met up with you!"

"You try shittin' in the woods for a few months and see how that suits you," said Jimmy. "Besides, all that food you was supposed to bring me never did exactly materialize. What the fuck did you think I was gonna do, eat the rest of my fingers?" For extra effect, he held up the mangled digits.

Boone bit his lip and gave no answer. He knew that Jimmy spoke the truth. When Boone yanked him up from Coppers Creek, they had put together their plan of escape, and Boone promised that he would keep Jimmy stocked with supplies while Jimmy hid out in this distant Gallatin County cabin. But it quickly became apparent that Boone couldn't regularly be away from Sewardville for hours at a time without

259

arousing the suspicions of the entire Slone family, so that promise fell apart.

So, yes, things hadn't quite gone as planned. Then again, he hadn't shot Jimmy in the face as planned, either. It didn't matter now. They were in a mess.

"I came up here before the winter," said Boone, "and I gave you some money, and told you to sit tight. That neighbor of yours at the end of the paved road got some money, too. He said he'd look in on you to make sure you stayed stocked in food and water."

"Yeah, well, he did," said Jimmy. "Sometimes he did."

Jimmy got up, went to the cot and grabbed one of the quilts. He wrapped the ratty blanket around his shoulders. The nip of the evening air already seeped in through the walls.

"Forget it. Main thing is, you're here now," Jimmy said. He produced a pint of Jim Beam bourbon whiskey from the inside of his jacket.

"I see where your money went," Boone said.

Jimmy tipped the bottle towards his brother, shook his head, laughed. "Now you gotta tell me why you're early," he said, ignoring Boone's last comment. "The plan was, you'd come up here a week after we got Walt out of the way and then we'd go down to the state police in Frankfort and turn witness on him. It ain't been a week yet."

"That's the problem. Walt's not out of the way."

Jimmy was stunned. "What do you mean, he ain't out of the way?"

"I mean, he ain't out of the goddamn way," said Boone. "He's laid up in a hospital bed, breathing through plastic tubes, but he's still alive. Maybe you ain't such a good shot after all."

"Well excuse the fuck out of me!" Jimmy snapped, and again he held up his damaged hand. "You try holding a rifle with half your fuckin' fingers blown off one hand. See how you do!"

Jimmy slumped back in his chair, looking like he'd just been told there was no God in Heaven. But just as quickly as he'd lost his composure, he put the bad news behind him. "So the fucker's still alive. So what. It don't change shit. We still go to Frankfort, turn state's evidence and bring every last goddamn one of them down."

Boone stood up and began pacing back and forth across the room. "It's not that easy," he said. "I thought we'd have a few days to cover our asses and get out of there once Walt was dead, but that ain't gonna happen now. The sheriff's lost it. He killed J.T. Rogers because he thought it was J.T. that shot Walt, but that ain't satisfied him. If he ain't got Elmer Canifax yet, he will. And he's gonna come after me, too."

"Why the hell would he do that?"

"Because I got between him and Rogers. Because I tried to keep more blood off our hands. That's why."

Boone stopped at the window, looked out into the moonbeam-soaked valley.

"I fucked up, Jimmy," he continued. "I thought everything was gonna work out just like we planned. I should have known better. We got a world of shit coming down on us and nobody but me to blame for it. I got a little nervous before the day come to shoot Walt and I tried to play Karen and her brother off of Elmer and Rogers. Tried to throw everybody off our trail that way. Now Rogers is dead, and he won't be the last if John Slone has anything to say about it."

"Then let's not wait," Jimmy pleaded. "Let's go right now. Fuck 'em Boone, let's go right now!"

"I can't."

"Why can't you?"

Boone turned away from the window and faced his brother again. "Because. Samantha. I can't leave her there with them. That was always part of the plan, that we'd take her with us."

Samantha was the key to everything. Boone had gotten his fill of doing Walt Slone's shit work, his fill of Sewerville in general, and he wanted out. More importantly, he wanted his daughter out.

He'd agreed to kill Jimmy for Walt, but when the deed was set to go down in the stormy waters of Coppers Creek, Boone finally realized that he could no longer remain a part of such madness. If Walt Slone would order Boone to kill his own brother, what would come next? His mother? His daughter? Karen? Who could tell. What started off with small time errands – deliver illegal fireworks here, pick up guns there – had evolved into a life of inflicting pain on others. For God's sake, Walt had paid Boone and Jimmy to kill his wife when they were barely legal adults. Boone wondered why he ever thought life with the Slones would get any better from there. Why did he think it would get any better? It could only get worse.

So, he'd pulled Jimmy up out of the swirling water and they'd concocted their plan on the banks of Coppers Creek. Sure, Jimmy sacrificed a couple of fingers, but those severed fingers helped convince Walt that Jimmy was out of the picture. And for most of the time, the plan worked to perfection. Boone knew some people who knew some people, and paid them enough money that they found Jimmy a remote place to stay for a few months where Walt would never think to look. That turned out to be this hidden Gallatin County valley, not far from the Ohio River, a hundred and thirty miles from Sewardville in a far-off corner that not even Walt's all-seeing eye could find.

From there, the plan went accordingly. Autumn passed, and winter, and into spring. Jimmy stayed at the cabin, and while Boone could not check in with his brother the way they'd hoped, the cabin's nearest neighbor was rewarded handsomely for ensuring that Jimmy never ran out of the necessities.

In the spring, the neighbor gave Jimmy the keys to a car with forged license plates. Jimmy drove back to Seward County with his favorite hunting rifle, climbed up in a tree at the far end of the Sewardville City Park, and waited there until the moment came that he had a clean shot at Walt Slone. And when he had that shot, he did not hesitate.

Jimmy and Boone were supposed to meet a week later. Boone would have Samantha in tow, and they would head off to Cincinnati to the open arms of the Federal Bureau of Investigation, who would no doubt love to hear the inside dish on one of the biggest interstate criminal empires in the entire Southeast. At some point after that, the Slone operation would crumble, the three of them would enter the witness protection program, and that would be that.

But then… well, then. They weren't meeting a week later. They were meeting now. And now, they had a mess on their hands.

Jimmy kicked Boone's chair and nodded towards it, silently asking Boone to sit back down. Which he did.

"Fine then," said Jimmy. "You go back and get your daughter. We'll work this shit out." He took another swig from the pint of Jim Beam and offered one to Boone, who politely declined.

"So how was my funeral?" he said, changing the subject now.

"Your funeral?"

"Yeah," said Jimmy. "I assume that I had one. What was in the coffin, anyway?"

Boone went with the new conversation. "I had Harley Faulkner burn up the leg off an old cow that I found layin' in the road. We buried that."

"You're shittin' me."

"Nope."

"Ol' Harley never asked any questions?"

Boone smiled. "Hell no," he said. "He just put it in the furnace and cremated that fucker right up. When it comes to Walt Slone's business, Harley's way past the point of asking any questions. He just takes the money and runs."

The brothers chuckled at the total absurdity of it. Their laughter echoed in the cabin, a brief but warm reminder of sunnier days which they had not seen together in far too long.

After things died back down, Jimmy asked, "Did Mama come?"

"Did she come to what?" asked Boone.

"To my funeral."

"Nah," Boone said, without hesitation. He saw no point in letting Jimmy get his hopes too high. "In case you didn't know, we ain't gettin' along very good with Mama these days."

Jimmy nodded his head and smiled, a wide grin that closed his eyes to barely more than slits. Boone knew from childhood that such a smile was when you really could tell that Jimmy was happy. Truly, honestly happy. He didn't smile like that often, but when he did, there was no doubt that he meant it. Perhaps their darkest days were behind them, and soon enough they could finally get back to living the way that brothers were supposed to live. Perhaps. Perhaps.

SURPRISE

Boone drove back to Sewardville shortly past one o'clock that morning. Despite the late hour, he felt as wide awake as he'd been in months. Seeing Jimmy had been just the shot of adrenaline he needed; once again he was convinced their plan would work, after all. Maybe they'd hit a little unexpected turbulence, but it wasn't enough to bring the whole airplane down. He could go back, fend off the sheriff for a day or so, then get Samantha – there would still be Karen, but he could deal with Karen – before finally heading back for Jimmy.

Goodbye Sewerville, hello, F.B.I., and how the heck are ya, brand new life.

The cell phone service in the hills of Gallatin County was spotty at best, but as he got closer to Owenton he picked up full bars again. Just as he drove past the Chevron station where he'd stopped earlier that night, his phone rang.

He checked the caller I.D.. It was Elmer Canifax.

Fuck.

Boone's first inclination was that if he picked up the phone, only negatives could result. His world already teetered on the verge of the steaming pit and he risked falling down there with the rusty farm equipment, the meth dealers and the mobile homes. It might not even be Elmer. It could just as easily be John Slone, having dispatched Elmer and scrolled through his phone to find Boone's number and solidify the belief that Boone was moving against the family.

But as the cell chimed on, Boone thought to himself: if it *was* Elmer, that might actually help. Just a few hours ago, it seemed sure that there were no more friendly faces in Sewardville, at least, nobody who might be willing to go all in against the Slone family. Not with J.T. Rogers dead, and Elmer likely so. But if Elmer was still alive… If Elmer managed to escape the sheriff's wrath, he would most certainly know that was only temporary, that sooner or later John Slone would come calling with blood in his eyes. When that day came, Elmer would need some force behind him. Boone could be that force for Elmer. Elmer could be that force for Boone.

Regardless, Boone was headed back to Sewardville and when he got there, would have to face the Reaper. Might as well not do it alone.

He picked up the phone. "Hello?"

"Boone! Where in the fuck are you?" Elmer's voice ran like a locomotive, as though he'd started his rant while alone, hit full throttle, then called Boone and kept right on going.

"Where are you?" said Boone, purposely ignoring Elmer's question.

"You gotta help me!"

"Slow down, Elmer."

"Goddamn Boone! Rogers is dead! Goddamn!" Elmer screamed. "The sheriff's comin' after us! He's on our ass and we're in some deep shit here we're fuckin' in some real deep fuckin' goddamn shit here where are you fuck fuck fuck fuck FUCK!"

Boone held the phone at length until Elmer finished his diatribe. When the voice on the other end of the phone settled back down, Boone said calmly, "Tell me where you are. I'll meet you."

Elmer breathed heavily, trying to regain some composure. "Rogers is dead."

"I know."

"The sheriff killed him. Sure as fuck, Boone, he did it, he fuckin' killed J.T., I'd bet anything."

"You're right. He did."

"Goddamn right he did." Elmer paused. "Wait. You know for sure?"

"Yeah, I know for sure," said Boone.

Another pause from Elmer. Then, "How?"

Boone heard sudden suspicion in Elmer's voice and realized that he couldn't tell the full truth here. If Elmer knew that Boone had been present when the sheriff killed Rogers, then he would believe with good reason that Boone and the sheriff were on the same side, that Boone had double-crossed them, got the deputy killed and now had Elmer square in his sights. Not true of course, but Boone didn't want to put any thoughts in Elmer's head. He couldn't lose his backup now.

"The sheriff came lookin' for me after he took care of Rogers," Boone said, not lying. "He knows I'm in with you. He'd have killed me, too, but I managed to get out before he could do it."

"You got out?"

"Yeah."

Elmer considered it.

"All right then," he said, finally. "Where are you now?"

"I can't say," said Boone.

"What's that supposed to mean?"

"It means that I can't say. What do you want, Elmer?"

"Meet me down at Coppers Creek, and I'll tell you."

Boone thought about it.

"Okay, I'll be there in two hours," he finally said, all too aware of the irony in the choice of location.

There was a long silence on the other end of the phone, as Elmer chafed. "What the fuck am I gonna do for two hours? Where are you, anyway?"

"I told you, I can't say where I'm at so don't you worry about it," said Boone. "If you want me to meet you, fine. Just go up to the creek. Sit tight when you get there. You ought to be glad I'm meeting you at all, with the way this shit's comin' down around our heads. Just be there." Then he hung up.

This changes things, Boone thought. He flashed to Jimmy in the cabin, saying they should hit Walt again. Now. Finish the job. Now. Maybe they would, after all.

Two hours later, Boone found Elmer just a few yards downstream from the same section of Coppers Creek where he'd taken Jimmy all those months ago.

Elmer crouched near the ground, behind a dense briar thicket that grew near the edge of the water and shielded him almost completely, especially in the darkness. Boone wouldn't have seen Elmer at all if Elmer hadn't caught his attention with a sharp "Hey!" at the moment Boone unknowingly walked within five feet of his hiding place in the briars.

Boone stopped as soon as he heard the familiar voice. He looked around, but didn't see anything. Then the thicket moved, and Boone reached for the pistol holstered at his side.

"Hold on! It's me, dammit!" Elmer said as he came out into the open.

"You really are a special kind of dumb, you know that?" said Boone as he took his hand off his gun. "I could have blown your head off."

Elmer shrugged and forced a sarcastic grin. "Yeah, but you didn't. Besides, who else did you think would be out here, anyway?"

Boone turned, headed back towards the truck, motioned for Elmer to follow. "We better get goin'."

"Hold on," said Elmer. "I ain't ready to go just yet."

Boone stopped.

"What's your plan?" Elmer continued. "I ain't so sure I wanna just jump in with you. Hell, for all I know, the sheriff put you up to meetin' me out here."

Irritated, Boone whipped back around and took two steps in Elmer's direction. "The way I see it, whatever plan I got, it's better than anything you got alone," he said. "Sooner or later, the Slones will track you down. If and when they track you down, you're deader than four o'clock. You come with me, at least you got a chance."

"I ain't stupid," said Elmer. "You wouldn't come out here if you didn't need me, too."

Boone knew he was right. Still, he didn't want to give him the satisfaction of actual agreement. The truth was, if either one of them hoped to avoid a spot on Harley Faulkner's embalming table, they needed each other. Otherwise, the sheriff would just hunt them one by one like deer on Thanksgiving. If the sheriff didn't do it himself, he'd surely call in some of the many favors owed to the Slone family from across the state of Kentucky, if not the whole southeastern United States.

They had to work together in these next crucial hours. That might give them a puncher's chance. If they could strike the Sheriff quick and hard before he got to them, then they could get through this. If. If. If.

Boone took a couple of steps toward the creek. There, he hooked his thumbs in his belt loops, paced around on the damp ground, thought about the situation. The creek flowed by in slow, watery whispers, lapping gently against the muddy bank. Boone stared out at the black water and saw Jimmy standing out there, with his hands duct taped behind his back.

"You're right," said Boone when he came back to reality.

"What about?" said Elmer.

"About me needing you," said Boone. "I need you, you need me. That's just the way it's gonna be. We might as well quit fuckin' around."

"Mmmm-hmmm."

"Mmmm-hmmm." Boone kicked at the ground, busting up the soft soil in clumps.

Elmer walked out from the safety of the briar thicket, until he stood next to Boone on the creek's edge. Together they silently looked out across the narrow waterway, their attention momentarily captured by the shimmering arcs of moonlight that danced atop the ceaseless current.

"You know how it is," said Boone, his voice as steady as the water before them. "There's only one way out of this for both of us."

"Yeah. I know. Get them before they get you, ain't that the saying?"

Boone inhaled the cool spring air. Each man faced the creek, not each other. Neither knew what to say next, but both felt like they should say *something*.

After five minutes of awkward quiet, Boone spoke up again. "You ever killed anybody before, Elmer?"

Elmer seemed shocked. "What do you mean by that?"

"I figured I may as well ask, given the circumstances," said Boone with a shrug.

Elmer rubbed his bald head, hesitated for a full five seconds even though he knew full well the answer. "Can't say that I have."

"You think you could?"

"Kill somebody?"

"Yeah."

"I don't see as how I got a choice in the matter," said Elmer firmly.

"That ain't much of an answer ," said Boone.

FAMILY

He digs in the dirt.
Jimmy digs in the dirt.
They dig in the dirt.

Her green eyes, the soft wrinkles around them, the wrinkles that squeeze together every time she smiles at him. Her sweet smell of powder and lavender lotion. She loves white orchids, the Mountain orchids, with their delicate white petals drooping together at the ends like tiny hands clasped in prayer.

Hundreds thousands millions of orchids, tumbling gently in the wind, falling all around like the softest rain.

The dig in the dirt.
They dig in the cold dirt.
They dig holes for orchids, there in the dirt, in the cold dirt. Their hands are frozen. Cold dirt packs in their fingernails, dirt up their arms, dirt dirt dirt.
They dig holes.
Holes for flowers.
They dig a hole.
A hole for a person.
A hole for Ellen Slone.
In the dirt, in the dirt, in the dirt.

She stumbles through the moonlit woods up around Coppers Creek. Her silver hair, tied up in a ponytail. It bounces high with each loping stride that she takes. He never forgets that, how high her silver pony tail bounced.

Her green eyes, her eyes with the soft wrinkles around them, hidden underneath a black blindfold wound tight around her head. Her hands are bound behind her back with grey duct tape.

They did this to her.

She runs, the best she can run, but she is old and her best isn't good enough. Boone chases behind her, and Jimmy behind him, and they run and they run and they run, and then she falls, and she cries, and she begs

Please don't

Don't do this

Please let me go please please

He wonders: could Ellen somehow get away? Should he let her get away? Just let her get up and run into the night, let her disappear, let it all disappear.

He can't kill her or anyone else. He is not a killer. Is he a killer? He is not a killer.

Please don't

Don't hurt me Just let me go I can run away, I won't tell anyone, I have money.

But they can't let her run away.

Why is Walt doing this to me?

Because he wants to.

Why are you doing this?

Because he wants me to.

She lays on the ground, begging him for mercy. Begging him to let her go. He can't do that. He wishes he could but he can't. He raises the pistol, aims at her head.

Please don't

Please don't

I'm sorry.

He holds the gun on her. He wants to let her go. They can't let her go. How did he get into this? He is not a killer.

He steadies his aim. He has to do this. Walt wants him to do it. Walt made him some promises, if he does this thing, if he does this one thing he can have Karen and be part of the family.

He closes his eyes because he can't watch. He will do it, yes, but he can't watch. She has such pretty silver hair. Her silver hair, tied up in a pony tail. He can't watch. He closes his eyes and keeps them shut tight. He readies himself for the deed, the terrible deed.

He is not a killer.

He will kill her.

But something goes wrong. Before he can squeeze the trigger, he feels a hard push in his chest, and he opens his eyes to find that Ellen has jumped up. Ellen has knocked him down.

Ellen is running away.

Maybe she can get away.

Maybe they can let her get away.

But she doesn't get away. Boone lifts his pistol and a gunshot cracks the chilled air, and another, and another, crack crack crack one right after the other. All four shots hit Ellen, he's not sure where but it doesn't really matter where. They hit her. That is all that matters. They hit her and she falls. The blindfold slips off. She dies. She dies with her eyes open and blood streaming through her silver hair.

But something does not seem right. He was supposed to shoot, but he can tell from the smoke that is not coming out of his gun barrel that he has not fired his weapon.

He hears Jimmy's voice behind him. *You okay?*

I'm okay, says Boone. *What the fuck happened?*

I got her, says Jimmy. *She tried to run, but I got her. You ain't got nothin' to worry about, brother. You ain't no killer, after all.*

It hurts.

ELLEN

Boone and Elmer drove by the hospital, and saw John's police cruiser and Karen's black Escalade parked close to the medical center's entrance. That confirmed it: all of the key players in the Slone empire were gathered there at the Sewardville Medical Center. So, Boone and Elmer headed back out of town, towards the big house on the hill. Walt's house.

Elmer couldn't help but feel nervous now. "What if somebody decides to come back up here?" he said, as they started up the incline towards the Slone house.

"They won't," said Boone.

"You don't know that."

"They won't," said Boone. "Right now, John and Karen won't leave their daddy's side unless they have to. And if they were lookin' for us, I'd imagine this would be the last place they'd come."

The driveway was empty, and the house dark save for a security light that cast its white light towards the corner of the house where the cars normally parked.

Boone shut his headlights off as he turned in from the highway. He turned the truck towards the house and then made a sharp cut into the dewy yard, leaving wet tracks in the grass as he drove across the steep face of the hill and eventually stopped outside the fenced-in grave of Ellen Slone. He locked in the emergency brake, picked up his pistol, and got out of the vehicle, leaving the engine running.

After a brief hesitation, Elmer followed Boone to the gravesite. The two men stood only a foot away from the black marble headstone that marked Ellen's final repose.

"Do you remember what you asked me about her, the other day?" said Boone, in a quiet voice. "Back at your house, when you showed me the guns and drugs you stole from Walt?" He nodded towards the tombstone.

"Not really," said Elmer.

Boone bit his lower lip. Of course Elmer didn't remember. But *Boone* remembered. "You asked me if it was true, what you'd been hearin' all these years, that Walt paid me and Jimmy to kill his wife for him."

A deep unease crawled down Elmer's gullet. He pondered his next words carefully, thought *this is a test,* as he glanced downward at Boone's hand inside his jacket, surely holding on to a pistol. Then he said, "Oh yeah. That," the safest words he could think of in the moment.

"You still wanna know that answer?" said Boone.

"Not really."

"Well, it's true," said Boone. "It's goddamn true. You're standin' here with a cold stone killer, everything you heard about me, it's true. I figured we ought to clear that up so we don't get into this and you start doubtin' that I'm capable of closing the deal."

They stared at the headstone, neither one of them comfortable now. A soft wind whispered in the woods on the other side of the gravesite. Boone took his hand out of his jacket, turned his collar up around his neck to ward off the breeze, then put his hands in his pockets.

Elmer relaxed, thinking he would not be shot. At least not for the time being.

He said, "Why'd we come up here, Boone?"

Boone pursed his lips, considered not answering. "I don't expect to be back this way again," he said eventually. "Thought I should see her one last time. You know how it is. I just figured if I was gonna confess, this was the right place do to it."

Karen sat in the chair next to her father's hospital bed, watching him sleep. She chose to believe that he was sleeping, anyway.

Walt hadn't opened his eyes since he'd been shot at the Orchid Festival. He'd laid there in his hospital bed, quiet and unmoving, with so many hoses and tubes hooked into his body that he looked like a middle-school science project. For all Karen knew, he might have been awake this whole time and been able to hear everything going on in the hospital room around him, just so heavily medicated that he couldn't open his eyes or move or say anything. Or, he could be on the precipice of death, waiting only for nurses to come in and shut the machines so he could drift off into the endless gloam.

Or, he could just be sleeping.

Karen glanced towards the corner, where Samantha slept in another chair with John's sheriff jacket draped across her. The exhausted child had gotten fussy and wanted to go home earlier, but when Karen made it clear they were staying right there for the rest of the night and probably the whole next day and night, too, her daughter crawled into the chair just after midnight and hadn't moved since.

Now, this late, the hospital was practically silent. No pitter-patter of visitors in the hallways, no chatter of doctors and nurses in the rooms.

"You hear from Boone yet?" John said, as he came into the room with two cups of coffee.

"No," said Karen. "Nothing." She declined her cup. Her brother put it put on the shelf near the bed, anyway.

"Can't say as I'm surprised," said the sheriff. He leaned against the wall, a few feet away from the foot of his father's bed. "Boone's a coward. He's gone against his own family, that chicken shit he pulled up at J.T.'s today. Whatever happened to Dad, Boone was in on it. Whoever pulled the trigger, Boone knows. Sure as the world."

"You don't know that."

"The shit I don't." John nodded his head with a preacher's conviction. "That no-good son of a bitch turned against us now. He may not have pulled the trigger, but as far as I'm concerned he's the bastard that put Dad in this hospital bed."

John's words came out strong and clear. Still, tiny doubts nagged at Karen. It all seemed so hard to believe, that her husband would risk so much – his wife, his daughter, his own life – so recklessly. Boone was a lot of things, but she never thought of him as reckless, especially when it came to their daughter, who he loved so much, who he put above all else.

"I know Boone well as anybody. He'll come back," said Karen. "Maybe not today, or tomorrow, or the next day. But sooner or later, he'll come back."

"I hope he does," John muttered. "Because whenever he comes back, I got a little something for him." He ran his hand along the handle of the 9mm pistol holstered at his side.

"You be careful about that," said Karen. "That's Samantha's father. It'd be awful hard to explain to her when she grows up that her Daddy went to be with Jesus in Heaven because her Uncle John shot him in the back of the head."

John smiled, let his gaze drift towards his father, towards the hoses and tubes. "Ah, you could figure out some way," he said, only half-kidding.

The room went quiet again. The sounds of white hospital noise once more overtook the moment: the hum of fluorescent lights, the breathing machine, the steady *beep beep beep beep beep* of the heart monitor.

"We should move Daddy," she whispered, finally. "Just in case."

"Move him? Where?"

"We can get all this equipment moved to the house. Bring in a nurse and doctor full-time, they can watch him there. The hospital's safe enough, but the house would be even safer."

"Don't worry about it. I'll watch him," said John. He walked towards her, picked up her hand, squeezed it in his. "I'll stay right here. I'm not going anywhere, not until he wakes up."

Karen leaned forward, into her brother. As her head found support against him, warm tears dewed the corners of her eyes. "Daddy's got a lot of enemies. They could come here," she said. "As soon as word gets out that he's laid up in the hospital, like this, they could all come."

"Let them," said John. "If any of them are that stupid, then bring it all on. The Slone family's never run from anything or anybody, and the way I see it, there ain't no reason for us to start runnin' now. I know Dad would say the same thing."

He bent down, and met her eye level.

"If anybody wants to walk through that door, they better bring the rest of hell with 'em. 'Cause the devil himself's gonna be right here waiting. Let them come."

FAMILY

From Walt's house, Boone and Elmer drove back to town and got on the Eastern Kentucky Parkway. As they traveled, Elmer asked more questions. Boone was stingy with his answers.

"Where are we going?" Elmer asked.

"To meet somebody," said Boone.

"Who?"

"Somebody."

Elmer squinted with aggravation. "You're telling me I gotta ride to God-knows-where with you and you're not even gonna tell me where we're going? How do I know you're not gonna just take me out in the woods and shoot me in the back of the head?" He considered that a solid point, given Boone's earlier admission about Ellen Slone.

Boone sighed. "You won't believe me until you see him."

"See who?"

"My brother."

"Jimmy?"

"Yeah."

Elmer looked out the window. The orange glow of highway reflectors whipped by in the darkness. "Okay. You're right," he said after a moment. "I don't believe you. Hell with that bunch of bullshit right there."

Boone adjusted the rearview mirror, subconsciously checking for a Sewardville police car behind him. "Me and him were gonna hold off a couple days," he said, "but now's the time."

"Right," Elmer said in a mocking tone. "You drove all the way out to Coppers Creek to get me, then into town, then back up to Walt's, and now you're gonna drive to God-knows-where to pick up this supposedly alive brother of yours. Which by the way, I still call bullshit on that. And then you're goin' back to Sewardville *again?* What the hell? Are you gettin' paid by the mile?"

"I came to get you because I thought we'd all be better off if you rode with me," said Boone. "Now we'll go get Jimmy, and all go after the sheriff together."

"You're serious," said Elmer. He kept his line of sight trained on the highway reflectors. "If this don't beat fuck all. You believe this stuff you're sayin'. You really goddamn believe it."

"Of course I believe it," said Boone. "It's the truth."

"Jimmy's alive?" Elmer swiveled back towards him now. "That's what you're tellin' me. He's alive. Right now."

"Yeah."

Elmer pondered that. "Let's say that maybe that really is true. How in *fuck* could you have pulled that off? What's it been, seven or eight months since his funeral?"

"Almost eight. October to April."

"How do you expect me to believe you've kept him hidden for that long?"

"It don't matter," said Boone. "He's alive. That's all you need to know. You'll see for yourself soon enough."

Suddenly, confusion reigned over Elmer. He felt disquieted again.

Boone laid his foot on the gas and they rocketed down the four-lane parkway, headed back to the wilds of Gallatin County. A minute later, Boone's cell phone rang. He saw that it was Karen calling, but didn't answer. He would talk to her soon enough, when he took their daughter Samantha with him for good, away from the madness of Sewardville.

Elmer blurted out, "You ain't gonna kill me, are you?"

"No," said Boone. "But I figure as long as you're right next to me, you can't do no more harm."

The remainder of the ride to Interstate 64 was quiet. When they exited at Frankfort, Boone stopped at a Shell station so he could fill his truck back up with gasoline.

Both men got out of the truck. Boone went to the pump, while Elmer headed for the inside of the store.

This surprised Boone. "Where do you think you're going?"

"Gotta piss," said Elmer.

"Hang on, I'll go with you," said Boone, not wanting Elmer out of his sight. Not this late in the game.

"What are you gonna do, hold my dick for me? Sorry, but I piss solo," said Elmer. Without breaking stride, he went on through the glass double doors and found the men's room in the back corner, past the walk-in beer closet.

VENGEANCE

Once Elmer made sure that nobody else was in the bathroom – checking under all the stalls and even in the small closet – he slid the deadbolt closed and locked himself in the third stall, the furthest one from the door. There, he hunkered down in the corner, took his cell phone out, and dialed.

Midway through the first ring, John Slone answered. "Hello?"

"Is this Sheriff Slone?" said Elmer, even though he knew exactly who he'd called.

"This is the sheriff," John said. "Who is this?'

"It's Elmer Canifax."

At those words, John Slone let out a weird cackle. "You're shittin' me. *The* Elmer Canifax?" snarled the sheriff. "The biggest piece of shit in Seward County if not the state of Kentucky, if not the whole damn country? The soon to be shot through the goddamn face Elmer Canifax? Well, ho-lee fuck."

After that, Elmer heard only breathing, envisioned that the sheriff sat straight up in his seat, maybe even leaned forward.

"Sheriff, listen, I know what you think about me, but I got something you wanna hear," said Elmer, already unsure that he'd made the wrong call.

"I hope you're enjoying your last days on this Earth," John answered in a tone like a drop off a twelve-story building.

Elmer swallowed hard. No turning back now. "I got something you wanna hear," he said again. "Real good information. Trust me."

The sheriff bellowed loud, mocking laughter in advance of a torrential storm of intimidation that would impress even the saltiest of Paris Island drill instructors.

"Trust you? Who is this, really?" roared John Slone. "I thought you said your name was Elmer Canifax. I wouldn't trust Elmer Canifax to dick-stroke the goddamn governor. Surely you didn't just tell me I should trust you, you stupid son of a bitch. Surely you didn't. Why don't you just tell me where you're at, and I'll come there right now and put you out of your fuckin' misery. There ain't no need for us to drag this out no more. I got J.T. already, I'm gonna get you next. I'm gonna get Boone, too. I'm gonna fuckin' bury the both of you stupid fucks with a bulldozer and a shovel, do you hear me? I'll throw you motherfuckers so far in a goddamn hole that the fuckin' worms won't be able to find your rotting asses. Let's go. Let's go. You little shithead. Did you really think you were gonna get away with this bullshit? Who the fuck do you think you are? Who the fuck do you think you're dealin' with, huh? You mother fucker. Cocksuckin' motherfucker. You goddamn, stupid ass, sonofabitchin', motherfuckin', cocksuckin' SONOFABITCHIN' GODDAMN, GODDAMN SONOFABITCH! I WILL FUCKING RIP YOUR HEAD OFF AND FEED IT TO YOUR MAMA'S DOGS! AND THAT'S BETTER THAN YOU DESERVE, DO YOU HEAR ME MOTHER FUCKER? DO YOU HEAR ME, YOU FUCK?"

Elmer held the phone away from his ear and let John's final few words rattle off the bathroom walls. Soon enough the rant ended, and silence followed. Elmer pulled the hand set back towards him, just as the sheriff said, "Are you still there?"

"Yeah," Elmer answered.

"Good, then. You're a dead man."

"Jimmy Sumner's still alive."

"I'll bleed you out, ya hear? I'll field dress you like a deer - Wait. What?"

Elmer cleared his throat. "Jimmy Sumner's still alive."

The line went quiet.

"Are you there, sheriff?"

"What do you mean he's alive? No fuckin' way."

Now, the dialogue took on a different tone. Sheriff Slone instantly lost his violent bluster. Elmer sensed he had a big one hooked now.

"There *is* a way," said Elmer. "I'm with Boone right now. He says we're going to get Jimmy, then we're coming back to kill you and finish off Walt. What do you think about that?"

"I think you oughtta tell me where you are," said John.

"I just told you where I'm at. I'm with Boone, and I'm on my way to get Jimmy Sumner. He's alive, sheriff."

"It's a lie."

"I don't think so."

"Boone's just trying to get you out of the way. He's gonna take you out in the woods and put a bullet in the back of your idiot skull."

"He could have killed me already. I think he's telling the truth." Elmer paused. "Do you really want to take the chance that he's not lying?"

Again silence. Elmer knew he'd landed this one.

"So what if he is alive?" John said. "Fuck him. Fuck you."

"I'm bettin' it was Jimmy and Boone that made the play on Walt. Hell, it could have even been Jimmy that pulled the trigger," said Elmer. "They played you, sheriff. You thought it was me and Rogers, but no. Boone and Jimmy played you like a cheap deck of Bicycle cards."

With no small amount of glee, Elmer envisioned John Slone now gnashing his teeth, ready to explode, his face flush with angry warm blood, as he realized that he'd been played. "Sheriff, I can't talk much longer," he said. "Boone's gonna come looking for me. I gotta go."

The sheriff said, "What do you want?"

"I want a deal," said Elmer.

Once more, the line went quiet. This time it stayed that way for a good thirty seconds, until finally, John said, "What makes you think I'd make a deal with the sorry likes of you, anyway?"

Elmer didn't back down. "Because you're a man that don't like problems. And we both know you got one *big* problem right now. And I'm in a position to take care of it for you."

"Let's say that happens," said the sheriff. "Say I do get that problem taken care of. What do you get out of it?"

"I get a target off my back." He let that point settle, then added, "And I get all the meth business in Sewardville."

John laughed into the phone. The extended chuckle went on for such a period that Elmer began feeling queasy, afraid he'd overplayed his hand already.

"You ain't askin' for much, are you?" said the sheriff, still laughing.

Elmer didn't say anything.

"Hell no, you ain't," John said, almost to himself. His laughter slowed and then finally died out completely. He muttered something under his breath that Elmer couldn't make out, then cleared his throat and said, "You got half a deal for each one of 'em you take out. Jimmy gets the target off your back, Boone gets you the meth business. But you gotta get both, all or nothin'. If you don't get either, I'm gonna kill you myself. Take it or leave it."

"I'll take it," Elmer said. Before those three short words were out of his mouth, he realized that the devil on the other end had already hung up the phone.

FAMILY

The tense atmosphere in Boone's truck relaxed as they crossed into the Owen County countryside. Boone and Elmer chatted, nothing meaningful, but still a welcome nothing that took their minds off the grim hours that lay ahead.

Finally, as they neared the Ohio River on the north edge of Gallatin County, Boone cut the wheel and left the final gravel road. They raced towards the hillside and the valley beyond. Soon enough the crude cabin where Jimmy Sumner awaited rose from a heavy fog that had settled in overnight.

As he pulled up near the cabin door, Boone looked down and saw that the truck's digital clock read six o'clock a.m. on the button. Morning approached quickly, heralded by the first needles of sunlight that crept through the spindly trees astride the valley.

Boone got out of the truck. Elmer moved to follow him, but before he could get out, Boone held up his hand.

"Stay here," said Boone. "I'll bring him out."

"I can't go in?" said Elmer, looking like he'd just been spit upon. "What's the big deal?"

Boone slammed the truck door shut. They stared at each other through the truck window. "You don't need to go in," he said. "Jimmy ain't expecting anybody but me. If he sees more than one person get out of this truck, he's liable to start shootin', no time for questions. I'll go in, tell him you're with me, then we'll all head back home and take care of things with the sheriff. That's how it works."

Elmer looked at him.

"You got a problem with that?" said Boone.

Elmer looked at him.

Boone didn't say anything else. If Elmer took one step out of that truck and Boone didn't like it, he'd just shoot him and move on. Boom. Done. They'd come too far to have their plan jacked at this stage, and if Elmer wanted to test Boone's resolve in this moment, that was his own ill-advised business. Boone would ace that test; Elmer would not. Boom. Done.

It never came to that, though. Boone headed for the front door, Elmer stayed where he was, and the morning continued as planned. For the moment.

Boone stepped into the cabin and found Jimmy's rifle pointed square at his chest. Jimmy sat upright in bed, but he recognized his brother and quickly lowered the gun.

"What are you doing back already?" Jimmy said without getting up. "I thought we had our plan, that you were coming back in a couple of days?"

"Plan's changed," said Boone. He grabbed Jimmy's jacket from where it hung on the back of one of the plastic chairs, and tossed it to his brother. "Get up. We're goin' after the Slones today. Now."

Jimmy caught the jacket with one hand. He rose from the bed, and with his other hand stood the rifle up against the nearest wall. He looked out the window, saw Elmer in Boone's truck but couldn't recognize him in the dim blue light of early morning. "You got somebody with you?"

"Yeah," said Boone. "Elmer Canifax."

Jimmy spun around, facing his brother again. "You got to be shittin' me!"

"No. I'm not," said Boone. "Sheriff's after him, same as he's after me, same as he'd be after you if he knew you were still alive."

Jimmy shook his head. "I can see already that this plan's fucked up. What the hell are you thinking, Boone?"

"I'm thinking we need as much help as we can get," said Boone. "We'll take care of the sheriff and then play it from there."

Jimmy gave his younger sibling a long, questioning look. He started to say something, stopped, started and stopped one more time, but let it go, sensing that there was no point now in trying to sway Boone's mind. Elmer was already up there with them. Hopefully, Boone had played it right. If not, they were dead anyway. Simple as that.

Jimmy shook that thought off. No point in worrying about it now. He took a couple of steps over to the cabin's table, picked up a ragged piece of paper, and offered it to his brother.

Boone saw it was a torn piece of grocery sack, covered in messy handwriting.

"Here. Take this," said Jimmy. "Guess it's a good thing I finished it after you left last night."

"What is it?" said Boone, trying his best to read the scrawl but without much luck, save for a few words here or there: *Me and Boone. I'm sorry. Love you. Be all right.*

"It's for Mama," Jimmy answered. "I want you to take it, just in case something happens. I want you to give it to her."

Boone handed it back. "Nah, you can give it to her yourself."

"Just take the damn thing," Jimmy said, pushing away Boone's gesture. "We ain't gotta argue over this. Just take it and give it to her. She don't want to see me no ways."

"She don't want to see me, either."

"Just take it."

"I told Mama you were dead," said Boone. "Don't you think she'll want to see for herself that it ain't true?"

Jimmy didn't answer, but doubted that Boone was right. He paced a few steps around the room, then lowered his head, and said quietly. "She's done with me."

"She's not done with you."

"Sure she is. She's been done with me a long time. She don't want to see me and in all honesty, I can't say as I blame her. It's better for everybody if she don't ever have to see this ol' boy again. I've let her down too many times already, no need to do it again, right? No need to do it again. Just take her that letter, I stayed up most of the night getting' it ready. It says everything I got to say. She can read. I wish I could tell her myself, but I just can't. I never was good at talkin' anyhow."

As he finished speaking, Jimmy looked back up. When he did, tears were leaking from the edges of his eyes.

Boone couldn't remember the last time he saw that.

He folded Jimmy's note and placed it in his shirt pocket.

"Thank you," said his older brother, as he wiped his eyes clean with his thumb and index finger. "Now let's go get that motherfucker." He slipped on his jacket, grabbed the rifle, and headed for the cabin door.

When Jimmy opened the door, he found Elmer Canifax standing on his front step, with a .38 special in his right hand. It was aimed dead at the center of Jimmy's face.

VENGEANCE

"**B**ack it up. Put the rifle on the floor," Elmer said. Jimmy did exactly as told.

Boone reached for the pistol inside his jacket. "Elmer, I told you, stay in the damn truck."

"Careful, Boone," said Jimmy. "He's got the fuckin' drop on us." He stepped backwards into the middle of the cabin, empty hands held out in front of him, careful that he didn't make any sudden moves that might set Elmer off.

Elmer worked his way into the room in slow motion, inch by careful inch. The old wood of the cabin floor groaned with each deliberate footstep. For the first time, the brothers saw that he actually had two guns - one .38 trained on Jimmy, and another pointed at Boone.

"Boone, if you're thinkin' about gettin' your gun out, don't do it," said Elmer, as he kicked the door closed behind him. "If you move so much as a cunt hair, I'll blow Jimmy's face on the wall behind him."

Boone hadn't quite drawn his pistol. Now, he let go of the grip, held his empty hand upward.

"What the fuck is this, Elmer?" he said.

"You know what it is. It's the end. The end of everything, boys."

Boone's heart leaped into his skull, thumping in his ears like fists on a heavy bag. He glanced at Jimmy, who looked shaky and wide-eyed, as though he might burst into full-blown panic any second. Two minutes ago, they were on their way out, taking the last few steps they needed to make Sewerville nothing but a shitty memory. Not now. Now, a new reality had kicked down the door and put them both at the wrong end of a gun barrel.

Jimmy looked his brother's way. "What the fuck is this?"

"Hold on," said Boone. "Don't move."

His mind raced. How stupid could he have been, to let this happen? He'd brought the fox into the hen house. His urge to strike at the Slone family had clouded his judgment so badly that he'd thrown in with one of Sewardville's shadiest characters, never stopping to think it through in any real way. How could he be such a fool?

Boone said to Elmer, "You made a deal with John Slone?" and as the words came out, he realized his voice was shaking and he couldn't do anything about it. "His deal was better than ours? Is that what this is?"

"Something like that."

"Elmer, you little fucker," hissed Jimmy, clenching his teeth. "I'll kill you myself."

Elmer shook his head, two quick movements to each side. "It don't look to me like you're gonna do shit, Jimmy. Now turn around and face that wall behind you."

"Don't you move, Jimmy," said Boone.

Elmer squeezed the trigger and a bullet whizzed past Jimmy's shoulder and splintered the wood in the wall behind him.

"Turn around, goddammit!" Elmer yelled.

"No, I told you, don't move," Boone told Jimmy again.

The gunshot had caused Elmer's hand to drop the pistol a bit, but now he raised it back up at Jimmy's face. "You either back the fuck up and turn around against that wall, or I shoot you where you stand. It doesn't make a difference to me."

Jimmy shrugged. "Do it then."

Elmer pulled back the hammer on the gun aimed at Jimmy. "What did you say?"

"Go ahead. Do it," Jimmy said. "Take your shot. Show us how big you are, big man."

Elmer pulled back, cocked his eyebrow, not quite sure how to react to that. He relaxed his grip, just barely – and Boone took note.

Now he had an opening.

With Elmer's eyes locked on Jimmy, Boone yanked his own gun out from inside his jacket and had Elmer's bald head square in his sights before anyone else had time to react.

Elmer moved to straighten his aim at Jimmy and reclaim the upper hand, but before that happened, Boone clicked back his own hammer.

And there they were.

Nobody moved. Their eyes glanced around the room, each man sorting out his new positions.

"Let's talk about this," Boone said to Elmer. "Before things get out of hand and somebody does something they don't really wanna do."

"Fuck him, Boone!" Jimmy chimed. "Shoot the sonofabitch and let's get out of here!"

"If you shoot me, I'll take both of you out before I go," said Elmer.

He was right. Boone didn't doubt it. Unless he got off a perfect shot (which wasn't likely under these circumstances) Elmer would surely manage some return fire, and in the cabin's tight space he could easily hit one or both of his targets no matter how wildly he shot. Their best chance was to either talk themselves out of it, or wait long enough that Elmer slipped again and gave another opening.

"Do you really think the sheriff'll let you get out of this?" said Boone to Elmer, as he watched Elmer shoot rapid glances back and forth between the brothers. "You kill us, you're just doin' his laundry, nothing more. The minute you're back in Seward County, he'll have somebody on you. You won't make it to midnight, I can promise you that. Do you really think he's gonna let you go? Hell no."

"I got my deal," said Elmer.

"There ain't no deals with the Slones," Boone answered. "If you ain't family, you ain't nothin' to them but a piece on a game board. You're bein' played. They're using you to take us out so they don't have to get blood on their hands. Then they'll use somebody else to get rid of you. That's how it works."

"You mean, like Walt used you to get rid of his own wife?"

"That's right."

"Well, you're still here, ain't ya?"

Now Jimmy looked at Boone, seemingly surprised by this turn in the conversation.

Elmer went on. "I might not be a cold killer like you, Boone, but I'm gonna do this and take my chances. Murder seems to be the way through the door. The way I see it, you killed Ellen Slone and that got you in with the family. Why should I be any different?"

Jimmy took a half step forward. "You ain't no killer. And Boone ain't no killer, either."

"Back up! Back the fuck up!" Elmer waved one gun, caught himself, steadied and checked Boone again. "Both you motherfuckers, back up now!"

Jimmy took another step towards Elmer. "Boone's right, you ain't gettin' out of this. Why don't you just put those guns down and let's figure this out, okay?"

"I'll shoot you right here, I swear to God."

"You won't," said Jimmy. "If you had it in you, you already would've done it by now."

Elmer glared at him, then at Boone, then back at Jimmy. He held the twin .38's aloft, but now his hands and arms started quivering. "Fuck you," he said. "Fuck you, I'll fuckin' do it."

Nobody answered.

"I'll fuckin' do it. Test me, motherfuckers!"

Jimmy moved up another step.

Boone pleaded, "Hold on, brother, just give him a minute."

Sweat beaded out on Elmer's forehead, dribbled down the side of his face. His hands shook even more now and he could barely hold the guns up.

Boone squeezed the grip on his pistol. This was it. This was the chance they needed.

"Come on motherfuckers!" Elmer screamed.

Jimmy muttered something under his breath – Boone would later recall it as, "I got this" – and then he rushed Elmer. For an instant, Boone thought he was going to make it, thought they were saved, thought this would end without bloodshed.

But a half step before Jimmy tackled him, Elmer fired three quick shots

Krak! KrakKrak!

that hit Jimmy in the chest and burst out his back, splattering hot blood on the floor and wall.

Jimmy stumbled back and went down, clutching his wounds. Elmer whipped his other pistol around and got off a couple more shots

Krak! Krak!

and those, too, caught Jimmy as he fell, one in the shoulder and one through his collarbone.

All of that took two seconds.

Boone froze in horror. As his brother crumpled face-down, blood oozing from his many gunshot wounds, the moment crystallized. Boone squeezed the trigger on his weapon, once, twice, three quick times. The first shot missed, but the other two did not. The second bullet caught Elmer in the jaw and blew out the other side of his head. The third one tore through the carotid artery, pouring blood out in a frantic scarlet gush.

Elmer staggered, and crashed backwards. He was dead before his body collapsed against the cabin door.

A moment passed.

Boone surveyed the suddenly quiet room, and found his eyes drawn to the smallest details. Wood splinters. Bullet casings.

Tiny specks of blood in odd patterns on the floor near his feet.

Then, he realized with some shock that he was still alive.

And so was Jimmy. Barely.

Boone rushed to his brother's side, knelt down beside him and pulled him up as best as he could. Now he saw the extent of Jimmy's mortal wounds and how much blood had been lost, and realized they didn't have much time.

"Jimmy, oh God, Jimmy –"

His dying brother breathed in heavy gasps that were getting shallower by the moment. His eyes seemed without focus, and his head dropped back against Boone's stomach as he cradled him.

Jimmy struggled to get his words out. "Boone... we got to get out... got to get out of here..."

"I know. I know. We're goin'," said Boone, choking back tears.

"He said it was you... said you killed Ellen Slone..."

Boone brushed Jimmy's bloody hair out of his face. "No, no," he said. "Don't worry about that."

"They thought... thought they had somethin'... on you... But they didn't... have nothin'..."

"Shhh. Shhh—"

Boone felt his grip on himself slipping away. His tears flowed freely now, off his face and onto his brother.

Then, Jimmy's eyes regained some of their focus. He looked up at his brother and said, "I just wanted... wanted to ask you..."

"Shhh, Jimmy. Hold on now."

"Did you ever think... that there was a way... we could have been any better?"

Boone looked down at him, blinking away the tears that ribboned from his eyes. He wasn't sure how to answer that. He wasn't sure if he *could* answer that.

But no matter. Not now. Jimmy managed a smile, looked up at his little brother one last time, and whispered, "I do... I do."

Boone pulled his older brother close, listening to the shallow breaths that he knew were the last Jimmy would ever take. He rocked gently back and forth, crying quietly but freely now. He cried for his brother, and he cried for himself. He cried for Mama, and Ellen Slone, and anybody else that he'd let down in all this mess. He cried for Samantha. Samantha. Samantha.

His head hurt; his heart hurt. Everything hurt. He wanted everything to be over. Soon, he knew, one way or another, it would all be over.

Jimmy closed his eyes, his shallow breaths stopped, and he was gone.

After that awful moment, Boone sat still on the cabin floor. Again his eyes found some small details that he thought beautiful, even in their emptiness when cast against the mortal coil. Spidery cracks in the aged wood floor. Flares of sunlight through the grimy windows. Dust particles dancing in the air. Snaky tendrils of gun smoke, not quite dissipated, floating towards the ceiling.

Soon, it would all be over. Boone laid Jimmy's body on the nearby cot and put his brother's hands across his chest. It seemed peaceful, the right thing to do. He kissed the still-warm forehead one last time, then covered Jimmy with the same blanket that had kept him warm during the fall and winter months since they had hatched their plan, their great plan, the plan which was supposed to save them but which had only led them into death. But Jimmy would not be the last to die; his little brother would see to that. Soon, it would all be over.

Boone picked up Jimmy's rifle from where it still leaned against the cabin wall. He took one last look at his brother's body. Then, he walked outside, and got in his truck. He left the quiet countryside of Gallatin County, and drove through Owenton and Frankfort on the way back to Sewerville, where he would face Sheriff Slone and anybody else that got in his way. He would face them, and he would kill them. Soon, it would all be over.

FAMILY

For Boone, the drive back to Sewerville felt like nine hundred years, like ten lifetimes, like an ice age. He rode with a ghost, one that whispered Jimmy's last words cold on the back of his neck.

I just wanted
to ask you
Did you ever think
that there was a way
we could have done any better?

He didn't know.

Now, Boone stood on his mother's front porch, the last stop before he found the sheriff. Mid-morning sunlight brushed his shoulders and there he stood, covered in his brother's blood.

He could see Mama inside, seated at the kitchen table, drinking coffee and reading her Bible. He knocked on the door, as he always did, figuring she would just walk away into the other room, like she always did.

But this time was different. This time, when she heard the rap at her door, and looked up to see Boone through the window, Mama closed her Bible and got up from her seat at the table. And to Boone's surprise, she came towards the door.

He wasn't sure what he might actually say to her. He had rehearsed this conversation hundreds, thousands of times, but the time had long past since he really expected to have it.

Then Mama opened the door. She looked him over and saw the dried blood on his arms and hands and clothes.

He thought she was going to slam the door back in his face, but she didn't.

She just said, "Come inside."

She went back into the house, and he followed her. A few steps into the living room, she turned back and faced her son again. "Stop right there."

"Mama, I need to tell you something," he said.

"No you don't," she said.

"It's about Jimmy. You need to know."

"I don't need to know," said Mama. "I don't want to know, either." She was a foot and a half shorter than Boone, shrunken and brittled by old age. But with the hard, angry way she looked at him now, Boone felt like the smaller person in the room.

In a firm tone, she said, "I didn't let you in here so you could talk. I brought you in to listen. Can you just listen for once in your life?"

Boone looked at her. He deserved this. He deserved whatever words came out of her mouth, he deserved whatever hate she felt in her heart.

"Mama, please," he said.

She held up one hand, quieting him. Once more, she examined the blood caked on Boone's clothes, but again she didn't offer comment. She just shook her head. Her smallest gestures shamed him.

He knew he deserved this.

"I want you to look around here," she said, waving her arm in a short arc above her head. "Look around this house, this house where you grew up. Every night I ask myself, how could a man like you come out of a home like this? I don't understand it."

"What did I do wrong?" she continued in the same steady timbre. "Tell me what I did, son. What was it that made you turn out the way you did, with all your wickedness? It just hurts my heart, Boone. I ain't never told you but I'm tellin' you now. It hurts my heart. I can't hardly sleep some nights, I just lay there in my bed prayin', wonderin' what kind of trouble you got yourself into now. Are you in jail? Are you hurt? Are you dyin'? Are you dead? I never know. Lord, I just never do know.

"All that evil, all that devil's work, all those demons that you've walked with for these years. All the people you've hurt, all the people dead because of you. What number of men have you killed? Don't tell me. I don't want to hear. My soul can't take knowing. Maybe you even killed your own brother. Don't think I haven't thought about that on some of these nights, don't think for one second that I ain't wondered if you was capable of that kind of wickedness."

She paused in her speech, breathing hard. Her cold stare tore through Boone's guts. He knew that he deserved this.

She said, "My Bible tells me that the Lord said, 'What have you done? Listen! Your brother's blood cries out to me from the ground.' And I know what He was sayin'. Jimmy's blood cries out to me, too. I hear it all the time.

"He was filled with wickedness, just like you're filled with wickedness. I realized a long time ago that you chose a life of devils and serpents, son. And I wonder, does your poor brother's blood ever cry out to you, the way it cries out to me? Does it? Does it? Or do you stay in that house so high up on the hill that you can't hear anything *but* them devils and serpents, 'cause the devils and the serpents are a part of you that can't be cut loose, just like you're a part of them that don't *want* to be cut loose? It's all just wickedness. Pure wickedness. Right there. In your heart. In your dark heart, the heart of the devil.

"You want to know why I let you in here tonight? I let you in 'cause I wanted you to get one last look at the place where you grew up. Go ahead. Take it. Take your last look around. Think about when you and Jimmy was little boys runnin' through this house. Lord knows I think about those days all the time, those days back before the wickedness took hold in both of you. I raised you two right, raised you up just like the Book says. It didn't matter. I stayed awake nights, prayin' for you, prayin' you'd find your way out of the dark, but that didn't matter. Nothing mattered.

"You been comin' to my house for all these years, knockin' on my door, like you think I ought to actually let you back in. Like I ought to let you bring your wickedness back in this house. Well now, here you are. I finally let you inside. And this is the last time. *The last time.* I don't want you to come back here ever again, do you hear me?"

He looked at her. He deserved this.

"Do you hear me?" she repeated.

"Yes, Mama," he said.

"Good. I want to make sure you hear. 'Cause I don't want to see you ever again. Not here, not anywhere else. You're not my son anymore, do you understand? You're not my son. Now get out. Go on. Just get out."

She turned and walked out of the room.

Her son waited for a moment, not quite sure if Mama was finished. Ten minutes later, he still stood there and she hadn't returned.

He deserved this.

He walked towards the door that led out of the house, the house where he grew up, the house where he was no longer welcome, ever again. He knew that he deserved this.

On the way out, he reached into his jacket and pulled out a curled piece of heavy brown paper, the strip of grocery sack on which Jimmy had scrawled his last letter to their mother. He unfurled the message, read the first few words to himself, then decided he couldn't go any further.

Mama said he was full of wickedness. She said that he lived with the devils and serpents, that he had darkness in his heart and blood on his hands and there was no prayer that could ever change that. Boone wanted to tell her she was wrong, he could give up the demons and the serpents, he could be better. But he couldn't tell her that. Because she wasn't wrong.

He laid Jimmy's letter on the couch and left the house forever.

Dear Mama,

If you are reading this, then you have talked to Boone and you know that I am not dead after all. I am alive, Mama. I am alive. I am sorry that I can not see you right now and tell you how sorry I am for making you think that I had died, but I hope you will find it in your heart to forgive me one of these days. This way is the best.

I am so sorry, Mama. For a lot of things. I never was too good with words but that is probably the best thing I could say even if I was good with them. Me and Boone have done a lot of things wrong in our lives and I know we have hurt you in a lot of ways. We have hurt a lot of people in a lot of ways. But I am writing you this letter to tell you that from here on out, everything is going to be different. Maybe that is hard for you to believe. I could understand if you don't want to believe that. But we are changing. Your boys are changing, you will see. I can not tell you too much about it right now, but you will see. I promise.

I love you Mama. I just want you to hear that. I love you and Boone loves you. We have put you through a hell in your life that you did not deserve. There is nothing I can say that will ever undo all the awful things me and Boone have done. There is nothing I can do to give you back all those nights you spent worrying about us, wondering what kind of trouble we was in or if we was ever coming home or if we was even alive. If I could, I would. I would take it all back. But I am sorry that I can not. Life does not work that way.

These last few months have been so hard. I have spent a long time by myself, hiding out up here (can not say where) and waiting for the day that I could come back and see you again. To be honest, I never thought it would be this hard. But if anything good has come out of my time alone, it is that I have had a good chance to do a lot of thinking. Now I understand the type of person I was, and the type of person I should have been. And they are not the same person.

There is so much evil back home. All the drugs, and the whiskey, and guns, and fights between men, and so many other things I couldn't tell you here. But we both know what I am talking about. And me and Boone, we have been right there in the middle of it for too long, and like I said, we have caused a lot of hurt on too many people. Especially on our own family. While I am not like Boone (I do not have a family of my own other than my Mama and my little brother) I still do know that when you hurt the people around you, you are hurting yourself at the same time.

So that is why I am writing this letter. To help me stop hurting. To help you see that it will all be different now.

I am sorry. That is what I want to tell you, I am sorry. So so so sorry. I am sorry as I can be, from the deepest corner of my soul. And I love you. I have always loved you, Mama, and I hope that you can someday find love for me again. I would like to see you and hopefully after things settle back down, you would like to see me, too.

Well I had better go now. My fingers are getting cold. I am writing this letter by candle light and it is about to burn down. Getting dark in here, but hopefully soon there will be plenty more light for us all.

Your son,
Jimmy

FAMILY

As he drove towards the hospital, Boone picked up his cell phone and dialed his wife's number. Samantha answered, which surprised him but also brought him a measure of warmth. Her sweet voice, an island of innocence in the midst of so much spilled blood.

"Hello?" she said.

"Samantha? It's Daddy."

"Hi, Daddy."

"Is your mommy there?"

"Are you coming to see me?"

"I am, baby. I am coming to see you." He cleared his throat. "Are you at the hospital with Grandpa?"

"Yeah."

"Is Mommy there?"

"Mmmm-mmmm."

"Is your Uncle John there?"

"Yeah."

His mouth felt dry. "That's good," he said. "Baby, I need to talk to Mommy right now. I'll see you soon, okay? I'll come and get you and we'll go away on a trip. How does that sound?"

"That sounds good, Daddy. Can Mommy come with us?"

Boone hesitated. "We'll see," he said. "Is Mommy there in the room, right now?"

"Yeah."

"Can you put her on the phone?"

"Yeah."

"Samantha?"

"What?"

"I love you."

"I love you, too, Daddy."

She handed the phone over to her mother. He heard Karen's muffled voice say *Who is it?* and then everything went quiet.

"Boone?" Karen said a moment later, her voice coming clear through the phone now. She did not sound happy. "Where are you?"

Boone waited a moment before he answered, hoping that would make his wife just a little bit less comfortable. Then he said, "Jimmy's dead. Rogers is dead. Elmer's dead. They're all dead."

"What are you talking about?" she asked.

Her question showed a contrived ignorance that Boone found more laughable than insulting. He said, "If I know the Slone family, you've cleared all the other patients off Walt's floor. The only people up there are you, John, Samantha, and your Daddy. The nurse comes by to do her scheduled check-ups every hour on the hour, but you make sure she comes alone and that she leaves the very second she's finished. Nobody else comes within ten yards of that hospital room unless they call you first. That sound about right?"

Utter silence, on the other end of the phone.

He continued. "I doubt there are any guards around, either. There oughtta be somebody there, but I doubt there is. John thinks he can take care of it. He thinks he's the number one big dog daddy, and he'll keep this shit under control. Do you think he's the number one big dog daddy? I guess we'll find out soon enough. But besides that, you all don't want anybody carrying a gun around there unless they got Slone blood in their veins. Tell me I'm wrong."

Again, Karen offered nothing in response.

"I'll be there soon," he said.

"How soon?"

"What, you think I'm gonna tell you that so you can have the entire Seward County sheriff's department waiting on me?" he said. "Come on. I may be dumb, but I ain't stupid. When will I be there? Soon enough, that's when. Soon enough. And I'm only tellin' you that much so you can get Samantha out of there before the shit goes down.

"You take her, and you get out of the hospital right now. I will meet you at our house at midnight. If you don't meet me at our house, I will find you wherever you are, and I will get my daughter. If I get close to the house and find any surprises waiting for me — a deputy's car, state police, whatever – I will turn around, and I will find you later. And I will *still* get my daughter. No matter what happens, no matter what it takes, I will get her. Do you hear what I'm saying, Karen? You won't keep Samantha from me."

Karen yelled now. Even through the cell phone, Boone heard her voice echoing off the hospital tile. He pictured his wife on the verge of angry tears, her body shaking with each brutal word.

"Who do you think are? Where are you? You tell me!" she raged. "John will find you. We know everything. We know how you've gone against the family. What do you think you're doing? We will find you, do you understand?"

"It won't be difficult," he said. "I'll see you soon."

He hung up, and tossed the phone aside. Before the handset hit the seat, he pulled into the hospital parking lot, fully aware that after the exchange he'd just had with Karen, the Slones would be expecting him. Just not now.

VENGEANCE

"He's on his way," Karen said.

"Good," said John. "Let him come."

"What are you going to do?"

"Well, if all goes as planned," he said, "I aim to kill that damn husband of yours."

Fifteen seconds later, Boone burst into the lobby of the Sewardville Medical Center with the butt of Jimmy's shotgun pressed against his shoulder. His own 9mm dangled in the holster that hung around his chest. He moved straight ahead, focused, firm. Ready.

"Get down! Everybody get down!" he shouted at the two girls working the reception desk, waving the barrel at them, leaving no doubt that he meant business.

One of the desk nurses reached for the phone, her eyes wide with panic.

"I said get down!" he barked. "Now, dammit, now!"

The girls yelped and dove for cover, sending loose papers flying across the length of the desk, spilling onto the floor on both sides.

Boone kept coming. A nurse walked into the middle of the scene just as Boone got past the front desk, but she dove for cover when he gave the shotgun one hard pump in her direction.

Now, he saw the elevator. It looked no more than ten running strides away. The double doors were opening, and he ran for them, knowing that if he didn't get in at that moment he would be wasting precious seconds that might jeopardize everything.

A skinny male nurse with a scraggly beard stepped out, but Boone threw him to the floor before the nurse had a chance to do anything about it. As he got into the lift, he shouted, "If I hear a police siren any time in the next five minutes, before they get me, I'm gonna come back down here and kill every one of you motherfuckers! Count on it!"

Less than one minute had passed from the time he entered the medical center. Then the elevator doors slid closed, and he started moving upward, where the Slone family waited, where his destiny waited, where the end of everything waited.

*

Sheriff Slone looked out the window. He saw people running out the front door en masse and had little doubt what sent them scurrying.

"He's here," he said, with no hint of emotion.

Karen stood up. "What now?"

"Take Samantha and go up to the next floor," John said. "I'll come and get you when it's all over."

While driving to the hospital, Boone had somehow kept his head clear enough to calculate six, maybe seven minutes to find Walt's room and finish this business before the police could get there. No doubt, as soon as he walked into the lobby and pulled out his gun, somebody in the hospital would find a way to hit the emergency call button. He would have only a few crucial minutes. He could surprise Sheriff Slone and Walt, work his way through them, then get out the fire escape and back to his truck before the first police car showed up.

Now, in the elevator, time wrenched forward in slow, desperate groans. Boone felt as though everything around him had rusted nearly to a halt, while he fought through at full speed. It would be less than ten seconds until the door opened again and he was on Walt Slone's floor, but the way his heart bass-thumped in his throat it felt like that journey might take an hour. And it already felt like *two* hours had elapsed since he'd hit the button for the third floor and begun his ascent.

At least there was virtually no security presence in the hospital. He expected that. Counted on it. One, it was the middle of the day and there wasn't much activity of any sort in the medical center. But two – and this was crucial to Boone's plan – John Slone surely believed that his very presence would plenty deter anyone that might come gunning for his dear old Dad. The sheriff wouldn't need extra law enforcement stationed in the building; they could go on about their day. He would stay there with Walt as his personal bodyguard and that would be all that was needed. This would be John's way. He believed in his own abilities.

And Walt would be the only patient on his floor. Count on that, too.

Boone heard a faint chime, and felt the elevator slow to a stop on its hydraulic lifts.

The doors opened back up.

He held his shotgun high, against his shoulder, ready to fire at whomever awaited him —

And there stood Karen.

With Samantha in her arms.

For a second, everyone froze. Then Karen turned, thinking she could run back to her father's room, but Boone grabbed her by the shoulder and pulled her and Samantha into the elevator with him.

He slammed a glowing button near his waist, and the doors closed again.

"Let me go!" shouted Karen, as their daughter began crying.

"Shut up, Karen," said Boone.

She hauled off and slapped him, but he barely felt it.

"I'm taking Samantha. We're leaving," he said. "When these doors open, I've got a couple more things to take care of here, then we're gone. Gone where you'll never find us, you understand?"

"You think so. You think you're just gonna run off, is that right?" Karen said.

"Damn right, I am" he spat back at her. "I suggest you go downstairs and wait for the cavalry to arrive."

"John was right about you!" Karen snapped. "You bastard! You've gone against the family, and you think we're just gonna let you walk out of here?"

Boone didn't say anything else. Instead, he reached for Samantha, and she for him. Karen pulled back, but he was too strong, taking the little girl by the waist and prying her from her mother's grip.

"You can't do this."

"That's where you're wrong, Karen," he said. "I can do this, and I will. I should have got away from here a long time ago, but you're not stopping me now."

He pushed the button, and the elevator doors slid open again. He was standing between Karen and the exit; she looked past him, down the hallway, as if she might run for it, but he silently pointed the shotgun's barrel at just enough of an angle that it sent the clear message to his wife without showing Samantha anything.

Boone shook his head. *Don't try it.* He put one finger to his lips, telling her to stay silent.

Karen glared hard at him, but she got the message. "What are you gonna do, shoot me in front of our daughter?" she said.

"Let's hope it don't come to that," he answered.

"John will kill you, you know."

"We'll see about that."

"Is that all you've got to say to me?"

It *was* all he had to say to Karen. The time for talk had long since passed. He gave her a hard shove towards the back wall of the elevator, hit the button that would send her down to the first floor, and jumped out with their daughter just as the doors closed between them.

With Karen out of the way now, he turned his attention down the hall, and took his first steps toward Walt's room.

He led Samantha into the first open room he saw, at the end of the corridor nearest the elevator. There, he bent to her eye level, and said softly, "Samantha, honey, I need you to stay here by yourself for a minute, okay?"

She just looked at him. Soft tears ran quietly down her face. "Where did Mommy go?"

"Mommy went away. Can you stay here for me?"

The child nodded.

"Good girl," said Boone. "I'll be back in just a couple of minutes. I'm gonna close the door, and whatever you do, you don't open it for anybody else but me. You got that?"

Once more, she nodded her understanding. He ran his fingers through her hair, kissed her on the cheek, and went back into the corridor, closing the door behind him.

Boone's thoughts swam in the air while his heart quickened under his breastplate. He looked down the corridor and found John Slone standing outside of Walt's room.

"Karen said you'd be joining us," John hissed. "I have to say, I don't think she was expecting you this soon, though. She was just here a few minutes ago. Maybe you saw her?"

"I did," said Boone.

A moment passed between them, a long enough moment that both men realized this was not going to be a verbose Hollywood ending where each of them launched into a powerful monologue about righteousness and betrayal. This was not Hollywood, this was not the movies. This was Sewerville. There could only be one ending here, the same ending that befell so many other unfortunate souls in this place – Jimmy, Deputy Rogers, Elmer Canifax, Ellen Slone, countless pill heads and meth addicts, anyone who got trapped in the clutches of the vile Sewerville beast. Boone and the sheriff had oft witnessed this ending. But now, both men knew that one of them would finally experience it for themselves.

That end was death.

Each of them recognized the moment at precisely the same time. The sheriff reached for the pistol in his waistband, but Boone was quicker to grab his weapon from the holster against his chest. He drew and fired

KRAK! KRAK! KRAK!

The first shot missed. The next two didn't. One bullet hit the sheriff in the abdomen and lodged there; the other spun through his right shoulder then blew a chunk out of his back on exit. Blood splatted a wet butterfly pattern across the wall and doorway.

The sheriff crashed to the floor, and managed to crawl into Walt's room for cover.

Boone stood there and watched him.

Is that it?

So fast?

"Daddyyyyy!" he heard Samantha wail from behind the closed door of the room where he'd hidden her.

"Stay in there, honey!" he answered. "Daddy's OK! You just stay in there and I'll come and get you!"

No sooner had he gotten the words out of his mouth than the sheriff whipped his gun barrel haphazard out the doorway and fired a wild shot. The bullet ricocheted down the corridor, whizzed past Boone's shoulder, too close.

Boone sprinted across the hall, into another empty room, on the opposite side of the hallway from Walt's.

"I'll get you, motherfucker!" yelled John.

"You got a ways to go," yelled Boone back.

Boone stood just inside the hospital room, diagonal from John and Walt, waiting for the sheriff to fire his next bullet and hoping like hell that shot would be as wild as the first one. His heart thumped in his ears so hard that his vision blurred around the edges.

A minute passed. Nothing.

Two minutes. Still nothing.

"Fuck you," said the sheriff. "Fuuck you, buuddyyy." He sounded weak. Fading now.

Boone's pulse slowed a bit – still a steady thud but at least he could see clearly again – as he realized that the first volley was over and he was still alive. Still he knew that John could be, and probably was, just waiting for Boone to make the next hasty move, the final fatal mistake, that would allow him to line up a clear shot at the center of Boone's skull.

With that in mind, Boone peered around the edge of the door frame. He could see his adversary's foot, and part of his leg, enough to know that the sheriff was in no position to line up anything at that moment. Instead, he looked like he was sitting up against the wall, barely moving. Probably not far from death

Boone called out "Fuck you, John!"

"Fuuuck yooouuu budddyyy," answered Sheriff Slone. Boone heard weakness in those words; he knew he'd hit the sheriff twice, was pretty sure one of the bullets had struck gut. John could be bleeding out already.

Boone felt his heart jump again. "I'm gonna come over there and finish you off, you son of a bitch," he said. "I'm gonna be the last thing you see before you leave this godforsaken Earth, straight on to Hell. The Hell where you belong. You hear?"

"Come... come... get... some," said John. He fired off a round that didn't even make it into the corridor, cracking instead into the wall beside Walt's bed.

Boone could hardly believe it. His life's climactic confrontation, his final stand against the damned Slone family, overlords of not just his life but all of Sewerville, had come down to this. Karen was out of the picture, and though she would surely be back soon, he didn't have to worry about her at that moment. Walt was incapacitated in a hospital bed. And the sheriff was shot through twice, propped up a few feet away, weakening by the second and likely dying.

All in the span of two, maybe three minutes.

Sewerville, which had taken decades to reach its current sorry state, changed forever in two or three minutes.

The sheriff got off two more shots

KRAK!

K-KRAK!

but both went far awry. Boone heard them ricochet around Walt's room and wasn't sure where they landed.

It didn't matter. The sheriff's foot kicked from side to side with the recoil of the gun, seemed out of control from the rest of his body. His injuries were so bad that he couldn't otherwise move.

John slurred his words, as if he spoke from a luminal space, between wake and dream.

"Now... now you're... now you're messin' with... a sonofabitch...."

Boone called out, "In one minute, I'm gonna walk over there and put this shotgun in your mouth. I hope you're ready, you worthless bastard."

Then, he saw thick blood pooling out the door of Walt's room, and any remaining fear subsided.

"Now you're messin' with... a sonofabitch..."

KRAK! He fired.

KRAK! He fired.

Useless. There was the sound of glass breaking, as one of these bullets careened into a window. The sheriff seemed no more of a threat now than did Walt. It occurred to Boone that the two people he hated above all else were both over there, at his mercy, easily available for him to come and finish them off.

"You hear that, John?" he said. "You hear that sound? Those are my brother's footsteps. He's comin' for you. He's comin'. Do you hear?"

The sheriff gave no answer.

Boone walked out into the corridor. He took a long, slow breath. This was almost over. His heart slowed; he felt a strange calmness wash across his soul. He went to Walt's room, pushed the door open the rest of the way, and saw John lying face-up on the floor, pale as a sheet of cheap notebook paper, gurgling up his own blood. The sheriff clutched at a small bullet hole in his abdomen, and with the scarlet lake expanding from his back, Boone knew he was shot through. Another jagged wound gaped just below the neck, surrounded by bone fragments where the shoulder had blown up.

He'd dropped his gun next to him, too. Though it was only a few inches away, it might as well have been miles.

Boone stepped over the dying man, stood over him with one leg on either side.

The sheriff looked up at him with fading eyes. "Now you're... messin' with... sonofabitch... you... sonofabi—"

Boone stuck the black barrel of Jimmy's shotgun into the mouth of his tormentor. John took it, too depleted to do anything else.

"I bet you never thought it would end this way, huh? Can't say that I did, either, but here we are," said Boone in a calm, flat tone. "So what's it like, to be at the other end of the gun barrel for once?"

John closed his eyes. He kicked one foot weakly, nowhere near enough to move Boone.

"Look at me!" Boone commanded.

The sheriff's eyes fluttered back open, and Boone could tell that for John Slone, opening his eyes that one last time was a final, desperate act of willpower.

Boone stared down the barrel, into the eyes of the man beneath him. "Around Sewerville, it always ends like this," he said. "It always ends with one person on the wrong end of the barrel. I hope you think about that. I hope you think about all those people you put on the wrong end. The end where you are right now. *I hope you think about them while you're in hell, do you hear me, John?*"

But John couldn't hear him. Not anymore.

Before Boone had a chance to pull the trigger, the sheriff's eyes rolled over white and shut again. He took a quick breath, and another, then let out his final death rattle and breathed no more.

Boone watched him for a moment, in near disbelief that John was dead. But he was dead. He was dead. The devil was dead.

In the distance, the first police sirens screeched from the edge of town towards the hospital.

Boone stepped away from the corpse, towards Walt's bed. The old man lay there, still hooked to all the hoses and tubes, still looking like a middle school science project. Or some kind of monster.

Boone drew his pistol and pressed it against Walt's forehead. "Goddamn you, Walt," he said. "Goddamn you for all of this. Goddamn your son, goddamn your daughter, goddamn you and everything you ever touched. You deserve this, you son of a bitch." He cocked the hammer back and held it fast. He held the gun there, held it hard, held it until his hand shook, his arm shook, his shoulders shook, his entire body shook from the core of his soul on out, as he tried to hold back all of the pain that the Slone family had caused him in his life.

He had to kill the old man. He had to see him off to hell, where he could spend eternity with his demon son.

But he couldn't do it.

The day had seen enough death already.

In his hardened heart, Boone knew that. He tried to work up the murderous nerve, but he didn't really have that nerve in him. He liked to think that was exactly what separated him from the likes of Walt Slone.

He lowered the pistol and walked towards the door —

And he changed his mind.

To hell with Walt Slone.

Boone spun around quickly, fired

KRAK! KRAK!

KRAK! KRAK!

in Walt's direction, and would have fired more if the clip hadn't emptied and his last few pulls of the trigger produced more than sharp metallic clicks.

The police cars drew ever closer.

Boone figured he now had two minutes, at the most.

He ran down the hallway and grabbed Samantha, then took off for the fire escape. When he shoved the door open, the alarm went off. The fire alarm. A final absurdity in Sewerville's epoch of absurdities. He raced down the metal steps with his daughter in his arms, came down in the parking lot, and jumped in his truck. The engine cranked, he stomped on the gas, and he tore out of the parking lot with his daughter strapped into the seat next to him. They hit the East Kentucky Parkway before the first flashing blue lights arrived at the medical center.

SAMANTHA

They drove.

"Where are we going?" asked the daughter.

"We're going away," her father answered. "Far away."

"How far?"

"Far, baby. Don't worry. Everything's going to be fine."

"I know." She stared out the window. "When will we see Mommy again?"

He hesitated. Although he knew he would have to answer that question eventually, now didn't seem like the best time. "Soon enough," he said. "We'll see Mommy soon enough."

"Do you promise?"

"I promise."

That satisfied the daughter, for now. She leaned her exhausted head back against the seat of the truck, but found sleep difficult despite teetering on the edge of exhaustion.

A few minutes later, the roll tide of distant thunder combined with rain's delicate cadence on the windshield, orchestrating a lullaby that enticed the child into slumber. Her eyelids dropped close, like butterflies landing, and her hands came together, petite fingers interlaced on her chest. When her father looked over, he saw tiny hands clasped in prayer, just as the petals of the pearl white Mountain orchid seemed like tiny hands clasped in prayer. The Mountain orchid. The Mountain orchid. The mountain orchid, the flower which shimmered only on the hillsides of Seward County, Kentucky. The Mountain orchid that adorned the grave of Ellen Slone, the Mountain orchid that she loved so much, so many years ago. So many years before everything tumbled into the darkness. So many years before Sewerville. So many years.

FAMILY

After they switched cars in the next county (with some help from Harley Faulkner), Boone and Samantha headed for Frankfort. There Boone asked for a meeting with representatives of both the Kentucky State Police and the state Senate. He told them that he expected full immunity from prosecution, in exchange for all the information he could provide on the Slone family's criminal empire. After some discussion the authorities granted his request and a day later, that meeting took place.

JIMMY

He sensed his brother, there, with him.

"It is only those who have neither fired a shot nor heard the shrieks and groans of the wounded who cry aloud for blood, more vengeance, more desolation."

William Tecumseh Sherman

THE
END

ABOUT THE AUTHOR

Aaron Saylor grew up in Kentucky and still lives there with his wife, Leslie. He loves movies, comic books, the Kentucky Wildcats, and the Cincinnati Reds. Let him know if you've got a good poker game going.

1478612R00182

Made in the USA
San Bernardino, CA
19 December 2012